WOLF BORN

N. GOSNEY

feb 2016

To Dawn
Lovely to meet you
at TU7 :)

Natalie Gosney

First published in Great Britain in 2013 by N. Gosney

The Wolf Born Saga™

Copyright © 2013 N. Gosney

The moral right of the author has been asserted.

ISBN : 978-0-9575273-0-0

Layout and Typesetting by Philip Gosney
Cover Illustration by Philip Gosney

Cover Illustration Pieces Supplied by 123rf
www.123rf.com
Werewolf Font by Lettering Delights
www.letteringdelights.com

This book is dedicated to Phil.
For his seemingly endless patience and help.

CHAPTER ONE

Chocolate wrappers all over the desk, uneaten sandwiches sitting on saucers on the dining room table, empty tissue boxes littering the sofa…

Carly sighed wearily as she surveyed the damage. You'd think that a small tornado had blustered through the house given the amount of rubbish strewn around, but no, this was merely the work of one fully-grown and very untidy man.

"It's not fair", she muttered to herself as she gingerly lifted a cushion to see what might be lurking beneath it. "Why do I have to deal with all of this?"

She knew the answer of course; nobody else would do it. Her boyfriend Rob was incredibly lazy, and despite Carly's constant nagging, he never seemed to lift a finger to help her around the house. He couldn't even throw away his leftovers, much to her frustration. Not that she had been particularly organised prior to living with Rob; Carly was prone to procrastination, and her mother had always complained about how much work she used to make for her when she was younger. However it seemed that since Carly had taken the adult step of moving into her first house with Rob, she now tended to appreciate keeping things neat and tidy. Unfortunately Rob seemed oblivious to her desperate pleas of "put things away! Throw garbage in the trash!" and insisted on creating mini-mounds of chaos everywhere. He acted as if he were still about fifteen years old.

Carly decided that the only way she was going to be able to tackle this mess was with a little bit of help from Alice Cooper. She headed over to her computer, quickly searched on YouTube, and then smiled as the opening sounds of 'Poison' blasted out of her computer speakers. She picked up her sweeping brush and began to twirl around the living room with it. She closed her eyes and started to spin. She was just in the middle of belting out the chorus, when she had an overwhelming sense of somebody watching her. Her eyes sprang open and she saw two shining eyes staring through her living room window. It was dark outside, and the eyes glowed as though they were on fire. Carly let out a small yelp and instantly the eyes disappeared. She scuttled over to the front door, flung it open, and stuck her head out. She looked left and right to see if anybody was there, but nobody was in sight; she wondered if she had imagined it. Suddenly a chill came over her; the last thing she wanted was to be outside, so she couldn't imagine what had possessed her to open the front door in the first place. Hastily she slammed it shut, locked it, and wandered back into the living room. She quickly closed the curtains, stood still for a few moments collecting her thoughts, and then picked up the sweeping brush once again. Alice's voice was still blaring out from her computer speakers, but Carly didn't feel in the mood to listen to him any more. She crossed the room and turned off the computer.

"What the hell was that?" she said aloud. Then she shook her head. "You know, talking to yourself is the first sure sign of madness", she continued. That must be it, maybe she was going mad. There was obviously a logical explanation. It was probably next-door's cat or something. It was at times like this though that she wished she had a pet dog to keep her company when Rob wasn't around. As it happened, Rob wasn't around a great deal at all lately. At the moment he was with his friends - a sort of sports, beer and pizza evening apparently, so Carly was on her own. He worked full days as a mechanic, and in the evenings it seemed that he always had somewhere to be. She got out her cell phone and sent him an SMS message.

'just seen something peering in thru the living room window. scared the hell outta me xx'

She hit send, and waited for a few minutes for a reply back, but received none. That was just typical of him; he never seemed to message her back. He was supposed to let her know what time he would be home, but she thought it was likely that he wouldn't bother; it never seemed to be a priority for him lately. Ever since they had moved in together, Rob had seemed more distant than usual; he picked fights with her for practically no reason. She looked at her phone again, but there was still no reply from Rob. She thought she'd send a message to her friend John instead.

'*just had a fright - somethin was staring @ me thru the window. freaked me out!*'

It didn't take long for her phone to beep at her. She flicked to new messages; John had replied.

'*grab a knife. could be a burglar*'.

'Oh, brilliant,' she thought, 'I feel much better now that he's said that…not!' She snorted and put her phone back into her pocket. She shook her head and decided to stop thinking about it; she had tidying up to get on with after all, so that was what she was going to do.

An hour and a half later, and the house was looking much more reasonable. Carly threw herself down onto the sofa and surveyed her handiwork. Everything was more or less in order, except for…

"Argh! A *speck!*" She leapt off the chair and dived to pick up the offending white piece of fluff that was clearly visible on her dark coloured rug. Carly hated that rug. It was one of those rugs that you can vacuum up to six times in a row, and yet you'll still manage to miss one or two specks of white fluff. Why the fluff always had to be white, Carly couldn't imagine. She assumed it was some sort of cruel prank that the universe was playing on her. She felt sure, of course, that if her rug had been white or cream coloured, the fluff would undoubtedly be black. It was simply inevitable. Someone out there had it in for her; of that, she was absolutely positive.

"Okay fluff, I've got you now", she cackled, slightly manically, holding up the small offending article and scowling at it as though she had just vanquished her mortal enemy. All at once, she heard a small scratching sound coming from her front door. Carly groaned. "Blasted cat." Next-door's cat, as cute as it was, was forever wanting to come into the house expecting to be fed. Carly didn't really mind this most of the time, but not when she had just tidied up. She didn't really want to be faced with cat hairs after she had just strived so hard to get her house clean.

"Go away cat!" she called, a little irritably. She didn't know the cat's name. Her neighbours had never bothered to put a collar on the creature. Carly didn't know whether this was out of sheer laziness, or whether they actually secretly hoped that the cat would one day run away or be catnapped. It was a sweet little thing though. The cat was pure black, and Carly, being a little superstitious, always hoped that she would gain good luck from the fact that it had crossed her path a great many times. She was paradoxically aware though that black cats are thought to be bad luck, but she thought she would adopt a British point of view on this matter. An English girl she chatted to online had once mentioned that they are considered auspicious in the U.K.

The scratching continued, and Carly began to get a little annoyed. "Darned cat is going to ruin my front door at this rate", she said, again speaking out loud. She had a habit of doing this, and always had done, though she felt a little silly speaking to herself when walking down the street because she sometimes attracted strange looks from passers-by. It was quite embarrassing actually; it ranked up there with tripping side-ways over your own ankle (Rob called it 'the amazing ugh-ankle thing'), or that really awkward one where you side-step to avoid somebody heading towards you, except that they side-step the same way, so you both simultaneously side-step back in the opposite direction, until you end up dancing with a complete stranger in the middle of the street. Unfortunately Carly had experienced all of these occurrences more times than she would have liked.

The scratching hadn't stopped. Carly tutted and walked over to the door. "Go away ca…" she began to say, and then stopped, puzzled. There was nothing there at all. As she stood gazing out of her door for the second time that evening, wondering if the neighbourhood children might be playing tricks on her, she caught a fleeting glimpse of something black out of the corner of her eye. It was only for a split second, and then it was gone. It had moved so fast that Carly couldn't be sure at all what she has seen. 'It was probably that cat', she decided. She looked left and right to see if she could see it, but felt a sudden pain in her neck that caused her to flinch, and she rubbed at it absently, thinking she must have pulled a muscle. "Go on cat, go home!" she called into the darkness. A low growl came from somewhere. Carly gasped. 'Why would a cat growl? Perhaps it was a loose dog that's wandered into my garden.' She closed the door hurriedly, not wanting to be mauled by some vicious stray.

"Okay, that's it, I'm not opening the door for anything else tonight", she vowed. "I've had quite enough of this!" Carly sat down and reached for the television remote control. She figured she might as well see what was on the T.V. as her boyfriend wasn't going to be home for at least another couple of hours. She flicked through the channels. Polar bears in the Arctic; no, she couldn't be bothered with polar bears. The secret life of a newsreader; no, she didn't want that either. A marathon back-to-back evening of Chums re-runs. Well, she wasn't a huge fan of Chums, not like her friend Daisy was. Daisy could reel off every episode of Chums word for word (and frequently did). Carly didn't mind watching Chums, but it wasn't something she actively sought out. Still, there didn't seem to be a better alternative, so she thought she would keep it on for the time being. It was quite a funny episode, and Carly began to chuckle whilst watching it. She had seen this particular one before, but not recently.

Carly was just getting into this episode of Chums, when without warning an almighty CRASH shook the whole house. Carly's heart leapt to her throat and began hammering wildly, and she accidentally knocked the remote control onto the floor.

"What the hell was that?" she shouted, leaping off the sofa. It had sounded as though an elephant had rammed her house (or a car perhaps, but Carly, for some strange reason, preferred the idea of an elephant! After all, if something large is going to destroy your house it might as well be an elephant.) 'At least that would be a story to tell the grandchildren!' she thought.

CRASH!

There it was again. Carly's ornaments fell off her shelf with a smash. "Oh God, no, not my beautiful hippo!" she wailed. Her favourite ornament had been a beautiful porcelain hippopotamus that her aunt had given her when she was about six years old. It was white, and decorated with hand-painted blue and pink flowers. Her aunt had died in a car accident less than a year later, and Carly had treasured that hippo dearly. Even though she had been only young, she had been very careful not to damage it, and until just this moment it had taken pride of place in the centre of her display shelf in the living room. Unfortunately it was now shattered in hundreds of pieces on the floor.

Carly didn't have any time to dwell on the loss of her beloved hippo though, for a third CRASH shook the house. Carly stumbled backwards, tripped over the rug, and landed heavily on the hard wooden parquet. The house began to fall apart around her. She could hear roaring and growling coming from outside. It sounded as though something was trying to claw and barge its way through her living room wall. Absurdly, as she lay on the floor petrified, the strangest thoughts began to run through her mind.

'Well, you'd think they could just use the front door bell', she mused, then she realised how completely ridiculous that was. She didn't know what she was dealing with. In order to make the house shake, it obviously must have been large. "Elephant sized I should imagine", she said aloud. "Oh my God Carly what is *wrong* with you?" she continued. "Some huge thing is tearing your house apart and you're talking to yourself about elephants?"

Cowering under the coffee table, she fumbled in her pocket for her cell phone. There was no way she could reach the hard-line; there were chunks of plasterboard falling freely now. Her hands were trembling so much that she could hardly reach her cell, but finally she pulled it out of her pocket. She punched 911 and pressed dial.

"Emergency services, which service do you require?" the voice came from the other side of the line.

"I d…d…don't know", stammered Carly, trying to collect her thoughts. "My house is falling down…something is knocking it down. I'm inside it…you'd better send the police, oh and maybe an ambulance, I could be dead soon! Actually you might need to send the fire department soon, I'll probably need to be pulled out of the rubble!" The gravity of what was actually happening hit her all at once, and she felt as though the breath had been knocked out of her chest. She began to cry and gasp.

"I'll dispatch a police-vehicle to your house", the operator said. "Calm down, it'll be okay. Can you tell me where you live?"

"By the time a police-vehicle gets here, I won't be living anywhere! I won't have a house!" wailed Carly. A large chunk of ceiling fell on top of the coffee table just above her head, and she let out an involuntary scream. "Please hurry!" she yelped down the telephone.

"Is there any way that you can get out of the house?" asked the operator. Carly peered out from underneath the coffee table. "I don't know; there's something outside. I told you, it's trying to tear down my house. If I go outside, it'll get me!"

"How about a back door?" suggested the operator, trying to keep Carly talking. Carly knew this tactic, because she had watched many programmes such as '911' when she was younger. Emergency service operators are trained in the art of trying to calm the person on the other end of the telephone down, and they keep them talking for as long as possible. This lets them know that the person is still alive. It's supposed to be reassuring to have somebody there to listen to you when you are panicking. To be honest though, Carly didn't feel particularly reassured in the slightest - she was terrified. She didn't know whether to stay where she was and risk being crushed to death as the house fell on top of her, or whether she ought to attempt to battle her way to the door, and face whatever was outside.

"Okay", she gasped, as more of the house caved in, "I'll try and get to the door." She didn't wait for the operator's response. She flung herself out from underneath the coffee table with all the agility of a pregnant warthog, and half-skipped half-fell across the room. "OWWWW!" she shouted, as a piece of brickwork bounced off her shoulder. She reached out for the door handle and tugged it; the door wouldn't budge.

"Come ON!" she screamed at the stubborn door, pulling for

all she was worth. Using strength that she didn't even know she had, she gave the door one final wrench and it flew open. Carly threw herself outside, ran as fast as she could across the street, and dived onto the garden of the house opposite, just in time, as the building collapsed behind her. For a few moments she couldn't move. She was lying face down in the grass motionless. Dazed and confused, she felt as though she should cry, but she couldn't. She wondered fleetingly if she might be in shock. She had been an ambulance cadet when she was about thirteen years old, and she vaguely remembered that if somebody is in shock, their legs are supposed to be elevated. She thought she would look a little strange though, rolling onto her back and lifting her legs into the air, so she didn't bother. She wondered why she was thinking about ludicrous things such as how stupid she would look with her legs in their air, considering the fact that her house had just fallen down. It was as though she couldn't think of anything other than totally irrelevant ridiculous things, because she couldn't quite grasp what had just happened. The gravity it was too much for her to handle right now.

She could hear panting and snarling; it was coming from over where the ruins of her house were. Carly remained frozen on the grass. The snarling grew louder. The creature was coming toward her. Every muscle in her body stiffened, and she felt ice-cold shivers running down her back. It came closer, and closer, and Carly could feel its breath on the back of her neck. She closed her eyes tightly, too terrified to move.

"Carly? Carly? Are you all right?"

Carly opened her eyes. Her neighbour, Graham, was standing over her, shaking her shoulder. Graham was a pleasant elderly gentleman. He lived alone since his wife had died three years previously. Carly didn't know him very well, but they sometimes had a little chat if they were both out in their gardens.

Carly noticed that she was now lying on her back. "I...I...I was on my front..." she mumbled.

"What?" said the old man. "I don't know what you mean. You're asleep on my front garden!"

Carly sat up. "My house! My house!" Suddenly she was

hysterical again. She turned around to face her house, expecting to see a pile of rubble in its place.

"What's the matter?" asked Graham. His wrinkled brow furrowed with concern. "I think we'd better get you home, you seem a bit confused. Perhaps you've been sleepwalking."

Carly wasn't really listening to him. She was staring open mouthed at her house, which was totally intact and unscathed in any way. "My house fell down!" she exclaimed, not tearing her eyes away from it. "It collapsed. It fell down!"

Graham looked bemused. He shook his head at her. "I think you've just had a bad dream dear! Come on, let's get you home."

Carly allowed him to take her hand and pull her to her feet. Her head ached, and her clothes were dirty. "What time is it?" she asked, putting her hand up to her forehead.

Graham looked at his watch. "2am", he replied. "I was only outside because I forgot to take the trash out before I went to bed. Woke up in the night to use the bathroom and I remembered the garbage, so I came to take it out. I can't miss the trash collection in the morning, my garbage cans are packed full."

Her neighbour walked with Carly back over to her house. She was in a daze. If it was 2am, where was her boyfriend? Was he inside the house? They reached the front door and Carly turned to Graham. "Thanks Graham", she said. "I'm sorry I was on your garden. I have no idea what happened."

Graham smiled. "It's okay. It's a little strange, but don't worry about it", he said kindly. "If you'll excuse me now I'm going back to bed. I have a chiropodist appointment tomorrow morning so I need my beauty sleep."

Carly smiled wearily and said goodnight. She stood and watched as Graham shuffled back to his house, went inside, and closed the door. She then turned back to her own front door. She reached out a hand and touched it gently; it felt solid enough. She didn't have the faintest idea how she had ended up on Graham's front garden, but her house certainly didn't seem to be in any danger of collapsing. She assumed that Graham must have been right - she must have just had a really bad dream. She couldn't see any other possible explanation. Her neck felt sore again, and she rubbed it once more. "Ouch", she said aloud. It was as if she had scratched it somehow. She gently ran her fingers over the rough lines she could feel there. She couldn't think how it could have happened, but then again, nothing about this night was making much sense at the moment.

Carly took hold of the door handle and pushed hard. It wasn't locked, and opened easily. The house inside was dark and quiet. She stepped softly over the threshold, wiped her feet on the bristled doormat and closed the door behind her. She walked into the living room and fumbled for the light switch. She couldn't find it at first; it didn't seem to be in the right place somehow. Carly's head was fuzzy and in the darkness nothing looked the way it ought to. Eventually her fingers made contact with the switch, and a pale green light flooded the living room. At least, that's the way it appeared to Carly. She blinked a few times trying to clear the cloudiness from her eyes, but the light still remained green. Everything seemed soft and very out of focus. She wondered if this was due to her wearing her contact lenses whilst she slept, so she stuck her finger in her eye, intending to wiggle her lens around a little.

"OWWWW!" she squawked. Tears poured down her cheeks, and she clamped her eye shut. She had poked herself in the iris; it started stinging. She sat down on the sofa and held her injured eye shut for a few moments until the pain subsided slightly. Once her eye had stopped watering, she carefully re-opened it and looked around the living room. It was strange; nothing was blurry any longer - at least, not from that eye. She glanced down at her t-shirt and saw her contact lens sticking to the front of it. It was torn almost in two.

"It must have fallen out when I poked myself in the eye", mused Carly. "But if that's the case, how is it that I'm able to see?" Indeed, when she closed her other eye, the one that had not been injured, and tried to see purely out of her contact-lens-less eye, everything was crystal clear. Lines were sharp and focused. The world had never looked so crisp to her before in her life! It was incredible!

Carly decided, experimentally, to remove the contact lens from her other eye as well. It was difficult; her nails seemed unusually long that evening. She had been a life-long nail biter until recently. She had been doing this ever since she could remember. Indeed, Carly could not recollect a time when she had begun, though clearly it was unlikely she had done it as a baby. She had tried to stop when she was sixteen, and resorted to wrapping her fingers in sticky tape, but had only succeeded for about three or four months or so before she reverted to old habits. However, she had recently managed to quit biting her nails once again. It had been five months so far and her nails were still very much intact. She had gotten used to having long nails now, and was usually able to skillfully remove her contact lenses without any problems, but for some reason tonight she was struggling quite a great deal. Her nails appeared to be unnaturally long, and slightly curved. 'More like talons than nails', she thought, getting irritated. She didn't want to hurt her other eye; one eye was bad enough, two would have been too much!

Finally, after a great deal of struggling (and eye-watering), she removed the stubborn article from her eye. "Wow!" she gasped, looking around the room. What had appeared clear already with one eye was now magnified by a thousand. She felt as though she was seeing the room through somebody else's eyes; a superhero's eyes, in fact, for Carly couldn't imagine that any human could see the world quite this vividly. The lines of her furniture were so sharp, that it seemed to her as though someone had drawn them in pencil like the lines of a cartoon. The colours around her were so vibrant that they took her breath away. Also, it occurred to her that she could practically zoom into objects that were far away. It wasn't as though they became bigger, but rather they were so detailed that when she focused her gaze on them, she could make out even the tiniest features.

Buzz, buzz. A fly was bouncing on her living room window. The noise was irritating, and Carly glanced over at the fly wishing it would leave. She could see every hair on the legs of the insect; she could make out every vein on its huge round eyes. The fly itself remained small in her vision, but she could see it perfectly. She had never experienced anything quite like this before.

Quite overcome with awe, Carly put out one hand to the living room cabinet to steady herself. She was feeling a little woozy; all these new sensations were throwing her sense of balance out of whack. She wondered if she might be high on some kind of drug. She hadn't the faintest notion how she could have done this though. She had never taken drugs in her life (save for alcohol, and prescription medication when she had been ill), nor did she intend to take any, which made this all the more puzzling, as she certainly wouldn't have done this to herself. She simply couldn't imagine where the drugs would have come from, if it was indeed drugs that were causing her to feel so strange.

Carly decided to make her way upstairs and see if her boyfriend was there. He certainly wasn't downstairs; the house was quiet and still. She assumed that he must be in bed. She flicked on the landing light and carefully made her way up the stairs, holding on to the banister as she went. She was afraid that in the state she was in she would tumble back down the stairs. "That's all I need right now, a broken neck", she said under her breath.

Reaching the top of the stairs, she turned to face her bedroom door. She pushed it open, and the sight that met her eyes hit her like a sledgehammer. Her boyfriend Rob was lying on the king-size bed they shared; his throat had been completely ripped out. The entire room was ransacked and covered in blood. Rob's eyes were wide open and fixed on the ceiling. Carly stood motionless for a few moments staring at the grisly scene before her. She became aware of somebody screaming, but she didn't know who it could be. It took a few moments before she realised that the sound was actually coming from her own mouth. She couldn't move, or even tear her eyes away. The screaming continued; Carly couldn't make it stop. She didn't feel in control of her own body at all.

After what seemed like an age, Carly forced her eyes shut. She still couldn't move her limbs, she was rooted to the spot, but she managed to close her eyes at least. The thought of the horrific sight was seared into her mind, like a big ugly scar. No matter what she tried Carly couldn't push the image away.

She opened her eyes again. "What the f...?" What she now saw before her was not at all the same as it had been a moment ago. The bed was neatly made, everything was in its proper place, and there was no sign of her boyfriend at all. No blood, no mess, and nothing to indicate that anybody or anything had been in there.

Carly sank to the floor shaking her head. What was going on? Was she losing her mind? First she thought that her house had fallen down, when clearly it hadn't, and now this. She felt sick to her stomach and lurched to her feet. She stumbled into the bathroom and hung her head over the toilet. Nothing happened though, yet the queasiness continued. Carly rammed her fingers down her throat in desperation, but all she succeeded in doing was retching, and her eyes started to water again. She didn't manage to bring up any vomit, much to her frustration. Finally, she slumped onto the cool bathroom tiles, brought up her knees to her chest, and put her head forward onto them. She closed her eyes and tried to clear her mind. She still felt dizzy, she had done ever since she had woken up on Graham's front garden, and she couldn't shake the feeling that she was missing chunks of time out of her evening.

It seemed to Carly that she had been in the bathroom for about five or ten minutes, when she heard a thudding noise coming from downstairs. She lifted her head up from her knees, stood up, and promptly fell back down to the floor again. Nausea and wooziness was flooding through her body. She tried again and managed this time to remain on her feet. It was surprising to see light coming in through the bathroom window. The glass in this window was frosted so she couldn't tell what the light was, but it looked suspiciously like daylight. 'But it can't be daylight, it was the middle of the night only ten minutes ago!' thought Carly incredulously.

She turned toward the bathroom door intending to head downstairs to investigate the thudding, but as she did so she caught sight of herself in the bathroom mirror. She gasped in shock; she was completely dishevelled. Her hair looked as though it hadn't seen a comb in a year, and her skin was pale, (paler than usual in fact, for Carly was naturally quite pale skinned). The right side of her neck was covered in deep red scratches. She winced as she examined them; they looked as though an animal had attacked her.

"No wonder my neck was so sore earlier", she said aloud.

However, the things that shocked Carly the most were her eyes. No longer were they their usual bright blue, but instead they were almost an orange, yellow, red colour, and they were glowing like fire, just like the eyes that she had spied through her living room window. That felt like it had been a million years ago, yet only a few hours had passed since that had happened. She hurriedly switched on the light, thinking that the glow was a result of some sort of strange reflection. However, even with the light on she could still clearly see her eyes glowing in the mirror. They looked surreal, staring out of her milky white complexion. Carly had witnessed so many strange things though this night that had turned out to merely be hallucinations, that she supposed she was merely imagining her appearance to be so unusual. She closed her eyes tightly, counted to sixty, and opened them again. She was disturbed to find that her eyes were still glowing, and she looked as messy as she had done earlier.

"I can't deal with this right now", she said, trying desperately to make sense of this all. The thudding had stopped, but she decided to go downstairs regardless. She turned the bathroom light off and walked out onto the landing. There was no need for her to put on the landing light, as the passage was quite bright. She glanced out of the window halfway down the stairs and saw that it was already morning. Carly didn't know how it was possible, but somehow the entire night had gone by in the blink of an eye. Where was her boyfriend though? Her heart raced as the anxiety coursed through her body. He should have been home hours ago. She tore downstairs and searched the house for any sign that he had come home, but there was none. Finally she went over to his desk, picked up his address book, and flicked quickly through his contacts to see if he had the number of any of his buddies he had been seeing last night stored there. She found one, Jackson. It was, in fact, Jackson's house where he had said he was going to be. She tried to call the number from her cell phone, but had not enough battery life for a phone call lasting longer than a few seconds, so she hurried across the living room and punched the number into the house phone.

"Just wasting time", she growled inwardly.

"Hello?" a lady answered the phone. She sounded a little startled, and Carly wondered if she had woken her up. Carly assumed it must be Jackson's girlfriend.

"H…hello. Sorry if I woke you up. I'm Carly - Rob's other half. He didn't come home from the guys' get together last night. I was wondering if he spent the night at your house by any chance?"

"Oh God!" the woman wailed. Carly was quite alarmed.

"What's the matter? What is it?"

"Rob was here, at the beginning of the night, along with Jackson, and Ian, Jackson's brother. Gary and Devon were here as well. They were watching football on the television for about an hour, and then I left them and went for a drink with my friends. I got back around midnight and nobody was here, nobody at all. The car is still in the garage, so it's not as though Jackson drove the other guys home. They must have gone in somebody else's car, so I thought, but I've since called Ian's fiancée, and she hasn't seen him, and Gary's girlfriend hasn't seen him either. Devon lives alone…" the woman tailed off, sniffling.

Carly digested what she had been told. "Well, is it possible that they all went off in Devon's car somewhere? Maybe back to Devon's house? Or perhaps they just randomly decided to go to a nightclub or something? I can't imagine why they would have, but you never know?" Carly suggested.

"No, I don't think so", said the lady. "None of them are answering their cell phones; Jackson's wallet is still here, and besides, Jackson has a severe muscle-wasting condition. He has to rest a lot of the time, and often doesn't get to leave the house. He wouldn't be in any state to be able to go to a nightclub. It would be extremely unlikely that he would even go to Devon's house. Anyway I tried Devon's house phone, and nobody answered."

"It's out of character for Rob as well", said Carly. "He goes out a lot but he's usually home by midnight, so this is very out of the ordinary. Strange things have been happening though…"

"What kind of strange things?"

"Oh, uh, just strange things in general…nothing to do with them all disappearing though…" said Carly, vaguely. 'Damn', she thought, 'I shouldn't have said that. I can hardly tell her about my hallucinations or my freaky eyes.'

"There's something else…" said the lady, her voice beginning to tremble. "I found a few spots of blood on the driveway, just next to our front door."

"Blood?" repeated Carly, horrified. "Are you sure?"

"Well, it was red, and looked, you know, like blood. Or red paint I suppose but it wasn't there earlier, and we haven't been using any red paint. Nor have any of the neighbours."

Carly didn't know what to say. Something in the gut of her stomach told her that it was indeed blood, but she didn't know how she knew that.

"Oh, God…" she managed at last.

"I'm going to call the police", said the lady, "report them as missing."

Carly nodded, and then realised that obviously she couldn't be seen down the telephone. "Yeah, good idea", she said. A lump began to rise in her throat. "Sh..should I ring them too?"

"Yes, probably, I don't know", the woman said, beginning to wail again. Carly felt too confused and sick to cry.

"There, there," she said weakly, "I'm sure they're okay". She wasn't sure in the slightest that they were okay. In fact, she had a feeling that they weren't, but she didn't trust her own instincts at the moment let alone anything else. As far as she was concerned, all this could be just another hallucination.

"I could be still watching Chums!" she said aloud.

"What did you say?"

"Erm…nothing." Carly stammered. She hadn't realised that she had verbalised her thoughts. "What's your name?"

"Beatrice", said Jackson's girlfriend.

"Oh, like the author?" enquired Carly. She didn't know why she was waffling like this, but for some reason she felt the need to make small talk. In some strange way it was helping her to feel more in charge of her own sanity.

"I don't know an author called Beatrice."

"Oh…well, maybe it's Beatrix then", Carly said flatly. The conversation fell into an uneasy silence.

"I'd better go and make the call then", said Beatrice. She sounded monotone now, as though the life had been drained out of her.

Carly nodded again, not caring this time that Beatrice couldn't see her do it. "Same here", she said. She knew how Beatrice was feeling, or at least she thought she did, for in addition to the nausea, dizziness, and confusion, Carly was now experiencing a hollow sensation inside her. She couldn't place the feeling, but she knew she had felt it before.

Carly put down the phone without saying goodbye first. She always hated it that in movies nobody ever seems to say "bye" before hanging up the phone. Rob and Carly had often mentioned this strange phenomena to each other, and had concluded that film directors must generally be in the habit of hanging up on people in this manner, hence this is why it is always portrayed this way in films and T.V. series. Carly always thought it was quite ridiculous that the film directors neglected to include proper telephone partings in their supposedly realistic films, however, here she was, behaving as though she were an actress in a film. She didn't care though really; it occurred to Carly, when she eventually later realised what she had done, that there were far more pressing concerns to worry about. Hanging up the telephone on Beatrice without bidding her farewell was not important in the slightest.

She picked up the phone again, dialed 911 and waited.

"Emergency services, which service do you require?"

Carly could have sworn that she had heard that voice before.

"Police please, my boyfriend has gone missing, and his friends", she blurted.

"Are you calling from number 8 Cherry Tree View?" asked the operator.

"Yes I am", replied Carly. She knew that the emergency services operator could see her address on the screen.

"Didn't you call a few hours ago? You reported that your house was falling down?"

Carly didn't know what to say. "I…er…" What the hell was happening here? Had she been hallucinating so much earlier that she had actually called the police? "Erm…" she stuttered.

"Madam, I'm sorry, but we don't take kindly to time-wasters. The officer we dispatched to your address earlier found nothing untoward with your house, and nobody answered the door when he knocked. If you don't want to find yourself in serious trouble, I suggest you stop calling us." The operator sounded extremely annoyed.

"I'm really sorry, something was happening earlier, it felt as though my house was falling down", said Carly feebly, knowing that sounded quite ridiculous. "My boyfriend and his friends are genuinely missing though. They haven't been seen since the evening."

"I'm sorry but they have to be missing for forty-eight hours before they can be officially reported as missing. I'll make a note of your call though."

Carly hung up the phone, again without saying goodbye; she just didn't see the point. She felt dejected and frustrated. Nothing was making any sense, and she had no idea where Rob was. Her stomach began to rumble and she realised that she was starving.

She got up and paced into the kitchen. She rummaged in the cupboards and searched inside the fridge, trying to find something she might feel like eating, but nothing was appealing. Even her usual favourite snack of crackers and cheese didn't tempt her. For some reason, she was craving a great big juicy steak, but she didn't have any steaks (or indeed any fresh meat at all) in the house.

In a vague attempt to distract herself, she wandered back into the living room and fished her cell phone from out of her pocket. *'Rob has gone missing. I'm craving steak and hallucinating about my house falling down and murders and stuff. I'm feeling weird - my eyes are glowing. I dunno what's going on with me, I feel sick'.* She was about to send the text to John, but after re-reading it she decided that she sounded like a weirdo, and deleted it all. Instead she sent a much simpler text stating, '*Rob is missing. police not willing to help. dunno what to do*'.

She didn't know what she was expecting John to say really. It's not as though he could do anything from where he was. She never found out whether or not he replied to her message though, for her phone chose that moment to bleep at her and switch itself off; it was out of battery. Carly began to pace the living room floor back and forth. She felt as though she ought to be out searching for Rob, or at least doing something constructive, but she didn't know what to do. Her stomach began to rumble again, louder this time, and she started to feel hungrier and hungrier. She went outside and spied a squirrel running across the field. As she watched it, she became oddly aware that her mouth seemed to be producing more saliva than usual. Normally, upon seeing a squirrel, her only thoughts tended to be of the "awww how cute" variety. Now, however, the squirrel before her looked oddly appealing. She could imagine sinking her teeth into the squirrel and gobbling it up. She felt somewhat disgusted at this thought, yet couldn't shake the fact that the squirrel looked delicious. She was ravenous, and she didn't know why! "Surely I can't be so hungry that I'm wanting to eat a squirrel for goodness sake!" she said to herself. "Go and have some cheese and crackers."

Carly tore her gaze away from the squirrel, re-entered the house, and quickly crossed the living room. She went into the kitchen and took the cheese from the fridge. Taking a knife, she cut two thick slices of half fat cheddar, and retrieved two cream crackers from one of the cupboards to accompany the cheese.

After two bites of the cheese and crackers, Carly knew without a doubt that she didn't want any more. The cheese tasted rancid to her tongue, and the crackers were altogether far too bland. All she could think about was steak, a rare steak, the rarer the better, which was odd because Carly didn't particularly like rare steak as a matter of course. She usually asked for her steaks well done (though she was fine with a medium as well). Today though, a rare steak was the only thing she wanted.

She threw the crackers and cheese in the trash and had a drink of water to wash the taste away. She was just contemplating where she could get hold of some meat, (wondering if it would be easier to drive to the supermarket, which was further away, or to walk to the butcher's shop at the top of the street. The butcher was obviously closer, but it opened at unusual hours, and not every day for that matter, so the possibility of it being shut when she got there was quite high), when there came a loud pounding on her front door.

Carly felt a shiver run down her spine. She could feel the hairs on the back of her neck stand up, and she suddenly felt very afraid. The pounding continued. Carly didn't know how she knew, but she had the distinct feeling that she knew who was outside. She suddenly felt inexplicably afraid, and decided that the best course of action was to remain in the kitchen, hidden, and hope that whoever it was would just leave.

No such luck though; the pounding continued, louder and louder, and despite Carly's intentions at staying hidden, she felt compelled to walk towards the front door. It was as though she had no choice in the matter, her body was taking her there against her will, as if she had a connection with the person on the other side of the door.

She reached the front door and opened it.

CHAPTER TWO

On Carly's front doorstep stood a man she didn't recognise, yet there was something oddly familiar about him. He was very tall, with broad shoulders. His hair was long, about shoulder length, (though still a bit shorter than Rob's), and a scraggly nondescript sort of colour (at best guess, Carly would have said it was dirty blonde). He looked perhaps a year or two older than Carly (who was twenty-two), though Carly herself would readily admit that she was not the best judge when it came to peoples ages, so the man could have been anywhere up to his late twenties she figured. He stared down at her without saying a word, but he had a smile on his face that seemed to suggest he knew her.

"Can I help you?" she asked, warily.

"Carly, Carly…" said the man, grinning broadly. The smile reached his eyes, and Carly felt reassured by this. She was always a strong believer that smiles should show in a person's eyes if they are genuine. This man's smile looked reasonably genuine. She relaxed slightly as the man continued to beam at her.

"Do I know you?"

"We met last night", said the man, winking. Carly was flabbergasted.

"What do you mean?"

"You don't remember? No, I suppose you probably wouldn't. That's all right, not to worry. Are you hungry?"

Carly blinked at him, taken aback by the question. What an odd thing for him to ask. It didn't strike her as a normal conservation opener from a complete stranger. On the other hand…hunger; oh God, yes, Carly was hungry. Hunger coursed through her entire body; she was on the brink of collapsing from being so hungry. She nodded frantically at the man; all other thoughts seemed trivial.

"I reckoned you would be. I brought you a gift."

From behind his back, the man produced a brown paper bag. He handed it to Carly. "What is it?" she asked.

"Dinner", replied the man, smiling again.

Carly took the bag gingerly, and peered inside it. Oh heavens, inside was the most delicious looking raw steak she had ever seen. Without even stopping to think, she tore the bag aside and sank her teeth into the bloody meat. She felt the blood dripping down her chin but she didn't care. The tenderness of the meat was exquisite. She had never tasted anything so delicious in all her life. As she ate, she became blissfully unaware of everything around her. The only thing that mattered was the flavours filling her mouth. Every gulp was euphoric. She could feel the chunks sliding down her throat and it was divine. It didn't take her long to polish off the entire steak. She looked up at the man, eager for more.

"Sorry, that's all I've got", he said with a chuckle. "That was a very nice cat I just gave you. I'd have had that myself, so be grateful!"

Carly's stomach suddenly lurched. Cat? She had just eaten a cat?

"What cat? Please tell me that wasn't next door's cat?"

"What, that black thing? Pfft no, that's a scrawny little thing. I wouldn't bother with that one. Don't worry about it - you don't know this cat. Put it this way, she was well fed before she died. Wouldn't surprise me if her owners put out a reward for her. She had a good life I can tell you!"

"Oh my God I've eaten a royal cat!"

The man threw back his head and laughed loudly. "You're a funny puppy you know."

Carly just felt confused, again, for what felt like the thousandth time that day. "Listen, if you know me, how is it that I don't remember meeting you last night?"

"Well, you went through a lot, put it that way. You won't feel right for a few weeks, but its normal. Allow me to introduce myself. My name is Kyle." The man stuck out his hand towards her. Carly cautiously took it, and Kyle pumped her arm in a powerful handshake. Normally, a handshake like that would have had Carly wincing, however today she felt strong enough to shake his hand back equally as strongly. She had the handshake of a weight lifter!

"Your strength is starting to come to you now that you've had something to eat!" said Kyle, looking satisfied. "Raw meat, that's what you need. That's your new diet from now on."

Carly didn't really want to know why he had said that, but she felt as though she ought to ask anyway out of sheer curiosity. Luckily though, she didn't need to ask, for Kyle volunteered the information without her even opening her mouth or saying a word.

"If you don't eat meat, you'll grow weak, and we can't be having that", he said. "I mean, you'll survive okay if you eat other things, dogs eat biscuits after all, but meat is what you really need."

Carly snorted. "I'm not a dog", she pointed out.

Kyle chuckled. "Well, not exactly..."

"What is that supposed to mean?" bristled Carly. Was that some sort of insult?

"You haven't clicked on yet have you?" said Kyle sounding slightly incredulous. "Are you always this oblivious?"

Carly put her hands on her hips indignantly. This wasn't the first time she had been accused of being oblivious. Once when she was about thirteen, her mother had bought her a new bike. She had put it in the garage, right at the front, where nobody could fail to see it if they opened the garage door. She then asked Carly if she could fetch her a plant-pot from the garage. Carly had opened the garage door, dutifully found a plant-pot, and brought it to her mother. Her mother had looked at her quite quizzically, as Carly had not mentioned the bike. Truth was that Carly hadn't seen the bike at all; she simply hadn't noticed it. It was only on returning a second time to the garage, that Carly had made a point of looking around a bit more carefully, and then she had spied the present. It was quite amazing that she hadn't seen it the first time, but that was Carly, quite unobservant.

So, despite her indignation, Carly admitted that Kyle had a point. She really did have the gift of obliviousness. "Okay, what am I being oblivious about?" she asked.

Kyle sighed, clearly finding the whole thing a little exasperating.

"Think about it", he said.

Carly cast her mind back over the events that had unfolded over the past several hours. "There were some glowing eyes peering in through the window", she mused aloud. "My eyes are glowing now too. I've been hallucinating. My boyfriend and his friends are all missing. I'm eating cats…oh and I'm stronger than I used to be."

Kyle nodded, as she spoke. "So, what does it all add up to then?" he asked, as though he was asking a small child how to spell a simple word.

"God I don't know. I'm a vampire and I've killed my boyfriend?" Carly hoped to goodness that she was wrong about that!

Kyle roared with laughter, so loudly that Carly jumped. "Oh Lord you've been watching too many movies", he said, trying to catch his breath. "Next you'll be expecting to start twinkling in sunlight! No you're not a goddamn vampire!"

Carly was somewhat relieved. She had felt stupid saying it anyway. "Okay, so what then? Spell it out!"

"You're a werewolf", stated Kyle, quite matter-of-factly.

"A what?"

"A werewolf. I assume you've heard of werewolves before?"

Carly rolled her eyes. "Stop messing with me. Seriously, what's going on? Stop talking crap about werewolves and really tell me."

"I'm being deadly serious", said Kyle. Indeed he really did look now as though he was being deadly serious.

Carly narrowed her eyebrows. "There are no such things as werewolves."

Kyle smiled at her. "Watch", he said. He rolled up his sleeve and held out his bare arm in front of him. He closed his eyes, and breathed heavily. His arm began to mutate before Carly's eyes. It began to grow thick sandy coloured fur, and changed shape, until it entirely resembled the foreleg of a dog. His hand shrank and turned into a paw (albeit a large paw), and long sharp talon-like nails sprung from it.

Carly gasped in horror. "Oh my God…" she said. She couldn't believe what she was seeing. She looked up to see if the rest of Kyle's body had changed, but no, it was just his arm. After less than a minute, Kyle opened his eyes. His arm quickly regained its human form, and he gave it a little shake, and rolled his sleeve back down.

"What the hell was that?" asked Carly.

"Once you get more in control of being able to shift, you will learn that you can control individual body parts, and change them at will."

"You're serious…I'm a werewolf? And you're a werewolf?"

Kyle nodded. "Yup."

Carly felt as though she was going to faint. She managed to remain standing for a few seconds, before her knees buckled under her, and she lurched forward. In a split second, Kyle reached out his arms and grabbed her. He stopped her from falling to the floor.

"Thanks", said Carly, as he helped her to steady herself.

"You're welcome."

'A werewolf with good manners', thought Carly. 'You don't see that every day.' She shook her head. What was she thinking? You don't see werewolves at all, ever, let alone ones with good manners!

"I don't know what to say", said Carly. "I'm a werewolf? That's…"

"That's a lot to take in, I know, I get it", replied Kyle, voicing what she was thinking.

A thought occurred to Carly. "How is it that you can control when you turn into a wolf then? I thought that werewolves turn into wolves under a full moon, and that it's uncontrollable?"

"Yes, there is that part of it, that's what makes it a curse", admitted Kyle. He seemed a little melancholy all of a sudden. "It hurts like hell when that happens. It's too fast, and you can't control it. Plus…you don't exactly turn into a wolf under the full moon, but more a sort of beast-like version of a wolf. Your human spirit has gone, and you become, quite literally, a vicious killing machine. The rest of the month though, you're the one in control. You decide when it happens, you decide how it happens, and you can take your time with it. It's a bit like the difference between getting into a swimming pool by using the ladder, and then bobbing gently on the surface, or being tackled into a swimming pool by a sumo wrestler, who then pins you down under the water for several minutes before letting you up to breathe."

"Oh…" said Carly. "That makes sense." 'What am I saying? None of this makes any sense', she thought. "Do you know where Rob is?" she asked.

"Rob?"

"My boyfriend."

"Oh, is that his name? Well…we'll get onto that subject in a minute." Kyle seemed slightly agitated at the question.

"No, Kyle, we'll get onto that subject NOW please!"

"Okay, okay, well…truth is…Rob's in the woods, I think, somewhere, with Seth, and the others."

"Who is Seth?"

"My brother. He's a bit older than me, bossy, you'll probably find him kinda annoying!"

"I find *you* annoying!" retorted Carly, flicking her long mahogany hair over her shoulder. "Is Rob okay? Why is he in the woods with your brother?"

Kyle sighed again. "Okay look, sit down, you're beginning to make me nervous", he said, looking furtively left and right.

Carly grunted, and walked into the living room. Dramatically, she threw herself on the sofa. "Go on then, spit it out."

Kyle began to pace around the living room in front of her. He shook his head and stretched his arms out a little, as though warming up before exercising. Finally he began to speak.

"Seth and Devon are friends, they have been for a few years. About a year ago, Devon came to me and asked me to scratch him. He told me that Seth wouldn't do it, but he was desperate to be one of us. I tried to talk him out of it, but he pleaded with me so badly that I did it. My scratch passed on the gift of lycanthropy…"

"Lycanthropy?" asked Carly.

"Werewolfism", explained Kyle.

"Werewolfism? Is that actually a word?" interrupted Carly.

"Does it really matter?" snapped Kyle. Carly decided to hold her tongue. "Sorry," she whispered, "go on".

Kyle cleared his throat. "Anyway, Devon, Seth, and I have been meaning for some time to expand the pack and get some new recruits, but we've been a little busy so sort of didn't get around to it. We got talking a few weeks ago, and Devon told us about his old uni buddies that he still hung around with. A group of guys, around the same age as us, who are already on friendly terms with each other; it seemed like the perfect opportunity to gain a pack."

Carly gasped. "You mean all this time, Rob and the others have been hanging out with a werewolf, and just didn't realise?"

Kyle clicked his tongue impatiently. "Yeah, well, it's not as though you can tell when we are in human form. So, getting back to the point of all this, we decided that last night was going to be the night when we formed the pack, so after Jackson's girlfriend left the house, Seth and I arrived there, and together with Devon we welcomed Jackson, Rob, Ian and Gary into our pack, so to speak."

"You turned them into werewolves?"

"Yes, but it wasn't pretty, Jackson got badly wounded." Kyle paused at this point, a troubled look etched itself upon his face. He rubbed his brow in a nervous gesture. We never meant for it to turn out that way, I would never have gone along with it if it hadn't been for the fact that Seth had said it would be all right. Devon said that he had told the others about becoming werewolves, and that they were all hyped up about it. Turns out that they didn't actually know about it at all."

"That explains the blood that Jackson's girlfriend found outside her house", said Carly. It was beginning to make sense now.

"Quite so", agreed Kyle. "The four of them began to hallucinate quite badly. Rob was screaming about a herd of stampeding elephants trampling on him. Gary and Ian started attacking each other - both seemingly convinced that the other was trying to murder him. Jackson was so badly wounded in the fray that he was knocked out. We managed to drag them into Devon's car, which was parked outside, and took them to a cabin we have in the forest, which contains medical supplies. It wasn't the best formation of a pack, put it that way. We didn't really think it through particularly well. With hindsight we ought to have turned one at a time, it would have been much easier to deal with, rather than taking on all four in the one go! Plus, I think they should have known about it and given their permission."

"So they're all there now, in the forest?"

Kyle looked sombre. "Jackson didn't make it", he said quietly. "We've buried his body near the cabin."

Carly's head was spinning; she still couldn't believe what she was hearing. Then, suddenly, she felt a surge of fear. Here she was standing talking to a monster! "Have you ever killed anybody?" she asked, almost not wanting to hear the answer.

Kyle lowered his gaze. "I have killed somebody yes, once", he said softly. "The first time I shifted during a lunar change…" he broke off, clearly unable to continue speaking.

"Who did you kill?" asked Carly gently.

Kyle pulled his wallet from his pocket. It was a battered black leather wallet that looked as though it had seen better days. He opened it up, and withdrew a creased photograph from it. He handed the photograph to Carly.

Carly held up the photograph and peered at it. A pretty girl of about nine years old was holding a red rose and smiling out of the photograph. Her hair was long and loose and the same colour as Kyle's. She was wearing a denim blue skirt and a pale pink t-shirt. Carly remembered when she was a girl having a denim skirt very similar to that one. She wore it once to a school disco and a rather unpleasant boy had been sick on her lap as a result of eating too many mini sausage rolls. Carly's mother had thrown the skirt away after that incident; apparently she hadn't even been able to wash it, it had been too badly soiled.

"Who is she?" asked Carly.

"My little sister Gemma", replied Kyle, taking back the photograph. "You see, my father was a werewolf too, something my parents never told me. With werewolves, you inherit the condition, even if only one parent is a werewolf. It gets passed down, as it's a very dominant trait. You start to experience signs when you are going through puberty. It's up there with voice breaking and pubic hair growing! Anyway, one day, when I was thirteen, about a week or so after my birthday, I felt ill, started to hallucinate, felt dizzy and sick, I'm sure you know what I'm talking about!"

Carly nodded, she knew only too well the feelings that Kyle was describing, having experienced the same thing very recently.

"I took myself off to bed, not knowing what was happening to me. I thought I was probably sick with the flu or something. My mom was out at work, and I was at home with Seth and Gemma. Seth was babysitting us. Honestly, after I got into bed, I don't remember anything else. As it turns out, at some point later that evening, Gemma had come to my room to see if I was okay. We were very close. I played with her more than I did Seth really, back then, because he was a bit of an asshole at the time. Mind you he's a bit of an asshole now as well. Anyway, when I came round the next morning, Gemma was dead, and half our house had been demolished."

Carly gasped. "You killed Gemma…"

Kyle nodded.

"Oh God Kyle I'm so sorry, that's terrible. It's not your fault though, you had no idea you would turn into a werewolf!"

Kyle exhaled. "I know, I know, I've had years of trying to come to terms with this."

"What about your parents? Where are they now?"

"My mom died when I was sixteen; lung cancer", said Kyle, his voice trembling. "As for my dad, I don't know where he is, nor do I care", Kyle's eyes flashed angrily. "He walked out on us when I was ten and we never saw him again. He should have told me. It's his fault it happened. I don't know if my dad is alive or dead and frankly I'd prefer it if he were dead, I'd never have even the remotest chance of bumping into him in future then!"

Carly didn't say anything. The rage Kyle felt for his father was obvious, and she didn't feel it was her place to press him on the matter. She remained silent for a few minutes. Then something occurred to her. "Seth is your older brother isn't he?" she asked.

"Yeah, three years older, why?"

"Well, if you were thirteen when you first changed, that would have made him about sixteen. He would have already changed wouldn't he? Didn't you click on from him being one, that you actually might be one too?"

Kyle grunted. "Seth didn't bother with me very much in those days, kept himself to himself. That was his moody teenage phase."

"And Gemma?"

"Gemma was only just turned ten when she died." Kyle pressed his lips together tightly, turned his back to Carly and lifted his arm up to his face. It looked to Carly as though he was wiping his eyes with his sleeve. She reached out a hand and gently brushed her fingers against his shoulder. He stiffened up at her touch.

"I'm really sorry for your loss", said Carly. Kyle didn't reply. After a few moments he turned around.

"So, Carly, anything else you want to know? I'm here to help with the transition. It's always easier if somebody is there to help you out and keep you at least semi-sane while all this is going on."

"I'm feeling all right for the moment, I'm not hallucinating right now anyway, so that's something!" Carly was actually surprising herself by how well she was handing all this. She wasn't sure it had really sunk in yet, so that was probably partially the reason behind how calm she was feeling.

"Good, that'll be the meat that helped with that", said Kyle.

"I do have another question though, actually."

Kyle raised his eyebrow and looked at Carly. "Fire away."

"Why did you recruit me into your pack? How do you even know me? Through Rob? I don't understand, why me?"

Kyle looked slightly embarrassed. "Well actually that wasn't my doing at all, that was Rob."

"Rob wanted me to become a werewolf?"

"Not exactly." Kyle began pacing around the room again. He seemed restless, in much the same way a caged tiger paces around, wishing to be free from the confines of its cage. Carly was feeling a little restless herself. The four walls of her house seemed to be closer together than usual, and Carly had a slight sense of claustrophobia that she couldn't shake. She had the urge to go outside and run, which was very unusual because Carly was not the type of person who enjoyed running in the slightest. Carly had never liked sports or exercising of any sort, other than walking. Walking she could tolerate, but running - never!

"When we turned all the guys at Jackson's house into werewolves, and then tried to get them into the car to drive them to the cabin in the woods, it was a bit like trying to round up sheep. In the confusion, Rob managed to run away. We wolves can run very quickly, that's something that you'll experience for yourself soon. I followed him as soon as I had helped Seth and Devon to separate Gary and Ian who were at each other's throats. Rob had a head start on me, and he ran all the way back to his house, back here."

"Oh my God, that's what I saw peering through the window last night. Those glowing eyes -I assumed it was you!"

"No it wasn't me, that was Rob", said Kyle. "By the time I caught up to him, it was too late, he had already scratched you."

"I don't remember him scratching me at all!" Carly paused. "My neck started hurting, but I don't remember a scratch. Surely I would remember being approached by a werewolf and it scratching me?"

"No, actually, you probably won't. Like I said, your memories will be confused and hazy for quite some time. You won't remember much about last night at all other than hallucinations I shouldn't imagine. You did open the door though to him, do you remember that?"

Carly thought hard. "Yes, I opened the door. I saw something running away."

"That'll be it then, he'll have scratched you but you've forgotten."

Carly reached her hand up to her neck. She could feel the claw marks were still there, but they didn't feel as deep as they did last night. They didn't hurt as much as they had done previously either. Kyle took her hand and moved it away from her neck. He softly ran his finger over the scratches there. "Do they hurt?" he asked. Carly shook her head.

"Not now they don't, well not much anyway", she said.

"Wounds heal quickly for us, as long as we aren't starved of meat", said Kyle.

Suddenly, quite unexpectedly, Carly felt anger bubbling up inside her. "I don't understand though", she snapped sharply. "If you know it's a curse to be a werewolf, and you've killed your own sister because of it, why would you want to form a pack? More people becoming werewolves? More innocent lives at risk?"

Kyle furrowed his brow. "We need a larger pack, we're not surviving very well with just the three of us really. Hunting is becoming more and more difficult, and without meat we're pretty weak; not only that, but Seth is the one who suggested it, and he's the pack leader."

"Why is he the pack leader?"

Kyle shrugged. "He's the oldest", he said simply.

"So just because he's the oldest, that's it, you have no say in the matter?"

Kyle looked sheepish. "Pretty much, yeah."

"Why, what will he do if you disobey him? Kill you?" Carly wasn't serious, but the look on Kyle's face immediately told her that she had hit the nail on the head. "You're kidding? But…he's your brother!"

"I know, yes, he is," Kyle sighed, "and he would do anything to protect his pack, including me, but you've got to understand we're *wolves*. If another wolf in the pack challenges the Alpha, there is a fight to the death. The winner would then be the pack leader."

"Oh", said Carly. "I can't believe he'd actually kill you though."

"Well either that, or I'd kill him, and I tell you now I'd rather die a thousand times over than be responsible for the death of my brother. After what I did to Gemma, hell would have to freeze over before I let that happen."

Carly was beginning to understand. She never had any siblings, so she didn't know what it feels like to love someone like that. The closest she came to it was having cousins. Carly had lots of cousins; two on her mother's side, and twelve on her father's side. Yet she wasn't amazingly close to any of them. Some she had been closer to than others, but not recently. People talk about the bond that siblings have, and Carly wondered what that must be like.

She looked at Kyle now, taking him in properly for the first time since he had arrived at her house. He was about six foot tall and had a medium build. There wasn't an ounce of fat on him from what she could see. Rather, he looked muscular and lean, in much the same way she would imagine a healthy wolf's figure would be. His shoulders were quite broad, though not excessively so. He looked strong, and his legs were fairly long. She could well imagine that he would be able to hold his own in a fight, though obviously she had never seen Kyle's brother Seth in order to draw up a comparison between the two!

"What's Seth like?" she asked Kyle, slightly hesitantly. Kyle pulled a wry face.

"He's an asshole I told you", he replied.

"That's not terribly descriptive!" pointed out Carly, rolling her eyes slightly. "What does he look like?"

"What does it matter? You'll meet him soon anyway", said Kyle, clearly reluctant to talk about his brother.

"Just indulge me please", insisted Carly. She didn't know why she was so curious, but she really wanted, for some reason, to find out what she was getting into. She wanted to know what to expect when she finally met the pack leader.

"Well, he's not much taller than me. 'Bout half an inch maybe at the most. Uhh…black hair…"

"Black hair? Gosh that's different to you and your sister."

"Yeah well Gemma and I look like our parents. Seth doesn't", said Kyle shrugging. "Maybe his looks skipped a generation, I dunno."

Carly's stomach rumbled. Kyle looked at her sharply. "You hungry again?" he asked abruptly.

Carly instantly pictured a slab of raw meat in her mind's eye. Her mouth began once again to salivate. "I guess I am, yeah."

Kyle sagged his shoulders and made a guttural noise. "It's always the same in the beginning. Until the first full moon, which isn't due for another two weeks, newbie werewolves are always starving. Come on we'd better get you some more meat before you start spacing out again." He took her hand and started to pull her toward the front door.

She yanked her arm back and planted her feet on the floor, steadfast. "Where are we going?"

"To get some meat. Didn't I just say that?"

"Well hang on a minute I need my wallet."

Kyle looked at her incredulously for a few moments, and then his face broke into a broad grin. "You don't need a wallet for meat! You're not going to buy it."

"I…I'm not?"

"No you silly, we're going to catch it!"

"Catch it ourselves? As in…"

"Grab it, kill it, eat it!" clarified Kyle.

Carly felt the same way she had done earlier when she had been watching the squirrel, a mixture of disgust and longing. Finally she nodded at Kyle. She wanted to do this; she needed to do this.

Without saying another word, Kyle took hold of her hand again and they left the house. Carly forgot to set the burglar alarm and didn't even remember to lock the front door. It couldn't have been further from her mind. She was starting to feel jittery and shivery, as though she was coming down with a fever.

Kyle obviously felt her hand shaking as he held it; he looked at her with a concerned expression. "Are you okay?" he asked.

"Oh…ww…w…wonderf..f…f…ful", she stammered, her teeth chattering.

"Hmm, let's stop a minute, sit there", instructed Kyle, pointing at a nearby tree-stump. Carly hadn't been paying much attention, but they had been walking for several minutes and were now just about to enter a forest. There was a very large forest area in very close vicinity to where Carly lived. There were also many lakes. The abundance of natural space was what had attracted Carly and Rob to their home in the first place. They had been fed up of living in the city, where everybody is practically on top of everybody else and the noise of buses keeps you awake at night. Here the scenery was much more pleasant, though they were still very close to shops and nightlife if they wanted to go out, which they did quite frequently.

Carly sat down on the tree-stump. Her head was beginning to spin. She felt a tickling sensation on her leg, as if something was crawling up it. She looked down and saw a rather large spider scuttling up her shin towards her knee. She gave a small yelp and shook her leg - the spider fell off. She shuddered; she hated spiders with a passion. She glanced up at Kyle; he was looking at her rather oddly. "I hate spiders", she explained. He was still looking a little puzzled and didn't reply.

Carly felt more tickling on her leg. "Oh Jesus!" she screamed, and leapt to her feet. There was a great swarm of spiders now running up her legs. They were huge and hairy - she had never seen spiders like that before; they looked more like the sort of spider you would expect to see in a jungle. She began swatting wildly at her legs, screaming and half crying. She picked up a stick that was lying on the ground next to her and began hitting the spiders, scratching her legs badly in the process and leaving giant welts on her skin.

"Carly, woah! Stop!" Kyle grabbed hold of her shoulders. Carly was still screaming with fear. She was kicking wildly and accidentally booted Kyle in the leg. It was a hard kick, but Kyle barely seemed to notice it. He grunted slightly, but that was all. Instead, he kept a firm grip on her shoulders.

"Carly, look at me", he ordered.

"Get them off me, get them off me!" she screamed, not hearing him at all. The spiders were everywhere now - on her back, on her shoulders, on her head. The more that fell off, the more climbed on. She didn't know where they were coming from, but they only seemed to be crawling on her. They weren't approaching Kyle at all.

"LOOK AT ME!" roared Kyle.

Carly was shocked by his tone, and momentarily stopped her hysteria. She looked at him; his eyes were glowing brighter than usual. She imagined she could almost see them emitting flames.

"It's not real", he told her. "It's a hallucination. Okay? Just a hallucination."

'Not real? Surely something this realistic couldn't just be a figment of my imagination. Mind you, I did see the house falling down, and the image of Rob dead in bed.' Carly cast her mind back and grimaced. She took a deep breath. "Okay, not real, not real, not real." She looked down at her legs; the spiders were still there. "Not real, not real, not real, not real!" She shut her eyes and continued to chant to herself, an edge of desperation resonating in her voice.

"Stay there for a minute, can you do that for me?" Kyle spoke softly, close to her ear. Carly nodded, still muttering to herself, with her eyes firmly closed. She didn't dare to move in case one of the nonexistent spiders attacked her. She felt Kyle letting go of her shoulders and his footsteps padded away from her until she could hear them no longer.

She felt alone and exposed in the woods by herself. Her eyes were still closed and she imagined she could hear strange sounds all around her. Eventually, after what seemed like an age, she heard the distinctive sound of Kyle coming back towards her. She sniffed the air and could smell his aftershave - Brut, her favourite. Rob wore the same brand sometimes.

"Kyle?" she called out. He didn't answer until he was practically standing beside her. He took her hand and placed something small and furry into it.

"Eat", he commanded.

Carly didn't open her eyes. She didn't want to see what she was holding. It smelled wonderful though and she lifted her hand to her mouth.

"It's a rabbit", announced Kyle, just as she was sinking her teeth into its back. Carly wouldn't have cared if it had been another cat at this point as she was so hungry. As it so happened, she had eaten rabbit before. When she had been a little girl, her father had sometimes bought rabbit meat from the market and made rabbit stew. She hadn't had it for many years though due to the price being so expensive. She struggled to rip open the rabbit to avoid the fur and get to the delicious meat underneath, but she ended up chewing some of the fur regardless.

"You'll get the hang of that", said Kyle reassuringly. "Anyway, after your first lunar change, you'll be able to grow more appropriate teeth for this sort of thing."

Carly nodded, unable to speak due to the rabbit hanging out of her mouth. Kyle looked away. Carly managed to break off from eating long enough to ask "what's the matter?"

"I'm feeling kinda hungry", he confessed.

"Oh, why didn't you say so? Do you want a bite?"

"No, no it's okay, you have it, you need it more than I do", insisted Kyle. "Besides I can always find another rabbit later if I need to. They're not very big, you won't have enough to keep you going for a while if you share it with me."

Carly wasn't inclined to argue with him about that. She felt as though she could eat ten rabbits, but she settled for the one she had. 'It's strange,' she mused inwardly, 'that I'm not squeamish at all about ripping open this bunny. At one time, even seeing something like this on the T.V. would have put me off watching it.'

Kyle smiled at her. "You develop a tolerance for killing other creatures when you're a werewolf!" he said.

Carly was astonished. "How did you know what I was thinking?"

"Lucky guess", shrugged Kyle.

Carly turned her concentration back to the rabbit. Smacking her chops and not caring whether or not she looked completely undignified, Carly savagely gulped down the meat until at last she was left licking the bones. She looked up.

"Satisfied?" he asked.

"For now", she replied, wiping the blood from her face with her arm.

"We'd better get moving then." Kyle took her hand again and they walked together through the trees. Carly didn't quite know why they were holding hands; it certainly wasn't usual for her to hold hands with a relative stranger, but for some reason it seemed completely natural. She felt as though she had known him her whole life. She cast her mind back to an hour ago when he had shown up at her door. She had felt drawn towards him even then, and now she felt as comfortable with him as she did with any one of her close friends - perhaps even more so.

"Where are we going?" she asked, realising that they weren't heading back in the direction of her house.

"To Seth's cabin…the pack's cabin", said Kyle. Carly stiffened slightly, and Kyle squeezed her hand reassuringly. "It's okay, really, we're a pack now, we look out for each other."

They walked in silence for about an hour. Carly marvelled at the size of the forest; she had never actually ventured far into it before. She was beginning to wonder if they would ever get there, when suddenly Kyle stopped walking. He let go of her hand and pointed into the distance. "There it is."

Carly's gaze followed his finger and she squinted. She couldn't see anything at first, but then she managed to make out a tiny light. "We're pretty close then", said Carly. It was more a statement than a question.

"Well, about fifteen minutes walk", replied Kyle.

"Fifteen minutes? That can't be right. How would we be able to see it already if it were that far?"

"You can see much further now than you used to", said Kyle. "Or hadn't you noticed?"

Actually, as it happened, Carly hadn't noticed. To be sure she had noticed how clear her surroundings were, and obviously she didn't need to use her contact lenses any longer, but in terms of distances she hadn't really acknowledged that aspect of her new vision.

"It's kind of cool really", he continued, running his hand through his hair. It was quite dark in the wood, though it was still early, due to the canopy of leaves above her head obscuring the sunlight. Even in the shade of the dense foliage, Carly couldn't help noticing that Kyle was far from being bad looking. She didn't know why she hadn't seen it before. More than likely it was because the dramatic events that had taken place that day had been a little more pressing on her mind. Now, though, as she looked at him, she began to appreciate his chiselled features. He looked as if he belonged in an aftershave advert on television. She felt herself suddenly unable to tear her eyes away from him.

"Come on, we'd better go", said Kyle, breaking her out of her reverie. He took hold of her hand again and Carly felt her cheeks grow warm. She knew she was blushing, so she quickly lowered her head, aware that Kyle's werewolf vision would have no problem in picking up her abrupt change of complexion.

Kyle seemed completely unaware of any of this and continued walking quite steadfastly towards the cabin. He had a focused determined look on his face and he took long strides, in an apparent attempt to quicken his pace. Carly had to jog to keep up with him as she was only 5'4" herself so her legs were much shorter than his, but she didn't cause her any problems. On the contrary, she felt herself itching to move even faster. She wanted to run. Merely jogging in this way seemed very restrictive. The feeling grew stronger and stronger, until at last it was so unbearable that she tore her hand out of Kyle's and began to tear through the forest at full speed.

The wind pulled her hair from her scrunchie and her long auburn locks blew backwards freely. Her legs kept going - faster and faster. She felt her body rushing past the trees; if any branches snagged her as she ran, she didn't feel them. She felt truly free for the first time in her life. She forgot who she was, she forgot who she had been, she forgot her friends, she forgot Rob, and she forgot about everything except the way she felt right then, running. She was easily as fast as a greyhound on a racetrack. She was graceful and agile, bounding easily over fallen logs and stumps. Her heart was pounding yet she was barely breaking a sweat. A tree stump at least as high as her shoulder was in her path. Carly saw it too late to avoid it, so she braced herself for impact. Just as she was about to hit it, instinct took over, and she leapt as high as she could; to her amazement she found she was sailing easily over the stump, landing in the mud on the far side of it with all the ease of a gymnast. She paused briefly for a moment, revelling in what she had just done, then once again broke into a sprint. She didn't know where she was going and she didn't care.

All of a sudden, she saw something leap at her. It slammed its body into hers with full force and knocked her tumbling to the ground. She lay there for a moment, stunned. Then Carly heard a snarl behind her. She sat up hurriedly and spun around. A huge black wolf was standing, watching her. It was panting heavily. She stared into its glowing eyes and it stared back at hers. Carly felt as though she was in a staring contest with the beast. She didn't know who would win but she didn't want to look away. The wolf began to growl and bare its teeth. Carly didn't feel afraid, but rather exhilarated. After what felt like an age, she heard a howl coming from somewhere over to the left. Then there were footsteps, and rustling in the bushes. From the corner of her eye she saw another figure of a wolf appearing on the scene.

This wolf was a sandy colour, not dissimilar to the colour of Kyle's hair. It was almost the same size as the black wolf in front of her, though very slightly smaller in build. It headed straight for Carly and began to lick her face.

Carly felt as if a very large dog was licking her. As a general rule she wasn't very fond of dogs licking her face, but she didn't mind this in the slightest. She broke her gaze from the black wolf and stood up.

The black wolf closed its eyes and crouched down on the floor. It began to transform itself into a human being. The transformation didn't take longer than ten seconds, yet it seemed to take place in sections. First the limbs, then the torso, then lastly the head. There, crouching on the ground now, was a man. He was entirely naked except for a strange pendant in the shape of a capsule, which he wore around his neck on a gold chain. Carly was fascinated by what she had just seen. She stared at the man in front of her in awe.

"I suppose you're Carly", the man said. He stood up now, seemingly unashamed of his own nudity.

Carly was a little taken aback by this and tried to keep her eyes on his face rather than the rest of his body. "Y…yes", she stammered. Once again she could feel her cheeks beginning to grow warm.

The man noticed this and looked pleased. "I take it you like what you see?"

"Are you always this cocky?" asked Carly, then realised, too late, her unfortunate choice of words.

The man laughed. "Only when there are pretty girls around."

Carly felt slightly mortified and looked away to the side of her, expecting to see the second wolf there. Instead, Kyle was now standing in its place. To make matters worse, he was also completely naked.

"Oh my God", said Carly involuntarily. She brought her hands up to her eyes. "Don't you two think you'd better put some clothes on or something?"

Both Kyle and the other man, who Carly presumed was Kyle's brother Seth, began to laugh.

"You're part of a pack of werewolves now sweetheart; you're going to have to get over your modesty hang-ups! Just think of this as a nature camp!" said Seth cheerfully.

Carly was flummoxed. "Erm…erm…" she stuttered, her hands still over her eyes, not quite knowing what to say.

Kyle chuckled. "It's ok, look, my clothes are just back in the bush where I changed, I'll go and put them on."

"Okay", said Carly, still not looking. She heard Kyle's footsteps walking way.

"My clothes are back at the cabin, so you're going to have to put up with me like this until we get there", announced Seth, once Kyle had gone. "I'm Seth, by the way."

"Yes, I figured you were", said Carly, lowering her hands and keeping her eyes on Seth's face. "Kyle has told me about you."

"Oh really? I bet he has. All good I presume?"

"Well, he didn't really say a great deal, just…told me that you're his brother, that's all, and that you're the pack leader."

"As if you couldn't tell just by looking at me", winked Seth.

Seth really looked nothing like Kyle. Both were good looking, but Seth had an entirely different nose and chin, and his hair was short, black, and spiky. Both had glowing eyes though, of course, as Carly now did herself.

"I was wondering something", said Carly. "How do you hide your eyes when you're out in public?"

"We tend not to go out in public really, but if we have to, then sunglasses or coloured contact lenses, both generally work ok", said Seth shrugging. "I don't really have many friends other than Kyle and Devon these days anyway, and you'll find that strangers just seem to assume that glowing eyes are some sort of funky contact lenses even if they do spot them, so it doesn't tend to be a huge problem."

"The beauty of being a werewolf in this day and age then I suppose," mused Carly, "as opposed to way back when sunglasses and contact lenses weren't readily available".

"Mmm yeah, can't have been easy for them back then", agreed Seth.

They both fell into an uneasy silence. Carly shuffled around in the grass and leaves underneath her feet. It was nearing the end of summer. In a few weeks the whole forest would be carpeted with a thick layer of red and gold leaves. For now though the trees were still lush and green.

"Do you know who I am then?" she asked him. She presumed he obviously did, but she wanted to break the ice a little.

"You're Rob's other half", replied Seth. He looked her up and down, taking in her slender figure. "Lucky guy."

Carly blushed openly. "Thanks", she said, feeling flattered but embarrassed. Carly wasn't very good at taking compliments, she always felt as though they ought to be directed at somebody else.

"If you ever get fed up of him, I'm always here you know."

"You're very sure of yourself", said Carly, half-smiling. "What makes you think I'd be interested in you?"

"I'm the pack leader, I'm the one with the power. Who wouldn't want to be with the top dog?" asked Seth. Carly looked at him curiously wondering if he was joking, but no, he seemed quite serious.

"Well, I'm perfectly happy with Rob", she retorted. Her eyes flashed.

"Suit yourself, but you'll change your mind."

Carly was just trying to think of a suitably indignant comeback, when Kyle reappeared from behind a tree.

"You were a long time, what were you doing?" asked Seth, a little snappily.

"Forgot where I left my clothes", said Kyle.

"You what? What kind of a retard forgets where he's left his clothes?"

"Sorry", said Kyle. He lowered his head in a submissive gesture.

Seth sighed. "Let's go, they're all waiting for us at the cabin."

Without waiting for Kyle and Carly, Seth set off running. Carly peered after him but within a matter of seconds he was out of sight. The cabin was also no longer visible, as Carly had inadvertently run the wrong away, away from it.

Kyle looked at Carly and pulled his hand out from behind his back. In it was a pretty bunch of wild flowers. "These are for you", he said, looking slightly bashful.

"Oh, wow!" Carly was taken aback. Nobody had ever presented her with a bunch of flowers before. Even Rob, who she had been dating for two years, had never seen fit to buy (or even pick) her any flowers. "They're beautiful, thank you! Is that why you took a while to get back to us, because you were picking flowers?"

"Yeah, well, I thought you'd like them. They're to welcome you to the pack."

Carly took the flowers and held them up to her nose. They had a beautiful fragrant scent, which Carly appreciated more now with her new heightened sense of smell than she would have done when she was a human.

Kyle smiled, and held out his hand to her once again. "Shall we go?"

Carly took his hand and they continued walking.

CHAPTER THREE

Before long they reached the cabin. It was quite large, for a cabin - at least the size of a regular three bedroomed house, though it was all on one level much like a bungalow. It was entirely made out of logs. Carly felt as though she had been transported into a Heidi storybook. As they approached it, the door flung open and out ran somebody that Carly recognised. It was Rob.

"Carly!" he screamed, hurtling towards her. Then he stopped dead in his tracks and looked at Kyle. He looked back at Carly, then at Kyle again, and then at their hands which were still entwined together.

Carly quickly let go of Kyle's hand. "Kyle was just leading me to the cabin", she said. "He has been very kind to me."

Rob looked at the flowers that Carly was carrying. His face contorted in anger. Carly had never seen him pull an expression like that before, as Rob was usually quite a mild mannered guy.

"I bet he has", said Rob, sarcastically. He stared at Kyle threateningly, who, in turn, took a step backwards.

"Look man, there's nothing going on", he said, putting his hands up in surrender.

Rob didn't appear to be listening though, and he snarled in a very wolf-like manner. "What the fuck do you think you're doing?" he growled, his teeth gritted.

"Look, can we drop this, you're being silly; Carly is here to see you!"

Rob dropped to his knees and let out a cry that sounded as if he had witnessed something terrible. He turned to Carly. "I can't believe this, I've been waiting for you here all this time, and what do I get in return? I can't believe you're fucking this guy, and you have the cheek to do it right in front of me? How could you?!"

Carly's mouth dropped open. "Rob, what are you talking about?"

"You filthy slut, get your clothes on", wailed Rob, beginning to rock backwards and forwards.

Carly looked down at herself, wondering if she was hallucinating again. Her clothes were still there. She looked at Kyle and whispered "Kyle, I'm not naked am I?"

"No, you're not", he replied. "I think Rob is seeing things."

"What was I ever doing with you in the first place?" Rob was muttering to himself. "You're nothing but a fucking bitch. Well, I'm glad I've been sleeping with Jennifer, serves you right. She's hotter than you anyway."

Carly gasped. "What the…?"

"It's the hallucination talking, just try not to listen", said Kyle reassuringly. Carly gulped and nodded.

Without warning, Rob suddenly leapt to his feet and lunged at Kyle, biting and scratching. Kyle dodged out of the way and instantly grabbed Rob's right arm, bending it up behind his back while tripping him over; this manoeuvre resulted in Rob being pinned to the ground. Rob squirmed and thrashed around, but Kyle held him there with very little effort.

"I'm a lot stronger and faster than you, so you need to calm down and stop fighting me", Kyle said calmly. Rob paid him no heed though and began roaring and bellowing. "Will somebody get some goddam meat for this guy before he does himself an injury?" yelled Kyle in the direction of the cabin.

Seth strolled out of the cabin looking amused by the scene before him. "Having a little trouble there Kyle?" he asked, smirking.

"No, but Rob here could use some dinner", replied Kyle, still holding down Rob.

"Do I have to do everything for you little brother?" asked Seth. He disappeared back into the house and returned with a dead squirrel. Carly's eyes widened at the sight of it and her taste buds began to tingle. The smell of it wafted over to her with the wind and she lifted her nose to the air to sniff hungrily.

Seth tossed the squirrel to her and she caught it easily. "There you go, that's for Rob", he said with a grin.

Carly moaned. She desperately wanted to eat the squirrel but she knew she had to give it to Rob. She took two steps towards Kyle and Rob and then stopped. Her hands started to bring the squirrel to her mouth. It took every ounce of her willpower to stop herself from tearing into the creature. She concentrated hard and managed to force herself to walk the extra two steps to where they were lying.

She bent down and placed the squirrel in front of Rob. Rob craned with his neck and snapped at it, taking a huge chunk out of its back. He closed his eyes and began to chew, making appreciative noises. As he ate he stopped throwing himself around, and Kyle cautiously released his hold on Rob and stood up.

Rob remained on the floor eating the squirrel. When he was finished, he slowly stood up and looked at Kyle and Carly. "I'm sorry", he said.

"Who is Jennifer?" asked Carly.

"Oh…nobody…she's nobody…in fact, I don't know who she is", said Rob, stammering.

Rob looked down at the floor and didn't meet Carly's gaze. Alarm bells started ringing in her mind, but before she had chance to question him further about it, Kyle interrupted her train of thought. "Let's go inside, shall we?" he said.

Rob seemed relieved at this suggestion, and quickly scuttled back into the cabin again.

Kyle gave Carly a comforting smile. "After you", he said.

Carly took a deep breath and pushed open the wooden door. Stepping inside, she found herself in a very sparsely furnished living room. There was a tatty three-seater sofa to her left. It looked as though it was once blue, but now it appeared grey and worn. Two wooden carver chairs were on the other side of the room and several beanbags and cushions were scattered on the floor. There was an electric radiator against one wall, which was heating up the room quite nicely. There didn't appear to be a television or any sort of table in sight.

Sitting on the sofa was Ian. Carly had only ever met him (and

Gary and Devon) once. Ian's face was drawn and his eyes, though tinged with the same glow that Carly's herself now had, seemed red, and Carly could tell that he had been crying. Gary was next to him and had his arm around Ian's shoulders.

Carly briefly wondered if Ian was upset about having become a werewolf; then she remembered what had happened. She felt a lump rise in her throat and she headed straight over to Ian. He looked up as she approached.

"I'm so very sorry for your loss", she said. "I didn't really know Jackson very well, but he seemed like a good guy. I've never lost a sibling, so I can't say I know what you're going through, but I really am very sorry."

Ian nodded but didn't say anything. He pressed his lips together tightly and a single tear rolled down one cheek. Gary squeezed his shoulder.

Carly felt awkward, she didn't know what else to say. She thought it was best if she left them to it for now. She looked around but didn't see anybody else in the room, so she headed for a door in the far wall.

Going through the door, she found a fairly large bedroom. In the bedroom there was a bunk bed and a single bed. Some reasonably thick curtains hung from the windows and a simple oval shaped rug was on the wooden floor. Carly thought how much nicer real wooden floors are compared to parquet flooring, which is what she had in her own house. Despite the very minimalistic furniture, she really liked this cabin. She walked up to one of the walls and appreciated the detail of the natural knots and markings, which appeared in the wood there. She softly ran her fingertips over the wall, enjoying the sensation of the varnish under her skin.

"There's another bedroom exactly the same as this one", came a voice from behind her. It was Kyle, standing in the doorway.

Carly spun around quickly. "Sorry, I didn't mean to intrude, I didn't know where to go really. Ian seemed like he needed a moment, and Gary was with him. I didn't know where the rest of you had gone."

"That's fine, don't worry about it", said Kyle. "There are three bedrooms; two like this, and one with a double bed in it. There was always supposed to be seven of us, Jackson obviously being the seventh. Seth wanted to have the double bed to himself, and the room on his own, as he's the pack leader. Now, though, well I guess you'll be having that room. Seth will have to bunk in with the rest of us. We weren't planning on a girl being here!" Kyle grinned sheepishly and a lock of his hair flopped in front of his face. He ran his hand through it, pushing it back into place.

"What if I don't want to be part of the pack?" said Carly. "I'm beginning to feel as though I have no say in the matter!"

Kyle looked surprised. "Don't you feel as though you belong? As though this is where you're meant to be? With us?"

Carly thought about it for a moment. She hated to admit it, but he was right. She felt connected to each and every one of them, even though, with the exception of Rob, she barely knew them at all. She honestly felt as though she would be lost if she were on her own without being with at least one of her pack mates.

Kyle had been watching the expression on her face. "You do feel it, don't you?" he asked.

Carly nodded. "I can't describe it", she said. "I've never felt like this before."

"I know; it's an odd feeling isn't it? You feel as though you'd gladly give your life for the others in your pack", said Kyle. "I feel the same."

"I almost feel as though I love you all, so intensely", said Carly. She wondered if she had said the wrong thing, but she genuinely wanted to know if this was how she was supposed to be feeling.

"Yeah, that's normal", said Kyle. "All of us feel the same way about you as well." He suddenly stopped and looked embarrassed. "I mean…umm…" he stammered.

Carly smiled. "Thanks", she laughed. "Like one big happy family then?"

"Well, well, what's going on here?" a voice came from behind Kyle. Kyle moved sideways and Seth stepped through the door.

"Nothing really", replied Carly. "Kyle was just telling me about the bedrooms here. I believe I'm going to have to take your room.

Sorry about that!"

"Take my room? You must be joking?" said Seth, raising his eyebrow. "Kyle was only messing with you."

Kyle looked incredulous. "What's wrong with you? She can't bunk in with all of us lot!"

"What, are we all in pre-school?" scoffed Seth. "Ewww girls are disgusting!" He feigned mock horror at the sight of Carly and started to squeal in a high-pitched mocking tone. "Get her away from me!"

Kyle gave him a light punch on the arm. "Shut up man, you know what I mean. She might want a bit of privacy!"

"*I'm* the pack leader. She's not having my goddam room!" he bellowed. Kyle lowered his head in submission. Seth turned to Carly. "You're quite welcome to share it with me though", he winked.

Carly wanted to smack him, but something stopped her. "Thanks, but I'm taken", she said. She didn't know why she hadn't said anything more forceful. It was as though she had an inbuilt sense of duty towards Seth. She assumed that this was because he was the pack leader and it irritated her greatly. She wanted to stand up for herself, but the words simply wouldn't come.

She must have looked frustrated though, for Seth began to chuckle. "I can show you a damn good time if you reconsider!"

Carly kept quiet. She felt as though her blood were boiling. She glanced over to Kyle, who was clenching and unclenching his fists. He looked as if he might burst, but, like Carly, he had his teeth gritted and was saying nothing.

Seth took a step towards her; she stiffened up. Reaching out his hand, he stroked her hair very gently. Carly just wanted him to go away, but she stood still and tolerated it. Then, with a smirk, he turned and left the room.

As soon as he had gone both Kyle and Carly relaxed their stances. "I told you he's an asshole", said Kyle, looking very apologetic.

"It's okay, it's not your fault", she said. "I suppose I've no choice then but to be in one of the rooms with you guys."

"Well, Gary, Ian, and Devon have already decided that they want a room together", said Kyle. "I guess that leaves me, you, and Rob, in the other room."

"Don't you think that's going to be a bit awkward after what just happened outside?" asked Carly, raising an eyebrow.

"I tell you what, we'll put up a partition of some sort if you like. I'll go on the single bed, and you and Rob can take the bunk beds. We'll divide the room down the middle."

Carly smiled at him gratefully. "Sure, thanks, that would be helpful."

They stared into each other's eyes in silence. Carly could feel the hairs on the back of her neck standing up, as though they were near static electricity. The room was quiet apart from the beating of their hearts, which Carly realised to her astonishment she could hear if she listened very carefully. Her own heart began to beat faster inside her chest and she could hear that Kyle's had also picked up the pace. Kyle's eyes began to glow brighter, and it almost seemed to Carly that tiny sparks were flying out of them. The room around her started to lose focus; she could see nothing but his face. In that moment they were the only two people in the world; she felt herself inching closer towards him.

Just at that moment, a loud bang made her jump. It had come from outside. "What was that?" gasped Carly, quite startled.

"It sounded like a gun shot", replied Kyle breathlessly. He grabbed hold of her hand and pulled her back through the door into the living room. Gary and Ian were on their feet now, both looking worried. Devon was with them.

"Where are the others? Where's Seth?" asked Devon sharply. Gary shook his head. He seemed confused.

Kyle let go of Carly's hand and strode quickly across the room to the front door. "Stay here", he instructed, then exited the cabin, quickly followed by Devon.

Gary, Ian, and Carly remained where they had been standing. None of them spoke, none of them moved. Each was wondering what had happened. After about five minutes had passed, Carly turned to Gary who was next to her. "I'm going to see if I can find out where they've gone."

Gary looked shocked. "You can't do that! You heard what he said, we've got to stay here!"

Carly rolled her eyes. "I don't always do as I'm told", she replied. She didn't wait for him to argue with her. She walked across the room, took hold of the front door handle, and pulled it open.

"Wait Carly!" called Gary, but she ignored him and stepped outside.

She didn't know how it had happened, but it was dark outside. It couldn't be that late, surely? Carly estimated that she had only been at the cabin for about half an hour at the most. It couldn't be nightfall already. She didn't have a lot of time to think about that, though, for out of the darkness came a staggering figure. It was moving slowly, groaning. Carly squinted to try and make out whom it was. It was Rob. She ran towards him and was about to call out his name when he collapsed on the ground. "Rob!" she shrieked, and ran faster to reach him. He was writhing on the ground and his breathing was shallow. "Oh my God, Rob, what happened?"

"I've been shot", gasped her boyfriend.

Carly lifted up his t-shirt and clearly saw the wound in his side; it was bleeding. "We need to get you to a hospital", she said, tears filling her eyes. "You'll be okay, don't worry." She was far from sure that this was the truth, but she didn't want him to panic, as this would have made him feel worse. She didn't know what to do - she had never encountered a gunshot wound before.

Rob scrabbled to find her hand. "I'm sorry", he whispered.

"For what? You've got nothing to be sorry for", replied Carly. She was crying freely now.

"I'm sorry about Jennifer", he gasped. "I don't deserve your tears. I should have ended it with you as soon as I realised I was in love with somebody else, instead of cheating on you. I'm sorry."

Carly felt her breath catch in her throat at his words. At that moment, Seth, in wolf form, came bounding out of the forest. He quickly changed into a human and scooped Rob off the floor and into his arms. "I've got medical supplies", he said, before running the short distance back to the cabin, still carrying Rob.

Carly was left standing amongst the trees feeling helpless. She was still crying, and she didn't feel as though she would ever stop. She couldn't believe what Rob had said, and now he was probably going to die. It didn't feel real at all, none of it did. "Wake up Carly!" she began to scream. "Wake up Carly, wake up Carly, WAKE UP CARLY!" She slapped her own face several times and pinched herself on the arm. Again and again she pinched, but nothing happened. She was still here in the forest. She fell to her knees and sobbed into her hands. She cried as though her heart were breaking, for indeed, she felt as though it was. The events of the entire day began to wash over her like a flood and it was as if she was losing control. She didn't know who she was anymore; she didn't think she would ever feel right again.

After a while her tears subsided. Her face was red and blotchy and her hands and sleeves were completely soaked. She imagined that she must have cried enough to fill a river. Still sniffling, Carly wiped at her face, trying in vain to dry it. She wasn't terribly successful though as her hands were also wet. She stood up and looked around. She could see the cabin not far away. She decided to head back to it and see how Rob was doing. She was dreading what she might find; she didn't think she would be able to cope if he hadn't survived. Despite what he had said about cheating on her, she couldn't imagine life without him. She wondered who could have shot him, and why. Had they mistaken him for an animal of some sort? Rob was a new werewolf like her so he couldn't turn freely into a wolf yet, not until the first lunar change - at least that's what she gathered from what Kyle had told her, so it was hardly as though he had been running around the forest in wolf form. What reason would anybody have to be shooting at him?

Carly was still thinking about this, when she caught a glimpse of something moving at the side of her. Slowly, ever so slowly, Carly turned her head to see what it was. A raccoon; it was sniffing at the floor, seemingly unaware that she was sitting there. Carly stared at it and her stomach began to call out to her. She could feel her tongue starting to tingle. She really didn't know how she could be hungry again, as she had eaten quite recently the squirrel that Kyle had brought her, but he had warned her that she would be frequently hungry for the next couple of weeks.

Without moving a muscle, Carly watched the raccoon and prepared herself to pounce. As the creature neared her, she felt a great surge of energy coursing through her body; she grabbed it with lightning fast reflexes. She couldn't believe she had caught it, she felt so triumphant! Once, when she had been about nine years old, she had managed to catch a mouse that had made its home in the cellar of the house she lived in. Her mother had been putting down poison, but the mouse must have been very intelligent, as it never seemed to touch the stuff. So Carly had fashioned a mousetrap of her own using peanut butter as bait and had managed to successfully catch the mouse all by herself. She had kept it after that in a cage as a pet and it had lived to a ripe old age for a mouse. Carly had felt a little mean putting it in a cage, considering it had been a wild animal, but it was being a pest in the house, and she figured that it was kinder to take care of it than poison it! She had been extremely proud of the fact that she had caught that mouse, but the feeling she had then was nothing compared to how she felt now, catching the raccoon.

Carly quickly broke its neck and tore into the raccoon ravenously. She didn't feel a shred of remorse at killing it, which actually surprised her a little. She supposed it was normal though, considering her present circumstances, that her perspective had changed somewhat. She was mid-way through devouring the animal when Kyle approached her. She knew instinctively that it was he who was coming, even though she wasn't looking up as she was concentrating on eating. Her new advanced sense of smell alerted her to his presence; she now recognised his scent.

"You caught that yourself?" asked Kyle, sounding quite impressed.

Carly nodded, still tearing into the creature's flesh.

"Congratulations! Your first kill! You're the first actually, none of the others who were turned yesterday have managed to catch their own food yet." Kyle paused, and when he spoke next he sounded sombre. "Carly…" he began falteringly. "There's something I need to tell you."

Carly could tell from the tone of his voice that this was serious. She lowered the raccoon and looked at him. "Is it Rob?" she whispered, hardly daring to speak the words.

"He's not doing well", said Kyle. "We've given him meat, and treated the wound, but he was shot with a silver bullet laced with aconite."

Carly had watched enough films to know that silver bullets and werewolves do not mix. She didn't know anything about aconite though. "What is aconite?" she asked.

"It's a plant, known more commonly as wolfsbane; it's always deadly to werewolves", replied Kyle. "Well actually it's not exactly great for humans either, but it's particularly bad for werewolves. The poison from the aconite is in Rob's system, and there really isn't anything we can do to help him. The meat is prolonging his life by giving him strength. The stronger he is, the longer he'll last, but it's matter of time."

Carly's heart leapt into her mouth. "What about an antidote? There must be an antidote?" she said frantically.

His expression told her that there wasn't. "You never know, he might survive it; if only a very small amount of aconite was present, and if we can keep his strength up with the meat, his body might manage to pull through", said Kyle feebly.

"You don't think that will happen though, do you?" asked Carly. The tears were falling freely from her eyes once again.

"I don't want to get your hopes up", admitted Kyle. "Hunters usually aren't shy about using a lethal dose of aconite in their weapons."

"I need to see him, take me to him, please", begged Carly sobbing.

Kyle took her hand and led her back to the cabin. Carly could barely see where she was going as she was so blinded by tears. She kept thinking back to when she had first met Rob two years previously. She had been walking down the street one day and had dropped her cell phone (or rather, it had fallen from her pocket).

Rob had been walking nearby and the phone had bounced over and landed at his feet. He had picked it up, and handed it to her, and she had felt an instant attraction to him. She had then done something quite out of character; she had given him her telephone number. Her heart had been pounding in her chest the whole time and she had gone home quite convinced that the handsome stranger from the street probably thought she was a lunatic. She had not had any faith at all that he would call her, but sure enough, later that evening, he rang and asked her out on a date. The rest, as they say, is history. They dated for a couple of years and after Carly left university they moved in together, and had now been living with each other for about six months. At first it had seemed wonderful, but lately things between them had changed.

They reached the cabin; Kyle stood back to allow Carly to enter. She put one hand on the door to push it open, but faltered.

"Go on, you'd better go", said Kyle.

Carly took a deep breath and went into the cabin. Nobody was in the living room, so she crossed over to the door of the bedroom she had been previously looking at and went inside. The others were all gathered there, blocking the doorway, but they moved out of the way when Carly entered. She could see past them that Rob was lying on the single bed; Seth was squeezing water from a wet cloth onto his head.

Carly approached the bed. Rob was pale and his breathing was shallow. Carly could hear his heart beating irregularly. She sat down at the edge of the bed next to him and took his hand. "Rob?" she said softly, "can you hear me?"

Rob was muttering something she didn't understand. He was talking about sailing on a boat with Jennifer. Carly looked at Seth.

"He's not with it, really, you're not going to get anything coherent out of him", said Seth. 'He's feverish and hallucinatory. No amount of meat seems to be bringing him out of it."

"What can I do? Tell me. He needs help. Isn't there anything you can do?" sobbed Carly, clinging to Rob's hand.

"I'm sorry." Seth shook his head.

Carly turned back to her boyfriend and lay her head down on

his chest, weeping. "I love you Rob, you need to fight this - do you hear me? You need to get better. I need you to get better!" she said, starting to sound a little hysterical.

Kyle entered the room and walked over to her. He knelt on the ground beside the bed and took hold of her other hand. She barely even registered that he was there. "We've tried everything Carly. You need to just be here for him now, quietly, make it comfortable for him", he said gently.

Carly couldn't stop crying. She didn't know where all the tears were coming from. She thought she had used them all up when she had been in the forest, but here they were, flowing freely once again. Ian, standing behind her, was also sobbing, but Carly didn't notice. Her head was still resting on Rob's chest and she could hear his heartbeat now growing weaker and weaker. She knew he was fading away.

She lifted her head and looked at him. His mouth was still moving but now no words were coming out. Carly shook her hand away from Kyle's, and, with her hand trembling, she ran her fingers across Rob's lips, to feel them as they moved. As she did so, she heard him take one last shuddering breath and then he stopped moving. He lay still and quiet. Carly couldn't hear his heart beating any longer.

The room was silent now apart from Carly's sobs as she lay still with her head on Rob's chest. It seemed to her as though time had stood still. The fact that Rob was dead just didn't seem real at all. She expected that any minute he would open his eyes and tell her that it was all a big sick joke, the whole thing, him being dead, this whole werewolf thing, everything. If only that were true, she vowed she wouldn't even be cross with him for playing such a mean trick on her, or even for cheating on her; if only she could have him back.

Or even if it had been a dream, that, too, would be fine. She knew it wasn't either a trick or a dream though. She suddenly felt extremely nauseous; she was going to be sick. Carly dived to her feet, ran out of the room (nearly barrelling poor Gary over in her haste), and raced through the cabin until she reached the front door. She had barely enough time to fling it open and step outside when she began to retch. She vomited violently five or six times. Her whole body felt as though it was on fire, yet she began shivering. It was as though a fever had suddenly struck her, though she knew that wasn't possible. When she had finished being sick, she stood up and found herself surrounded by shadows. She could hear whispers all around her. She turned around in fright, expecting to see the open doorway of the cabin behind her, but instead there was just darkness and more shadows.

The whispers grew in number. There were more and more of them all around her. She couldn't make out what they were saying. They were all whispering above each other, saying all different things. Carly was terrified and put her hands over her ears, trying to block them out, but it made no difference. In a panic she began to run, not knowing where she was going. She couldn't make out the trees of the forest at all - there was just mist and shadows everywhere. The shadows looked like silhouettes of people, though there was nobody there. It was like running through a nightmare.

As she ran she became aware of one whisper, slightly louder than the others, and it caught her attention.

"Carly", it said. "Carly!"

Carly ignored it and continued to run. Her heart was pounding and she had never been so afraid in her life. She couldn't seem to outrun it though. No matter which way she went, it was exactly the same, whispers and dark shadows everywhere. Her foot caught on something solid, and she fell forwards. Instinctively, she put her hands out in front of her, but her body slammed into the ground regardless for she fell awkwardly.

"Ow!" she yelped, as her ankle twisted. She grabbed hold of it in pain.

"Carly!" a whisper directly in her right ear made her jump. She looked to the side of herself and to her astonishment she could see Rob there beside her. He was there, yet he wasn't there. Carly couldn't figure out what was wrong with the image she was seeing. He looked almost like a shadow with drawn on features.

"This isn't real", she said. "You're not real. You're a

hallucination."

Rob didn't appear to have heard what she said, but he held his hand out to her. Carly didn't react at first, then she hesitantly reached for his hand and tried to touch it but it merely passed through him. They remained like that for a few minutes, their hands passing through each other's hands. The whispers of the other shadows rustled around Carly like leaves on trees in the wind. At this point she didn't care if it was a hallucination. Rob was here with her again and that was all that mattered.

"I love you Rob", whispered Carly. Her whispers mingled with the others that surrounded her, and she could her it bouncing around her like an echo. Rob smiled again. She didn't know if he had heard her, as he didn't reply. Then she noticed that his features were less obvious than they had been a moment ago. With a start, she glanced to her left and right. The shadows were growing lighter. She was beginning to see the trees of the forest once again. Carly hurriedly looked back at Rob; she observed that she wasn't able to see him very clearly. He was fading fast.

"Don't go Rob!" she cried, but it was no use. The vision melted away like a mist and the forest was once again the only thing surrounding her. Carly was still sitting with her hand held up, but now there was nothing in front of her.

Slowly Carly lowered her hand to her knee and rose to her feet. She didn't know why the hallucination had ended, as she hadn't eaten any meat; she wished it hadn't ended at all. She tried to get her bearings but she couldn't pick up the scent of the cabin. Everything smelt strange and unfamiliar. She decided to just try and find her own way back by other methods. Her mother had always told her that if she ever got lost, it would be better to stay in one place, so that somebody would be able to find her, rather than wandering off and getting even more lost. However Carly didn't actually think anybody would be able to find her where she was because the forest scents here were, for some reason, quite strange, so she figured she had better make her own way back if she could.

She wasn't stupid though, she knew enough to try and track footprints. The problem was that her footprints didn't lead very far.

She saw four of her own footprints and then there were no more. Carly couldn't figure out why this was. Thus, as both her sense of smell and sight were not much use to her, she tried her hardest to hear any sounds that might lead her back to the cabin. At first there was nothing but the sounds of the trees rustling in the wind and the calls of birds and animals, but after straining with all her might, she managed to pick out a noise coming from the left which she couldn't hear from any other direction. It sounded a bit like growling, which, under normal circumstances, ought to have sent her running the other way. Now though Carly associated growling with wolves, therefore this was exactly the way she began to walk.

She was beginning to feel hungry again but this time she ignored it. She didn't want to start hallucinating in the middle of the forest, nor did she fancy being out there alone for longer than necessary. She just wanted to get back to the safety of the pack. It was odd, she thought, how much she needed them. She felt exposed and vulnerable on her own; this was understandable considering she was in the middle of a forest, which is quite an intimidating experience at the best of times, most people would agree, but as a werewolf she thought she ought to be more comfortable in this natural environment. Without the other members of her pack though, Carly just had a sense of being lost.

She quickened her pace and continued to follow the direction the growling had come from. She couldn't hear it any longer, though, so she began to wonder if she was going the right way. Then she heard it again, louder this time. She must be close to the cabin she thought. Then she saw it - a large grey wolf ahead of her in a clearing. It was standing at the bottom of a great oak, growling viciously at something up the tree. The bottom-most branch of the tree much higher than the wolf's head and Carly realised that there was no way the wolf would have been able to reach it. Carly peered upwards, and saw a man roughly ten feet above the wolf. He only looked quite young, perhaps in his early twenties. He wore green and brown camouflage clothing.

The man looked terrified. Sweat was pouring from his brow and his trouser legs were torn. Carly could smell blood so she knew he must be bleeding from some wound or other. On the ground, a little way away from the tree, Carly could make out what appeared to be a gun. 'Kyle spoke of hunters', she thought. 'I wonder if that man is a one of them.'

She peered more closely at the wolf; she didn't recognise it. Granted, she had never seen Devon in wolf form, but somehow, when she had seen Kyle in wolf form previously, it had looked like him. She had known who he was. Seth too looked like himself in wolf form. It was very hard to describe. This wolf before her now didn't appear to be one she knew. She didn't feel any sort of connection to it, so she knew in any case that this was nobody from her pack. In fact, she actually wasn't sure whether or not this was a real wolf as opposed to a werewolf, but the sheer size of its body indicated that this was no ordinary wolf.

Carly wasn't sure what to do. She hadn't realised there were other werewolves (though with hindsight she supposed it had been a little foolish to assume that her pack was the only werewolf pack in existence) and she certainly didn't know the protocol of how she should behave towards other werewolves. She didn't feel any animosity towards it, but thought there might be customs that she wasn't aware of. Carly simply didn't know.

She decided, on impulse, to make her presence known. She was sure that the young man in the tree must be a hunter and her blood began to boil. A vision of Rob's face filled her mind and her eyes flashed wildly. In that moment she wanted nothing more than to tear the man in the tree apart. Choked with rage and despair, she pictured her life without Rob. Fighting back the tears, she threw her head back and let out a wail of despair, which sounded extremely like a wolf's howl.

Both the man and the other wolf froze. Their heads swung around to look in her direction, but a split second before they spotted her something flung itself onto her back and knocked her to the ground. She hit the floor behind a bush, hidden from view. She thrashed wildly but something strong was pinning her down firmly. Carly opened her mouth to scream, but someone's hand was clamped firmly over her mouth

"Shhh!" a familiar voice hissed in her ear. "Do you want to get yourself killed?!" It was Kyle. Carly stopped struggling when she heard him and when he was satisfied that she wasn't going to scream, he released his vice-like hold on her. Carly rolled quietly onto her back and looked up at him. He was lying low to the ground now next to her. She turned on her side to face him. His eyes were familiar and comforting. Carly was overcome by a sense of relief that he was here; without thinking much about it, she leant in close and rested her head against him. Kyle put his arm out and pulled her towards him protectively.

After a few minutes, Kyle carefully lifted himself up so that he was peering above the bush. He seemed content with what he saw and very slowly reached for Carly's hand. She held it out to him and he pulled her up to a sitting position. Then he beckoned with his finger, indicating that he wanted her to follow him. She nodded, and without saying a word, Kyle began to crawl through the forest away from the bush. He was very stealthy and she tried to copy his almost silent movements.

They crawled and crawled; Carly began wondering why Kyle had not decided to turn into wolf form. It would certainly have been kinder to his knees! Carly's own knees were hurting a little from crawling over twigs and brambles. She wished she could turn into a wolf, and cursed the fact that the first lunar change wouldn't be happening for two whole weeks (not that she was looking forward to the first change particularly, as she was rather afraid of the whole concept of changing, but she couldn't deny that paws instead of knees would have been preferable right now).

When they had crawled some distance away, Kyle stood up. He held out his hand and helped Carly to her feet. She looked down at her knees; her trousers were torn and her legs were bleeding.

"They'll heal quickly if we get you something to eat", said Kyle. "Well, they'll heal regardless, but it would be quicker if you had some meat."

He bounded away without waiting for her to speak and returned swiftly with a mouse in his hands. It was still alive and was squeaking. He handed it to Carly, who tore into it with her teeth, killing it instantly. She ate it in two mouthfuls, and although she wished she had more, it seemed to do the trick for her knees; the wounds healed almost immediately. Kyle looked pleased.

"Thanks", said Carly. "That helped."

"No problem. Now what on earth were you doing over there? Do you have any idea what you were dealing with?"

Carly shook her head. Of course she didn't know what she was dealing with. Nobody had told her very much. She pointed this out to Kyle.

"Okay you're right", he conceded. He exhaled. "Well, that guy in the tree is a hunter."

"The hunter that shot Rob?" asked Carly.

"Honestly I don't know. I didn't see who shot him, I was a little way away from him when it happened."

"What were you all even doing in the woods just then anyway?" asked Carly.

"Seth, Devon and I had gone out to hunt", explained Kyle. "We knew you guys were likely to be hungry and it's a lot easier to hunt in wolf form. As you all can't shift properly yet, we thought we'd stock up on supplies."

"So what was Rob doing out there?"

"I can only assume he followed us. I don't know if Seth saw what happened. All I heard was a gunshot. At first I didn't know if anybody had been hit, but then I heard Rob speaking to you."

"You heard that?!"

"Well, yeah, I wasn't trying to eavesdrop or anything, but we do have rather good hearing."

"It's okay", said Carly.

"I headed straight back to the cabin, but by the time I got there, Seth had already brought Rob inside. I helped to tend to him and then I came to find you. You know the rest yourself."

"I…" Carly stopped. She wanted to tell Kyle about the shadows she had seen earlier and that she had seen Rob, but it sounded so ridiculous that she couldn't find the right words.

"What?" asked Kyle.

"Never mind, it's stupid."

"What's stupid?"

Carly sighed. "I had a weird hallucination", she said. "Not long ago, just before I found that other wolf and that hunter."

"What kind of a hallucination? Did you eat something to get rid of it? How did you manage to hunt while you were hallucinating?"

"No, I didn't eat anything, it just sort of…went away, on its own", said Carly. "It was very freaky this one."

"What was it?"

Carly told him what had happened.

Kyle listened intently. "That was no hallucination", he said. "You were spirit walking."

"I was what?"

"Sit down", said Kyle, perching on a nearby tree log. Carly sat down beside him. "Okay, there's a lot to explain about werewolves really. Basically, spirit walking is when you enter the land of the dead."

Carly must have been looking quite thunderstruck by this, because he chuckled slightly.

"Don't worry it's perfectly safe. It's like, well, heaven, for want of a better word. It's where the souls of the dead go."

"How on earth did I manage to go to the land of the dead?" asked Carly incredulously. "Do you mean it's like astral projection?" She had read books on astral projection before, and knew that it is when somebody can meditate themselves into having an out of body experience. Their spirit leaves their body, but is still tied to it by a sort of shimmering string or cord, like an umbilical cord. In some cases, people have claimed to have the ability to project astrally to the place where the souls of the deceased are.

"No, not exactly", he said. "Werewolves don't need to astrally project to get to the land of the dead. We can just…go there."

"What, as in, our actual bodies go there?"

"Yeah", affirmed Kyle. "It requires concentration, but intense emotion can also trigger it."

"That explains how I ended up there then", said Carly. "I was pretty emotional."

Kyle nodded. "I'm glad you got to see Rob once again", he said.

"If I can go there anytime I like, then I can see him all the time!" said Carly getting very excited. Kyle looked grave.

"It's not really advisable." He took her hand. "Wanting to see people you love on the other side is so natural, but it can drive you crazy."

"What's wrong with wanting it?" asked Carly. "Being with your loved ones is good isn't it?"

"It can be, yes, and finding yourself in the land of the dead is all very well and good if you do it accidentally and it remains a one off, but it's not that simple. It's like a drug; it becomes addictive. The more you go, the more you want to go. You can end up living your whole life in the land of the dead. There have been werewolves in the past who have found themselves in that situation. Others have tried to bring them back, but they were so immersed in being with the people they have lost, that they couldn't be brought back. It's a curse Carly, you would be lost forever if that happened. You would, in effect, be dead!"

"But if you're happy, then what's the problem?" insisted Carly, tears pricking her eyes.

"The problem is that it's committing suicide!" said Kyle. "We werewolves are creatures of life, not of death."

Carly pulled her hand away from his. "If I want to see Rob again, I shall. I can't believe you could say that it's wrong to do so!" she cried. "I'm not stupid, I wouldn't live in the land of the dead. You need to have some faith in me!"

"No, you're wrong", said Kyle softly. "You are a young werewolf, you can't possibly understand what I'm saying until you have experienced it yourself. I thought exactly the same way you did, that I would be able to stop myself at any point from going, but I was stupid. Alcoholics, smokers, and gamblers all think the same way, but they, too, are stupid."

Carly struggled to control herself. She was getting very worked up and frustrated at Kyle's stubbornness. She didn't feel as though she needed his permission to re-enter the land of the dead whenever she chose to do so. He wasn't the pack leader after all.

In fact, she wasn't even sure that she would feel any differently if it were Seth himself giving her the same advice. She decided to change the subject, but inwardly vowed to promptly ignore his advice. "Let's just drop it now", she said.

Kyle raised an eyebrow. "Do you accept what I'm saying?" he asked. "You can't let your emotions control you like that. You need to let Rob go, and not cling on to the thought of seeing him in the land of the dead whenever you feel like it."

Carly nodded rapidly. "Yes, yes I get it, lets just drop it", she said quickly.

Kyle looked unconvinced, but he did as she asked and didn't continue to speak about it.

"Who was that wolf?" queried Carly, changing the subject. "He wasn't one of us."

"No, he wasn't. I don't know him personally, but I suspect I know of his pack. There's only one other pack in this forest, so it's not difficult to guess that he's likely to be a member of it. There are many of them - it's a fairly large pack, larger than ours. I think there might be about thirty or forty werewolves in that pack, give or take a few."

"Gosh that's a lot!" said Carly. "Is that usual, a pack of that size?"

Kyle shrugged. "There are packs of all different sizes. It's no more usual than a smaller one. Hunting is easier with a large pack, and there is more protection - safety in numbers and all that; then again there are more mouths to feed, and more members to look out for."

"Do you socialise with them?"

"God no, we don't socialise between packs. They're our competition. It wouldn't matter so much if they were in a different forest, but as it is, we're all going after the same prey. We try and stay out of each other's way. They usually don't come as far as our cabin and we don't go near their side of the forest. I wouldn't trust them as far as I could throw them though."

"Oh, why not?"

Kyle hesitated. "Just a feeling", he said at last.

Carly could sense that he wasn't telling her everything, but she didn't pry further.

"Anyway, just make sure you stay away from them…and the hunters. Especially the hunters!" he warned.

"Why are there hunters? What do they want?" asked Carly, feeling a little ignorant.

"Hunters, well werewolf hunters in any case, hate werewolves", said Kyle.

"Yeah I got that, but why?"

"Come on Carly, don't you watch T.V.? They don't know what we're like - they just think of us as being the big bad wolves that live in the forest. To be fair, we are pretty scary at the lunar change, but that's only once a month, and we prepare for that; we make sure that we stay away from humans so that we don't hurt anybody."

Carly looked at him inquisitively, so he continued. "We have no control over our actions during the lunar change. We're like mindless beasts. When I killed Gemma, I had no idea I was doing it, and I don't remember doing it either. We're bigger, stronger, faster, and, from what I've been told we walk upright during this time, though obviously I couldn't tell you first hand what we would appear like to a human, because I've never seen myself like that, or, if I have, I don't remember it."

"God, that sounds awful", said Carly. "I don't want to be a monster like that!"

Kyle put his arm around her shoulder. "You have no choice," he said gently, "but I'll be here with you when it happens. We can support each other."

Carly looked up into his eyes and felt reassured. He was gazing at her tenderly, and she felt her stomach flipping over slightly, in a good way. Then she shook her head to try and shake off the thoughts she was having. Rob had only just died, what was she doing having feelings for Kyle? She felt ashamed of herself and wriggled out from under Kyle's arm.

Kyle pulled a face, but his expression wasn't easy to read. Carly ignored it. She was feeling very confused and couldn't face dealing with that at the moment.

"So, hunters try to kill werewolves then? Do they often succeed?" Honestly, Carly was quite terrified at the thought of being shot. Despite the fact that she wanted to be with Rob, she didn't like the idea of being killed by a hunter. Not in the slightest.

"They're good at what they do, I can't deny it", said Kyle. "That being said, Seth and I are still alive, so we're obviously doing something right." He paused and furrowed his brow. "Actually I'm kind of surprised that the hunter you saw had been cornered so easily by that other wolf. He looked to have dropped his gun, but that's unusually sloppy for a hunter. That wolf got lucky, but I don't know what he's going to do now. The minute he turns away from the tree, the hunter will dive for his gun. They're at a stalemate at the moment."

"Don't you think we ought to go and help that other wolf then?" asked Carly.

Kyle shook his head. "Didn't I just say that we stay away from any other packs? It's not our fight, we aren't going to interfere!"

"But…" Carly began to protest. Kyle put his finger up to her mouth and shushed her. "Look, trust me. You do trust me don't you?"

Carly nodded. "Of course I do."

"Right then, so you'll stay away from the other pack?"

Carly nodded again.

"Good. Right, we'd better get back to the cabin. We were all wondering where you had gone. You can't be out roaming around by yourself like this, not while the hunters are around. If anything happened to you I'd…"

Kyle didn't finish the sentence, but Carly could see that he was genuinely concerned about her. Once again she could feel butterflies dancing in her stomach. The last time she had those was when she had been dating Rob, before he had started acting strange for the past few months. She knew it was a clear sign that she was attracted to Kyle, but she dared not admit it.

She cleared her throat. "Yes, okay, let's go back." She jumped to her feet and turned to look at Kyle behind her. He stood up and took her hand. Carly felt as though she ought to shake it off, but considering how often he had been holding her hand it would have seemed as though something was wrong if she did, so she just allowed her hand to be held. She was rather afraid of how much she was enjoying having her hand held by him. She felt like a schoolgirl with a crush.

CHAPTER FOUR

Kyle took the lead and steered her through the forest back towards the cabin. As they neared it, the forest became more familiar; Carly knew her way now. The others came out from the cabin to greet them.

"Where have you been? We were worried about you", said Seth, walking towards her. "There are hunters in the wood, you shouldn't be out there by yourself."

"Yeah I know, Kyle has been telling me all about it", said Carly. She felt a little impatient by the way everybody seemed to be treating her like a child.

"She went to the land of the dead", said Kyle.

Seth gawped at her. "Wow!"

"Well, I was upset, obviously. Kyle said that emotion could have triggered it."

"True, it can be triggered by heightened emotion", agreed Seth.

Devon was looking rather impressed. "I've never been to the land of the dead, yet I've been a werewolf for just over a year." He paused. "What was it like?"

"A little scary actually", admitted Carly. "There were lots of shadows and whispering. I saw Rob though."

The group fell silent. "That must have been comforting", said Ian in a quiet tone of voice.

"It was, sort of."

"We buried him", Seth interjected. "Would you like to see?"

Carly nodded hesitantly and Seth beckoned her to follow him. He walked around to the back of the cabin. There, a few feet away from the cabin, Carly could see a mound of earth. It looked as though it had been freshly dug.

"We were going to put a plaque there or something, but we don't currently have any material to make one", said Seth apologetically.

"That's okay", said Carly. She looked around; there were piles of twigs and sticks lying on the ground. "Do you have any string?"

"Yeah I think there's some in the cabin. Wait there." Seth disappeared and returned almost immediately. Carly was somewhat relieved that he had returned so speedily because she felt a little strange being left alone at Rob's grave. Seth handed her a fairly large ball of string. "Here you go. What do you want it for?"

Carly took the string without explaining and picked up two strong sticks. She fashioned them into a cross shape and used the string to bind them together so that they would remain in the shape of a cross. "Bite that off for me would you please?" she asked, holding the string up. Seth obligingly changed his teeth into sharper canine fangs and bit through the excess string.

Carly walked the two or three steps over to where Rob was buried and planted the bottom of the cross she had made into the earth. She pushed it down a little further to be sure that it wouldn't fall over. Then she stood looking at the grave for a while. She wasn't really thinking about anything, she was just looking, taking it in visually.

"Would you like to have a...well...a service for Rob?" asked Seth. "You know, saying something about him, that sort of thing?"

"Rob wasn't religious," said Carly, "but I am, well, to a certain extent. I'd like a service yes, please. I could say a few prayers."

"Let's go into the cabin and tell the others to come then", suggested Seth. Carly nodded. She followed him into the cabin. They found Gary, Ian, Devon and Kyle all gathered in the living room. They looked up as Seth and Carly entered. Kyle stood up.

"Are you okay?" he asked.

Carly smiled thinly. "Yeah, thanks, I'm okay."

"We thought it might be a good idea to have a small funeral service for Rob." Seth paused. "We could have one for Jackson as well, if you like. I know that they have already been buried, but it seems like an appropriate gesture." Seth looked at Ian as he spoke.

Ian shrugged. "I don't really want to think about it to be honest", he said, his head downcast. "I suppose we could do one. It still doesn't seem real."

"I know what you mean", said Carly. "I can't quite believe that Rob has gone. I'm sure you feel the same way about your brother."

"At least you got to see Rob again though. You went to the land of the dead!" Ian's eyes sparked angrily. "That's hardly fair is it? Your precious Rob, who was cheating on you anyway, yet you got to see him. My brother loved me, he was my brother for God's sake, there were never any trust issues between us, yet I don't get to see him again?"

Ian stood up abruptly and pushed his way past Seth and Carly. He left the cabin, slamming the door behind him. Carly's mouth was agape. Embarrassed, Devon and Gary looked away from her.

"So, he was cheating on me then", stated Carly after a few moments. She had been hoping that it had been just crazy talk on Rob's part, though deep down she supposed she knew that it was real. Her voice was flat. "I suppose that'll be what he was talking about before he died." Nobody answered; Carly felt her temper growing. "Gary, Devon, you knew Rob, you met up with him two or three times a week. Did you know about this?"

"Actually we met up with him once every two weeks", said Gary. Devon elbowed him sharply in the ribs.

"No he used to go to meet you two or three times every week…" Carly stopped as she realised the truth. "You guys only met up like twice a month?"

Gary nodded.

"Oh." Her mind was whirling. It made sense now, how distant he had been during the past couple of months. He used to tell her every time he went out that he was meeting his buddies, so presumably all this time he had been seeing another woman.

"Who is she?" she asked, her voice wobbling. She wasn't sure that she wanted to know the answer, but she felt compelled to ask anyway.

"Jennifer, he said her name was Jennifer", said Gary.

"We don't know any more than that, sorry Carly", said Devon. "She's not somebody we know, but he mentioned her a few times."

Carly felt as though she had been punched in the gut. There was a physical pain inside her that hit her with full force. She put her hand up to her stomach and bent over slightly. Seth, beside her, despite being the pack leader, appeared not to know what to do. He fidgeted awkwardly. Kyle stood up, crossed the room, and put his arms around her.

Carly didn't cry this time. She wanted to cry, scream, and shout, but she didn't. She just stood clutching her stomach, being held by Kyle.

"Do you, er…still want to have a service for Rob?" asked Seth. Kyle glared at him.

"Shut up Seth", he said, in a semi-growling tone.

Seth immediately took a defensive stance and growled back.

Carly pulled away from Kyle. "Stop it both of you", she said. She thought for a moment. "Yes, I think we should have a service."

Kyle looked surprised. "Why?"

"Because…I'm better than he is", she said simply.

"All right; let's do it", said Seth.

"Don't you think we ought to go after Ian?" piped up Gary. "As there are hunters in the forest, we don't want him to get shot!"

"True enough, we'd better look for Ian first", said Seth. "Kyle and Devon, come with me. Gary - you and Carly stay here."

Kyle, Devon and Seth all simultaneously looked around the room. They stepped away from any furniture or walls. Carly watched them curiously, for they seemed to do this by instinct, as though it was quite natural for them to create some space before changing. Having done that, each of them began to take off their clothes. Carly couldn't help but notice Kyle's ripped abdominal muscles, though she tried to tear her eyes away, for the thought of Rob's death was still eating at her. Finally, their clothes in piles on the floor, the three men changed into wolf form. It was almost instantaneous, one smooth fluid motion. Like a sudden wave of fur rippling from their heads down to their feet, their features changed from human to wolf. It was impossible for Carly to see the specific moments that their features changed - it happened too quickly. She could appreciate why they had stepped away from the furniture, as the room was far from massive, and the wolves were much larger than ordinary wolves. Devon was slightly smaller than both Kyle and Seth. His fur was dark brown, just the same shade as his hair. Carly found herself being swatted by Kyle's tail as the wolves brushed their way past her. Gary, similarly, was pinned up against the wall by Seth's shoulder and was looking rather startled. Although Carly had seen Kyle and Seth in wolf form before, she couldn't help feeling somewhat intimidated by these imposing but majestic creatures now filling the living room. She knew they wouldn't harm her, but she could feel her heart beating faster than previously. She realised she was holding her breath. Kyle gave a small whine, and the three of them swiftly exited the cabin and disappeared into the forest.

Carly turned to Gary. "How long had he been seeing her? Was it serious?"

"Are you sure you want to be asking all these things?" asked Gary. "You're not going to feel any better by the answers."

"I'm sure, I need to know", she persisted.

"I don't know how long he was seeing her for, but yes, it was serious. She was pregnant at one point by him but she had a miscarriage."

"Oh my God!" Carly brought her hand up to her mouth and stifled a sob.

"We told him he was being an idiot by being with her, but he didn't want to listen."

"It's not your fault he was a bastard", said Carly. Her mother had always told her not to speak ill of the dead, but at this point Carly didn't care. She had been so devastated at the thought of having lost him when he died, but now she realised that she had already lost him whilst he was alive. This realisation was even more painful than the fact that he had died. She knew it was irrational, but then again feelings aren't generally rational.

Just as she was pondering this over, the door swung open and Seth walked in, followed by a rather miserable looking Ian. Kyle entered behind them.

"Sorry Carly, I shouldn't have kicked off like that", said Ian, looking apologetic.

"It's okay, don't worry about it."

"No, really, I had no right to blame you. It's nobody's fault that I haven't been able to see Jackson in the land of the dead. What I said was awful, I'm sorry."

Carly walked over to him and gave him a hug. "Apology accepted." She gave him a small smile.

"Right, are we going to do this then?" asked Seth. Everybody trooped back outside and gathered around the two freshly laid graves. Ian's expression was one of heartbreak and sadness.

"He's in your heart", whispered Gary, giving his shoulder a squeeze. Ian looked grateful.

Seth began to speak. "Here lies Rob…" he stopped and looked at Carly. "What was his full name?"

"Robert Smith."

Seth cleared his throat. "Here lies Robert Smith, taken from this Earth before his time. We pray that he will find happiness in the land of the dead."

Carly had intended to say a few words, but she was so choked up that she couldn't speak. Silently, she cast up a prayer for Rob. She knew now without a doubt that she would not ever intentionally try to visit the land of the dead. She didn't want to see him again, but she also couldn't bring herself to hate him. She hoped he would be at peace.

"Amen", said Kyle.

"Amen", echoed Carly, Gary, Ian and Devon.

"We also pray that Jackson…" Kyle paused again.

"Jackson Oliver Williams", supplied Ian.

"We pray that Jackson Oliver Williams, a good man, also taken from this earth before his time, finds eternal peace and happiness in the land of the dead."

"Amen", chanted everyone in unison. There was a brief pause.

"Do you want us to give you a minute here alone?" asked Kyle, breaking the silence, looking at Carly.

She shook her head emphatically. "No thanks, I don't want to spend any more time here to tell you the truth", she said.

Kyle nodded understandingly and put his arm around her

shoulder. The group headed back to the front of the cabin and entered it.

"I bet you're starving", said Kyle. Carly was indeed feeling hungry again.

"They'll all be starving", said Seth. He looked at Ian and Gary. "Aren't you?"

"God yeah", confirmed Gary.

"There's some meat in the fridge that we caught earlier today", said Devon. He went into another room that Carly had not yet seen and returned with three dead squirrels. He gave one to Ian and one to Gary; the third he passed to Carly.

"Thanks", she said, and bit it. The taste exploded in her mouth and Carly wondered, for the umpteenth time since becoming a werewolf, how raw meat could be so delicious. Meat, even cooked, had never tasted this good before. She ate it all and felt satisfied. Smiling, she looked at Kyle. He smiled back, leaned over, and gently used his thumb to wipe some blood from the side of her mouth.

Out of the corner of her eye, Carly became aware that the others in the room were watching her and Kyle intently. She felt her cheeks heat up and she took a step backwards from Kyle and cleared her throat in embarrassment. Seth's eyebrows were narrowed; he appeared to be angry. Carly didn't understand what could be the matter. She didn't like the glint she saw in his eye.

"Kyle", he said through gritted teeth in a slightly growly voice. "Could I have a word with you please?"

Kyle looked worried, and he obediently walked over to Seth.

"Outside", barked Seth, motioning to the door.

Both of them left the cabin and began to talk in hushed voices outside. Carly strained with her new found hearing trying to make out what they were saying, but she couldn't hear a great deal for some reason. She wondered if it might be because the door was made of very thick wood. She looked at Devon, Ian and Gary – they also appeared to be straining to eavesdrop.

"What do you think the matter is?" whispered Carly.

"It's about you, I think", said Gary looking pained. He tiptoed over to the cabin wall and pressed his ear against the logs there.

"Seth sounds kind of…jealous."

"Jealous of what?" asked Carly, incredulously.

"Shhh!" hushed Gary, for Carly had inadvertently raised her voice. Carly pressed her lips together.

"Well, that makes sense", whispered Devon. "You're the only female in this pack. Seth will probably be wanting you to be his."

"To be his?" echoed Carly faintly. "His what? I don't want to be Seth's anything, other than a member of this pack!"

"Yes, but…you're the only female", repeated Devon slowly, as though he were speaking to a small child. "Don't you understand?"

Carly understood all too well, but she most certainly didn't want to have anything to do with Seth. She admitted he had been kind in regard to the passing of Rob, but his earlier arrogance was still fresh on her mind. Despite the fact that he was quite handsome, he had an air of conceit that Carly didn't find appealing at all.

"I don't like Seth like that though", she hissed indignantly.

"But you like Kyle", stated Devon matter-of-factly. Carly blushed and she quickly lifted up her hands to hide her flushed cheeks.

"Don't be ridiculous", she replied, entirely unconvincingly. "I've only just lost Rob."

Gary crossed over to her and touched her arm. "Carly, you know you lost Rob long ago, I'm sorry", he said.

Carly didn't want to hear that. Her eyes welled up with tears and her bottom lip began to quiver. "He told me he was sorry though, right before he died", she said, blinking furiously. Her voice was getting louder now - Seth and Kyle outside would be sure to have heard her, but she didn't care.

"Maybe he was, I don't know, but what he did wasn't very nice."

Carly gave him a little shove and turned away from him. She was crying now and didn't want the others to see how badly affected she was by this.

"Just so you know, you can't be Kyle's. You're Seth's now that Rob has gone", whispered Devon.

Carly whirled around angrily and flew at him with her fists clenched. He caught hold of them easily and held her at bay.

"How can you possibly say something like that? Rob has been

dead all of five minutes and you're telling me I'm now Seth's? Like I'm some second hand antique that is lying around for anybody to pick up?" she yelled furiously.

Seth and Kyle re-entered the cabin.

"You're all making an awful racket", remarked Seth cooly. He had a smug smirk on his face, as though he had gotten what he wanted.

Kyle was looking angry. He looked as if he was holding back the rage that was building inside him.

"Carly, there's not a great deal of point being cross sweetheart", said Seth in a self-satisfied tone of voice. "Don't worry though I'm not going to rush you into anything, but Devon is right, as the only female in a pack of male werewolves, it's normal that you should become the partner of the pack leader. That leader being me, of course."

Carly stopped struggling with Devon and stood still, staring at him. In that instant she hated the man in front of her. No longer did his presence fill her with feelings of safety; now she just felt upset, angry, and confused.

"I'll never be yours." She noticed that her voice had a slight growly edge to it. Devon took a step towards her, but Seth turned and glared at him, which stopped him in his tracks.

Carly didn't know where to turn. She knew she didn't want to stay there any longer. "I want to go home!" she cried, and barreled past them out of the door. Behind her, she could hear Ian sigh exasperatedly. She didn't care what he thought. She accepted that she was acting childishly, but she just felt as though she couldn't breathe. She wanted to go home, to forget all of this had ever happened, to go back to her uncomplicated life which involved nothing more taxing than hanging out with her girlfriends and surfing the internet.

Running through the trees, she didn't know where she was going. Night was beginning to fall, and having never navigated the forest in the dark, everything looked unfamiliar. She could smell many scents that she would never have usually picked up on as a human, but she didn't know how to distinguish one from the other.

She could make out other creatures easily enough and knew what the scents of her pack members were, but in terms of making use of the smells of the forest to find her way home, she had to admit she was completely at a loss as to where to start.

Carly looked up at the moon, which she could see above the forest canopy. It was a clear night, and it shone brightly. It was only at half fullness, which made sense, considering Kyle had told her that the next full moon would be in two weeks' time. She wished she could see the stars to be able to use them to navigate, but then again she didn't know how to navigate by the stars, so that was a little useless. Carly had always been interested in astronomy in theory, but in practice she had never really taken the time to actually study it in depth. She could pick out some of the constellations by name and sight, but that was about as far as her astronomical skills went, which wasn't much use to her right now.

Carly decided to follow the moon anyway, even though she didn't know where it would lead her. She figured that at least it would ensure that she was always going in a more or less straight line, as opposed to walking in circles, so at some point she was bound to reach the edge of the forest.

She began walking carefully, instinctively picking her feet up out of the way of branches. She was much more sure-footed than she had been as a human and found that her eyes were excellent at helping her to see in the dark. It was though she had suddenly acquired permanent night vision, which was strange, but useful. She could see the eyes of other nocturnal animals peering at her from behind trees and bushes, and felt the brush of a bat's wings as it swooped low above her head, but she didn't stop to kill anything. She wasn't hungry again yet and she desperately wanted to get home.

She walked and walked, sometimes breaking into a slight jog. She didn't feel tired although she must have been walking for at least two hours. The moon began to climb higher in the sky, and Carly had to crane her neck upwards further to be able to see it. Still she did not reach the edge of the forest though, and Carly was beginning to wonder if she might be walking the length of the forest instead of the width. She had hoped ideally to have walked width-ways through the forest as this would have ensured that she reach the edge of it sooner. She toyed with the idea of turning sideways and keeping the moon on her side (either the left, or the right, Carly didn't suppose it really mattered a great deal), but then she decided that was probably a bad idea. It's a bit like the lottery, she thought. You play the same numbers week after week after week and they don't come up. Then one day you change your numbers and that's the week that your regular numbers hit the jackpot. Or it's like switching lanes in a traffic jam, or a queue in the supermarket - as soon as you do, the queue that you left starts to move more quickly than the one you just joined. Chances are that she might actually be walking the width of the forest, so if she changed direction now, she might find that she had longer to walk, because she would be turning length-ways. She really had no way of knowing, but decided to plod on the direction that she had been already following.

Carly continued to walk; her thoughts about the day's events were plaguing her mind. She still found it hard to comprehend that Rob was gone and that their seemingly ideal relationship had in fact been a lie. Kyle, well, that was another story. She couldn't deny that there was an unmistakeable attraction between them, but she couldn't see how it would be right to pursue it so soon after Rob had died. In addition, the very fact that she was a werewolf was mind-blowing in itself.

She shuddered when she cast her mind back to the visions she'd had when she was scratched. The image of Rob dead in bed; could that have been some kind of premonition? True enough, he hadn't been ripped apart in bed at home, but the outcome was the same, he was dead. She wondered whether or not she was going to return home only to find a pile of rubble there!

"That would be just typical", she muttered. Then all at once she had an overpowering sense of being followed. She spun around but could see nobody there at all. She didn't know whether or not she was imagining it, but she had been quite certain that somebody was following her. She acknowledged that her mind could be playing tricks on her, but she didn't want to take the risk.

She looked over to a tree at the side of her. The branches were quite high and there were large spaces between them. Mentally she calculated the distance between branches and concluded that she probably would be able to scale up it, at a push.

'One, two, three', she silently counted, then took a running leap up to the first branch. She managed to grab hold of it with both hands, and her legs flailed wildly for a few seconds.

"Oomph!" she grunted, and tried to get her legs and body to swing rhythmically in order to lift her legs high enough to be able to wrap them around the branch. Once she had managed to do this, she hung there horizontally, clinging to the underside of the tree quite sloth-like whilst she regained her breath. Mustering up her strength, she was able to turn herself around so that she was now sitting astride the bottom-most branch.

'There, now, I'd have never been able to do that when I was a human', she thought satisfied. She was quite pleased with how she had conquered the tree. She stood up on the branch, maintained perfect balance, (without even the need to hold her arms outstretched, or hold onto the tree trunk), and looked up. The top of the tree seemed very far, but now that she had apparently discovered that she possessed a talent for tree climbing, she wanted to see if she could make it all the way to the uppermost branches.

Deftly, she moved from branch to branch, looking very much like a modern-day female Tarzan. The further she climbed, the easier it became, until she felt almost at one with the tree. Up and up she climbed, until at last the top of the tree seemed within her grasp. With one final heave she managed to scale the last few branches. She stood up, so that her head was poking up through the canopy of the forest.

The view was quite breathtaking. All around her was a sea of leaves, and although it was night, she could see perfectly. The bright moon also helped with that, and the stars were now clearly visible. Carly had never seen a sky quite so full of stars. Usually the pollution from street-lights in the city makes it difficult to see more than the most obvious brightest stars, but here tonight the sky resembled a river of diamonds,

Carly surveyed the density of the trees around her. On either side, the forest seemed to stretch out as far as the eye could see. In front of her though, Carly thought she could make out a glimmer of light far in the distance. She guessed there might be some houses or buildings there. Perhaps she had indeed been heading in the right direction towards the edge of the forest.

Carly didn't want to get down yet. The air felt fresher up there and not quite so leafy as it did within the forest. Not that she minded the leafy smell particularly, it was rather pleasant, but she also liked the crisp cool freshness of the air above the canopy; it was easier to breathe. A desire came upon her to throw back her head and howl, but she resisted the urge. She was in unfamiliar territory and she didn't want to alert any potential hunters to her whereabouts.

After having one last look around, Carly began the long descent back to the base of the tree. She had climbed down about a third of the way, when voices from below came drifting up to her highly attuned ears. Instantly, she froze on the spot.

"That stupid boy, I knew he would get himself in trouble." A man's voice speaking in hushed tones floated her way. She didn't recognise it.

"He was careless, yes, but I'm sure he won't make the same mistake again." This time it was a woman speaking. "He's still picking it up. At least we managed to wound one of them."

"Didn't manage to kill it though!" The man sounded angry now, and his voice became a little louder.

"No, but the wound was quite serious. Unless it manages to get the bullet out, it's going to die anyway. At least it's nowhere near the full moon yet; we still have time."

"Two weeks is hardly a great deal of time", snapped the man angrily. "We don't even know who the wolf born is. Nor do we know where he is. We're going to have to do better than this."

"I know," said the woman calmly, "but if we kill every single one we meet, that pretty much guarantees that we'll succeed".

"Which is why we should have killed that monster today!"

"He didn't look like a pack leader, it couldn't have been him", she replied.

The voices were beginning to be more difficult to hear, and Carly could hear the sound of their footsteps walking away. She struggled to make out any more words. Only their muffled unintelligible voices were now audible, and soon they had completely gone.

Carly remained where she was for a few minutes, straining her hearing to make sure they had definitely gone. When she was satisfied she was alone once more, she quickly skimmed down the tree and landed silently on the ground on her hands and feet like some sort of ninja.

She didn't know what the couple had been talking about exactly, but she could hazard a guess that the guy they had been referring to had been the hunter up the tree she had seen earlier - a novice hunter perhaps? That would explain how he had been so careless as to drop his gun and get himself into such a predicament. So, the wolf had been injured. Carly half wished she had ignored Kyle and stayed to help him. She didn't know why the packs had such a firm rule about not socialising with other wolves. Carly thought it was quite logical really, the enemy of my enemy is my friend, and the hunters were the enemy; therefore it made sense for the packs to be allies.

The part that was puzzling her was when the man had spoken of a "wolf born leader". What did that mean? Somebody who had werewolf parents? That would be Seth then she assumed, unless the other pack also had a wolf born leader. What could they want with Seth specifically? Why was it so important that he be killed, above other wolves?

Carly dithered at the foot of the tree as she pondered what she had heard. She felt a duty of obligation to head back to the cabin and warn Seth that he was apparently the hunters' prime target, but on the other hand she still felt quite a considerable amount of disdain for him after the way he had behaved earlier, and she still wanted to go home. She obstinately began to walk in the direction of the moon again, but as she did so she felt her stomach begin to churn. This time it was not hunger, but pack loyalty, that was making her feel nauseous. She couldn't bring herself to walk away now that she had this new information regarding the hunters. Granted she didn't know quite how much use it was going to be, since the hunters themselves had said that they were planning on killing every single wolf in any case, but at least now she knew who they were really aiming for. She didn't know why however.

'Maybe they just think he's a prize jerk like I do', she thought, as she reluctantly turned around and began walking now with the moon behind her. She let out a weary sigh. Physically she wasn't tired, but it was disheartening to think how far she had walked, merely to end up heading all the way back to the cabin again. She didn't walk too fast, for the hunters had come this way and she didn't want to bump into them if they had stopped to rest anywhere. She didn't see them again though; the walk was fairly straight-forward without any disturbance. She had to stop and catch a raccoon along the way, for her stomach had begun to rumble, but she did this with ease, and she realised that she was beginning to adapt to her new werewolf skills quite well.

To Carly's surprise, the return journey didn't take as long as it had taken to walk in the opposite direction. Perhaps that was because she had an easier end destination to reach, thanks to the fact that she was just retracing her own steps. Before long the cabin was in sight. She groaned inwardly at the thought of being back there, and vowed to leave (for good this time) if Seth should be a jerk again. Sighing, she strode up to the door and gave it a small push. It was locked. Carly rapped on it sharply, expecting somebody to come and open it, but nobody did.

"I wonder if they're all out looking for me or something", said Carly aloud, talking to herself again. "I wish they had just stayed put!"

Carly felt a little guilty now for having left. She was causing a lot of bother by running off every five minutes, and it just wasn't safe for them to be out in the forest with the hunters around. The last thing she wanted was anybody getting shot. It wasn't everybody that had upset her, after all. Her mind flicked to an image of Kyle, and she winced at the thought that he might get hurt on her account. She decided to try and track which way they might have gone.

Looking at the ground, she could make out two sets of footprints, and several paw prints, all starting from the same place. From there they went in different directions. The footprints headed together to the right of the cabin, and the paw prints, although they walked together for a few feet over to the left of the cabin, they then separated as though all three wolves had headed in different directions.

Carly used a little logic and looked to see which paw prints were the largest. Seth was the tallest man, and the largest wolf, therefore it would make sense that he had the largest paws. If there was one thing that she remembered from when she had a pet puppy as a child, her mother had always said "if you want to know how big a puppy will grow to, look at its paws; the bigger the paws, the bigger the dog."

One set of paws was just a fraction larger than the other two, so she assumed that must be Seth's prints. As much as she wanted to find Kyle, it was Seth who she really needed to warn, so she set off following the larger set of prints. They weren't easy to follow; in places they were quite faint, and in those areas Carly had to rely on her sense of smell to help her along the way. Seth's odour was quite recognisable to her, and she picked it up as she went.

Carly walked for a long time following Seth's tracks. They just seemed to go on and on. She was beginning to wonder if he had gone all the way back to her house looking for her. Then she noticed something peculiar. More paw prints came leading out from the forest and joined Seth's. First one more set of prints, then two, and then later more and more, until eventually it looked as though a whole pack of wolves must have been following him. Carly couldn't understand it at all.

The scent she had been following had also changed. First she picked up Devon's scent in around the same place where the first set of tracks joined Seth. 'Devon and Seth must have met up here', she thought; but then other scents, clearly of other wolves, wolves she did not recognise, began to mingle with the scents of Seth and

Devon, until there were so many that she could no longer pick them out. "Oh hell, what if they've been attacked by that other pack or something?" she said aloud. She looked at the tracks; they were still positioned as though walking forwards and there didn't appear to be any sign of a fight or scuffle.

Carly was baffled, but she continued to follow the tracks, though she remained on her guard, and tried to prick up her ears so that she would be able to hear if anything or anyone was following her. Eventually she began to pick up distant voices ahead of her. She moved closer, slowly, and listened. She immediately recognised Seth's voice - it sounded quite loud and as arrogant as earlier. Carly rolled her eyes. She couldn't make out what he was saying though, so she moved even closer. She still couldn't see anybody, but she thought it was probably better that way. If Seth and Devon were with the other pack against their will, she didn't particularly want to be found lingering around their territory. She ensured that she could hear what was being said, then found a large tree and went to sit down behind it.

"We've lost one of them", Seth was saying, in a somewhat authoritarian tone. He sounded like a headmaster speaking to an assembly of children. "Hunters shot him. I understand one of you nearly took down a hunter though today?"

Carly could hear some whispers and shuffling between whoever else was gathered there. Eventually a voice that sounded like an adolescent boy piped up. "Yes it was Darren."

"Where is Darren then?" asked Seth.

"In his tent, with Ben. He got shot. Ben is working on trying to extract the bullet."

"How unfortunate", said Seth sarcastically. "Still, the hunters will assume that their bullet was fatal, so that will give them false hope. They haven't realised that they're using the wrong weapons."

"They don't know much about us then", stated another male voice. This one sounded older, perhaps even middle aged.

"Well, they know enough to be dangerous", said Seth sounding stern. "We just need to keep them off our back until the full moon. Once we obtain the power of the beast we can just kill the hunters without any problems. These puny wolf bodies aren't enough to get the job done."

"So how many werewolves you got left then?" asked the last man who had spoken.

"Three, and Kyle," piped up a voice that Carly recognised as Devon's, "and one of the three is a female".

A series of wolf-whistles and cheers broke out amongst the crowd. "Taking a mate Seth?" called another male voice.

"She's all over me," said Seth sounding smug, "but she's just a decoy like the others. Collateral damage."

"And how're you gonna get Kyle to come here then before the full moon?"

"He's my fucking brother you moron," snapped Seth, "why wouldn't he come with me?"

"Sorry, sorry", came the reply.

"Devon and I are going to have to leave you now and get back to that bunch of snivelling idiots", said Seth. "Make sure Ben gets that bullet out of Darren. I want you all out scouting for those hunters. Be the predators, not the prey!"

With that, there came chattering, scuffling and movement as though the crowd was breaking apart. Carly used this opportunity to run as fast as she could away from that place. She didn't think that her steps would be detected amongst the noise from the people there. She moved as quietly as possible, yet bounded swiftly over any obstacles in her way.

She ran so fast, that even though she was no longer human, she began to pant and gasp from exhaustion. She realised she was desperate for a drink, and the hunger was once again calling out to her. 'Oh God, no, don't let me hallucinate here, let me get back to the cabin first, please', she pleaded, but there was no escaping the inevitable. She felt her head become woozy and everything around her started to spin. She could see little rainbows dancing all around her, and small green leprechauns were waving to her from behind bushes. 'Well, this is different', she thought, partially aware that what she was seeing wasn't real. 'This isn't like a proper hallucination, it's more like tripping on acid!'

She began to stagger around, and then became aware of a figure in front of her. It was Kyle, and he was naked. In that moment he looked like the most stunningly handsome man on earth. "Kyle," she gasped. "Take me! I want you!"

Carly began to rip off her clothes until she was down to her bra and knickers. She couldn't see properly; everything was blurry. The rainbows and leprechauns had gone now, but her head was still spinning. The sensation was not unlike being completely drunk. She giggled and launched herself at Kyle, but his body was cold, hard and rough. "Ouch", she yelped, as her shoulder struck Kyle's stomach. He didn't move, but just stood there smiling at her.

"What the hell?" she said. She reached out her arms and put them around him, but still he didn't move. She didn't understand what was wrong with him. "Kyle?" she said.

Finally, giving up, she sat down on the ground and looked at him. She tried to adopt a sexy semi-reclined position, but still Kyle just stood there. Carly didn't know why she had suddenly turned into a nymphomaniac, but she felt consumed by it. She closed her eyes and lay down, suddenly very fatigued.

As she lay there, she felt something touching her elbow, shaking it. "About time", she slurred. "Kyle, I want you!"

"Eat this", came a voice, and then she felt something cold and delicious pressed against her lips. She licked it and it was divine. Quickly, she ate it, her eyes still closed, revelling in its flavour. When she had finished she opened her eyes. Kyle's face hovered above hers. He was looking concerned. Carly glanced down at his body, and saw that he was fully dressed.

She struggled to sit up, trying to make sense of what had happened. Her head was feeling much clearer now. She was very embarrassed at being half naked in the middle of the forest. "What happened?" she asked.

"I think you were hallucinating", said Kyle kindly.

"It didn't feel much like a hallucination", said Carly doubtfully.

"You can experience all sorts of weird things in the run up to your first lunar change", said Kyle. "Just because it didn't feel like the hallucinations you had earlier, doesn't mean it wasn't. You seem very tired as well, which can often make the hallucinations a bit weirder than usual."

Carly thought back to how desperately she had wanted to make love to Kyle. She blushed furiously. If Kyle noticed, his face didn't display any emotion.

"Did I…say anything?" she asked hesitantly.

Kyle paused for a moment, and then replied "No, nothing. But you appeared to be attacking a tree with your shoulder."

Carly was sure that he was lying about not having heard her say anything, but she was grateful he did. They would both just pretend it never happened. Kyle held out a hand and pulled her to her feet. She stood up, and realised how close she was to Kyle. She looked up, and saw that he was gazing down at her. Their breath was practically intermingled, and their lips were only millimetres apart. Carly wanted nothing more, in that instant, than to inch up just that tiny bit further and make them meet, but she couldn't move. She knew there was something important she needed to tell him about what she had just seen, but it had gone completely out of her mind. All that registered right then was the two of them, together, in the forest.

It was Kyle who broke the spell. He stepped backwards and picked up her trousers from where they lay at his feet. He handed them to her with a small smile. "You're gonna need these", he said. He then walked a few steps over to where her t-shirt had caught on some brambles, and retrieved that also. "Catch", he said, throwing it over to her. Carly deftly caught it and quickly got dressed again. Kyle stood watching her, but Carly didn't feel uncomfortable at all. To the contrary she felt strangely thrilled, but also rather confused by his sudden unresponsiveness. Didn't he like her, or was he concerned about her feelings considering Rob had died earlier that day?

As she thought about it, the events of the past few hours came flooding back to her. She turned to Kyle with a panicked look on her face.

He noticed her expression. "What's wrong?" he asked.

Carly shook her head, not quite knowing where to start. "Okay, well, I was out in the woods, and I was climbing a tree…"

"What were you climbing a tree for?"

"Well that's not the point", said Carly impatiently. "I was climbing it and I saw some hunters talking under the tree."

Kyle looked slightly horrified "God Carly, that's a bit dangerous to be spying on hunters. You could have been killed if they had seen you!"

Carly clicked her tongue. "Shush, they didn't see me, I'm fine. Look that's not the point either! The point is that they were talking about the fact that the person they really want to catch is a wolf born werewolf; a pack leader. That's their real target. I assumed by this that they meant somebody whose parents were werewolves?"

"Seth?!" gasped Kyle, turning slightly white. "We have to warn him."

"So I was right then?"

"Yes. A wolf born is what we could call somebody who is a natural wolf. Somebody who has at least one werewolf parent – like Seth and I. We've got to find him and tell him what you overheard."

"Well yeah, I know, that's what I thought too, but when I went back to the cabin to find you all, there was nobody there…"

"That's because we were all out looking for you," interjected Kyle.

"I know, but listen, I followed Seth's tracks and they led me to the other wolf pack den!"

"Seth wouldn't go there; why on earth would his tracks be leading there?" Kyle paused. "'Oh man, you don't think they attacked him and dragged him there or something do you?"

"No, there was no mistake, he was there of his own accord."

"Did you talk to him?"

"No, I listened from behind a tree", admitted Carly.

Kyle looked sceptical now. "Seth has always warned us against mingling with the other wolf pack. He was out looking for you. There's no way he'd go there. Perhaps you were hallucinating again."

Carly felt like stomping her foot in exasperation. "It wasn't a goddamn hallucination. Maybe you just don't know your brother as well as you think you do!"

Kyle's eyes flashed angrily. "What would you know? You've only just met us! You don't know anything about us!"

Carly realised it was unlikely that she would get Kyle to listen to what she was saying, but she persisted regardless. "He was with Devon. They were talking to the other pack about us. Seth said that we were snivelling idiots, and referred to us as collateral damage."

Kyle gawped at Carly, and turned away, obviously not wanting to hear anything else.

"There's more", continued Carly softly. "Seth spoke of wanting to access the power of the beast. I didn't know what he meant though."

For a long time Kyle said nothing. Then he spoke, his voice shaky. "The beast is what we become during the lunar change, like I told you about. I don't know how you could get power from that though, the beast side of us cannot be controlled."

"D…do you believe me now?" asked Carly hesitantly.

Kyle shook his head obstinately. "What you're telling me doesn't make any sense", he said. "Seth would never side with the other pack over us, why would he do that? He's my brother. You're wrong. I believe you think you heard what you did, but you didn't, it wasn't real, it was your mind playing tricks on you."

"You're not going to tell Seth what I've told you, are you?" asked Carly.

"Why not? He's our pack leader, we tell him anything involving our pack."

"No, you can't tell him." She wasn't sure why exactly, but she felt certain that it wasn't a good idea for Seth to know that she had followed him and Devon to the other pack's territory.

Kyle sighed. "Look, Carly…" but he didn't get to finish his sentence, for all of a sudden Seth and Devon came running out of the woods towards them. Carly shot Kyle a warning glance, which Kyle pretended not to notice.

"Carly! There you are! We've been looking everywhere for you!" exclaimed Seth. He beamed broadly, but the smile didn't quite meet his eyes. He stepped towards her and lunged forward, looking as though he was going to kiss her. Carly turned her head to the side, so he missed and ended up appearing as though he was head-butting thin air. Devon stifled a snigger.

"She's all right", said Kyle. "She was hallucinating when I found her, so I caught her a rabbit. She's fine now."

"Great, that's great. Have you seen Ian and Gary?"

"No, we've not come across them", admitted Kyle.

"Maybe we should head back to the cabin and see if they're there", suggested Devon.

"Yeah, all right. I'm beat - wouldn't mind hitting the sack when we get back", said Seth. He looked slyly at Carly. "And you'll be joining me my dear."

"In your dreams", snapped Carly angrily.

"Seth, back off", said Kyle, stepping in front of Carly. "She doesn't need this. She's not your property."

"Aww, is lovestwuck widdle Kyle going to fight his big bad wolf brother over a girl?" taunted Seth.

"Look, just stop it", said Carly. She could see that Kyle was beginning to seethe, and she didn't think there needed to be another argument of this sort right now.

"Fine, fine," Seth threw his hands up in mock surrender, "but you can only resist me for so long if you want to be a member of this pack".

That was the final straw. With a howl, Kyle tore off his clothes, changed into his wolf-form, and lunged at Seth. Seth didn't have time to react quickly enough, and found himself in human form pinned underneath a snarling Kyle.

"You don't want to do that, little brother", said Seth threateningly. Kyle, teeth bared, kept his massive front paws on Seth's chest. He brought his face close up to Seth's and growled. The two stared at each other for a few minutes, then Kyle stepped off Seth and changed back into his human form.

Seth stood up and brushed the leaves from his clothes. "If you do that again," he said, in a calm chilling voice, "you'll be dealt with". He turned and walked away in the direction of the cabin, quickly followed by Devon.

Kyle stood panting, watching them leave. Carly approached him and ran her finger down his naked torso. "Thank you", she said breathlessly.

Kyle shrugged, turned from her, and put his clothes back on. "He's an idiot, but he's still my brother, and he wouldn't betray us the way you said."

"Let's not talk about it now", said Carly, trying to appease him. She needed Kyle to believe her, but simply telling him without any proof was turning out to be a futile exercise. "We'd better get back to the cabin."

Kyle nodded and began to walk with her towards the cabin. He didn't take her hand this time; she felt as though he was shunning her, although he obviously still cared enough about her to defend her. They reached the cabin and went inside. Sure enough, Ian and Gary were already back there. They stood up to greet Carly as she entered. She quickly made it clear that she was very tired, and she headed into one of the bedrooms to lie down on the single bed there.

Despite the fact that she was exhausted, Carly couldn't sleep. The events of the day kept replaying themselves in her mind's eye. She tried to make sense of all that had happened. What had Seth meant when he was talking to the other wolf pack? The things he had said were so confusing; all that business about the hunters using the wrong weapons, what could that possibly mean? Carly tossed and turned, until eventually she heard the bedroom door open. She could tell from his scent that it was Kyle who had entered. Carly lay very still, pretending to be asleep. She heard his footsteps cross the room over to her bed, and then, much to her huge surprise, she felt him kiss her gently on the cheek. Then he turned and climbed into the top of the bunk bed on the other side of the room.

Carly smiled, and drifted into a light sleep, filled with dreams of werewolves and ghosts.

CHAPTER FIVE

It wasn't even light outside yet when Carly was awoken by a sound coming from the room next door - Seth's bedroom. She opened her eyes and sat up in bed. Carly glanced over at Kyle who was still fast asleep. Gary and Ian wouldn't have been likely to have been disturbed by any noises from Seth's room though as theirs was not adjacent to it. She listened carefully, and heard footsteps in Seth's room crossing over to the door, and then the quiet but distinctive sound of his door being opened. Again, she heard more footsteps cross the living room, and then the sound of somebody leaving the cabin.

Carly waited a few minutes, her heart in her mouth, to hear whether there were any returning footsteps, but she heard nothing further. Quickly, she flung back her quilt, put her shoes on, and tiptoed out of her bedroom. The living room was empty. She hurried over to Seth's bedroom door and pushed it, praying that she had been right about the footsteps and that it had indeed been Seth who had left the cabin. It was closed, but not locked. Carly gave it a shove and entered the room. She didn't know what she might find in there (though she assumed she probably wouldn't find anything incriminating), but she thought she would have a look around anyway.

Seth had a huge soft double (or perhaps king-size) bed. She was too afraid to put a light on in case Seth was standing outside. The light would be visible from the window, and she didn't want to alert Seth that she was snooping around in his bedroom.

Carly rummaged around in the dark, trying to use her night-vision. Recognising objects was not as easy as she had anticipated because, even though her eyes were now accustomed to the darkness, objects had no colour. It was like trying to watch a black and white film - certain details are unclear when viewed this way.

Carly crouched down and tried to look underneath the bed but she couldn't get her head low enough to see. She assumed she wouldn't find anything as the gap was so small, but she stuck her hand underneath anyway and began to swipe around, hoping to find something there. It was to no avail, and she stood back up frustrated.

There was a large old-fashioned wooden wardrobe in the far corner of the room. She opened it and found several changes of clothing; nothing particularly out of the ordinary. She shoved the clothes around a little but didn't find anything else. One jacket caught her eye. It was a smart looking jacket with large dark buttons down the front. Carly couldn't make out the colour but it seemed to be a pale hue, possibly beige. It appeared oddly out of place in Seth's wardrobe, which was riddled with denim and leather. Carly felt it. It was quite soft, as though it was made from a high quality material, although Carly wasn't sure what exactly.

Aside from this jacket, the wardrobe was filled with clothes Carly would expect Seth to wear. He had been wearing fitted navy blue jeans (torn at the knee) a t-shirt of a rock band and a leather jacket earlier today. The rest fitted in with this general style. Kyle himself wore a similar style of clothes. Carly had wondered previously if they had shared clothes when they had been younger.

Carly couldn't find anything of interest. She closed the wardrobe door and sighed, not knowing where else to look. Her eyes scanned the room but she didn't see any other potential hiding places. Frustrated, she left the room. She was just in the process of tiptoeing back into her own bedroom when Kyle suddenly confronted her. Carly nearly jumped out of her skin. She clutched a hand to her chest and panted hard.

"Jesus Kyle, you nearly scared me half to death!" gasped Carly, her heart pounding like a frightened rabbit's.

"What were you doing?" asked Kyle in hushed tones. "I thought I heard some noise coming from Seth's room."

"I just…went to the bathroom", said Carly. "Why? That's okay isn't it?"

Kyle looked slightly suspicious, but he nodded. "Of course you can go to the bathroom, don't be silly", he said. "I wonder what Seth is doing, I don't think he's asleep, I definitely heard some movement in his room."

Carly tried to look nonchalant. "Oh did you? Well maybe he got up, who knows!" she said with a neutral tone to her voice. 'Crap, he knows I was in there', she thought. Her face didn't give her away though.

"Yeah, maybe. Are you coming back to bed?" asked Kyle.

Carly nodded, and followed him to the bedroom. Once they were inside, Kyle shut the door, and looked at Carly. "You know," he said thoughtfully, "we'd better get you some changes of clothes".

Carly blushed, but in the dark she didn't think Kyle would be able to tell. She was still wearing the same clothes she had been wearing for the past day and a half, and she knew she looked very worse for wear. Even more pressing was her desire for a shower. Her hair was matted and she was pretty sure it also had some stray leaves in there. Kyle, by contrast, was bare-chested and wearing a pair of grey jogging bottoms that Carly presumed he kept for nightwear. "I must look a mess!" she said, noting how crumpled her t-shirt was.

Kyle smiled. "No, you look beautiful", he said.

Carly returned his smile. She couldn't quite work it out; he seemed to like her, yet he wouldn't make a move. On impulse, she leant forwards and gently touched her lips to his. Kyle blinked, as though taken aback, but then he took hold of her shoulders and passionately kissed her back. Carly closed her eyes and melted into his embrace. This was just the way she had imagined it would be. The touch of his lips against hers made her feel alive and safe.

Just as suddenly though, Kyle abruptly pulled away from her. Carly opened her eyes, confused. "What's the matter?" she asked.

"We can't do this Carly, no." He turned and dived onto the top of the bunk bed, leaving Carly standing looking up at him, confused.

"Why not? What's the matter?" she repeated.

Kyle sighed and rubbed his face with his hands. "I won't let Seth lay a finger on you if you don't want him to," he said, "but…it's true what was said earlier, generally the pack leader gets his first pick of female in the pack. You happen to be the only female."

Carly was flabbergasted. "You just said you wouldn't let him lay a finger on me!" she protested.

"And I won't, I promise, but it's not my place to have you myself", he said. "If you're not Seth's mate, then you can't be anybody else's mate either."

"That's the stupidest thing I've ever heard!" said Carly feeling quite crestfallen. "Do you like me or don't you?"

Kyle sighed again and jumped down from the bunk. He took her face in his hands, and tilted it upwards slightly. "You don't really need to ask me that, do you?"

"So I don't understand then why this stupid rule is a rule at all!" she said. "Surely Seth can't get everything he wants?"

"No, he can't, but neither can the rest of us", said Kyle trying to explain. "I've been a wolf for a long time now. Trust me, I know how packs work. We stick to a certain dynamic that we don't change, it has been like this for hundreds of years."

Carly pulled his hands off her face, and her eyes flashed angrily. "I can't believe you actually accept that drivel", she whispered, in the crossest way a whisper can sound. She spun around to face away from him angrily. Doing so, she accidentally knocked Kyle's jacket off the back of a chair situated at the foot of her bed.

Kyle reached down to pick it up, but a smallish rectangular object fell from his pocket onto the floor next to Carly's feet. It was Kyle's wallet. She bent to pick it up, but as she did so it came open. Inside the wallet were two photographs. The first, Carly had seen before; it was the one Kyle had shown her of his sister Gemma. The other though, Carly didn't recognise. She looked at it for a moment. It was a nice looking photo of a woman, a man, and three children. The eldest looked to be a boy aged about thirteen, another boy aged about ten, and a little girl, aged about seven, who Carly recognised as Gemma. They were standing together posing for the photograph at what appeared to be a family picnic. It was hard to see the features clearly in the dark though.

"My family, as we used to be", said Kyle, as way of explanation. He quickly reached to take the wallet back from her, but Carly held tight to it and flicked the light switch on with her other hand. She peered hard at the photograph. Kyle was watching her intently.

"You haven't changed much", said Carly smiling. "Gemma was really pretty", she added softly.

"Yeah she was a lovely kid", said Kyle suddenly sounding quite sad. "She always used to pretend to be a princess. She would try and dress me up like a princess too, but I didn't like it much. Still, she was sweet, we had a lot of fun together."

"I'm sorry Kyle", she said, rubbing his arm.

He didn't flinch. "Well, what can you do?" he asked rhetorically.

Carly looked at the photograph again. Kyle's father, she noted, looked a lot like Gemma and Kyle. He had a similar looking face shape, with almost identical features to Kyle, and his hair was exactly the same colour. Kyle could almost have been a mini version of his dad. Except for the clothes; Kyle's were much more modern. 'Just a minute', thought Carly. 'That jacket, I've definitely seen it before.' The man in the picture was wearing a pale beige jacket with large dark brown buttons. Carly gasped. It was exactly the same one she had seen just a little earlier in Seth's wardrobe. What could he be doing with his father's jacket, she wondered. "Was Seth close to your father?" she asked trying to sound casual.

"Nah not really. Dad was fairly busy when we were kids. He worked late hours and usually didn't come home until we were all in bed so none of us really spent much time with him."

"So, he never gave you any presents or anything like that?" pressed Carly.

Kyle raised an eyebrow. "That's a very specific question. Why do you want to know that?"

"Oh no reason, I just wondered that's all. I mean, I've still got a necklace that my mother gave me when I was a kid, so I thought your dad might have given something or other to keep safe for him while he was away from you all."

Kyle shook his head, looking slightly baffled. "No. Well, not as far as I know", he said.

98 - N. Gosney

"Oh right okay", replied Carly, thinking she had better just drop the subject for now. Kyle obviously thought it was a strange question. It was, really, she admitted to herself, and she would have looked odd if she continued to question him about it. 'Besides,' she reasoned to herself, 'maybe Seth just has a very similar style of jacket to his father's'. She also considered that the jacket would have been a peculiar present in any case. She looked at Kyle who was carefully putting the photograph back into his wallet. "I think I'm gonna go to sleep now", she announced.

"Same here, it'll be morning soon, we should probably get some rest", agreed Kyle.

They both said goodnight and climbed into their respective beds. Carly lay awake for a few minutes listening to Kyle shuffling to get comfortable. Her ego still felt somewhat bruised from when he had turned down her advances. As she was dwelling on this though, a twinge of guilt washed over her when thoughts of Rob entered her mind. She felt cross with herself for feeling guilty. 'Why should you feel guilty?' she inwardly chastised herself. 'He had been cheating for months.' A lump threatened to form in her throat. 'But he's dead, that's why you should feel guilty.' A picture of Rob's face formed in her mind and silent tears started to trickle down her cheeks.

Carly didn't remember falling asleep at all. The last thing she remembered was crying in bed. She could only assume, therefore, that she had cried herself to sleep without even realising it. Here she was, though, being woken up by the sound of a commotion in the living room. It sounded like an argument of some sort. She opened her eyes blearily; light was pouring in through the window, which admittedly had curtains but they were so thin they might just as well have not been there at all.

Carly glanced up at the top bunk; Kyle was not there. His bed was neatly made and his jogging bottoms were dangling from his bedpost. She felt absolutely starving, and was amazed that she could feel so hungry without being in a hallucinatory state. 'I'd better get some food!' she thought. She flung back her blankets and stood up, yawning. She didn't know how many hours she had slept, but it must have been only a few. 'Mind you, the previous night hadn't exactly been restful either', Carly thought. 'I wondered how much sleep werewolves actually need in order to function properly.' She could still hear heated voices coming from the living room.

"You're mad! We've got enough on our plates right now with Gary, Ian, and Carly. Three new wolves are enough for the time being. Look what happened to Jackson and Rob. Accidents happen when we take on too much, you know this. I can't believe you want to recruit even more!" That was Kyle's voice, and he sounded very agitated.

"More recruits means the pack will be stronger Kyle", replied Seth's voice, sounding calmer than Kyle's. "We can protect each other better from the hunters."

"More people hallucinating and getting shot you mean!" retorted Kyle. "You know that new werewolves are especially vulnerable. They can't even change yet. We'd have a lot more to deal with if we were running around after any more!"

Seth growled, a vicious sounding growl. "I'm your leader Kyle. You are my subordinate!" he said threateningly. "Watch your tongue."

Kyle let out a growl of his own in exasperation. He flung open the door to the bedroom and stomped in, slamming it behind him. He barely seemed to notice that Carly was awake, and began to pace the room, muttering and growling to himself.

"Kyle?" said Carly gently.

Kyle jumped slightly at the sound of her voice, as though she had broken him out of his reverie. "What?"

"Are you okay?"

Kyle frowned and began pacing again. "Meh, I'm ok, I'll survive", he said, shrugging.

"You don't really mean that", stated Carly pragmatically.

Kyle shrugged again.

"Would you tell me if you weren't all right?" she asked.

"No, probably not", admitted Kyle. He managed a small smile.

"Did I overhear right? Seth's wanting to recruit some *more* members into this pack?"

Kyle stopped pacing and sat down on Carly's bed. He ran his hands through his hair in a frustrated motion. "Yeah, that's what he's been going on about this morning. Most stupid idea I've heard in a while. It's taking us all our efforts to stop you from running off and getting shot, let alone bringing in even more clueless newbies right now."

"Erm…thanks Kyle…" said Carly, feeling a twinge of annoyance that he had apparently just lumped her in the 'clueless newbie' category.

"Sorry," said Kyle, "no offence meant".

"Well," said Carly, pausing for thought, "for what it's worth I agree with you, I think it's pretty poor timing on Seth's part. Why not wait until after the full moon to bring in new members? That way Gary, Ian and I will have gone through our first lunar change. We'll no longer be susceptible to hallucinations, and we'll be able to change into wolves. We won't have to be constantly chaperoned by you, Seth and Devon."

"Well that's it, that's what I told him, but he's having none of it. Stubborn idiot!"

Carly hesitated, wondering if she ought to bring up again what she had heard Seth discussing with the other wolf pack. She had her suspicions though that although Kyle and Seth didn't always see eye to eye, Kyle would still be reluctant to believe anything said against his brother. He was loyal to a fault. In a way, Carly admired this, although in this situation she felt like shaking him. 'It's so exasperating not having him believe me!' she inwardly grumbled. Carly didn't have a chance to say anything anyway, because Kyle interrupted her train of thought.

"I've got something for you," he said, "wait there". With that he disappeared swiftly out of the door.

Carly didn't know what he could possibly have for her, but she did as he had said and waited patiently. He returned about a minute later holding a folded pile of clothes.

"I got these for you", he said, smiling. He held out the clothes and Carly took them.

"Wow, thanks", she said. "Where did you get them?"

"Some people were camping in the forest. They had left some clothes out to dry just next to their tent."

"Oh my God, you stole them?"

Kyle looked embarrassed. "Well, yeah, I guess. Listen it's the law of the jungle - dog eat dog. I left them a rabbit though for their dinner to make it up to them."

Carly shook her head. "I can't accept these, you took them from somebody else!"

"How do you think we survive Carly? We're not like regular people. We're werewolves!"

Carly didn't know quite what to say to that. She stood holding the clothes, feeling a little taken aback. 'I suppose he's right", she thought resignedly. 'I live in a cabin now in the wilderness. What else am I going to wear other than stolen clothes?' she conceded. "Thanks for the clothes", she said again.

"No problem. The bathroom is free if you want to use it. I've left a towel in there for you. There's even some shampoo."

A bath! Carly had longed for a bath! A nice warm bath was just what she needed! She forgot about the origins of the stolen clothes and headed straight past Kyle toward the bathroom. This was something she didn't need telling twice about!

Entering the bathroom, Carly put down her bundle of clothes and walked over to the tub. She turned on the tap and held her hand under it, feeling the cold water and waiting for it to start to turn warmer. It didn't. The water was icy and showed no signs of getting any warmer. After a good few minutes, Carly walked out of the bathroom and into the living room. All the others were in there, sitting on sofas chatting.

"How do you get the water to run warm for the bath?" she asked, not directing her question at anybody in particular.

Devon and Seth burst out laughing. Kyle had a small smile on his face but he had the good grace not to laugh at least. "You don't", he said. "We can't get hot water here."

Carly's heart sank. 'So much for the nice warm bath I had been looking forward to!' She turned and walked back into the bathroom and looked at the bath, which was now about three quarters full of icy cold water. "You have got to be kidding me", she said aloud. She stripped off her clothes, lifted up one leg, and gingerly dipped her big toe into the water. It was absolutely freezing. She yanked her toe back out of the water and yelped. "Come on Carly, you need a wash, you can do this", she told herself, trying to feel brave.

She had never been the kind of person to leap into cold swimming pools or jump straight into the sea. She always had to inch herself in, little by little. Last year she and Rob had gone on holiday and the hotel swimming pool had been extremely cold. Rob had dived straight in but it had taken Carly a full hour before she had been able to inch herself into the pool. She knew that was completely impractical for this bath though.

"Okay, okay, just go for it." Plucking up her courage, she lifted her leg up once again and plunged it into the water. The water only came up as high as her shin, but that was high enough. She closed her eyes, gritted her teeth, and jumped straight into the bath. Her shrieks echoed through the cabin, and the others in the living room erupted into fits of semi-hysterical laughter, which didn't impress her at all. It was probably the quickest bath she had ever had in her life. Half an hour later she was dried and dressed, and she emerged from the bathroom with her teeth still chattering. "That wasn't very nice guys", she said, in mock anger.

"Now you know what we have to put up with", said Kyle, grinning.

Carly looked at her watch; it was mid-morning already. "I'm hungry", she announced. Devon stood up and walked over to the fridge. He retrieved some meat and threw it towards Carly, but just as she was about to catch it, Kyle stepped in front of her and caught it instead. "Hey!" protested Carly.

"You don't want that", he said with a smile. "You want fresh meat! Come on, I'm going to take you hunting. It's about time you learned how to hunt."

"I already know how to hunt", said Carly indignantly. "I caught a raccoon - you know I did!"

"Yes, that's true, you did…" agreed Kyle, "but raccoons are easy.

What you really need to learn is how to catch a larger dinner!"

"Larger? Like what, a deer?"

Kyle said nothing, but the twinkle in his eye told her that she had guessed correctly.

"Now come on, don't be silly, how am I supposed to catch a deer? I can't turn into a wolf!" said Carly doubtfully.

"That's true, but you can watch and pay attention to what I do. When you gain the ability to change, you'll be coming with us on hunts. A deer can feed the whole pack, it's much more efficient than taking down tiny things like squirrels and rabbits."

Carly got ready to go out, as did Kyle, and they set off into the forest together. Carly noticed that he no longer made any attempt to hold her hand. She felt that the dynamic had changed between them since he had rejected her kisses last night, but she still felt comfortable around him, although now she had resigned herself to just having a platonic friendship with him.

They walked for quite some time. Carly was growing hungrier and hungrier and was starting to get a little worried that she might start flipping out again over some imaginary vision or other. Suddenly Kyle grabbed hold of her shoulder and pulled her to a standstill. Without saying a word, he motioned with his eyes over to the side. Carly followed his gaze, and saw in the distance a young roe deer.

Without warning, Kyle stripped off his clothes, making very little noise in the process. The deer didn't flinch; it appeared to be quite occupied in eating some morsel or other; grass presumably. Once he was completely naked and his clothes were lying in a heap on the ground, Kyle quickly turned into his wolf form and began to move silently through the under-brush towards the deer. Carly didn't dare move, and watched with bated breath to see what would happen.

Closer and closer he crept yet the deer remained blissfully unaware of his presence. When he was quite close, he crouched in a bush and then leapt out towards the deer. The creature, instantly startled, began to run through the forest. Kyle was in hot pursuit, just a few steps behind. His lupine legs moved so quickly that they would have appeared as mere blurs to human eyes. Carly, too, began to run, so that she could keep watching the action, though she kept a reasonable distance away so as not to become an obstruction. The wind rushed past her and took her breath away. She was painfully aware that in comparison to Kyle her body was clumsy and awkward; not streamlined and sleek as a werewolf in wolf form. She could hear the deer's heart pounding faster and faster and the only thing she could think about was how much she wanted to eat it. What Kyle was doing seemed so exhilarating, and she wished she could have changed too. She wanted that freedom; that rush. She longed for the ability to chase after a creature such as this one and to have the strength and stamina to overpower it. Hunting was her instinct now and she didn't want to have to fight it back. Knowing that she had the ability to easily outrun a human being was not nearly satisfying enough for her.

Kyle ran even quicker and gained on the deer. His jaws snapping, he managed to clamp his teeth around one of the deer's hind legs. It began to limp. That was just the opportunity that Kyle had been looking for. He lunged upward and sank his teeth into the deer's throat. The deer fell to the ground with Kyle still clinging to it. His fur mingled with that of the creature, and, for a moment, they looked as though they were one and the same animal connected together. Then he released his grip on the deer and looked triumphantly at his kill.

Carly hurried over to him. "Wow, Kyle, that was amazing!" she said in genuine admiration.

Kyle gave himself a shake, and promptly turned back into a man again. "Aww shucks, it was nothing", he said, feigning modesty. Then he looked serious. "Did you pay attention? Did you see what I did?"

Carly nodded. "I couldn't look away!" she admitted.

"Good; well the day after your first lunar change I'm taking you out for your first deer hunt…solo!" he said. "Right, let's find my clothes." Once Kyle had re-dressed himself, together they carried the deer back to the cabin. It was very heavy, as deer tend to be, but with her newly found strength she didn't find it a problem. In fact, even if Kyle had not been there, Carly was sure she would even have been able to carry the deer on her own.

Carly and Kyle's arrival back at the cabin was greatly appreciated by Gary and Ian. Both were in the beginning stages of hunger-induced hallucinations. Gary was muttering something about toxic crocodiles and Ian was waltzing around the living room with an imaginary dance partner. Seth informed Carly, when asked about it, that he had not given them any meat from the fridge because he had every faith that Kyle would bring back a deer, so he had made them wait for lunch, so to speak. Carly thought that was a little unfair, but at least Gary and Ian's hallucinations didn't appear to be causing them too much bother.

Kyle, Seth and Devon took the deer out to the back of the cabin to dissect it on a wooden table. "Ordinarily," explained Kyle, "the three of us just sort of…got stuck in…but there are six of us now so it would be a bit awkward not to get in each others way if we all herded around the deer!"

Carly wasn't concerned that the table wasn't sterile. She was a wolf; it didn't matter to her now. The usual rules on food hygiene didn't exactly apply any longer! Carly waited patiently in the living room, keeping an eye on Gary and Ian, until at last Kyle brought her a plate of meat. It was the most beautiful meat she had ever seen in her life. Blood was oozing from it and it was a delicious pink colour. After taking one bite she felt as though she had died and gone to heaven! It was so tender and delicious, much nicer than the rabbits, raccoons, and squirrels that she had eaten earlier. She resolved to make it an absolute priority to learn how to hunt deer as soon as she possibly could.

The rest of the day passed without much happening particularly. There didn't seem to be much to do to pass the time in the cabin. Carly felt restless. She decided to go for a run which prompted the whole pack to leap to their feet in agreement that there was nothing better to do than run; so run they did. The whole pack tore through the forest together, though admittedly three were in human form and three were in wolf form. The wolves easily outran the humans, though Carly, Gary and Ian were much faster than normal humans would have been. Carly was a little concerned that they might bump into the hunters, but this didn't happen, and they returned to the cabin all panting.

Carly fell asleep almost instantly as her head hit the pillow that night. She had gone to bed particularly early (it must have only been around 8pm or thereabouts), not expecting to drop off right away, but she had clearly underestimated how exhausted she was from the events of the past several days. She slept so deeply even an avalanche outside wouldn't have woken her.

Days passed by without event. First one day, then three, then five, until at last a week had gone by since she first arrived at the cabin. Carly was finding her stay in the cabin to be quite frankly mind-numbingly boring. Her companions seemed to be content with sitting around all day just chatting or running or hunting. There was no television, no music, in fact very little at all that Carly could class as being entertainment save for a few books. She realised she was a werewolf now but she still felt like a human inside. She craved something more than such a dull existence. She brought it up with Seth a few times but he had scoffed and called her a difficult woman, which Carly had taken great offence to. Seth himself seemed to disappear, in any case, for hours at a time. Sometimes Devon went with him. Kyle said he didn't know where they went and he had no interest in finding out. Carly was sure that they were going back to the other wolf pack but every time she tried to bring the subject back up with Kyle, he clammed up and refused to talk about it.

Carly didn't know what to do. She was growing restless. She wanted to return home but Seth had warned her that she couldn't do that. "You're a werewolf now", he told her. "You need the protection of the pack. Imagine what would happen if you started having a hallucination in front of ordinary people? They're hardly going to go and rush to feed you a dead rabbit now are they? And what if the hunters found out who you were? They would be round at your house quicker than you could blink and you wouldn't be well prepared to defend yourself, being on your own, not having even had your first lunar change."

Carly agreed that he was probably right but she felt claustrophobic in the cabin. Also Seth's antics from the previous week were never far from her mind and she was itching to find out what he was up to. Lying on her bed that night, she made up her mind to follow Seth the next time she should see him leave the cabin. She was determined to find out if she could learn any more about why he was liaising with the other wolf pack. She didn't trust him one bit after having overheard what he had said about them.

She fell asleep and began to dream. Usually her dreams were fleeting unimportant dreams that were quickly forgotten the next morning. This dream was different; it didn't feel like a dream at all. She was running through the forest at night but she was not herself. Her arms and her legs were in motion and when she looked down she saw that her hands were not hands at all; they were paws. She was running in the form of a wolf, moving swiftly, streaking like a black blur through the trees.

She had no idea where she was going. She didn't have any control over the body she was in. She felt like a passenger on a ride who had lost their map. It was as though she knew the way to wherever it was she was heading (though how she knew, Carly couldn't say). She headed straight for the edge of the forest and into the town. The houses there were dark and quiet. Nobody seemed to be around. Carly felt sure it must be the middle of the night in this dream, though she knew that was ridiculous as dreams don't follow conventional time frames. Still this was the most realistic dream she had ever been in. She walked up to a house that had a glow emanating from behind the thin curtains of a downstairs room. She assumed it must be a lamp or something of the sort, as it wasn't particularly bright.

Carly growled, a low rumbling growl, a growl that would have sounded terrifying to anybody hearing it. The curtains moved slightly and a man's face appeared at the window. He was a pleasant looking middle-aged man, glasses and slightly chubby cheeks. He looked a lot like her old music teacher Mr. Brown. Involuntarily she growled again. She could see her own reflection in the window. Her eyes were glowing brightly in her black wolf head. The man caught sight of those eyes now and gasped. Carly felt as though she was in a déjà-vu situation for she remembered well how it felt to catch sight of Rob's glowing eyes through her window prior to having been turned into a werewolf!

Carly reached out a paw and, with one sharp claw, began to carve a line in the glass window. She didn't know why but she knew she had to get inside the house. When she had carved a line from top to bottom she walked back a few steps then ran, leaped and hurled herself at the window. It shattered instantly and she found herself standing in the man's living room shaking glass off her back.

The man was standing in the corner of the room with an absolutely petrified expression. He was shaking like a leaf and made no attempt to run. His mouth was open, as though he was trying to scream but simply couldn't manage to do so from sheer terror. Carly felt pleased, which surprised her. She wanted the man to feel that horror. She bared her teeth and growled again and paced towards him slowly. The man closed his eyes. He appeared to muster up all the courage he had, and with fingers fumbling clumsily, grabbed hold of a telephone that was beside him. He threw it at Carly who dodged it easily. She loved how afraid he was; she felt powerful and in control. He smelled like dinner and she couldn't hold herself back any longer.

Carly took a flying lunge straight towards the man. He screamed; a terrible bloodcurdling scream that filled Carly with sheer delight. Putting out his hands, he clawed at Carly's neck, pulling out great clumps of fur in a desperate attempt to wrestle her away, but Carly barely felt it. Her gaze was fixed on one thing - his tender looking neck. A dribble of saliva trickled from her mouth, and she ran her tongue over her sharp teeth. Wasting no further time, she knocked him to the ground with her enormous paws, and plunged her teeth into his jugular. She felt nothing but pure satisfaction as warm blood gushed from the wound and into her mouth. The man's tortured screams echoed around the room. Carly held back from tearing him apart immediately, for she wanted to revel in his pain.

She let go of his neck and looked to see his expression. His eyes were now rolling in his head and he was twitching, blood oozing from his mouth. She couldn't resist having a little more fun with him; moving to different parts of his body, she used her front teeth to tear out chunks of flesh, in several places on his arms, legs, even his cheeks. With every new bite mark she made the man let out a low guttural groan. As his groans began to sound quieter though, Carly realised he was dying. 'Well that's no fun', she thought sulkily.

Enough was enough, it was dinner-time anyway. Lifting one front paw she used her talon like nails to rip into his torso and began devouring his intestines. A final gargled cry escaped his lips as the man choked on his own blood. Carly looked up as the screaming stopped; the man was dead. Greedily she once again sank her jaws into the man's flesh and continued to gorge herself. He tasted familiar, like she had eaten human beings many times before. She lapped up his blood as though she was eating an ice cream; her black fur stained a deep red colour. She was just relishing her meal when she felt something tapping her on the shoulder. She broke off from eating and looked around but there was nobody there. She knew she wasn't going to stop with just this one man tonight, no, she wanted to do it again and again, she wanted to terrify as many people as possible. Nobody was safe whilst she was out and that was the way she wanted it.

The tapping on her shoulder continued, getting stronger and stronger. Carly noticed the scenery around her growing dimmer.

"Carly, Carly, wake up", a voice called close to her ear, sounding a little desperate. "WAKE UP!"

Carly jumped and found herself in her bed. Kyle was shaking her shoulder. She sat up in a panic and looked down at her body; it was very much human. She was panting and sweating from the dream. How could she have dreamt such things? She felt nothing but repulsion for the way she had gloated over eating that man. Come to that, she felt physically sick at the whole dream. Nausea welled up inside her and she knew she didn't have enough time to make it to the bathroom. She raced over to the window, flung it open, and vomited outside.

"Woah, Carly, are you okay?" asked Kyle.

Carly managed a weak smile. "I had a really bad dream!" she said.

"Wow that must have been some dream!" said Kyle. "I'd ask you what you dreamt about but there's no time now, I need you to come and give me a hand."

"With what?" asked Carly.

"Gary has been shot."

Carly gasped and immediately hurried back over to him. "How badly?" she asked semi-frantically. She didn't want another pack member to die - she didn't think she could face that.

"Not too badly, it's only his leg. I think it's just a silver bullet without any aconite in it judging by the fact that his condition isn't worsening, but we need to remove the bullet. I want you and Ian to hold him still while I deal with it. I haven't got any pain killers so he's going to thrash around a fair bit as I dig into the wound."

"Where are Seth and Devon?" asked Carly fearing she already knew the answer to that question.

"No idea, out hunting somewhere I assume", said Kyle. He looked quite firm on the matter and Carly could tell that he didn't want her to bring up the other wolf pack again.

"Okay, let's do this", said Carly.

She followed Kyle into the living room. Gary was lying on the sofa wincing in pain. One of his trouser legs was torn up as high as it could go. The wound in his thigh was obvious.

"Are you ready for this?" Kyle asked Gary. "You need to brace yourself."

Gary nodded. Ian went to one side of him and placed his hands on Gary's body, ready to keep him held down if he moved. Carly went round to Gary's other side and followed Ian's lead. Kyle sat down on a stool at the side of Gary's leg and quickly turned his fingernails into claws. He reached into the wound and began to dig around, feeling for the bullet. Gary roared in pain; his body lurched. Carly and Ian kept a firm hold on him. "It's quite close to his artery, so I need to be really careful", said Kyle, furrowing his brow. "I don't want him to bleed to death!"

Upon hearing that, the colour (what little colour there was left) drained from Gary's face. He made a huge effort to try and keep as still as possible; he couldn't help flinching at times though.

Kyle's face was a picture of worried concentration. At last he held up a small metal object. "I got it", he announced, looking quite suitably relieved. Gary smiled weakly. Kyle quickly applied a material pad to the wound which he bound up with a bandage.

Carly exhaled; she had been holding her breath in trepidation. "Is that it?" she asked. "Is he going to be okay?"

"Hopefully yes, I should think so", replied Kyle. "It wasn't a particularly life-threatening shot, it was just in a very awkward place!"

"Where was he to get shot like that?" asked Carly anxiously. "Were hunters near the cabin?"

"About ten minutes run apparently", said Kyle. "That's right isn't it?" he asked Gary and Ian.

"Yes, about ten minutes north of here", replied Ian.

"See, I wouldn't know, because I was asleep in bed! I had no idea these two donkeys went out by themselves!" said Kyle.

Gary had his eyes closed but Ian looked somewhat sheepish at Kyle's words of reproach. "We were hungry and there didn't seem to be very much in the fridge", he said, sounding apologetic. "Seth and Devon weren't here, and you and Carly were asleep, so we thought we would go out and hunt some raccoons or squirrels or something."

"You could have woken me up", said Kyle, sounding a little irritated. "What if you had been killed? You know there are hunters in the forest!"

"Well, we were hungry..." repeated Ian lamely, his sentence tailing off.

Kyle sighed. "For your own safety it's better if you hunt at least with one of us who has already gone through the change. Seth, Devon and I have been dodging hunters for a while now. We know what to look out for, how to handle ourselves. Please, promise me you'll let one of us know if you want to go out hunting again and we'll come with you. I don't want any more deaths in the pack!"

Ian solemnly nodded. Gary appeared to be asleep; Kyle didn't attempt to wake him. "He needs to rest", said Kyle.

"I think I'm just gonna sit here and wait for him to wake up", said Ian. "I've got nothing better to do really." With that he retrieved a book from the bookcase and sat down in a nearby armchair.

"Okay", said Kyle, and he walked towards the front door. "Coming Carly?"

Carly obediently followed him out and closed the door behind them. She had been impressed by the way he had taken charge when dealing with Gary and by what he had said to Ian. She told him so.

"It was nothing", Kyle said, shrugging.

"No, really, you sounded like a leader Kyle!" said Carly being quite sincere.

"Don't be silly. Seth is the leader. I just know what I'm doing that's all; I've been a werewolf long enough. Anyway, are you going to tell me what you dreamed about?"

The dream! It came rushing back to Carly instantly and the nausea she had felt upon waking welled up in her stomach again. She clutched one hand to her throat, trying hard not to be sick again.

"Crikey that dream really rattled you!" said Kyle, noticing her reaction.

Carly nodded and forced herself to calm down. Hesitantly she told him what had happened.

"Well", said Kyle. "Well…"

"Well what?" asked Carly getting very nervous.

"Well it wasn't a very nice dream, that's for sure, but it was just a dream, you mustn't think about it any more", he said. "Remember I told you that your mind can play funny tricks on you when you're in the run up to your first change."

Carly wasn't convinced by his tone that he was telling her everything she needed to know. A thought occurred to her. "Kyle, do you have any books on werewolves?" she asked trying to sound cheerful.

"Most of the books we have are about werewolves", he chuckled. "Why? Are you wanting to swot up on yourself?"

"Something like that yes", she replied.

"The big bookcase near the window in the living room has most of the werewolf books. Help yourself."

Carly thanked him and went inside. Gary was still asleep. Ian was so engrossed in his book that he didn't even flinch or look up when she entered. She headed towards the large bookcase by the window. It was an old looking mahogany bookcase with beautifully carved legs. Carly remembered her aunt (the aunt who had given her the hippo ornament) having had a sideboard made out of the same wood, with very similarly carved legs. It had been highly polished and well taken care of; it was a beautiful antique. By contrast though, this bookcase appeared to have seen better days, like much of the furniture in the cabin.

The doors to the bookcase were closed but not locked, despite them having two small keyholes. She pulled the doors open and cocked her head sideways to read the titles of the books.

"The curse of the werewolf; stare of the wolf; werewolves, mermaids, and myths…" she read aloud. She finally settled on one entitled 'lupine experiences'. She pulled it from the shelf and took it into the bedroom. Carly made herself comfortable on her bed, propped up by pillows, and began to leaf through the book. It was full of beautiful pictures of wolves, with large passages of writing describing the ways in which a human being can control their change into a werewolf, details of a werewolf's outward appearance and other general facts.

Eventually she came to a section entitled *'First lunar change'*. Carly's eyes widened for this was what she had wanted to read about. The drawing to accompany this title was terrifying. It was of a humanoid wolf-like figure towering over a human being. The beast depicted must have been about eight or nine foot tall at least. Despite it being only a drawing, it was the most hideous creature Carly had ever seen, even in horror movies! Admittedly she didn't watch too many of those types of movies.

Carly bit her lip and began to read. A lot of information Kyle had already told her, regarding hallucinations occurring in the run up to the lunar change and being perpetually hungry. One paragraph stood out to her though that Kyle had omitted to tell her about. It was written in the form of a verse:

Tas, kurš gaida pirmā pilnā mēness
var pieredzi redzes caur citu vilka acīs.
Sapņi bieži ir realitāte
tāda ir dzīve jaundzimušajam vilkacis

Carly didn't recognise the language, and were it not for the translation underneath, Carly would have had no idea what it said:

She who awaits the first full moon
can experience sight through another wolf's eyes.
Dreams are often reality
such is life for the newborn werewolf.

Carly read through the passage two or three times digesting what it said. Her mind flicked to her dream (or nightmare, as Carly inwardly referred to it as). "What if it wasn't a dream after all?" she said aloud. "What if I was seeing through somebody else's eyes?" The horror of what this implied washed over Carly like a wave. She realised that if this was the case, then she really had just experienced the killing of a man and had even tasted his flesh. It was as though she had done it herself, even if she wasn't responsible. She clamped her hands on either side of her head and shook it slowly. 'No, it can't be possible. Surely it was just a dream?' she thought. "Please let it have been a dream, please let it have been a dream, please let it have been a dream!" she begged. She wasn't sure whom she was talking to but it didn't seem to matter. She just needed to get the words out, to hear her desperation vocalised. Tears fell from her cheeks and she felt herself shivering slightly. She curled up on the bed crying pitifully, until at last her sobs subsided.
She lay quietly - her mind full of horrors that she didn't want to

comprehend. There came a knock at the door nearly an hour later. Carly's cheeks were cold from where her tears had fallen. The backs of her knees were aching. She stood up stiffly, walked across the room and opened the door. It was Kyle. "Why are you knocking? It's your room as well!" she said, sniffling slightly.

"Well I didn't know what you were doing in here, did I?" replied Kyle. "You could have been sleeping or getting changed!"

"Considering the fact that, in a week's time, I'm going to have to be stripping off like you all do in order to change into wolf form, that seems a little reserved of you, wouldn't you say?" quipped Carly. She was glad of Kyle's company, she didn't feel quite so despondent when he was around.

Kyle wiggled his eyebrows playfully. "Well you already started throwing your clothes off in the forest I suppose. You're right, I should have just barged in!" He laughed as Carly flung her pillow at him in mock anger. This lighthearted banter felt good. Given the way she had been feeling, it was nice to take her mind off the vision she had seen in her dreams. "Did you find any interesting books?" he asked, calming down his laughter.

Carly was a little taken aback by the question and didn't know quite what to say. "I suppose so..." she replied, trying to sound noncommittal. "Why do you ask?"

"Just wondered!" replied Kyle. "I was only making conversation." He peered suspiciously at her. "Why so defensive?"

"I wasn't being defensive!" Carly realised that she sounded even more defensive by saying that. She sighed. "Okay, Kyle, I need to ask you about something." She figured she might as well show him what she had read in the book.

"What is it?"

Carly held the book out to him, open on the page with the foreign verse inside.

"That's Latvian", he said, after reading the text aloud.

"Is it true, what it says about dreams being real, and having the ability to see through another werewolf's eyes?"

Kyle looked a little somber. "Yes, it's true", he admitted. "I've only ever known it happen in female werewolves though, and it stays with some permanently even after their first lunar change."

Carly felt her stomach lurch. "Why didn't you tell me that when I told you about my dream?"

"I didn't want you to start freaking out. You've been through a lot lately, finding out that you've become a werewolf, losing Rob, visiting the land of the dead…I thought it would be a bit much to handle."

Carly's eyes flashed angrily. "You should have told me Kyle, I had a right to know. I was in the body of another werewolf and they killed somebody! *I* killed somebody!"

Kyle put his hands on Carly's shoulders. "No, you didn't kill anybody, don't ever think that!" he said firmly. "The other werewolf killed somebody, not you. You had no control over it."

"But I wanted to do it! I enjoyed doing it!" cried Carly, feeling distraught.

"That's what the other werewolf felt Carly, not you! You were feeling what they felt; that's true empathy. It doesn't mean you are a killer."

Carly began to cry. She wanted so badly to believe Kyle. She wanted to believe that she wasn't a murderer but her mind kept flicking back to how much satisfaction she had gotten from terrorising that man and ripping his body to pieces. She couldn't differentiate her own emotions from the emotions of the wolf whose body she had involuntarily invaded. It terrified her.

"Hey hey, calm down", said Kyle trying to sooth her. He sat her down on the bed. "Being a werewolf isn't easy, I'll be the first to admit that. The build up to the first lunar change is probably the most confusing time of all; you don't know whether you are coming or going. We are here for you though, your pack. I promise I won't keep things from you again, if you promise you won't run away again, how does that sound?"

Carly smiled through her sniffles. "Okay, deal", she said.

"If anything is troubling you, anything at all, at any time, I'm here for you. You know that, right?"

Carly nodded gratefully. As if by magic, Kyle produced a pack of Kleenex from somewhere about his person and handed it to Carly.

"Thanks", she said and took the packet.

"No problem. Listen, I was thinking of taking a run into town tonight to fetch some supplies. Do you want to come?"

'A run into town?' Carly couldn't quite believe her ears. She had assumed that she would never leave this forest again! "We...we get to go into town?" she asked incredulously.

"Well sure, that shampoo didn't just materialise out of thin air", said Kyle with a wink.

"Oh, so you don't just steal things from unsuspecting campers then?" laughed Carly, feeling a little calmer now.

"Erm...well not just from campers no. Campers don't always have everything we need and they aren't that frequent really either. I wish I could tell you that we're going to just buy things but I'm afraid we have no money..."

"We're going to steal things from town?"

"From closed shops, yes. I don't go around to peoples houses though, I prefer the faceless victim." Kyle looked at her crestfallen face and gave her a hug. "I don't like it any more than you do but Seth insists it's the only way. He's right of course; we can't ever go home, not permanently anyway. It's not safe, not while hunters are around. With no money, what else can we do?"

"Sell deer meat?" suggested Carly, only half jokingly.

Kyle smiled. "And get arrested for poaching? Not a great idea! We can't be drawing attention to ourselves like that. Don't worry, I'm not going to start stealing forty-two inch televisions or anything! We only take what we need to survive."

Carly hesitated. She wasn't sure she wanted to be party to theft.

"Are you going to come tonight or not?"

"Oh, ok", said Carly eventually. She did see the practical need for what they were going to be doing, but that didn't mean she was very comfortable with it. "Can I go home? I really want to pick up some of my things."

"If we're careful you can, but we won't be able to stay long", said Kyle.

The rest of the day passed quickly, and when night fell, Carly felt impatient to get going. "Is it time to go yet?" she asked Kyle.

"Go where?" enquired Seth. He and Devon had returned a few hours prior.

"I'm taking Carly into town to get a few things that we need", explained Kyle.

Seth growled. "You didn't consult me on this."

"You weren't here", said Kyle calmly. "You know we need to gather some supplies, you said so yourself a few days ago."

"You can go alone", said Seth, looking obstinate.

"I want to go with Kyle. I can be useful", protested Carly.

Seth growled again, this time at Carly. "I want you here!"

"What for?"

Seth struggled to think of something to say. "Because I said so, and I'm the pack leader."

"Pah! Pack leader my ass! You're never even here! You rarely bring back food, you weren't even aware that Gary got shot by hunters…Kyle does more for the pack than you do!"

Seth let out what could only be described as a ferocious sounding bark-howl and lunged at Carly. He had his claws extended, and they tore through Carly's t-shirt right across her stomach. Carly gasped and stumbled backwards, clutching at her body where she had been attacked. The pain from the scratch seared into her, yet she did not cry out.

Instantly, Kyle and Ian leapt in front of Carly, shielding her from Seth. Kyle's expression was as black as thunder.

"Get away from her", he said, in a low threatening voice.

Seth stepped forwards but a hand on his arm from Devon stopped him from going any further. "Let's go and get something to eat", suggested Devon. "I'm hungry." Seth and Kyle were staring at each other, neither wanting to break the other's gaze, but eventually Seth looked away and followed Devon out of the cabin without another word.

Kyle turned to Carly. "Are you okay?" he asked. Carly nodded. "Let's take a look at that scratch", he continued. Carly lowered her hand and Kyle carefully lifted her t-shirt to expose her midriff. Four deep claw marks were present.

"Is it bad?" she asked, not daring to look down.

Kyle sucked in his breath through his teeth. It was the same kind of noise that Carly had heard car mechanics make before when she had asked how much it would be to fix her car. It was a sound that didn't instill much confidence in her. "Well, put it this way, we're tough us werewolves. We heal faster than humans do. It's not a serious wound in the grand scheme of things. Having said that, you'll probably be left with a pretty scar there."

Carly looked down and winced at the sight of the scratches. They felt sore, and she half-wished she hadn't opened her mouth and said all those things to anger Seth. She didn't know what he was capable of, but if he saw fit to be so violent towards her, it really did seem likely that he had meant what he had said to the other pack about them all being nothing but collateral damage.

"I think you'd better have a lie down for a bit", suggested Ian.

"I really wanted to go with Kyle to town!" she said petulantly, feeling like a chastised schoolgirl.

"I'm not going right away. We can't go until the middle of the night; we need to be sure nobody will be around. It'll be several hours before I'm ready to leave, and by that time your wound will be considerably better. I'm sure you'll be able to come, don't worry."

Carly was sceptical. "After just a few hours? Werewolves heal that quickly?"

"If it's not silver, or aconite, then yes we do heal that quickly."

Carly brightened up a little. As much as she'd had her reservations about stealing provisions, she was anxious to return to somewhere familiar, somewhere other than this forest and this cabin. "Oh good!" she said pleased.

"Go and rest now, you need your strength for tonight. If you over-exert yourself, it will take longer for the scratches to recover. You'd better eat something as well, that will help."

Carly did as he suggested. She retrieved three mice from the fridge Devon had brought back a little earlier and ate them hungrily, then headed back to her room to lie down. She leafed further through the book hoping to find out something more about werewolves, but the rest of the pages didn't hold any further secrets. Everything else, she was already familiar with.

A few hours passed by. Carly had been drifting in and out of sleep, as she had not had anything else in particular to do to kill time whilst lying on her bed, until eventually Kyle entered the bedroom. Carly stirred as he creaked open the door, and she turned her head to look at him.

"Sorry, I didn't mean to wake you", said Kyle.

"No that's okay I was only dozing. Is it time to go yet?"

"In about an hour I should think. How is your stomach?"

Carly lifted up her top and peered at her midriff. The wounds had healed into much shallower scratches now and weren't feeling nearly as sore as they had done earlier. "A lot less painful than they were", she said.

Kyle looked at them. "Hmm, they could be better, but they'll do I suppose. It's not as though we're going into battle or anything, it's a simple stealth operation. Get in, get what we need, and get out. I don't think you'll be overly exerting yourself."

"Don't forget we're stopping at my house as well", Carly reminded him.

"I hadn't forgotten", said Kyle. "By the way have you given any thought as to what you're going to do with your house? Sell it?"

Carly hadn't even thought about the long-term prospects of her house. The question hit her quite hard as she still wasn't used to the idea of not being able to live there any longer. "Well I don't own it, I lease it, so I'll need to give my landlord notice", she said. She was surprised at how upset she felt at this thought. She had never wanted it to be her home forever; she and Rob had intended to use it as a stepping-stone whilst they saved up for a place of their own. Now that would never happen of course; she was stuck being a werewolf in a cabin full of relative strangers for the rest of her life. Mind you, she no longer thought of them as strangers. A week in the pack and she felt as though they were her kith and kin, but she figured that was sort of beside the point; it was the principle here that mattered.

Kyle noticed her glum expression. "Well we can talk about it a bit later on", he said kindly. "It's not something that you need to think about right away."

Carly was grateful for that. She really didn't want to face the prospect of officially leaving her house. It would be as though she was finally admitting to herself that it was real, that Rob was gone, and she was a werewolf. She knew these things already, of course, but she still had her home tying her to her old life, which in a way was a comfort.

"Shall we get going?" asked Kyle, breaking her free from her thoughts.

Carly eased herself out of bed, being careful not to brush against anything with her stomach, and stood up. "Yeah, I'm ready", she replied whilst pulling on her sneakers.

CHAPTER SIX

Together Kyle and Carly walked out of the cabin into the night. It was dark even by werewolf standards as it was cloudy that night. Not even a glimmer of the moon was visible to shine through the branches of the trees. Carly experienced a thrill of anticipation running down her spine. They walked for about two hours and Carly felt quite cheerful. "Kyle", she whispered. She didn't know exactly why she was whispering. She knew that sound carries further at night and she didn't want to alert anybody to their presence - not hunters, nor members of the other werewolf pack.

"What?" Kyle whispered back.

Carly was about to ask him how much further the town was, when suddenly she stumbled on a root. She immediately had one of those mini-heart attacks that you get when you accidentally step off a curb without realising it's there. Luckily Kyle's reflexes were on top form. As quick as a flash he reached out his hand to stop her from falling.

"Thanks", she said, her heart pounding wildly.

"No problem", said Kyle. "Be careful though, your wounds still haven't healed properly."

Carly waved her hand in a dismissive gesture. His concern for her was sweet but she didn't think he needed to worry. She told him so.

"Well, I'm your pack member, we worry about each other. That's what we do", whispered Kyle, smiling.

"So how long until we reach the town?" asked Carly, finally able to get her words out.

"About an hour from here. It's no different from the journey we took last week when you first arrived."

"I can't remember how long that took though", admitted Carly. When she thought back to that day, sometimes it seemed as though they had walked only ten minutes to reach the cabin; other times it seemed more like ten hours. Her sense of judgment and perspective that day had been completely thrown off. This was hardly surprising considering everything she had been through at the time.

They continued walking in silence. Kyle kept one hand on the small of Carly's back to guide her. He was ready to grab the back of her t-shirt in case she stumbled again. Carly felt a little bit smothered and was quite sure that she didn't need to be treated like a baby, but she did rather like his attention so she didn't grumble about it. The hoot of an owl made Carly jump. Without warning a searing pain coursed through her leg and she let out a howl of agony. Kyle tried to grab her clothing but was unable to stop her collapsing to the ground.

"Oh hell, it's a trap!" cried Kyle peering down at her leg. Carly couldn't speak; she felt as though she might pass out. It was incredibly painful and she actually thought her leg might have been almost severed.

"Hold still! Hold still", said Kyle urgently, trying desperately to grapple with the trap to free Carly's leg. "We've got to get you out of here. If there is a trap, the hunters might be close!"

Carly knew she was making some kind of involuntary grunting noises at this point but she couldn't help it. At this stage she really didn't care how she sounded. Kyle pulled at the teeth of the trap which had sunk deep into her leg but it was too much for Carly to bear. She felt woozy and the next thing she saw was blackness as she slipped into unconsciousness.

Bouncing up and down, that's what she could feel. She could feel arms around her and hands supporting her, the sensation of bouncing and the sound of running feet. She opened her eyes and saw Kyle's face above hers; a look of concentration furrowed across his brow. She realised that he was running and he was carrying her. Her leg was throbbing and she could smell blood; this scent was so familiar she immediately knew it was her own, tinging the night air with its aroma.

"What happened?" she asked. Kyle didn't answer at once but when he did, his response was short and sharp.

"Hunters...after us", he said, in a brisk semi-barking tone.

A chill ran through Carly. "Wouldn't we be quicker if I ran instead of being carried?" she asked.

"You can't run - hell you can't even walk right now", panted Kyle, still not breaking his pace. "That trap nearly took your leg off. You're lucky it didn't; we can't recover from amputations! You lose a limb, then you lose a limb, that's it, no healing that!"

Carly was dismayed that Kyle would have to continue to carry her. She knew it was a hindrance to them. On the other hand the sheer delight she felt, knowing she was definitely not going to lose her leg, was immense. "My leg will heal though won't it?" she asked.

Kyle looked a little irritated. "Yes, but it will take a couple of days. That's one of the worst trap wounds I've ever seen." Carly didn't care; she was just so glad that she could keep her leg. She didn't have time to dwell on this for very long though, for the sound of gunshots rang out from behind them. "Oh hell", muttered Kyle. He increased his pace. Sweat poured from his brow and he appeared exhausted.

"Put me down", urged Carly, feeling increasingly worried about whether or not they would make it alive considering that Kyle had her weight to bear as well.

"Don't be silly, that's not even an option", panted Kyle. "We'll make it don't worry."

Carly was worried though. It was all very well and good Kyle telling her not to be, but as far as she was concerned he was probably just saying that so that her mind wouldn't be troubled. "I'm so sorry Kyle, I should have been looking where I was going." She though it was important to apologise, because she felt quite useless in every other respect.

"It's not your fault", reassured Kyle.

Carly could tell he was having some difficulty breathing whilst talking as they were going so fast, so she decided it would be better if she kept quiet and let him concentrate on running.

"Are they still behind us?" gasped Kyle after a few minutes. Carly peered over his shoulder and looked all around. She couldn't see anybody. Raising her nose to the air, she took two or three long deep sniffs. She couldn't smell anybody either.

"I don't think so", she said.

Kyle slowed his running down to a gentle jog and eventually came to a stop. He carefully set Carly down on the ground. He pulled up her trouser leg which was now soaked with blood and examined her leg. "It's a very deep wound", he said. Carly had no doubt about that, it was certainly painful enough. She winced as Kyle tore a strip from his t-shirt and used it as a bandage for her leg. "It will heal but it will take some time. That trap was made out of silver."

"How do you know?" asked Carly. "It just looked like a metal trap to me."

"I could feel it burning my hands when I was trying to free you from it", said Kyle. "That is why it was so painful to you...well, that and the fact that it nearly took your leg off!" Kyle finished wrapping the bandage around Carly's leg and tied off the ends. "There", he announced. "It will take a good few days to recover from that. At least we can be sure that there isn't any silver left inside your body. A trap is thankfully not like a gun. Bullets can shatter inside somebody, but a trap, well, once you remove the trap, you're not in contact with the silver any longer."

"Are we close to town?" asked Carly hopefully.

Kyle raised an eyebrow. "Well we're not far now, not after all that running, I'd say maybe ten minutes walk, but you're hurt!"

"I'll manage", insisted Carly. She turned around and clung onto the trunk of a tree behind her. Mustering up all of her strength, she pulled herself up, holding onto the tree for support. It was a large old tree, so she couldn't wrap her arms all the way around the trunk as it was far too wide, but she did the best she could. "There", she said triumphantly, standing on one leg. "I'm up, let's go!"

"Don't be ridiculous, you can't walk on that", remarked Kyle.

"Of course I can, watch!"

Carly put down her injured leg and attempted to take a step. Instantly, intense pain seared up her leg and she collapsed to the ground with a small scream.

"I'm saying nothing…" said Kyle rolling his eyes slightly at her stubbornness and quickly bent down to attend to her. He helped her to sit comfortably against the tree, then stood up and began to scratch his head. "I suppose I could carry you there," he said, pacing backwards and forwards in front of her, "but it's a good hour walk back to the cabin afterwards. With the best will in the world I can't carry you for an hour as well as carrying the provisions we need…" he muttered, seemingly talking to himself. "I'm strong, but I'm not superman."

"Maybe we could find a bike, or a horse or something, for me to ride on to get back to the cabin?" suggested Carly.

"Erm…no." The look on Kyle's face told her that he thought that was quite a ridiculous idea.

"Well leave me here then, whatever, come back for me tomorrow", retorted Carly feeling a little cross.

"There's only one thing we can do I suppose, but I don't like it", said Kyle, ignoring her semi-sarcastic tone. "You're going to have to stay in town for a few days until you're strong enough to walk back to the cabin."

"Are you serious?" asked Carly incredulously. "Won't Seth be angry?"

"Yeah, of course he will, this is Seth you're talking about, it's a given!" said Kyle in a blasé tone of voice. "He's always cross about something or other these days. I'll deal with Seth, don't worry about it." Carly's leg was hurting far too much for her to even contemplate arguing with him. She nodded, feeling a little light headed. Kyle took his t-shirt off and began to unbuckle the belt of his trousers.

"What are you doing?" asked Carly, quite astonished.

"Well I said I was going to carry you didn't I?"

"You need to be nude in order to carry me?" Carly was not clicking on to what Kyle intended to do. She stared at him blankly.

Kyle peered into her eyes and chuckled. "I can see the cogs in there turning but you're just not…quite…getting it, are you?" he said, laughing. "Look, it's a bit of a pain carrying you in human form. As with anything, it's easier piggy-back. So, you're going to ride me."

"As a wolf?" asked Carly, disbelievingly.

"Well I can't turn into a horse now can I? Yes, of course as a wolf. I'm quite big enough to take you, or hadn't you noticed?"

Carly blushed. "Oh yes, I had noticed that you're big," she flirted, "definitely big enough for me".

Now it was Kyle's turn to blush. "Shut up", he said playfully. "Grab my clothes for me would you?" Kicking off the rest of his clothes, Kyle turned into his wolf form in front of her. With a shake of his head, he motioned for her to mount his back. Carly picked up Kyle's clothes and stuffed them into the little satchel she had hanging from her shoulder. She had packed meat and water inside the satchel as well, in case they should have needed it at any point. Once again she struggled to her feet. With the aid of the tree she managed, somehow, to swing her injured leg over his back, whilst balancing herself on the ground on her good leg. Then she hoisted herself into a comfortable seating position.

Carly had nothing to hold onto, so she grabbed the fur at the back of his head. Kyle let out a small whine and shook his head. Carly immediately let go of his fur and looked around desperately, wondering what she could hang onto. Finally she settled for leaning forwards, resting her chest against his back and putting her arms around his neck. Kyle nodded and began to walk forwards. Carly felt his body moving beneath hers. It felt so powerful, strong and muscular. At first she wobbled slightly as he walked, but as she got used to the sensation, she began to feel more at ease with shifting her own weight gently side to side to counter the natural sway which occurred when Kyle moved. She forgot completely about the pain in her leg, as she was too busy concentrating on not falling off his back.

He walked at a brisk pace, not a run, but he didn't really need to run, as sure enough, roughly ten minutes later, they reached the edge of the wood. Kyle stopped as they emerged from the trees. The moon had broken through the clouds now and to Carly the world suddenly seemed incredibly bright. The field in front of them was bathed in a silvery glow. Kyle, too, seemed to be taking it all in. He scanned his head from left to right, as though he was surveying the territory. Carly wished she could speak to him, but as he was in his wolf form she had no way of communicating with him. That reminded her that she actually meant to ask him whether or not werewolves can speak to each other once they are in wolf-form. Certainly, she assumed they must be able to communicate somehow. Even real wolves manage to control their packs, so there must be some form of language, even if it's only body language. She made a mental note to bring this up with him later.

"Come on then, let's go", she said at last, giving him a stroke on the back of his neck. This seemed to interrupt Kyle's thoughts. He gave a little shake of his head and began walking again across the field. Carly nearly fell off his back for she wasn't holding on. She had to quickly fling her arms around his neck again. The lights of the town shone in the distance, first as tiny twinkling dots, then bigger and brighter as they approached them. When they finally reached the other side of the field, Kyle stopped again and lay down on the ground. He gave a little whine, gesturing to Carly to dismount. Gingerly, she slid off his back, paying attention to the way she landed on the ground so she wouldn't further aggravate her injury.

Once sitting on the grass, Kyle reverted into a man. "Give me my clothes would you, it's cold", he said, shivering slightly. "Instantly losing my fur like that you see."

Carly rummaged around in her satchel, pulled out his clothes and tossed them to him. Kyle caught them deftly and quickly wriggled into them. "So, where to first?" asked Carly.

"We need to get you to your house", said Kyle. "You can't come with me to collect any provisions, you're too vulnerable. You'd be a sitting duck!" Bending down, he picked up Carly the way he had initially carried her and began to walk through the deserted streets. Not a soul was in sight, which wasn't really surprising since it was the middle of the night.

"The only person I've seen at this time before, round here, is Scully Jim", said Kyle.

"That sounds like a pirate", remarked Carly, wondering who on earth Scully Jim could be.

"No, he's not a pirate – he's an old homeless guy. Usually he stays close to supermarkets; begging during the day and sleeping at night. I've bumped into him a couple of times when I've been back for provisions in the past."

"Isn't that a bit dangerous, being seen by him?" asked Carly feeling a little anxious.

"Nah, he's a decent guy. If he's around, I fetch him some provisions while I'm picking up my own stuff."

"So you steal for Scully Jim as well?" Carly raised an eyebrow.

"It's not really stealing…" said Kyle innocently. "I'm a bit like Robin Hood!"

"Oh, sure, you're the saviour of the day", said Carly sarcastically.

Kyle looked at her in surprise. "What's gotten into you? You're a bit tense this evening!"

"I'm not tense!" snapped Carly, then caught herself. Kyle was right - she was a bit tetchy. She didn't know why she was being like this. She felt quite highly-strung. "Are all werewolves so stressed in the run up to the first lunar change?" she asked.

"Umm…sometimes yes. Though I've been around male werewolves more frequently than females, so maybe it's a girl thing", he replied.

"So there are female werewolves around?" asked Carly.

"Oh sure, of course there are. Some large packs have several females. Like I told you before, the pack leader, otherwise known as the Alpha, gets his pick from the females of the pack. The rest go to the strongest other males in the pack. The runts don't tend to find a female."

"That's really sad though", said Carly. "So, somebody quite skinny and weak looking, who might have possibly had a chance at love and happiness when they were a human if they found somebody who wanted to be with them, if they become a werewolf they'd have no chance at all of finding a mate? They'd have to spend the rest of their life alone?"

"Werewolves are never alone," said Kyle, "at least not the ones who are part of a pack. You should know this by now Carly - packs are families!"

"It's not quite the same thing though is it?" reasoned Carly. "Families are all very well and good, but they're not really a substitute for love; the kind of love you get when you find somebody you want to spend the rest of your life with".

"You're still thinking like a human", said Kyle gently. "Think of…erm…" he scratched his head, "think of Bambi. Bambi has to fight that other deer to win Faeline's heart, doesn't he?"

"Yes…" said Carly slowly.

"The other deer isn't strong enough to be considered a suitable mate for her because he loses the fight against Bambi. That's the way it is in nature; the strongest males who can prove themselves worthy end up with the female. The others don't get a look in. It might sound harsh but that's the way it is!"

"But…but…" Carly struggled to get her words out. "We're not wolves though, we're werewolves, we're half human aren't we? It's not the same as just saying we're like any other animal."

"You haven't been through your first change yet, you still have more human instincts than wolf ones. When you've transitioned for the first time, you'll understand. The law of the pack will seem much more natural."

Carly must have been looking dismayed at this prospect for Kyle gave her shoulder a little squeeze. "Don't worry, it's not so bad. I've never known a werewolf yet who has been discontented with his place in the pack. Besides, you don't need to worry, females always find a mate!"

Carly bristled with indignation. "I'm not just a piece of property for male wolves to fight over you know!"

"Oh I didn't mean it like that, I meant that the runt thing doesn't apply to females…" Kyle tailed off, for Carly was now fuming. She could feel her heart pounding angrily, and her eyes glowing brighter than ever. She could now tell when her eyes glowed or flashed more than usual for she felt a slight tingling sensation occurring behind her eyeballs which was an unusual but not unpleasant feeling.

"So you're saying I'm a RUNT?" bellowed Carly, forgetting to keep her voice down.

"Shhh!" urged Kyle desperately. "You're going to wake the whole town! No I didn't mean that you're a runt. Look, let's just forget about this, I'm digging myself a hole here and it's not intentional. I'm sorry if I upset you."

Carly's anger waned a little. 'at least he had had the good grace to apologise', she reasoned. 'If it had been Seth it would have been quite another matter! I doubt he has ever apologised for anything in his life.' She looked at Kyle. "I don't care how strong or masculine Seth is. The fact that he is pack leader doesn't impress me either. I'm never going to be Seth's mate", whispered Carly.

"Okay, okay, you told me that already", replied Kyle, "calm down".

"I am calm!" replied Carly in as loud a whisper as she could manage. She didn't know why she was feeling so irritable. 'My period has got to be due with the way I'm feeling!' she thought. At last Carly's house came into view. She felt a mixture of emotions on seeing it again; mostly happiness and relief, but also a twinge of fear and sadness. This had been the house where it all began, where she became a werewolf. She ought to have been returning to this house with Rob, together, but now that would never happen. Carly jumped a little as a single tear ran down one of her cheeks. She hadn't expected to cry.

"I hope you brought your front door key!" joked Kyle. "I don't fancy breaking your door down, that would attract a lot of attention."

Carly's mind flashed back to the dream she had had. "Could you not use your claw and cut the glass in the window and get in?" she asked.

Kyle stopped walking and looked at her in astonishment. "Not many wolves do that to enter a building", he said, quite surprised that she had mentioned it. "In fact, I think Seth is the only one who does. How did you know about it?"

Carly was shocked at his words. If Seth was the only one who entered buildings that way, then that could only mean one thing. The gravity of what this new information implied hit her like a ton of bricks but she managed to stay relatively cool and collected on the exterior. "Oh I think he mentioned it at one point", she said dismissively. Inside though her stomach was churning. Seth was the wolf she had been dreaming about? It was Seth who had torn apart that man and eaten him? Those were Seth's awful thoughts that she had experienced? Carly felt sick. It couldn't be the case, could it? Even though she knew Seth wasn't everything he pretended to be, she still couldn't believe that he was really a depraved murderer; that seemed too much to take in.

"Are you all right?" asked Kyle looking at her with a concerned expression on his face.

Carly gulped and tried to ignore the knot forming in her stomach. "I'll be all right, my leg hurts that's all", she replied. Her brain was whirring as she tried to rationalise the events. 'Perhaps there are some other wolves that enter buildings that way. Just because Kyle hasn't seen them himself, it doesn't mean it's not possible. Maybe Seth himself even showed them how to do it? Maybe it's a wolf from the other pack! That must be it, it must be, it can't be Seth!' On and on the conflict raged in her mind and Carly just wanted it to stop. "So, are you going to put me down?" she asked, trying desperately to take her mind away from Seth. She would have time to think things through more thoroughly later.

"If I did that, you wouldn't get very far now would you," said Kyle with a smile, "I'd just have to pick you back up again".

"Well the key is in my back pocket, and I can't very well reach it like this!"

With a small exaggerated groan, Kyle set Carly down onto the ground in a standing position, so that she was actually balanced on one leg. He kept hold of one of her hands for support. Carly wobbled slightly from left to right as she dug in the back pocket of her jeans for her key. She felt the warm metal object and pulled it out triumphantly.

"Here we go", she said, swaying dangerously from side to side whilst brandishing the key.

Kyle took it from her. "Okay, wait here a minute", he said. Gingerly he let go of her hand. Carly waved her injured leg around like some sort of balancing aid.

"You're not going to fall are you?" he asked.

"No, I'm fine", said Carly, not entirely convincingly. Despite having acquired an excellent sense of balance since becoming a werewolf, the pain from her raised leg was making her lose focus.

Kyle walked swiftly over to the front door and put the key in the lock. After struggling with it for a few seconds, he eventually took hold of the handle and pulled it sharply down. It opened.

"Oh God, I forgot to lock the door when I left!" realised Carly.

Kyle rolled his eyes and hurried back over to her. Swiftly he scooped her back up again. Carly was very thankful, as concentrating on not falling over had been very awkward.

"Let's get you inside to rest that leg", said Kyle, marching towards the house.

Carly felt an overwhelming sense of relief to once again be back at home. Any negative thoughts she'd had about returning without Rob seemed to melt away the minute she was over the threshold. Even in the dark she was pleased to find that everything seemed familiar and comforting. "There's a switch just behind the curtain on the left", she said. Kyle reached over and flicked on the light. The brightness of the bulb illuminated the room so brilliantly Carly had to shield her eyes. She had grown accustomed to the darkness by now, so at first the light was hard for her to handle. She squinted up at Kyle. "Thanks", she said.

Kyle, by contrast, hadn't even blinked when the light had come on. His eyes were quite wide open and he surveyed the room in front of him. "Do you want me to take you upstairs? Would you feel more comfortable in bed?" he asked.

Carly shook her head. "No thanks, just on the sofa will be fine." She didn't want to admit that after a week of nothing but dusty old books to read for entertainment, she was looking forward to watching the television! She thought it seemed a little too human a desire. She wasn't sure Kyle would understand. Kyle did as she

134 - N. Gosney

asked and put her down on the sofa. It was a wonderfully soft burgundy coloured sofa, with lots of orange and cream cushions scattered around on it. Carly sank into them happily. "Ahh that's really comfy", she sighed, smiling. Kyle busied himself, lifting her leg up and placing it gently on a small stack of cushions. "What are you doing that for?" asked Carly.

"It needs to be elevated", explained Kyle. "Didn't you ever do basic first aid?"

"Yes, but that was a long time ago", Carly said.

"It directs the blood away from the wound if you raise it up", he explained. "Okay, technically it would help if you raised it higher than your heart, but that's a little tricky unless you want your leg to be sky high!"

Carly laughed a little. "I think it'll be okay where it is", she said. "Thanks Kyle."

"That's not a problem. Now I really must go and fetch some provisions. I'll bring some meat back for you before I head back to the cabin. Is there anything else you need?"

Carly thought hard but she couldn't think of anything that she didn't already have in the house. "No thank you", she said.

"Okay, well I'll be back as soon as I can", said Kyle, giving her a little kiss on the forehead. He headed out of the front door and closed it gently behind him.

Carly wriggled a little on the sofa to make herself as comfortable as possible and reached for the television remote control. "Crap", she muttered. It was on the coffee table just past her fingertips and she couldn't get hold of it. She leaned over as far as she could but still couldn't reach it. She grunted as she gave herself a final thrust forwards and promptly toppled off the sofa. With an almighty scream she hit the floor; the pain in her leg was so intense she blacked out almost immediately.

She had no idea how long she had been lying there unconscious, but the next thing she was aware of was the carpet in her face. Groggily she tried to sit up but felt weak and unsteady. Carly took hold of the coffee table for support, and somehow managed to hoist herself back up onto the sofa, grabbing the remote control in the process. Her leg was throbbing and stinging at the same time. She felt badly in need of some pain relief. She thought she might have some aspirin in the kitchen but didn't feel able to drag herself in there to find out. She hoped Kyle would be returning soon with the meat he had promised her; she would ask him to check her medicine box on top of the fridge. She barely had time to turn on the television when the front door swung open making her jump. In walked Kyle. He had a full rucksack on his back and two bulging shopping bags in his hands. "You startled me", said Carly. "I wasn't expecting you back so soon!"

Kyle looked a little puzzled. "I've been a good two hours", he said. "How long did you think it was going to take?"

Carly couldn't believe it. 'Two whole hours? Surely I wasn't unconscious for that long!' she thought. "Oh, I fell off the sofa... and, well, I passed out", she replied hesitantly.

"Oh God are you okay?" he asked, concerned.

"It hurts", admitted Carly. "Can you please go and have a look in the kitchen for me? There's a box on top of the fridge - I've got some medicines in there. I think you'll find some aspirin. I could do with something to take the edge off this pain."

"Oh I've got something better than that", said Kyle. He set down his shopping bags, swung the rucksack off his shoulder and began to search in one of the side pockets.

"What are you looking for?" asked Carly.

Kyle didn't answer but continued to rummage. "Ah, here we are", said Kyle at last, pulling a small rectangular packet from the bag. "Morphine."

Carly was a little taken aback. She hadn't expected anything as drastic as that but she had to admit the sound of a strong pain-killer was inviting. "What did you do? Rob the pharmacy counter as well?" she asked wryly.

Kyle shrugged. "Well it's not as though it wasn't necessary. That leg is in a bad way. I brought some decent packing material and bandages so I can sort it out for you properly." With that he made his way into the kitchen and returned with a glass of water so she could take the tablets.

The water was icy cold and refreshing and Carly realised that she had been thirsty. She downed the rest of the water and then handed the glass back to Kyle. "Thanks," she said, "I needed that!"

"Let's have a look at this leg then", said Kyle. From one of his shopping bags, he pulled out what appeared to be more medical supplies. He sat down on the edge of the sofa next to Carly and began to unwrap the strip of t-shirt tied around her leg. Carly averted her eyes – she didn't want to see her leg. She could feel a strange sensation as Kyle put something cold into her wound. She jerked her leg slightly.

"Sorry, did that hurt?" he asked.

"No, but it felt strange."

"I've got to pack the wound, it will help it to heal."

Carly held still whilst Kyle finished fixing up her leg. When it was sufficiently packed he unwrapped a bandage from its cellophane packaging and wrapped it firmly but carefully around her leg, tying it off at the end.

Carly smiled gratefully. The morphine was beginning to take effect and her leg didn't feel quite as bad as it had previously.

"Do you want some meat now?" asked Kyle. Carly nodded; she was famished. Kyle retrieved a packet of extra lean beef venison burgers from one of the bags and tossed it to her. "I know how much you enjoyed that deer the other day", he said with a grin. "I'm afraid supermarket meat isn't nearly as good as fresh though but it'll have to do."

Carly tore open the packet and tucked into the burgers. Kyle was right, they were nowhere near as tasty as the deer he had caught a few days prior, but they would suffice for now. She certainly wasn't going to complain about them.

"I've got a fair amount of meat here, it should keep you going until I get back", said Kyle. "I'll go and put it in your fridge." Kyle busied himself stocking Carly's refrigerator whilst she finished her meal. "I feel really bad leaving you here by yourself", he called from the kitchen.

"Don't be silly, you've got nothing to feel bad for", called back Carly between mouthfuls. "I'll be fine, it's not like I can't manage in my own house!"

"It's not as safe as being with the pack though."

"Honestly, stop worrying, nothing bad is going to happen. I'm a big girl I can look after myself!"

Kyle walked back into the kitchen and gazed sharply at Carly's leg. "Uh-huh…" he said, in a very unconvinced tone.

"Oh hush, just because I walked into a trap…it could have happened to anybody!"

"Well I'm still not fond of the idea of leaving you here," said Kyle, "but there's not much I can do. The others really do need these supplies."

"It's fine, really, you'll be back soon!"

"Tomorrow night I'll be back, I promise", said Kyle. "If you're strong enough I'll take you back then with me. I won't have any supplies to carry."

"That's fine, I'll be okay", reassured Carly. "Stop fussing over me, I'm not a baby!"

"No but you're my responsibility!"

"You're not pack leader, I'm Seth's responsibility, aren't I? As are you!"

Kyle looked a little dumfounded at this. His mouth opened and closed like a goldfish's mouth. "I'm not sure that was necessary!" he said at last.

"Sorry", said Carly. "Look, the sooner you go and get some rest, the sooner you can come back to me."

Kyle stopped and thought about that for a minute. "How does that work out exactly?" he said with a laugh. "I'm coming back tomorrow night regardless of anything else!"

Carly gave him a little shove. "Go on, get out of here", she said smiling. Kyle bent down and gave her a hug, then walked out of the front door. Carly turned around so she could see him through the living room window. He walked down the path, stopped, and looked back to the house. Carly smiled and waved at him; Kyle smiled and waved in return. She watched as he continued onto the street. He began to walk along the sidewalk in the direction of the supermarket. He was nearly out of sight when a black car with darkened windows pulled up alongside him. Carly instantly felt prickles rising at the back of her neck. She ducked down so that only her eyes were peering out above the top of the sofa. As she watched, feeling her heart beating faster in her chest, she saw one of the back doors of the car open slightly and suddenly Kyle dropped to the ground in a heap.

Carly let out a little scream, then clamped her hand to her mouth in terror. 'Whatever happens, don't let them know you're here', she thought. She was petrified but couldn't tear her gaze away from the window. Two pairs of hands reached out and dragged Kyle into the car. The door then slammed shut and the car began to move. As it neared the house, Carly quickly put her head down so she wouldn't be seen from the window. Her mouth felt dry and her skin was clammy. The adrenaline was coursing through her body. She knew she couldn't just sit there and do nothing. She had no idea if they had killed Kyle or not, or who they were (though her gut feeling was that it had to be hunters), but if he was alive, she had to get him back. "Why would they take him with them if they had killed him?" she asked herself in a shaky voice. "They would have just left him there, surely? Unless they had to dispose of the body?" She felt sick again, which was a sensation that was quite familiar to her since she had become a werewolf! It seemed as though there was always some situation or other occurring recently which induced a feeling of nausea. She fought it back though, and after having taken a further peek out of the window to ensure that she wouldn't be seen, Carly struggled to her feet.

It was fortunate she had taken the morphine for she found she was able to stand now. It did still hurt when putting her weight on her injured leg but it was now just about bearable. She winced as she hobbled to the front door. Cautiously she opened it and looked outside. She listened carefully and sniffed the air; nobody was nearby as far as she could tell. Carly didn't know what to do. She wished to goodness that the others back at the cabin had cell phones on them, so that she could call them and tell them to come, but she didn't think that they did. "Oh God what do I do?" she whispered into the night air. "Help me, what do I do?"

Carly felt so helpless. 'I have no idea where the men have taken Kyle, and even if I did, what good would I be if I found him? I can hardly walk, let alone rescue him from hunters!' Carly thought, standing in her doorway dithering for a few minutes, trying to decide what to do. 'I really have no choice. I have to try and find him on my own, even if I do end up floundering once I get there!' she concluded. Carly briefly weighed up the option of taking her car, but decided against it. 'It would be too noisy and I highly doubt I could track them from inside my vehicle, that would be next to impossible.' Carly sniffed the air. "Right," she said, feeling very uncertain, "on foot it is then". Carly closed the door behind her and set off in the direction the car had gone. She could smell the rubber from the tires and the unfamiliar scent of some other people mingled with Kyle's scent. She bent down to the ground, rubbed her fingers on the tarmac and held them up to her nose to get a better whiff of the scent. She felt a little ridiculous but she knew her sense of smell was her best chance of being able to find him so she didn't particularly care how silly it seemed. 'I can't allow another person I cared about to die. I've been through enough with Rob being shot', she thought.

Hobbling down the road, Carly wanted to cry with every step she took. Her leg really wasn't fit to walk on. She almost turned back to dose up on more morphine. Only the thought of Kyle stopped her from doing so, (that and the fact she didn't particularly want to overdose.) Gritting her teeth, she limped on bravely. She didn't feel brave though, she felt anything but brave. Her knees were like jelly from fear; she could still hear her heart racing. She was puffing and panting from the strain of having to drag her leg along. Just bending it at the knee sent rivers of pain shooting upwards through her limb, even though the wound itself was much further down the leg, not far above her ankle. She could feel a cold sweat pouring from her. She fervently hoped she wasn't going into shock.

After walking a little, she stopped to check the smell on the tarmac again. Sure enough, the scent was still present. Carly tried to hurry as quickly as she could in case the trail should start to fade. If she lost her means of following them she would probably never find Kyle. At the end of the road was a T-junction; Carly didn't know which way they could have gone so she was forced to check all directions. The smell was definitely stronger on the road leading to the right, so that was the path she took. Her leg was hurting more and more as she pushed it to its limit. At last she could take it no longer and she fell to the ground in the middle of the road, clinging to her leg and crying despairingly. "You can't give up now", she sobbed out loud. "Come on Carly, get up, Kyle needs you." In that moment she truly wished that she could amputate her own leg, the pain was so intense. If somebody had passed by brandishing a chainsaw then and there she would have begged them to use it on her. Carly began to drag herself along the road. The gravel tore into her hands, but she didn't even notice. "I'm coming Kyle, I'm not giving up on you", she muttered under her breath. "Don't you give up either. You stay alive, dammit, you have to stay alive!"

Realising she wasn't getting very far, Carly wrenched herself up off the floor letting out a cry. Onward she staggered, half blinded by the pain. Just when she thought she couldn't walk any further, the trail she was following veered off the road and onto a dirt path. It was the kind of path where one might imagine farmers take their tractors onto, but it certainly wasn't a road. "Oh God", muttered Carly. She didn't know where it was leading her. The path veered upwards and she couldn't see over the brow of the hill. She had to be very careful not to be spotted. As quietly as she could, Carly made her way to the top. In order to listen and smell the air she kept stopping behind the trees lining either side of the path. They had definitely come this way, she could tell. As she neared the peak, she crouched down onto the ground and proceeded to crawl the remainder of the way. As it happened she discovered that crawling was an easier position for her leg as she wasn't putting any weight on it. This helped a little. Peering over the top of the hill, Carly found that she was looking down into a field. At the bottom, in the field, there was a large barn. Carly didn't know if it might have been a cow-shed or simply a hay barn; she wasn't particularly knowledgeable on matters of agriculture. Outside the barn was the large black car Carly had seen earlier; the one Kyle had been dragged into. It was the same car, she was sure of it. It was stationary and appeared to be empty. Carly held her breath and waited at the top of the hill. She didn't dare to move for fear of being seen. Logically, it was probably unlikely as there were no lights at all here. Carly could see perfectly well with her night vision, but a human being would have great difficulty to see in the dark even with the moonlight to help them, so the chances of anyone spotting her were quite small.

Eventually, after a good two or three minutes, Carly began to make her way down the hill towards the barn. She slid down on her back to try and blend into her surroundings. There didn't appear to be anybody present at the foot of the hill, or near the car or barn. Upon reaching the bottom she attempted a very undignified sort of army-crawl towards the car. The smell from the tyres was unmistakably the same smell that she had been following, so it was clear she was in the right place. She could hear voices coming from inside. There were a few trees around the back; Carly thought that could be a better hiding spot for the time being. She would be able to listen to the goings-on inside without being spotted, so she gingerly made her way around the building. Sitting down behind a tree near the back of the barn, Carly felt a little stronger. Her leg coped better in a seated position. She didn't feel as exposed as in the open near the front of the barn and on the hill. The conversation inside the barn was quite audible.

"I don't know what you mean", said a voice that Carly recognised to be Kyle's.

"Don't play dumb with us, you dogs have ways of knowing about each other", came a man's voice. It was unfamiliar to Carly and sounded harsh in tone.

"Tell us who the wolf born is and we'll let you go", said a woman. She spoke in a much quieter voice, which Carly assumed was intended to sound reassuring, but to her ears it resonated with falseness. Carly was sure that Kyle would also be able to make that distinction.

"Yeah right, like you hunters would let me go", scoffed Kyle. "I'm not telling you anything."

"It's no good to you trying to protect him you know", said the man beginning to sound angry. "Once the skinwalkers have the wolf born, they'll destroy all the rest of you ordinary dogs anyway, so what good do you think protecting him is going to do? You might as well hand him over now and let us deal with him. It would save you a lot of bother."

"I told you I don't know what you mean", said Kyle.

Carly didn't know what they meant either. 'Skinwalkers? What on earth are skinwalkers, and why do they want Seth? Is this why Seth was mingling with the other pack, did he know that these skinwalkers were after him?' she thought.

The man exhaled in a frustrated manner. Carly heard him tell someone (presumably the woman) to come with him. She heard footsteps walking through the barn and then the sound of the door opening on the other side of the building. Carly strained to hear them since they were now outside, much further from her.

"He's not gonna tell you anything", whispered the woman.

"Then he's no use to us. We might as well kill him."

"What about if we let him go and follow him to his pack den? We haven't found it yet, but I bet if we do the wolf born will be there."

"Tracking device?"

"Well, I'm not sure if that is such a good idea. He probably wouldn't head for his den if he knew we had put a tracking device in him", said the woman.

"True, but how likely is he to lead us to the wolf born in any case if we let him go? He knows we would be more likely to kill him than release him, so by releasing him, he's sure to realise we intend to follow him."

"So we're back to square one then. We can't let him go."

"No, we can't. We'd better hang onto him for now until dad gets here. He can deal with him. If anybody can get information out of someone, it's dad", said the man.

"I guess you're right. Dad would kill us if we let him go anyway.

He does know we caught one doesn't he? You did tell him?"

There was a silence. "I…er…" the man sounded a little flummoxed.

"*Bradley!*" The woman cried exasperatedly.

"Shhhh! He'll hear you!"

"God dammit *Bradley!* We'd better go get him and bring him here."

"And leave that dog in there on his own?"

"Nobody knows he's here, and he's tied up with silver; he's not going to get out, trust me."

"Okay, well as long as we're quick."

"We'll be quick, dad isn't going to mess around once he hears about this. Come on."

Carly heard footsteps, and the sound of car doors opening, then slamming shut. The engine roared deafeningly. Carly waited with her heart in her mouth until she was sure it had driven away, then cautiously emerged from behind the tree. Nobody was about, she was sure of that. Wincing, she limped as fast as she could over to the barn door. It was padlocked, but she easily broke through that and opened the door.

"Carly!" cried a weak voice from the far end of the barn. "Oh God Carly I'm so happy to see you!" There was Kyle, bound to a chair with silver chains. His face was cut and bruised as though he had been badly beaten. The skin, which was touching the silver, was red, burnt and sore.

"Kyle, wow what have they done to you?" Carly hurried over to him and reached out her hands to untie him.

"Don't!" shouted Kyle. "It will burn your skin."

"So how am I meant to untie you then?"

"Erm…" Kyle looked stumped. "Can you find anything to knock the chains away from me with?"

Carly looked around the room, but aside from Kyle tied to his chair there was nothing else that she could find. "No, there's nothing here", she said.

"You're going to have to go and find something then."

"There's no time for that, they could be back any minute. I need to get you out of there!" Reaching up to her shoulders, Carly took hold of the short sleeves of her t-shirt and ripped them off. Due to her werewolf's strength, the stitching holding the sleeves to the rest of the t-shirt came away easily. There wasn't a lot of material there, but Carly wrapped what she had around her hands and took hold of the chains binding Kyle to his chair. "Argh!" she exclaimed, as she felt the silver burning her hands like acid even through the cloth.

"Carly, don't do this, you're going to hurt yourself", urged Kyle looking very concerned. "Just go, get help or something, I'll be alright until you get back."

"Don't talk out of your ass, they are very likely to kill you!" cried Carly in desperation. "They've gone to fetch their dad and God knows what he's going to do to you! Judging by what they were saying to each other, their dad is a lot worse than they are!"

"But the silver, it'll…"

"It'll not harm me any more than it's harming you right now!" interrupted Carly. "Now shut up!" She must have sounded quite forceful, for Kyle stopped arguing and let her get on with untying him. The pain from the silver was intense, but she ignored it and steadily worked on unfastening the chains as quickly as she could. Finally, Kyle was free. "Right, let's get you out of here", said Carly. She helped him to his feet, but he was unsteady, as there had been chains tied around his ankles. Carly felt like the blind leading the blind as she could still barely walk herself.

Together, they propped each other up and limped hurriedly towards the barn door. "Can you hear a car?" asked Kyle, a look of panic suddenly crossing his face. Carly stopped walking and listened for a moment. Sure enough, she could hear the sound of an engine, quite close, but not directly outside the barn yet.

Carly looked around in a fright, trying to see if there were another exit anywhere, but no such luck. "Oh God Kyle, what are we going to do? They'll see us!"

"We're going to have to run for it", said Kyle. "I'll carry you, we'll get away quicker that way. I can run faster when I'm a wolf."

"You're in no fit state to carry me!"

"Don't fucking argue, we don't have time to debate this, now just get on my back!" Kyle started flinging his clothes off, and before she had time to protest, Kyle had turned into a wolf. Carly hesitated for less than a second before scrambling onto his back and throwing her arms around his neck. Swiftly, Kyle dived out of the barn door and began to run across the field away from the barn and the hill. Even though he was limping, he still moved very quickly. Carly could hear shouts coming from behind them for the hunters had noticed Kyle was missing. The hunters began to shine torch-lights around. One of the beams fell directly on them.

"Crap they've seen us", cried Carly. "Run, run!"

Kyle managed a small breathless growl as he pushed himself to his limit. Shots rang out behind them, but still Kyle kept running. Before long the voices grew fainter and the shots ceased. Carly didn't dare to hope the hunters might not be following them any longer. She was terrified that if they stopped, they would be caught. Eventually though, once they were within the relative safety of a cluster of trees, Kyle stopped. Panting heavily, he motioned with his head for Carly to disembark, so she did. She slid off his back and gave his fur a gentle stroke. Kyle lay down, still in wolf form, and rested for a few minutes. Carly sat down beside him and nestled against his warm soft body. "You must be exhausted Kyle", she said softly. "Are you okay?"

Kyle stood up, walked a few steps away from her, and turned back into his naked human form. Sweat was pouring from his brow. Now that Carly had chance to look at him properly she could see in the moonlight his limbs and torso were covered in bruises. It wasn't just his face, as she had initially thought. "Oh God, look what they've done to you!" Carly walked painfully up to Kyle and gently touched her fingertips to the bruises on his chest.

He took hold of her hand and held it against him. "I'm still alive", he said quietly. "You can feel my heart beating." He smiled kindly at her. "That's all thanks to you. If you hadn't come looking for me, who knows what might have happened. I owe you my life!"

Carly blushed. "Ahh, it was nothing really", she said, gazing up into his eyes.

"It was everything", replied Kyle in a whisper. He ran his other hand through her long hair and bent his head down towards her. When their lips touched, Carly felt as though she was in a fairytale. She instinctively pressed her body against his.

"Ouch", yelped Kyle, pulling away from her. That was it - the magic was broken.

"Oh no, I'm so sorry, I didn't mean to hurt you!" Carly felt terrible. 'What a stupid thing to do, pushing up against somebody who is covered in bruises!' she scolded herself.

Kyle laughed. "It's okay, I'll live." He gave her a little peck on the lips. "It was worth the pain."

Carly smiled back feeling relieved. Then something occurred to her. "I thought you said this couldn't happen…you know…you and me; because of Seth…" she tailed off.

Kyle furrowed his brow. "I know I did, but I can't help it, when I'm around you I feel complete."

"Why don't we break away from Seth and form our own pack, just you and me?" suggested Carly with a wink.

Kyle grinned. "Well I'm not sure about that, but don't worry, I'll handle Seth. I care too much about you to stay away from you, pack law or no pack law!"

"I was hoping you would say that", admitted Carly. She felt as though she should be experiencing some pangs of guilt, because of Rob, but she just wasn't. 'You can't help who you fall for', she thought.

Hand in hand (though Carly's hands were throbbing from where the silver had burnt them), Kyle and Carly walked through the trees. Kyle had said he knew where they were going, but Carly had to admit she had lost her sense of direction altogether. Both were half crippled, but they were alive, and they were together, which seemed to be all that mattered at that point in time.

They had decided to make their way straight back to the cabin. Provisions would have to wait until another day; they had to relay what had happened to them to the rest of the pack; that was their main priority.

CHAPTER SEVEN

It seemed to Carly that the journey back to the cabin took a long time. It was mid-morning by the time they finally arrived at their destination. Carly had felt a little chilly as they had walked, so she could only imagine that Kyle must have been freezing, despite him claiming to be fine, as he had no clothes at all. She wished that she had something to give him to wear, but she had only her now sleeveless t-shirt, and a pair of skinny jeans, so poor Kyle had been naked now for hours. She didn't mind though, she rather liked admiring his muscular form, and Kyle himself seemed perfectly at ease with his own nudity.

Carly felt a lurch of relief when they reached the cabin. All the other pack members were assembled inside, occupied with varying tasks. They looked up when the door opened, and their expressions changed to ones of shock as they took in the state of Carly and Kyle. 'We must look a right pair', thought Carly.

"Holy crap what happened to you two?" asked Seth in astonishment. Gary jumped up and ran to fetch some clothes for Kyle.

"It's a really long story", said Kyle, sinking into the sofa. Carly followed suit and sat down next to him, easing her leg up onto a beanbag in front of her.

"Your leg," said Ian, "what have you done? Were you shot?"

Carly shook her head. "No, it got caught in a trap", she said.

Seth walked over to her and took hold of her leg. Carly flinched as he touched her; she couldn't shake the vision of being inside his body, and him tearing open that man. How was she ever going to be able to look at him in the same way again, knowing what he did?

"Hold still, I just want to have a look at it", said Seth. Carly stifled her fears and allowed him to carefully unwrap the bandage from around her ankle. "Ouch!" he said, visibly wincing. "That looks nasty!"

Kyle lifted his head up a little to take a look himself. "It was worse at first", he said. "Carly was lucky, she nearly lost her leg!"

"And what the hell is with you?" asked Seth, turning to Kyle. "You fall in a pit?"

Kyle and Carly looked at each other. "Well…" began Kyle, and he proceeded to relay the entire nights happenings. Carly interrupted him now and again with her version of events, to add a multiple person perspective. The rest of the pack sat and listened in horror as they learnt what the hunters had done. When it came to the part where Kyle was describing what had happened in the barn though, he suddenly became very vague about what the hunters had wanted. "They kept asking me where the rest of the pack is", he said sketchily.

Carly raised an eyebrow. 'Why isn't he telling them exactly what the hunters said?' she thought. 'All that stuff about the wolf born and the skinwalkers?' She figured Kyle must have a good reason though for keeping quiet about it so she kept her mouth shut. She noticed he also omitted the part about their kiss. She wasn't sure if that irked her, or not. She could see why he didn't want to bring it up just yet, it probably wasn't a good time for him to be getting into an argument with Seth, but at the same time she hoped it wasn't because he was ashamed of being with her, or worse still, that it wasn't because he had changed his mind about being with her.

When Kyle and Carly had finished telling their story, the room was quiet for a few minutes. Gary and Ian were gawping at them, their mouths agape and their eyes wide. Devon and Seth didn't look quite as shocked, but they did seem to have taken it all in.

"Thank you Carly, for saving my brother", said Seth breaking the silence. "I don't know what I would do if I lost him."

"Well, he saved me from the trap, I was just returning the favour!" replied Carly feeling a little embarrassed.

"Even so, you did a remarkable thing, following the car with your leg in that state."

"It was nothing", said Carly. She felt as though she was repeating herself. "I'm really tired though guys so if you don't mind, I'm going to have to go and take a nap."

"Of course you're tired. Quite understandable", said Devon, helping her to her feet. "Rest as long as you need to."

"That sounds like a great idea Carly actually", said Kyle. "I think I'll do the same. It has been an exhausting night!" With a grunt, Kyle pushed himself up off the sofa and together they hobbled into the bedroom. Kyle closed the door behind him. He leant towards Carly and kissed her tenderly. She closed her eyes and kissed him back, making sure she didn't press against his chest this time. "Goodnight Carly", said Kyle when the kiss had ended.

"Night Kyle", replied Carly. Butterflies were fluttering around in her stomach and she felt ridiculously happy considering how much pain she was in. They both eased themselves into their respective beds and fell fast asleep within a matter of seconds.

On and on Carly slept but her slumber was far from peaceful. Once again she found herself inside the body of a large black wolf; a wolf she now knew to be Seth. It was daytime this time and she was running through the forest. She felt the wind in her fur and she knew instinctively that she was heading towards the den of the other wolf pack. Streaking through the trees like a bolt of black lightning, Carly eventually spotted some other wolves up ahead. She knew who they were, even though logically she realised that it must be Seth who recognised them, for Carly had no idea who they were as she hadn't ever seen them before.

"Seth", said one of them, bowing his head slightly and baring its teeth in a show of supplication. It wasn't words so much as growls and whines that came from the wolf, but Carly could understand what he was saying perfectly. 'Oh wow, I'm their leader!' realised Carly with a start. Although this surprised her, at the same time it felt natural. Carly realised that her emotions were conflicting with Seth's, though he wouldn't be aware of this. "What news do you have for us?"

"Kyle and Carly were attacked by hunters last night", Carly heard herself saying. "According to Kyle, they wanted to know where the rest of his pack is. I'm not sure if I believe him though, I think he's hiding something from me."

"Do you think the hunters know about us?" asked another wolf to Carly's right.

"I don't know, it's possible", she replied. "They're still using silver, so that's a good sign. I know they have been tracking me for a while now, ever since I killed that girl of theirs. We have to hope they just assume that all wolves in this forest are the same, just regular packs."

"If they find out we're not…" began the first wolf who had spoken.

"That won't happen, I'm sure of it. We've got only a few days until the full moon. After that, we can destroy the hunters and that other bunch of idiots, and then the world will be our oyster. No more hiding in the wood dressed in pathetic dog costumes!"

Carly cast her mind to Kyle and the other pack members, and she knew that she was different to them. Somehow, she had a sense that she, (well Seth, of course), was not the same, though it was difficult for her to understand why or how.

"With all due respect Seth, if the hunters get hold of Kyle again, they could kill him, and then our ceremony will be useless!" said the first wolf.

Carly felt a surge of anger course through her body and she lashed out at the wolf with her paw. He yelped as he fell to the ground. Carly could see that her claws had torn into his face; she felt nothing but sadistic pleasure at this. "Nothing is going to happen to Kyle", growled Carly. "In future I'd ensure that you have a little more faith in your leader. I wouldn't want to have to hurt you." The wolf on the ground rolled onto his back in a submissive gesture. Carly felt satisfied he wouldn't be making the same mistake again. How dare he question her authority? She would be able to keep her brother in check until the full moon, she was sure of it; she was the pack leader after all. As Carly was thinking these things the world around her began to grow dark. She felt herself being more and more aware of her own existence. She could feel that she was lying on a bed rather than being in a forest. Slowly she woke up back in the cabin in her own human body. She lay in bed for a few moments, dwelling on what had happened. 'I can't believe how arrogant and obnoxious Seth is!'

A loud commotion outside startled Carly and she bolted upright. Kyle, too, who had previously been fast asleep, shot up in bed as though a bee had stung him.

"What was that?" he asked, his eyes wide open. He had the appearance of a startled rabbit.

"I don't know", she said. The shouting outside continued, though it was largely impossible to tell what was being said.

Then gunshots rang out and Kyle leapt out of bed. "Argh!" he grunted as he hit the ground heavily.

"Be careful, you're still hurt!" warned Carly. She got out of bed herself, just as Gary, Ian and Devon dived into their bedroom, slamming the door closed behind them.

"What the hell is going on?" asked Kyle sharply.

"Hunters!" gasped Devon. "They've got the cabin surrounded."

"Damn!" Kyle rubbed his forehead with his fingertips. "They must have followed the trail that Carly and I left when we came back. With our injuries we weren't exactly light-footed. I bet it wasn't hard for them to track us."

Carly felt a chill run down her spine. "Oh God..." she murmured. "What are we going to do? Can we run?"

"Not a chance, they're everywhere", said Devon. Gary and Ian were looking as white as ghosts.

"Where's Seth?" asked Kyle.

"He's with the other p..." began Carly, then she stopped herself. "He's out", she finished lamely. She shot a look at Devon but he didn't seem to have been listening to her.

"How do you know that?" asked Gary. "You've been asleep!"

"Erm, I thought I heard the door open and close earlier", said Carly. She was aware that she was turning red and tried to calm herself down. She was not a terribly good liar. Fortunately for her, the others weren't paying her a great deal of attention; all of them had their minds on the hunters.

"Okay, okay okay okay", said Kyle, beginning to pace around the room, his brow furrowed. "Think Kyle think, what can we do?"

"I say we take them on. There's five of us, we're strong", said Devon, his eyes flashing.

"Carly and I are pretty badly hurt and Ian's leg still hasn't recovered either", reminded Kyle. "Not to mention the fact that only you and I can shift into wolves. The others are much more vulnerable."

"I'll fight, I can manage", said Gary bravely. Kyle smiled ruefully and shook his head. "No doubt we'll have to fight, but going out there without any protection is a really bad idea. We'll all end up getting killed."

THUD, THUD, THUD.

The whole cabin began to shake.

"They're trying to break down the door", said Ian looking slightly green.

"If only we could hide from them somewhere", said Carly, looking desperately around the room.

Kyle's eyes widened and he grabbed Carly's face. "That's it!" he exclaimed, and planted a kiss on her lips. "You're a genius!" The others were looking at Kyle in astonishment. "We'll hide on another plane. It's like going to the land of the dead, except not quite as difficult to get to. You phase your body out of this plane and onto another one", he continued.

Gary's jaw fell open. "How on earth do you expect us to do that?" he asked. "I haven't got a clue how to get to the land of the dead let alone another plane."

"It requires concentration or intense emotion", said Carly, remembering what Kyle had told her.

Kyle looked proud and puffed out his chest slightly. "That's right. Now we haven't got time to start meditating, well, at least, you don't. Devon and I can manage but we've had a lot of practice. You guys are new at this and it takes time to learn how to do it, so you'll have to go with the emotional route."

THUD, THUD, THUD.

"We'd better be quick about it, they'll break through any minute now!" said Devon looking anxious.

"Devon, you go first", said Kyle. "At least one of us can get out of harm's way. I'll help the others to get there."

Devon nodded and closed his eyes. His breathing began to get deeper and more rhythmic. Within a matter of about twenty seconds, he faded before their very eyes and disappeared.

"Frickin' hell!" exclaimed Ian. "He's gone!"

"He can still see you, he'll only be in the next plane, the one closest to our world. To get to the deeper planes it requires much more intense concentration. Now listen to me, I need you all to think of something that stirs emotion in you. Ian, think of Jackson. Your brother, he's dead, picture him. Think of his girlfriend and your parents - they don't even know he's dead yet. Remember when you were little together, best friends growing up. He's DEAD, Jackson is never coming back..." Kyle's drilling of Ian was intense and Carly felt extremely sorry for him.

'It must be awful for him to have to replay all those memories like that', thought Carly. She knew it was a necessity though, they were running out of time. Kyle continued to talk about Jackson to Ian, and ever so slightly Carly thought that she could see Ian's body becoming translucent. At first she thought she was imagining it, but then it became more and more apparent that he was indeed fading away. 'It's working, keep going', Carly silently urged him. Eventually, Ian disappeared the same way that Devon had. The last thing Carly saw of Ian before he vanished were tears pouring down his cheeks. Her heart ached for his suffering and she wished there had been an easier way to get him there, but she knew there wasn't.

Kyle turned now to Gary. "Gary, think of something sad, or something incredibly happy", he ordered. "Sad is easiest though, or angry. What makes you sad?"

"Ian being upset just then made me pretty sad", replied Gary.

"That's not enough," said Kyle, "it needs to be personal to you. Has anybody close to you died?"

Gary thought about it. "Not really", he admitted. "My great grandmother passed away when I was about five years old, but I barely even remember her."

Kyle tutted. "Come on Gary, think, *think*. There must be something?" He turned to face Carly. "Carly, I need you to think of something sad as well. Think of Rob; remember how you felt the first time you passed over to the land of the dead. You need to recreate that feeling. Get it back, do whatever it takes", he said. He put his hands on her shoulders and gazed intently into her eyes. "Please, do it for me."

Carly nodded. She knew it wasn't going to be easy though, as the way she felt about Rob when she had visited the land of the dead last time wasn't quite the same way that she felt about him now. She hadn't known for sure at the time that he had cheated on her for a start. Still, she would do her best. She concentrated really hard, and started to feel quite depressed, but still she didn't feel as moved as she had done previously. She changed tactics and began to think about her aunt who had died, the one who had given her the ornament of the hippo, but even that wasn't working. She began to panic. "I can't do it Kyle, it's not working!" she felt her bottom lip beginning to quiver, but it was out of fear more than anything else.

"They're going to get you Carly", said Kyle staring at her hard. "Those hunters, they're going to break in, and they're going to kill *you*. Don't you understand? *You're* going to be dead, stiff, cold, a corpse Carly. Your life is going to be over."

Carly began to shake and cry; she was absolutely petrified. "Stop saying that Kyle!" she begged, putting her hands over her ears.

"You're never going to get to run outside again, never going to see the sunshine, never going to grow any older, have children, see the world. In about two minutes' time you're going to have a bullet through your brain", taunted Kyle.

She could hear every word he was saying and they pierced through her like a knife. "SHUT UP!" she shouted loudly, crying uncontrollably. Then suddenly the room around her seemed slightly out of focus. She felt lighter than she had done previously and could once again see Ian and Devon.

"You made it, thank God!" said Ian giving her a hug.

"Scare tactics - sometimes it's the only way", said Devon.

Carly's heart was still pounding. "Is that what he was doing? Scaring me half to death?"

Devon laughed. "You might well call it that!" he said.

Carly could still see Kyle and Gary but they were somewhat blurry now. Kyle was trying the same scare tactics on Gary as he had done on her, but they didn't seem to be working as well on him. "Come on Gary, come on", muttered Ian beside her. Carly took hold of his hand and gave it a reassuring squeeze.

"I'm sure he'll manage to do it", she said comfortingly.

"Think of all the dying children in Ethiopia", Kyle was saying now. He had a desperate panicky tone to his voice. Carly found that she was gripping Ian's hand tighter and tighter.

"Come on Gary", she said aloud. The three of them were fixed on the scene before them. All the while the thudding of the cabin continued, louder and louder it seemed. An almighty CRASH indicated that the hunters had broken through the front door. Kyle only had seconds left to get both him and Gary to safety. Carly could hardly breathe.

"Gary, you fucking asshole! You're the biggest retard of the fucking lot!" shouted Kyle, and as Carly watched, Kyle pulled back his fist and punched Gary in the face. Gary stumbled backwards, then roared and lunged at Kyle. His eyes flashed, and all of a sudden he was in focus again. He had crossed over.

Carly's relief at Gary being safe was overshadowed though by the fact that Kyle was still in the bedroom, very much in the living plane. She thought she was going to faint. "Kyle!" she shrieked.

The bedroom door swung open and banged hard against the wall. In strode a tall burly middle-aged man with grey hair. His eyes widened as he saw Kyle standing in the middle of the room. "I've got one!" he shouted, and lifted his pistol up.

It was as though everything happened in slow motion. As the man's finger began to press the trigger of the gun, Carly saw Kyle begin to fade in the room. The bullet left the chamber and travelled through the air towards Kyle. Carly and the others watched in horror as it inched closer and closer to Kyle, heading straight for his heart. Just as Carly was sure that Kyle wasn't going to make it, his form faded to the faintest of shadows in the living plane. The bullet passed straight through him and hit the wall behind where he was standing.

Kyle appeared in front of Carly, a terrified expression on his face. "UGH!" he exclaimed loudly, jerking violently and patting his chest frantically. Carly threw her arms around him and began to cry from sheer relief.

"It didn't hit you buddy, it passed straight through you", said Ian, patting Kyle on the back. Kyle was breathing heavily, but Carly felt his tense body relax slightly as she hugged him. He embraced her in return.

"Well that was a bit close!" he said at last. He turned to Gary. "Sorry about that punch!"

Gary rubbed his jaw and smiled. "That's okay, you got me through, I appreciate it! Besides," he said with a grin, "I'll get you back one day!"

"Oh will you now?" joked Kyle.

"Hush guys would you, I'm trying to listen", said Devon, flapping his hand at Kyle and Gary. The group fell silent and watched the hunters in the bedroom. There were three of them now; the man who had shot at Kyle, a younger fellow, roughly in his late twenties, and a female, perhaps twenty two or three, Carly guessed. She recognised the younger pair as being the ones who had held Kyle captive in the barn. The older man she presumed must be their father whom they had gone to fetch.

"I thought you said there was somebody in here dad?" said the female hunter looking a little puzzled. She walked over to the wardrobe and pulled it open, but of course she found nobody hiding there.

The grey haired man was standing, mouth agog, still with his gun aimed forward. He reminded Carly of a goldfish, and despite the gravity of the situation she had to stifle a giggle. Kyle pulled a strange look at her. "What's funny?" he asked.

"That man, he hasn't got the faintest idea where you've gone!" she said, laughing out loud. She couldn't help it, the release of tension was so inviting, and soon the whole group found themselves laughing along with her. It was almost surreal, standing in the bedroom still, unable to be seen or heard by the hunters; Carly felt as though she were behind some kind of two-way mirror, like the kind the police have for victims of a crime, or witnesses, to stand behind when they pick a suspect out of a line-up.

"It was a ghost, it must have been!" spluttered the man at last, lowering his weapon. "He was here, right in front of me!"

The younger man put his hand on his father's shoulders. "Dad, it has been a long day", he said quietly.

"Shut up Bradley, I don't need to be patronised by you! I'm not some senile old coot I'll have you know! I'm telling you there was somebody in this room!"

"If dad says there was somebody here, then there *was* somebody here", said the young woman, closing the wardrobe door.

"Okay okay, I get the point", said Bradley, rolling his eyes slightly. "We'd better split up to look for him then. Jo you go with dad, I'll take a look around on my own." With that he stomped heavily out of the bedroom, his hobnailed boots clunking on the wooden floor.

"Are we just going to stay here until they've gone?" said Carly.

"Well that's the idea", said Kyle. "I'd rather not fight them unless absolutely necessary."

Devon rolled his eyes. "Come on, a girl and an old man, we can take them!"

"Devon, no, we wait", said Kyle sharply. Devon growled and looked obstinately away. "Isn't it better if nobody gets hurt?" continued Kyle.

Devon didn't reply, but Carly didn't think he would be so stupid as to try and take on three hunters on his own.

Gun shots and shouting from the living room snapped Carly to attention. "Dad, Jo!" It was Bradley yelling loudly. Carly could hear snarls and howls coming from there also. The other two hunters raced out of the room to join him.

"Holy crap it's Seth", said Devon, and instantly phased out of the higher plane and back into the real world plane again. Quick as a flash, he turned into a wolf and bounded through the bedroom door, his clothes tearing into shreds and falling onto the floor.

"Oh no", muttered Kyle, and in the blink of an eye he had done the same thing. Carly, Gary and Ian were left in the bedroom alone.

158 - N. Gosney

Carly was petrified; her heart was racing. "Come on!" she urged the other two.

The three of them, still in the higher plane, ran into the living room. The scene that greeted them caused Carly to gasp. The hunters were firing their guns at the wolves. Carly's heart was in her throat as she saw Kyle leap to dodge a bullet that was flying straight towards him. Carly had never heard a gun being fired from up close; the noise was so loud it caused her ears to ring. Together, Seth, Kyle and Devon were lunging at the hunters. They looked terrifying and Carly was glad she was not on the receiving end of their strength! She could hear snarls coming from their throats but they seemed almost faint as her ears were still half deafened from the sound of the gunshots. Jo let out a noise of annoyance and threw her gun down on the floor; presumably she was out of bullets. Seth barged past her and knocked Bradley to the ground. He stood over him for a moment, pinning him down. Carly could see that in an instant, Seth's teeth would have made contact with Bradley's throat.

BANG! Another shot rang out. Carly jumped and turned to see the chief hunter firing at Seth. She swung her gaze back to Seth and exhaled as she saw that he had leapt away from Bradley thus avoiding being hit by the bullet, which lodged itself in the cabin wall. Bradley scrambled to his feet panting. Jo's hand scrabbled to grasp at the nearest object to her, which happened to be a lamp. Carly heard a yelp come from one of the wolves as the lamp made contact with his body. She couldn't at all make out who it was that had been hurt, there was simply too much going on for her to be able to tell.

"How do we phase back in and help them", asked Gary desperately, turning to Carly with a wild look in his eyes.

"I...I don't know!" she admitted. She had to shout to make herself heard.

"But you've done this before, you've been to the land of the dead!"

"The land of the dead isn't like this at all! There are shadows everywhere, and...it's just different! Kyle said this is the very closest plane to our own; I've never been in this one!"

"Well how did you leave the land of the dead?" asked Ian, his voice quivering.

"It just sort of faded away around me, I didn't do anything at all!" said Carly. As scared as she was, she wanted to join in the fight as well. She felt so useless just watching the three wolves taking on the hunters. "Maybe if we concentrate really hard...?"

The three of them closed their eyes and Carly began to concentrate with all her might on being back in the real world plane. She could hear the sounds of the fight around her; she willed herself to be a part of it. It felt as though she had been concentrating for ages, but in reality it must have only been a couple of minutes. She opened her eyes and let out a little scream of frustration for the scene around her was still blurry. Glancing over at Gary and Ian she saw that they hadn't been any more successful at re-joining the real world than she had. 'It's a bit like one of those magic eye pictures,' thought Carly, 'everything is just slightly out of focus'. She forced her eyes to go crossed and stared at the bookcase on the far side of the room. Slowly, as slowly as she could, she began to uncross her eyes. Just before she had fully uncrossed them the world snapped back into focus around her. She blinked a couple of times and realised that she had done it - she had phased from one plane to the other. She didn't have time to celebrate though. The hunters hadn't yet seen her. They were standing with their backs to her, fighting Seth, Kyle and Devon. She dived to the ground behind the sofa and found herself lying on top of Seth's clothes. The handle of a butterfly knife was protruding from one of the pockets of his jeans. She grabbed it and quickly unfolded it. Leaping up she plunged it into Jo's back, the hunter nearest to her. Jo let out a scream and collapsed onto the floor in a heap. Bradley turned to look at her, which gave Seth just enough time to sink his teeth into him and tear out his throat.

The chief hunter, realising that his son and daughter had fallen, turned and raced out of the door. Devon and Kyle were hot on his heels, but he spun around and fired a shot at them just as they reached the doorway, hitting Devon in the rump. He yelped and fell to the ground; Kyle stopped to see to Devon, and the hunter managed to escape. Kyle and Seth quickly returned to their human forms. "Devon, are you all right?" asked Kyle worriedly.

Seth parted Devon's fur and took a look at his wound. "Silver again", he said, wiping the sweat from his brow. "We need to get it out otherwise Devon isn't going to make it. Help me lift him onto the sofa." Together, Seth and Kyle lifted Devon off the floor and placed him face down on the sofa. He was still in wolf form. Carly wondered why he hadn't changed back, but assumed it must be because he didn't have the strength to do so.

"Hand me the medical kit from the kitchen please Carly", said Kyle. Neither he nor Seth had bothered to put any clothes on yet, they were both too focused on Devon. Carly ran into the kitchen and spotted the first aid kit on the kitchen work surface. Hurrying back into the living room, she handed it to Kyle.

"Gary and Ian are still phased out", she reminded him as he rummaged in the bag. "I'd go and help them to get back, but I'm not exactly very good at it."

"I've got to deal with this bullet, they're going to have to hang on", replied Kyle. "Unless you can fetch them Seth?"

"I...er..." Seth stammered. "I'll take over getting the bullet out of Devon. You go and get them."

"I've got a steadier hand than you, you know that", protested Kyle.

"I'm telling you I'll deal with Devon. Go, now, get the others", said Seth sternly.

Kyle put down the bag and held up his hands in mock surrender. "Okay okay, if you insist. Don't see why you couldn't have just gone though!" Carly followed Kyle as he walked back into the bedroom to put his clothes back on. "Wait there", he said, turning to her. Then he closed his eyes, and faded away. Carly sat down on the bed to wait.

"Carly!" Seth's voice called from the living room. "Can I have a bowl of water, a towel, and another empty bowl?" Carly stood up and went to fetch him what he was asking for. Ordinarily she would have pulled him up for not saying 'please', but she figured now wasn't the best time to have a discussion about manners. Besides, the more she learnt about Seth, the more afraid of him she was growing. She had seen the way his mind worked, in particular his blood lust when it came to tearing apart that man in her vision, and she knew it wasn't pretty inside his head. He couldn't be up to anything good with that other wolf pack, she was sure of that.

"How's Devon doing?" she asked. He was lying quite still with his eyes closed, and his breathing seemed laboured.

"Not brilliantly, but at least it was only his butt that got shot and nowhere more serious", said Seth fishing inside the wound with a pair of tweezers. "As long as I can remove the bullet quickly he should recover. The problem with silver is that the longer you're exposed to it, the greater chance it has of killing you."

"Do you need me to do anything?" offered Carly, trying to be helpful.

"No, there's nothing you can do. Just let me get on with it."

Carly felt slightly like a spare part so she wandered back into the bedroom and waited for Kyle to bring Gary and Ian back. She didn't have to wait long for they gradually appeared into view before she had a chance to even sit back down again.

"Hey guys," she said, smiling, "nice to have you back".

"I can't believe you figured out how to phase back in all on your own!" said Gary admiringly. "We were trying for ages and neither of us could do it!"

"I sort of…crossed my eyes and then uncrossed them", said Carly, struggling to describe her actions. "It was a bit like trying to do one of those magic eye pictures. It changed my perspective."

"That's not the way Kyle just showed us", said Ian.

"That's right, we had to close our eyes and concentrate", said Gary.

"There are a few different ways to do it," said Kyle, "but fortunately for us Carly came back when she did and stabbed that huntress, otherwise we might not have been as lucky as we were".

"Is Devon alright?" asked Gary, his face displaying concern.

"He's just the same as he was. Seth is currently attempting to take out the bullet", replied Carly.

"He hasn't done it yet?" asked Kyle. "It would be better if I did it myself. I've healed more people than Seth has." He left the bedroom, giving Carly's shoulder a quick squeeze as he passed her.

Ian looked at Carly thoughtfully. "What's going on with you two?" he asked.

Carly blushed. "What do you mean?"

"Aww come on, it's so obvious you two are into each other", teased Gary.

"I've only just lost Rob. What makes you think I'm in such a hurry to move on so soon?"

"You and Kyle are perfect for each other", said Ian. "Rob wasn't right for you, he was cheating on you! Who does that to somebody they're supposed to love?"

"Shush", hushed Carly. "You mustn't speak ill of the dead."

"I'm not speaking ill of him. Rob was a great guy, one of my best friends, but he wasn't right for you, nor you right for him. Kyle on the other hand is a different matter."

"If Kyle and I are so perfect together, then what about the pack law? I'm supposed to belong to Seth remember?"

Both Ian and Gary looked slightly stumped. "Well, if it wasn't for the law, you'd be a great couple", said Gary lamely. He looked embarrassed.

"It's out, the bullet is out!" Kyle shouting from the next room interrupted the awkward conversation, much to Carly's relief. She didn't want to reveal to them too much about her feelings for Kyle. 'I hope Kyle gets a chance to tell Seth before these do. It would be much better coming from him', she thought. The three of them trooped back into the living room. Devon had changed back into a human, though he was still unconscious. Kyle had patched up his wound with what appeared to be a large band-aid. Carly grabbed a sofa-throw from one of the other armchairs and draped it over Devon as though it were a blanket.

She turned to Seth. "Your clothes are behind the sofa", she said.

"We'd better bury the two hunters, we can't leave them in the cabin." said Kyle. "Ian, Gary, give us a hand would you please?"

The five of them dragged the bodies outside. Seth and Kyle

began to dig holes for them. Carly had requested that the hunters not be buried too close to Rob's grave. So they were laid to rest a little further into the forest; just far enough for Carly to be comfortable with the distance. Once the burials were completed Kyle stood up and leaned on his spade handle.

His face had a muddy streak across it which Carly found rather endearing. "We can't stay here in this cabin", he said. "The hunter who got away will be back. He knows where we live now, where our den is, so it stands to reason that he'll be back. He might know more hunters and we've got little chance of winning against a group of them a second time round. We were lucky today, it could have been far worse."

"I'm not sure Devon would agree that we were lucky today", said Seth sarcastically.

"He should do. He's alive isn't he?!" exclaimed Kyle.

"Where are we going to live?" interrupted Carly. "Is there another cabin we can go to?"

"No, not exactly", said Kyle. "We have tents though."

"Tents?!" spat Carly. She couldn't think of anything less appealing than spending the rest of her life living in a tent.

"It's temporary, until we manage to find somewhere else to live", reassured Kyle.

Seth cleared his throat and everybody turned their attention to him. "Excuse me bossy boots, but I'll be the one to decide whether or not we're going to find a new place to live."

Kyle rolled his eyes. "You can't be serious? Christ, talk about childish. Just because I had an idea that you didn't think of first, you're going to get uppity about it?"

"I'm the pack leader", snarled Seth. He growled at Kyle. "You can't just make decisions concerning the whole pack like that without consulting me first."

"Okay whatever, just drop it now", said Kyle. "We'll talk about it later I suppose." For a minute, Carly didn't think Seth was going to let the issue go. His stance was still tensed up and the scowl he had on his face showed no signs of easing. Eventually though, he slumped his shoulders in an apparent acceptance of ending the conversation. Kyle appeared visually relieved. Carly knew that Kyle didn't enjoy confrontations with his brother.

"I'm going to check on Devon", Seth muttered and stalked back into the cabin.

Kyle watched him leave and sighed heavily. Carly put her hand on his arm. "It's not just that the hunter knows where we live", he said quietly, almost sounding as though he was talking to himself. "It's that we've killed his son and daughter. Imagine how riled up he's going to be about that; he's going to be beside himself!"

"I can't imagine what he must be feeling", admitted Carly. "It's a shame we had to kill them." Carly felt genuinely awful about what had happened. Under normal circumstances there was no way she would ever have considered killing anybody, but this was different, it had been self-defence. 'Well, I killed in defence of the pack', she conceded.

"I know, what a waste of two lives", said Kyle. "If only they hadn't chosen this path…but I suppose their father must have brought them up to be hunters. It's not their fault really, I don't blame them for the way they hated us. Hate breeds hate, and if that's all they knew to do, then…" he tailed off.

"I'm glad I didn't kill anybody, I don't think I would be able to live with myself", said Gary pensively. Then he clamped his hand to his mouth and looked horrified. "Oh wow I'm so sorry, how completely untactful of me", he squeaked. "Carly, I'm so sorry! I didn't mean anything by it. I'm relieved that they're not a threat to us any more, I really am."

"That's okay", said Carly. "It hasn't quite sunk in yet actually. I've never killed anybody before." It was true, Carly still hadn't had a chance to process how she felt about being a killer. She had felt so sick at the thought of what Seth did to the man in his house when she was occupying his body in her dream, she didn't even stop to consider that perhaps Seth had a good reason for doing what he did. Maybe that man was a threat somehow, she didn't know. Perhaps he had wronged Seth in some way, threatened somebody he cared about, something like that? She had been so quick to assume that Seth was an evil monster that perhaps she hadn't given him a fair chance. She realised if she was capable herself of plunging a knife into somebody's back, then maybe she was just as bad as Seth, or maybe he wasn't bad at all. These thoughts were spinning around in her head making her very confused. She was suddenly terribly unsure of everything she had believed to be true. She had the overwhelming urge to confront Seth about it all. She held this back though because she didn't want to start an argument with him. She couldn't imagine he would take kindly to her admittance of all the things she had thought about him.

Kyle presumed her silence was due to her emotional state after all that had happened. He put his arm around her shoulders. "We're all here if you want to talk about it", he said kindly. "You saved us all Carly, don't ever forget that. If you hadn't phased in and stabbed Jo there's no way of knowing how that fight would have gone! We might all be dead now if it weren't for you!"

"Oh give up, you'd have managed perfectly well. You were kicking their butts", scoffed Carly.

"Well I thought you did great", said Kyle.

"So did I", said Gary.

"You did, especially with figuring out how to phase back in like that so quickly!" said Ian.

Carly blushed. "Shut up, you're all inflating my ego", she said with a smile, feeling grateful for their support.

The rest of the day passed quite quickly and largely without incidence, though there was one unfortunate episode around lunchtime when Gary started screaming about the sandman coming to get him, but that was quickly rectified with a large slab of freshly caught deer. Devon's condition rapidly improved and by evening he was sitting up (albeit uncomfortably, considering the location of his wound), and conversing with the others. Carly herself realised that her leg wounds were barely noticeable now, and similarly Kyle was looking much less battered than he had done earlier. Though physically he was almost fully recovered, Kyle had grown more and more restless as time passed. Eventually, as the sun was setting, he pulled Seth to one side. Carly was close enough to hear what they were talking about. In fact, with their advanced hearing, any one of the others in the pack could have overheard the conversation if they had been listening, but nobody else seemed to be paying much attention.

"We need to move away from this cabin as soon as possible", Kyle said. There was such urgency in his voice that Carly knew he was serious.

Seth growled. "There you go again telling me what to do."

"I'm not telling you what to do, I waited for you to bring it up again, but you haven't said a word. The longer we wait the more chance we have of being attacked again."

Seth looked as though he was mulling it over. "Fine", he said at last, in a rather reluctant tone. "But Devon won't be able to walk very quickly."

"Then we'll walk slowly, and we'll help him, but we need to leave now!"

Seth turned away from Kyle and faced the rest of the group. Carly tried to look as though she hadn't just been eavesdropping. "We're going to be leaving the cabin", he announced. "I've made a decision, for the safety of the pack this is the wisest thing to do."

'Oh yeah, sure, you've made that decision have you?' thought Carly sarcastically. 'It had nothing whatsoever to do with Kyle!'

"Where are we going to go?" asked Ian.

"Well I don't know. It's a large forest and we need to get as far away from the cabin as possible to give us a better chance of steering clear of the hunters."

"There are some tents in the store-room", said Kyle. "Gary, give me a hand would you please to fetch them?"

Kyle and Gary went to fetch the tents and Carly took it upon herself to put together some rucksacks filled with necessary provisions such as first aid kits, food and blankets. Devon watched as the others busied themselves.

"I'm not going to make it", he said at last, shifting uncomfortably. "I can't walk very quickly."

Carly crouched down beside him. "Don't be silly, we'll help you." He gave her a weak smile and she stood back up. As she did so, she felt dizzy, the way it happens sometimes if you stand up too quickly. She closed her eyes and put her hand out to grab hold of something to steady herself, but her hand was grasping at thin air. Suddenly she found herself marching through the forest. On either side of her were men, lots of men - she was surrounded by at least ten or fifteen men and they were all walking along with her. Every man appeared to have an arsenal of weapons on his back. She spied crossbows, knives and guns of all shapes and sizes. "Thirty minutes and we'll be there", she heard herself saying. Her voice came out deep and masculine. 'I'm the hunter who was at the cabin earlier', she realised.

"Carly, CARLY!" Devon's voice shattered her vision and she was herself once again back in the cabin. "What's the matter?"

Carly sat down on the sofa at the side of him. She was shaking and felt light-headed. She couldn't believe this had happened during the day instead of in her nightly dreams as usual. She was also quite shocked that she had seen through somebody else's eyes other than Seth's this time. "They're coming", she whispered.

"What?"

"The hunters, they're on their way back. They'll be here in half an hour."

Devon's face drained of colour. "How do you know that?"

"I've seen it, in a vision."

"Are you sure it wasn't just a hallucination? How long ago did you eat something?"

Carly clicked her tongue impatiently. "Not long ago. It's not a hallucination, it's a vision!"

"Okay, okay, calm down", said Devon.

"Calm down about what? What's going on?" Kyle had entered the living room just in time to catch the end of the conversation.

"The hunters are coming, I had a vision", said Carly frantically. "We've only got thirty minutes to get really far away from here."

Kyle opened his mouth to protest, but thought better of it. "Right, we better get moving", he said.

CHAPTER EIGHT

The pack worked quickly to gather their belongings. In less than ten minutes they were assembled outside the cabin.

"I think that the best plan would be for us all to split up", said Kyle. "We can walk pretty far apart yet still stay within sight of each other, because we can see much further than humans can."

"What use is that?" asked Seth. "I think we should stick together."

"If we walk together the hunters will easily be able to follow our trail. There are six of us so we're bound to break a few branches or disturb a few leaves. If we spread out the hunters won't know which trail to follow. They could split up themselves and try to follow all the trails, which will mean they will be more vulnerable and easier to take on individually. On the other hand they might decide to stick together as a group and follow just the one person's trail; then whoever it is can just hide."

Carly nodded. "That sounds like a good plan," she said, "but we really have to move, *now!*"

The pack separated, each taking a different path following the moon, which was beginning to rise, apart from Devon who travelled with Seth. Carly could just make out Kyle to her left and Gary to her right if she squinted. She liked Gary; he seemed to be somebody she could get along with. She resolved to make an effort to get to know him a little better. Ian was quieter than Gary though he was just as pleasant most of the time. She missed her old friends from before she was a werewolf and figured that making friends with Ian and Gary would give her more people to talk to properly and help her recover some of her own personality. She still felt a little like a stranger around them despite the bond they shared by being part of the same pack.

After about ten minutes brisk walking, Carly turned and looked back to see if she could still spot the cabin; she couldn't. She didn't know whether or not the hunters had yet arrived but all that mattered now was to carry on walking and reach safety. She could hear the distant roar of a waterfall. Carly remembered how, as a human, she and Rob used to drive out to Lake Winnimaki every summer and camp there near a beautiful waterfall. Carly used to love swimming in the lake at the bottom of the waterfall; the fresh sparkling water would glisten in the sunlight and she had always felt so alive at that place. She liked the forest here too; it reminded her of those summer vacations. She had seen a lot of lakes in the forest recently. One closest to the cabin was strangely named Wolf Lake (so Kyle had informed her), which Carly thought was very apt

They walked for a couple of hours. Carly was beginning to wonder if they were ever going to stop. Eventually she looked over to her left and saw Kyle running towards her. Carly stopped walking and glanced over to the right. She couldn't see Gary at first but then she spotted him emerging from behind a tree in the distance. "What's going on?" she asked Kyle.

He panted up to her and she noticed he was no longer carrying his backpack. "Seth has found a clearing where we can pitch our tents. He thinks we have shaken off the hunters. Wait there", he instructed, and ran off in the direction of Gary.

Carly sat down on a fallen log. The moon was high and bright. She noticed how close it was to being a perfect full circle. 'Not long to go', she thought. She was feeling a little apprehensive about the first lunar change. She was no stranger to injuries, but according to the books she had been reading a few days ago, the pain of the monthly lunar change is the most intense pain imaginable. None of the other pack members had actually confirmed this to her though, not even Kyle; she assumed that they didn't want to scare her. She wanted to know about it - she wanted to mentally prepare herself. It had never come up in conversations though so she hadn't asked. She didn't know why she hadn't asked actually; perhaps it was because she was afraid of the answer. She knew she would rather be aware of what was going to happen though so she resolved to ask Kyle at the next possible opportunity. She would have to be brave about it no matter what he would tell her. 'Surely it can't be worse than childbirth. Women go through that quite readily!' she thought. 'Some even have ten, twelve, fourteen children!' Carly herself had a great aunt who had sixteen children and another who had fourteen. Carly had never met any of them, nor the great-aunts in question but her grandfather had told her about them before he had passed away. Carly remembered being quite awestruck when she first learned about them and had concluded that childbirth must not be as terrible as people make it out to be considering they willingly go through it so many times. She had voiced this thought to one of her friends who had children of her own. Her response of "ha, you'll see!" had been admittedly less than encouraging but Carly still reckoned she was strong enough that future childbirth would be a walk in the park for her. She agreed that perhaps she was being rather optimistic but she figured that without optimism she would go through life miserably so optimism was ultimately the best course of action. A noise in front of her startled her out of her thoughts. She looked up to see Kyle returning with Gary and Ian in tow. She stood up as they neared her. "So where's this clearing then?" she asked.

"Follow me", said Kyle. Gary, Ian and Carly obediently formed an orderly queue behind Kyle as he led them to the clearing Seth had found.

Carly chuckled inwardly as she realised how very like baby ducklings they were and Kyle their mother duck. Seeing the ducklings on the water following their mother was one of the things Carly loved most about springtime, though the thought of ducklings made her mouth salivate slightly. Eventually they reached a part of the wood where no trees grew. The ground underfoot was level and mossy; Carly felt as though there was a spring under her step as she walked upon it. Seth and Devon were waiting for them; Seth had already started to erect his tent. Between them all they had three tents, a one man tent, a two man tent, and a three man tent, so the sleeping arrangements would be the same as they were back at the cabin. Seth had insisted that this was preferable to bringing three two-man tents, as he apparently didn't want to share with anybody else. 'Typical Seth', thought Carly at the time, though she was quietly relieved that he wasn't hassling her to sleep with him.

"We'll pitch our tents here", announced Seth in a rather authoritative tone as they gathered around him.

Kyle walked to the far side of the clearing where he had left his pack. "Carly, give me a hand with this tent please?" he called.

Carly willingly crossed over to him and put down her own pack. She had been carrying other varying supplies including sleeping bags, clothes and food. She hadn't found it a heavy burden at all, which hadn't surprised her. She had never been very good at carrying heavy loads whilst hiking, but she remembered how easy it had been for her to carry the deer with Kyle that he had caught a few days prior. She realised it was due to her new werewolf strength of course. Gary and Ian followed suit and began to pitch their own tent close to Seth's. Devon hobbled over to join them and busied himself with the poles. Carly turned her attention back to the task at hand. "I don't know how to put up a tent", she confessed, feeling rather silly.

Kyle looked surprised. "It's not so difficult", he said. "Look, just put that piece in there, this piece in here..." methodically he instructed her on what she should be doing.

Carly thought she was being a nuisance asking "what shall I do next?" each time she completed a task, but if Kyle was irritated by this, he did a good job of not showing it. Finally all the tents were assembled. "I'm hungry", admitted Carly as she sat with Kyle together in the tent. Her stomach rumbled. She had thought she had seen a strange blue light flickering out of the corner of her eye a few times but every time she turned her head to see what it could be, it disappeared.

"I'll go and catch you something", said Kyle, making a move as if to crawl towards the entrance of the tent.

Carly shook her head. There were more blue lights now and they were really annoying her. In fact they were beginning to increase in number quite rapidly. Everywhere she looked there were blue lights, dancing and jiggling around like fireflies. "Go away!" she said swatting at them.

"Pardon?" asked Kyle.

"Those blinking blue lights, they're really annoying me", said Carly. They all started to dive-bomb her. Carly found herself having to duck as they swooped above her head.

"Erm, right, Carly you're hallucinating again!" said Kyle. "Can you hang on a minute while I catch you something to eat?"

"No!" cried Carly. She felt as though the blue lights were trying to attack her. It was making her very nervous. She couldn't even see what was going on around her any more. There were simply too many blue lights in the way. She ducked and weaved in an attempt to get away from them.

"Okay well I'll have to get a steak from your rucksack", he said. He quickly retrieved one for her.

Carly took it and tucked into it hungrily. "Mmmmm", she said, letting the succulent flavour fill her mouth. As she ate, the blue lights faded away until they were completely gone. "That worked, thank you Kyle", she said smiling.

"You're welcome." Kyle pulled her towards him and kissed her softly. "That's what I'm here for!"

Carly allowed him to wrap his strong arms around her and she cuddled into his chest. "Have you mentioned us to Seth yet?" she asked, knowing full well that he hadn't.

"No", replied Kyle. "I don't know when will be a good time to bring it up."

"Perhaps it would be better if there was no us", said Carly. That wasn't what she wanted at all, of course, but she wanted to see what he would say!

"Don't be ridiculous, that wouldn't be better in the slightest. Don't worry I'll talk to him, at some point…"

"Kyle?"

"What?"

"How come you didn't question it when I said I had seen a vision of the hunters? Devon thought I was just hallucinating, but you didn't, you believed me. Why?"

Kyle looked at her pensively. "I don't know really. I guess it's because I know that visions can occur in the run up to the first lunar change, but largely in females. You don't get many males who experience visions. One or two maybe but it's not very commonplace. Also…" he stopped and rubbed his nose awkwardly, "I like you, a lot, so what kind of person would I be if I didn't take you at your word?"

Carly smiled and ran her fingers through his hair. "I like you a lot too", she said. They began to kiss again, more passionately this time. Carly began tugging at his t-shirt to pull it off over his head. He responded in turn, sliding his hand under her t-shirt and fondling her breast. Carly pulled away from him for a second and breathlessly pulled her top off. They resumed kissing, almost frantically now. Carly had butterflies swirling around in her stomach. Her heart was pounding quickly. She wanted Kyle so badly. She was so focused on him that she didn't hear the zip of the tent quietly unfasten. Neither did Kyle apparently, for when Devon asked them if they had a spare sleeping bag, they both leapt a mile and sprang apart from each other immediately. Devon's eyes widened as he saw them together.

"Shit, you can't tell Seth!" said Kyle, grabbing his t-shirt.

Carly, although shocked by Devon's sudden appearance, was a little miffed to hear Kyle say this. She quickly yanked on her t-shirt over her head and folded her arms in annoyance. 'Why shouldn't he tell Seth?' she thought. 'Kyle said he was going to tell Seth himself, he should have done so by now!' She wondered if he was ashamed of his feelings for her or whether it was simply a matter of Kyle wanting to avoid any confrontation with his brother.

Despite his apparent initial surprise, Devon now simply shrugged his shoulders. "What you do is your business", he said uninterestedly. "If Seth asks me, I'm not going to lie, but I doubt he'll ask. I won't mention it if he doesn't."

Kyle nodded. "I understand you not wanting to lie to him. He is our pack leader after all."

"Anyway, you got a spare sleeping bag? Mine has a hole in it."

Kyle looked over at Carly who shook her head. She knew there weren't any spare sleeping bags. She had been the one to distribute them.

"Alright, well thanks anyway", said Devon turning to leave.

"How are you feeling now Devon?" asked Carly, genuinely concerned. "Is your wound any better?"

"I'll live," he replied, "I've taken some pain killers". With that he left their tent, zipping it up after himself.

Carly had to admit that even by the dim light of the torch they had in their tent, his complexion looked healthier than it had done earlier. Carly and Kyle sat in silence for a few minutes. Carly didn't know what to say that wasn't going to sound as though she was nagging him to tell Seth about their new relationship.

"Well," said Kyle, breaking the silence, "that was awkward".

"I guess", said Carly. She waited for a few minutes to see whether Kyle was going to offer any further contribution to the conversation, but he remained silent. "I think I'm going to go to sleep now", she said. "I'm pretty tired and it's really late."

"Okay, goodnight Carly."

"Night Kyle."

Kyle leaned over hesitantly and kissed her quickly on the lips. She returned the kiss but didn't push things any further. Kyle turned off the torch and they both snuggled down into their respective sleeping bags. Carly fell asleep quite quickly. It hadn't been a lie about being tired; she genuinely was exhausted.

It wasn't long before Carly found herself having another dream-vision. She recognised it for what it was this time; she was now getting quite used to them. Just as before, she found herself in the body of the chief hunter. She experienced the familiar rush of emotions caused by conflicting interests. She realised she was hiding in a bush and pointing a gun at her own camp-site! Part of her, the part that was viewing the world from the hunter's perspective, felt elated that she and the other hunters were to finally be rid of them for good. The other part of her felt terrified that the hunters were now at their camp - this was the part which was still in control of her own emotions rather than those of somebody else.

Carly looked around at the other hunters. All of them were

armed and aiming their guns at the campsite. She motioned silently to one of the tents. Everyone including Carly (in the hunter's body) aimed and fired their guns directly at it. The noise of the gunfire startled Carly out of her sleep and she sat bolt upright in her tent.

Kyle too had woken on hearing the sound and was looking quite alarmed. "What the hell?" he whispered loudly. He began to crawl to the front of the tent.

"NO!" hissed Carly, grabbing hold of his arm and pulling him back. "It's the hunters, they're here at the camp. They must have followed us. They've fired on Seth's tent. We need to get out of here!"

"They've fired on S…" Kyle's lower lip wobbled slightly.

Carly shook his arm impatiently. "We need to go *now* Kyle!" Kyle nodded. Using his nails and teeth he tore a hole in the back of the tent just large enough for them to get through. Carly crawled out quickly, followed directly by Kyle, who bumped into the back of her in his haste to leave the tent. Once out, Carly whispered frantically. "We needed to rescue Gary, Ian, and Devon." She wasn't in any doubt that they would be unlikely to think of exiting their tent from the rear. 'If they exit from the front of the tents they will surely be killed.' She thought. Kyle inched his way through the brambles, which tore viciously at his clothes and flesh, until he reached the other tent. Carly waited further back in the forest with bated breath - she knew the hunters wouldn't be able to see her. They didn't have anywhere near the same level of vision as the werewolves had in the dark, and in her vision as a hunter she had seen no evidence of any night-vision goggles anywhere.

As Carly watched, Kyle tore into the back of the tent and emerged less than two seconds later with the others behind him. They looked confused and bleary-eyed but they didn't hesitate to follow Kyle to where Carly was standing. The five of them together now fled from the campsite as quickly as possible. Kyle was at the front, Carly at the rear. She turned and looked back at the camp just before it was out of sight. To her astonishment she saw a large black wolf spring out from behind the trees on the far side of the clearing and lunge for the throat of one of the hunters. She stopped walking and stared at the unfolding scene. Then, from the darkness of the forest, came a great pack of wolves, all with teeth bared, snarling at the hunters. She didn't realise how many there were at first, but then she realised there must have been at least thirty or forty wolves emerging from the shadows. She hadn't known the other wolf pack was as large as that. Carly didn't wait to see what was going to happen. Gary, Ian, Devon and Kyle were already very far ahead and she needed to catch up to them. As she turned her back on the campsite, she heard gunshots being fired and the tortured screams of the men as the wolves attacked them. Carly felt a shudder running down her spine but she didn't look back. As fast as she could, she tore on until she managed to spot the others. They were racing through the forest, though not as quickly as they would have done if Devon hadn't been injured. Carly fell in line behind them; silently they kept running. They didn't stop but kept going through the forest until they were far from the campsite. Eventually Kyle slowed them down to a gentle jog and they came to rest beside a large tree.

"I thought I faintly heard some sort of commotion back there, what was happening?" asked Kyle.

"I don't know, I wasn't able to tell", replied Carly, lying through her teeth. She desperately wanted to tell Kyle what she had seen, but with Devon present she didn't think it was wise. Devon was clearly part of whatever Seth was up to. He had been there at the other wolf pack's territory with Seth, that first time she had followed him. Therefore as far as Carly was concerned, she wasn't prepared to disclose what she knew in front of him. Kyle slumped down on the ground and held his head in his hands. Carly put her arms around his shoulders. She wished she could comfort him and tell him Seth was still alive, but to do that, she would have to reveal she had seen him.

To her great surprise though it was Devon who piped up. "Seth told me he was going out tonight," he said softly, "so don't worry Kyle. The chances are he wasn't in his tent tonight at all."

Carly looked at Devon in astonishment. 'Did he know that Seth had been with the other wolf pack tonight? It would make sense that he would have been told, as he seemed to be involved with them. Obviously he couldn't have gone with Seth though as he was still recovering from having been shot!' she thought.

Kyle lifted his tear-stained face and stared at Devon. Carly could see hope in his eyes. "Are you serious?" he asked incredulously. "Oh God Dev I hope you're right!"

"I'm really sure he wasn't there", assured Devon. "He said he was going…hunting." Carly heard the pause in Devon's voice but Kyle didn't seem to have noticed it.

"Well then," said Kyle wiping his eyes, "we'd better move on and try to find him".

"But the hunters are still out there! What if we bump into them again?" said Ian. Both he and Gary had been quiet during this whole time; they looked quite afraid. Carly realised she was starting to get used to this sort of thing; she didn't think this was necessarily good though. Getting used to being attacked isn't exactly a sign of leading a safe life!

"We'll be able to smell them long before we can see them. If they're far enough away for us not to be even able to see them, they definitely won't be able to see us", said Kyle. "If we stay out of their way we should be okay. We need to try and get to Seth; he'll be wondering where we are. I don't want him to run into the hunters on his own either."

"Seth's a big boy, he can take care of himself", said Carly blandly. She knew full well that Seth wasn't going to need their help considering he was already accompanied by the entirety of the other wolf pack; not to mention they may very likely have already killed all the hunters already. She knew, from having seen the other pack, that the hunters would have been severely outnumbered. Kyle looked contemplative. "I dare say he'd be able to smell the hunters in any case and would stay away from them. Even so, if he's been hunting, the smell of whatever he's carrying could put him off and he might not realise there are hunters at the camp. He wouldn't stand a chance against a team of men with guns, not on his own. We've got to find him before he runs into them", she continued.

Carly sighed and began to follow him. Gary, Ian, and Devon tagged along, seeming slightly reluctant as their feet dragged a little as they walked. Carly noticed that Devon was limping slightly. She asked him whether he needed a shoulder to lean on.

Devon looked a little embarrassed at having been asked. "No thanks," he said, "I'll manage". Carly could see though that he was struggling.

She jogged up to Kyle and quietly asked him if he could slow down a little. Kyle didn't appear to get the hint. He merely insisted that they had to find Seth as quickly as possible and kept on going at the same pace. Eventually Carly was forced to tell him quite plainly that Devon was limping. "Oh, wow, I forgot that he's injured", exclaimed Kyle somewhat too loudly, immediately slowing a little.

"You're talking about me aren't you", called Devon.

"No!" lied Carly, knowing full well that Devon wouldn't believe that for a second.

"Well, thanks", said Devon. "I would appreciate it if we went a bit slower."

"Why didn't you say so?" asked Kyle. "I'm really sorry man, my mind was just on finding Seth."

"Ehh it's okay, don't worry about it", said Devon.

The group continued at a more reasonable pace. Gary and Ian also seemed comfortable going a little slower. It was still fast by human standards, but for werewolves it seemed almost like a stroll compared to usual. They walked on for a good hour but couldn't find any scent or sign of Seth.

Eventually Kyle stopped and scratched his head as though trying to think of the best course of action. "Perhaps we should go back to the camp", he suggested.

Gary and Ian looked horrified. "What if the hunters are still there?" exclaimed Ian.

"Well, that would be a bit silly of them wouldn't it, to wait around in a deserted campsite for an hour? They probably realised that we fled and aren't going to come back", replied Kyle.

"But what if you're wrong?" said Gary. "What if they're

expecting us to go back, because we would be expecting them to expect us not to go back?!"

Carly tried to wrap her head around that but quickly gave it up as a bad job!

"You're over thinking things", said Kyle. "They scared us, we ran off, we're not going to come back as far as they're concerned. I have to check Seth's tent so we're going to have to go back. I need to know for sure one way or the other. Don't worry we'll be careful."

Gary and Ian hesitantly agreed. Devon seemed on board with the idea right away and Carly saw no reason why they shouldn't go back. She couldn't imagine that the wolf pack would have stuck around, though she could only guess at what sort of battle scene would greet them when they returned. It took a while to get back to the campsite as they had walked so far. Carly, Ian and Gary had to catch some badgers to eat along the way as they had all begun to feel the pangs of hunger again. It would have done none of them any good if they had started hallucinating at that time. As they neared the clearing where their tents had been pitched, the scent of fresh blood wafted over to where they were gathered. Carly's stomach lurched and her mouth began to salivate at such a smell.

Kyle put his finger to his lips and motioned for them all to stay where they were. The four of them crouched down in the brambles and waited as Kyle walked tentatively forward towards the camp. "Holy shit!" Kyle's exclamation was loud and unexpected.

Carly and the rest of the pack jumped up instantly and ran towards him. "Holy shit!" echoed Carly, as she took in what was before her. Gary, Ian, and Devon didn't say a word, but stood with their eyes wide and their mouths frozen open. Expressions of mixed horror, relief and disbelief were etched on their faces. Carly couldn't tear her gaze away, though what was before her was quite terrible to behold. There were bodies everywhere, all of them human and most of them torn apart as though they were mannequins. The entire campsite resembled some sort of grisly mass murder scene. Limbs lay strewn on the grass; they barely looked real. Mingled in amongst the dissected corpses were a few dead naked men who appeared to have been shot, rather than attacked by wolves. Almost all of them had their eyes open. Carly found this unnerving. The vacant expressions on their faces made her shudder. 'They must be werewolves from the other pack', she thought, crouching down and tentatively closing the eyes of one man who was lying close to her feet. Her hand trembled as her fingertips made contact with his freezing skin. She hurriedly stood back up. 'They must have turned back into their human forms when they died.' She didn't recognise them as the ones that Seth had spoken to when she had had her vision.

The smell of blood from the bodies was becoming overpowering. It was taking all Carly's strength not to plunge her teeth into the body she was stood over. At the same time she was overwhelmingly repulsed by her own desires. The sight of the massacred men was so horrific that she wanted to close her eyes and run from it, but the smell…the smell was a different story altogether. It didn't matter that the bodies were human rather than animal - her senses were screaming that she should indulge in the fresh meat presented to her. Carly heard a retching sound coming from behind her. She glanced back and saw that Ian had been sick in the brambles. She didn't blame him - he was obviously struggling with his inner turmoil at the scene before him also. Kyle looked pale; he gulped and then bravely stepped out into the clearing. His eyes had a wild look. He was biting his bottom lip as though trying to control himself. Carly took a deep breath and stepped into the clearing beside him. She took hold of his hand and he gave it a squeeze.

"This is…" he said. He couldn't finish his sentence.

"I know", said Carly, she knew exactly what he meant, he didn't have to say it.

"Well, I suppose we don't have to worry about the hunters coming after us any more", said Kyle. His voice trembled; Carly could tell he was quite shaken at being surrounded by so much death. She felt the same way though she was holding it together much better than she would have expected to.

Out of the corner of her eye, Carly spotted Gary wandering around the clearing surveying the bodies. He seemed somewhat less agitated to be around the delicious smell of blood than *she* was feeling. 'How is he managing to keep himself under control?' she thought.

"What's this?" he asked, pointing at something on the ground. Kyle, Carly and Devon came over to have a look.

"It's a...wolf skin", said Kyle in great astonishment. "What's a wolf skin doing here?"

"Maybe the hunters had killed some wolves and were carrying their skins", suggested Devon hurriedly. Carly looked at him curiously - his tone of voice had sounded a little anxious. She cast her mind back to her last vision, from when the hunters had been aiming their guns at Seth's tent. 'I definitely didn't see wolf skins on any of the hunters', she thought. She looked at Kyle. "The hunters just had weapons and hunting gear, they didn't have anything like this."

"Well, maybe they managed to capture one of the wolves who attacked them and skinned it?" said Devon.

Kyle raised an eyebrow. "So where's this skinned wolf then? He's got to be around here somewhere!"

Devon appeared lost for words. "I don't know", he admitted.

"Come to think of it," said Kyle, "why would the other wolf pack attack the hunters here like this? How would they have known that the hunters were after us? Unless we were being stalked by them."

"Could be that they were aware of the hunters and so they were trailing them", said Devon.

"And then what? They waited until the hunters were attacking us, then launched their own attack on the hunters?"

"It's possible!"

"Possible, but not probable. We've always been told to stay away from the other pack and they stay away from us. If the other pack saw our campsite, why would they stick around? They'd have just left, wouldn't they?" said Kyle looking puzzled.

"Maybe they just saw it as an opportune moment to jump on the hunters and finish them off once and for all", said Devon. "I mean, the hunters were after all werewolves, not just us. The other pack was obviously feeling threatened by them as well. It makes sense that they would want to be rid of them as much as we do."

"I guess so..." said Kyle, not sounding very convinced.

Carly, meanwhile, was taking in the conversation with great interest. She couldn't figure out if Devon was lying or telling the truth.

"Guys, there's another wolf skin here", said Gary. He had moved a little way away from the original skin and was now standing beside the body of another dead man. This one had taken a bullet to the head. Carly presumed he must be a werewolf. Next to him on the floor was another shaggy grey wolf skin.

"Geez", said Carly. "What is with all these wolf pelts?"

"I have no idea", replied Kyle. As they wandered around amongst the bodies they found more. The skins were just lying on the ground.

"Werewolves don't shed their skins when they die do they?" asked Gary.

Kyle shook his head. "No of course not. We just die!"

"I think we ought to try and find Seth", said Devon, changing the subject.

Carly looked at him with her brow furrowed. 'You know something, don't you', she said inwardly, aiming her thoughts at Devon. 'You know what the deal is with all these wolf skins.' She couldn't come out and ask him though, but she intended to find out one way or another.

"Right, yes, Seth!" Kyle's attention switched back to his brother at Devon's mention of him. Swiftly Kyle strode over to Seth's half flattened tent, and looked inside. "He's not here, nobody is here!" he called. Carly could hear the relief in his voice.

"Good!" she called back. "That means he's probably safe then, because I don't see him here anywhere."

"I hope the other pack haven't taken him as their prisoner!" said Gary sounding concerned.

"Now why would they do that?" asked Devon.

Carly didn't say anything but looked down at the floor. She knew very well that the other pack wouldn't be taking Seth prisoner as he appeared to be their leader, but she certainly didn't want Devon to be aware she knew this. Kyle emerged from Seth's tent and walked back over to them. He gave Carly a sharp glance. "Carly had this crazy notion that Seth has been having meetings with…"

"…that Seth might have gone to town to fetch provisions!" interrupted Carly, speaking as loudly as she could over Kyle.

"That Seth what?" asked Gary. "I didn't catch what you said."

"Oh I just thought that Seth might have gone to town to fetch provisions", repeated Carly. She gave a false little laugh. "You never know with Seth!"

"I don't think he would have done that without telling us first", said Gary.

Devon was staring very hard at Carly, which was making her feel uncomfortable. 'Oh hell, he knows that I know!' she thought. Her mouth suddenly became very dry and she could feel beads of sweat beginning to form at the back of her neck. "Let's just look for him then, shall we?" she suggested.

"Where's Ian?" asked Gary suddenly, looking all around. The four of them quickly looked to see where Ian could be.

"He might be back over where he was sick", said Carly. "He didn't look as though he could stomach all this gore."

"I'll go and have a look", said Gary. "Devon, you wanna come with me?"

Devon agreed. The two of them went to see if they could find Ian in the forest on the far side of the clearing.

"What was that all about?" asked Kyle.

"What do you mean?"

"You never said that you thought Seth had gone into town at all!"

Carly sighed. "Kyle, you were going to mention about what I told you a few days ago weren't you? About when I followed Seth to the other wolf pack?"

"I was going to mention it yes, because it's just not true - it was all part of your imagination."

"So why mention it then?"

"I dunno really, it just popped into my head."

Carly stared into his eyes. "You can't mention it in front of

Devon."

"Oh yeah, I forgot, you fantasised that Devon was there too."

"It wasn't a fantasy!" Carly was beginning to feel incredibly frustrated now. "You told me earlier in the tent that you believed my visions because you like me, so why are you being so stubborn about this? Damnit I wish I had never mentioned it to you at all; you clearly just don't believe me. Please don't mention it in front of Seth or Devon though. Even if you don't believe me, surely you can humour me? If you care about me at all you will keep it to yourself."

Kyle's expression turned to one of concern. "Of course I care about you Carly", he said, wrapping his arms around her. "Okay I won't mention it. Just please remember that Seth is my brother and I care about him too."

"I know you do", whispered Carly, resting her head on his chest and fighting back the tears.

"Look, let's get out of here, this place is giving me the creeps!" said Kyle. Carly completely agreed with him on that. Hand in hand they headed in the direction Gary and Devon had taken. When they reached the denser part of the trees, Carly expected to see the others waiting there for them, but nobody was in sight.

"Gary, Ian, Devon?" called Kyle, looking around. There was no reply.

"Guys where are you?" shouted Carly. "That's really odd, where could they have gone?" she mused.

"No idea, but I wish they had stayed in one place!"

Carly felt the familiar rumble in her stomach that could only mean one thing. "I'm hungry Kyle", she said.

"Oh, okay, we'll find you something to eat in a minute", said Kyle seeming distracted. "Where have they gone?" He lifted his nose into the air and sniffed hard. "I am picking up their scent but it would be easier if I were in wolf form. Can you grab my clothes for me please?"

Carly nodded and Kyle began to whip them off with remarkable speed. "Get on my back", he said and transformed into a wolf. Carly quickly gathered up Kyle's clothes and tried to tie them together as best she could, but they kept coming undone. Eventually, in desperation, she put his t-shirt over her own, tied the legs of his trousers around her neck and tied his shoe-laces together, which she flung over her shoulder like the strap of a handbag. She knew she must look quite strange, but there wasn't much she could do about that. Then she scrambled onto Kyle's back, leant forwards and wrapped her arms around his neck.

With a bound Kyle set off through the forest, pausing every now and then to sniff the ground. They journeyed through the night. Although Carly was not doing any walking herself, a feeling of tiredness started to wash over her. It seemed that a full night of uninterrupted sleep wasn't something she had experienced a lot of since becoming a werewolf. The rocking motion of Kyle's body beneath hers was lulling her into a state of relaxation. Her eyes were beginning to feel heavy. She yawned and her eyelids drooped.

"Ow!" Carly awoke with a start as her body slammed onto the ground. She had fallen asleep and had slipped off Kyle's back. He stopped running immediately and turned back around. "That hurt", groaned Carly, rubbing her elbow. Her pride had been hurt more than anything but it had still been unpleasant falling off like that. Kyle's clothes lay in a heap beside her. Kyle nuzzled her neck with his nose and gave her a lick on the cheek. Carly reached up with her hand and stroked his head. Then she heard a growl coming from his throat.

Puzzled, Carly looked up at him bleary eyed and was shocked to see that his teeth were bared in a vicious snarl. She looked behind her to see what this new enemy could be, but there was nothing there. Surely it couldn't be, could it? Kyle couldn't be snarling at *her*? Slowly, almost not daring to breathe, she turned her head back around until she was face to face with Kyle. His expression was one of pure hatred and the growl emanating from him was terrible to hear. Carly gasped and began to shuffle backwards on the ground, inching away from him.

Kyle didn't move but lowered his head in a menacing stance. He began to circle her slowly.

"What are you doing Kyle?" she cried. "What's wrong? What

have I done?"

Kyle paused from circling her for a moment to throw back his head and howl. Carly didn't hesitate. She leapt up from the ground and began to run as fast as she could through the forest. She didn't look back, but ran faster and faster and faster until she thought her heart would explode. She knew Kyle was right behind her - she could hear the padding of his paws as he gained ground; she could practically feel his breath on her, he was so close.

"Leave me alone!" she screamed, as she tripped headlong over a branch and found herself sprawling on the ground. She felt a sharp pain in her leg and realised that Kyle had sunk his teeth into her. 'I'm going to die', she thought. The world went dark around her.

When she regained consciousness the first thing she felt was something in her mouth. It was quite tough but delicious. Even before she opened her eyes she realised that her mouth was automatically chewing this delicacy. She swallowed it with a gulp and opened her eyes. To her great surprise she was lying with her head in Kyle's lap. He was smiling down at her. "Wakey wakey beautiful", he said smiling.

Carly let out a small shriek, sat bolt upright and began to slide away from him. "Y...y...you bit me! You were going to kill me!" she said.

"Sheesh, that's some hallucination! No wonder you were running around like a frightened rabbit screaming at me!" said Kyle.

Carly relaxed slightly. "That wasn't real?"

"What do you take me for? This wouldn't be a very good relationship if I went around trying to kill you now would it?"

"Oh." Carly felt dreadfully embarrassed. "I'm sorry Kyle, I can't believe I thought you were capable of such a thing."

"Hey, it's okay. Those hallucinations can be very realistic. It overrides any sense of logic that you have and just takes over. I know, I realise that, don't worry I'm not offended."

Carly slid back over to him and he kissed her on the forehead. "Let's rest now", said Kyle. "You're obviously exhausted otherwise you wouldn't have fallen asleep on me."

"But what about Gary, Ian and Devon?"

"They're likely to all be together. Devon can take care of the other two, I'm quite sure of that."

"But…" protested Carly.

"Shush now, you're tired, we're going to sleep, don't argue with me!"

Carly didn't want to argue about that; she really was very tired. Without another word she cuddled up in Kyle's arms, and despite the fact that the forest floor was far from comfortable, she quickly fell fast asleep.

CHAPTER NINE

Carly groaned a deep pained groan and opened her eyes. She was in an unfamiliar place, lying on a bed and covered with fur blankets. She looked down at her body. Her bare torso was wrapped in bandages and almost every part of her hurt. It was even painful to breathe! She remembered being with the other hunters, fighting a mighty pack of werewolves in the forest. Carly knew who she was; she was the hunter who had shot Devon. She was astonished that she was even alive; the last thing she remembered was a large black wolf hurling himself at her. She must have blacked out. That wolf - he was the reason she had become a hunter in the first place. It was him, she was sure of it.

Carly (the part of Carly that actually still managed to distance itself from the mind of the hunter), tried to search the depths of the hunter's memories to discover more of what he knew about Seth. The hunter however wanted to think about his injuries and where he currently was, so it was difficult. Carly felt as though she had some sort of split personality, which was very confusing. She was both herself and the hunter at the same time.

She found that she had to follow the hunter's train of thoughts and wondered where she was. Who could have picked her up and tended her wounds? The room she was in was simple but tastefully furnished, but the dream-catcher above her bed gave it away. 'I'm in a reservation', she thought. She had encountered the Native Americans a few times when she had been hunting. It was safe to say they didn't share the same views about werewolves. The Native Americans seemed to hold the spirit of the wolf, as they called it, in high regard, and weren't terribly fond of hunters. Carly shuffled uncomfortably in her bed.

"You need to rest. Lie still", said a male voice, which came from the far end of the room.

Carly looked up in surprise. She hadn't noticed anybody was there. "Thank you for helping me", she said, in a gruff manly voice.

"What kind of person would I be to leave you to die in the forest?" asked the man. He approached the bed carrying a glass of water, which he held out to Carly. "I'm Pat", he said. Carly eagerly took the glass and drank. The pain from the physical action of drinking coursed through the hunter's body, but it was a much-needed drink. Carly drank it all at once and handed the glass back to the man gratefully.

The man was, as Carly had suspected, a Native American. He was in his early fifties she guessed and had long black hair streaked with grey and tied back in a ponytail. He wore a checked maroon and white shirt and a pair of blue denim jeans. "You were hunting werewolves", Pat stated.

"Yes," replied Carly, "and I make no apology for it either. If you only knew what they did…"

"In our culture, wolves are known as The Pathfinders", said Pat, sitting down in a chair at the side of Carly's bed. "We respect the wolf. Why do you fear them?"

"These are no ordinary wolves, these are werewolves. There's a huge difference", said Carly stiffly.

"Do you respect your fellow man?" asked Pat.

Carly felt a little as though she were on trial. "Yes, generally, if they are respectful to me."

"If one did not show respect to you, would you tar all with the same brush?"

"No", admitted Carly.

"How does one become a werewolf?" asked Pat.

"You should know, shouldn't you? Werewolves are part of your culture!"

"I *do* know, but I am asking *you*", replied Pat with a smile. "Humour me."

"By being bitten or scratched by a werewolf, or by inheriting it from a werewolf parent."

"Yes. The nature of a person does not make them a werewolf. Do you agree this is correct?"

Carly grunted a reluctant acknowledgement.

"Good people, through no fault of their own, find themselves as werewolves", continued Pat.

Carly sighed. "You're missing the point. I know what I'm dealing with here. These are not perfectly decent people."

"I am sure you have your reasons for feeling the way you do. However the fight with the werewolves has only brought death to your friends."

"As long as we took some of those brutes down with us then they didn't die in vain", said Carly. She felt angry with Pat. 'How dare this man presume to know why I did what I did! I did it because I had no choice', she thought. "They killed my family. My wife, my children…" Carly shouted. The emotional pain in her chest was immense; she felt as though she would explode if she didn't release the pressure building inside her.

"Calm, you must be still", said Pat, putting his hands on her arm. Carly struggled against his grasp for a moment, then stopped and sank back into her pillows. "Do you want to talk about it?" Pat asked.

Carly shook her head. She didn't want to tell a complete stranger her family history; but then, without even realising it, she began to speak. "It was five years ago; I was at home with my wife and two of my children - my son and daughter. We were in the living room watching television. My other daughter Jessica was out somewhere with some of her friends. She came home at around half past ten, said she felt tired, kissed us goodnight and went to her room. Half an hour later my son and other daughter went to bed and then my wife Annie and I retired also. We hadn't been in bed very long when we heard talking coming from Jessica's room. It sounded as though she was talking to a boy. It wouldn't have been the first time she had sneaked boys into her room through her bedroom window. She had a bit of a rebellious streak did Jessica. She was eighteen so we didn't want to make too much of a fuss about it. She was going through a phase where she craved her own independence and we didn't want to be the type of overbearing parents that push their kids away from them.

At first we heard talking and giggling but then it sounded as though she was having an argument with somebody. My wife said she would see what was going on. She got out of bed and went to investigate. I heard screams. I dived out of bed with my shotgun and ran into my daughter's bedroom. My son and my other daughter had heard the noise and also came out of their rooms. We flung open the door of Jessica's bedroom and found the bodies of my wife and Jessica lying on the floor. Their throats had been ripped out. There was a man standing over them, though in the dark I couldn't make out more than his outline. He had no weapon on him at all. He was completely naked. As we watched, he turned into a huge black wolf and leapt from Jessica's bedroom window."

Carly stopped for a breath. The tears were pouring freely from her eyes. She wiped her face with her hands. Pat reached over and handed her a tissue. She took it gratefully. "This is why I became a hunter. My son Bradley and my daughter Joanne trained hard - they wanted justice for their sister and mother. I threw myself into tracking down that werewolf. In the process I discovered there were others. I've done my research; I know there are at least two packs in this forest. The training wasn't easy, it has been a slow process but I'm not a bad hunter, I've killed a few in my time. We discovered there were other people too who had lost loved ones to werewolves and we invited them to join us, to train as hunters.

I wanted to find the one who had killed Annie and Jessie - that was the most important thing to me. We questioned every werewolf we captured but none of them were him. The last wolf we interrogated though, a couple of months ago, revealed to us something we had never expected."

"What is that?" asked Pat, leaning forward in his chair.

Carly looked at Pat with his eyebrow raised. "I'm not sure if I should tell you sir, given your affinity to werewolves. I hope you understand."

Pat shrugged and sat back again. "Keep your secrets if you prefer it that way", he said, quite nonchalantly. "So your son and daughter, they are still alive?"

Carly felt a pang of sadness in her heart. "They were killed yesterday by a pack of werewolves we tracked to their cabin", she said. The words tasted bitter in her mouth. "I'm alone now, I have no family left."

Pat touched her shoulder softly. "You have suffered much sorrow. Your heart is heavy, I cannot imagine losing all of my family; it is no wonder your hatred of werewolves is so great."

"So you understand then?"

"I understand, but that does not mean I agree with you", said Pat, quite seriously. "You cannot blame all werewolves for the death of your family."

Carly tried to sit up but the pain in her ribs prevented it from happening. "They're all the same", she said savagely. "To make matters worse I'm fairly sure that Bradley and Joanne found something out about the werewolves that they wanted to tell me. They said they had something important to share with me after our last hunt, but they didn't leave that hunt alive so I have no idea what it was. I found a note in Bradley's bedroom a few hours ago. It simply said 'skinwalkers', but I don't know what that means. I haven't had a chance to look into it yet."

Pat's face seemed to change drastically. Carly looked at him in surprise. His skin turned ashen and his expression grew grave.

"Are you sure that is what it said?" he asked. Carly thought she could detect a slight waver in his voice.

"It's in my jacket pocket", she said. Pat reached over to a small table where the hunter's jacket was placed. He felt inside one of the pockets and pulled out a small sheet of paper. Written in black pen was the unmistakable scrawled word 'Skinwalkers'.

Pat muttered something in a language that Carly could not understand. He quickly folded the paper and put it back into the hunter's coat pocket.

"You know what skinwalkers are, don't you?" asked Carly. "What are they?"

"I must not speak about them, and neither should you", said Pat, standing up quickly. "It is late, it will be dawn soon. You must get some rest."

"No, please, I have to know." Carly reached out and grabbed hold of Pat's sleeve.

He hesitated, just for a moment. "I cannot, we do not…" he stuttered, seeming at a loss for words. "It is not something we talk about", he said finally.

"Please." Carly felt tears spring into the hunter's eyes. "It would help me so much to know what my son wished to tell me about."

Pat sighed, his indecision etched on his face. Eventually he sat back down in the chair. "I will tell you", he said.

"Thank you", said Carly.

"The Navajo people, *my* people, tell of such witches who have the power to turn into other creatures."

"The same way werewolves do?" asked Carly.

"No. Werewolves are not evil. Being a werewolf is part of who they are. These witches are truly evil. They bring this upon themselves, it is not inflicted on them. In order to gain the power to perform this sorcery they must first study the magic they require. Then they kill a member of their own family. After that they take the pelt of whichever animal they wish to turn into. It is from this that they can change at will into their chosen creature."

"Aside from killing a family member, what makes them evil?" asked Carly.

Pat's eyes widened. "Their hearts are filled with hatred", he said. "They torture and kill for pleasure and want nothing more than the destruction of others."

"That sounds like the werewolves", snorted Carly, crossing her arms.

Pat shook his head. "No, they are nothing like werewolves. You do not understand. Werewolves are not to be feared - rather they should be respected. They are the chosen ones who carry with them the spirit of the wolf."

"Well if I come across any skinwalkers they can get a taste of my silver bullets as well. See how they like it."

"Silver bullets will not kill a skinwalker my friend. Only bullets dipped in white ash will have any effect."

Carly blinked. Pat's face was fading in front of her eyes. The next thing she knew she was gently waking up to the sound of bird-song. It was daybreak. Both her legs had gone numb. She was once again lying on the forest floor with her head in Kyle's lap. She looked down at her body and was relieved to see that she was female once again! She was back in her own body. She glanced at Kyle; he was still asleep sitting upright leaning against a tree.

Very slowly she moved his arms off her body and tried to stretch her legs out to regain some feeling in them. This only resulted in pins and needles shooting from her feet up to her thighs. Carly had to restrain herself from yelping out loud.

At last her legs began to feel a little more normal again. Carly stood up quietly and gave them a gentle shake.

"Morning beautiful", said Kyle, opening his eyes and smiling at her.

Carly jumped. "Oh, you scared me!" she said. "Good morning." She bent down and gave him a kiss.

He responded by grabbing her around the waist, pulling her onto his lap and kissing her in return. "That was a nice way to wake up", he said, winking at her.

Carly smiled but couldn't take her mind off the vision she'd had. 'Now I know what skinwalkers are, how do they tie in with everything else?' Carly couldn't understand it. 'Were there some skinwalkers in the other pack?' she thought. 'It certainly sounded this way when Pat had spoken of how silver wouldn't work on them. Seth couldn't be a skinwalker though – surely he is the wolf born pack leader the skinwalkers are supposed to be trying to find?' she pondered. 'Presuming I am correct in thinking that the other pack contained skinwalkers, why would they be trying to find the wolf born if the wolf born is their own pack leader - Seth? Shouldn't they realise who he is?' It didn't make any sense to her. 'Could it be that Seth is afraid the skinwalkers will kill him if they discover he is the wolf born? Surely not. Being the leader of their pack must mean that they are acting on his orders. Why though would Seth want to capture himself?' It really was peculiar. Carly tried to think back. 'Joanne and Bradley had said that the skinwalkers would destroy all the werewolves once they had the wolf born, but how?' she thought.

Carly shook her head. She was trying to make sense of it all but nothing seemed to fit together. It was like a riddle that she couldn't solve. It was frustrating her immensely.

"What's the matter?" asked Kyle.

Carly hesitated. She didn't know whether she ought to tell him or not. She decided she might as well. "I had a vision while I was asleep", she said. "I could see through the eyes of the hunter - the one who shot Devon."

Kyle looked shocked. "Is he still alive?" he asked, sounding horrified.

"Yes, he's wounded though. He has been taken in by a Native American called Pat", replied Carly.

"Oh my God! If he's still alive maybe more of them managed to survive the fight", said Kyle, gently lifting Carly off his knee and springing to his feet. "The others could be in terrible danger. We have to find them!"

"Kyle…" said Carly.

"What?"

"Never mind." She would have to tell him the rest later. She did not think it was the best time to bother him with what she had learnt about skinwalkers.

"Here", said Kyle, reaching down and effortlessly grabbing hold of a small mouse that had just scurried out of a bramble-bush to the side of him. He squeezed its neck for a second until the mouse stopped wriggling and then threw it to her. Carly caught the mouse and ate it without hesitation. "I don't want you freaking out thinking I'm trying to kill you again!" he said.

Carly managed a small laugh. "I would have caught myself something before allowing that to happen again, but thanks for the breakfast in bed."

Kyle smiled then promptly turned into his wolf form again. Carly climbed onto his back and Kyle began to run through the forest. Carly had no idea where they were going and Kyle couldn't exactly tell her right now, so she had no choice but to just hang on and trust that he actually had an end destination in mind.

She allowed her mind to wander as they sped on through the trees. She was still thinking about the skinwalkers. She couldn't figure out how they were unaware that their leader was the wolf born itself. 'Surely he would have already told them. It just doesn't add up. why would he keep something like that a secret from them? Unless the hunters were wrong, and the skinwalkers weren't looking for the wolf born at all', she thought. 'After all, why would they be? What could they possibly gain from a wolf born werewolf? Some sort of new power perhaps?' Carly had no idea. She also considered the possibility that she could be wrong. 'Perhaps the other pack was just a pack of werewolves after all.' She thought back to snippets of conversations that she had overheard from the other pack. They had spoken of the packs being different and mentioned that the hunters had been using the wrong weapons on them. Carly had also seen the dead naked men from the other pack lying next to animal pelts. Kyle had assured her that this is not something that happens to werewolves when they die. It all added up quite convincingly. 'The other pack must be a skinwalker pack; nothing else made sense!' She was still thinking about it when Kyle slowed down and came to a stop.

Carly looked up to see the cabin in front of her. "What are we doing here?" she asked, climbing off his back. "Surely it's dangerous to be here. What if you're right and there are some other hunters still alive? They know where the cabin is! They could be coming back here!"

Kyle turned back into a man. "The rest of our pack could have come back here so I thought it was worth checking out. We'll be quick don't worry. I don't fancy sticking around here for long myself either."

"Well I guess you can pick yourself up some clothes while you're here", said Carly.

"Oh, yeah." Kyle looked down at his naked body in surprise. "I forgot you dropped my clothes last night!"

"How can you not be aware of whether or not you're naked?" asked Carly, quite incredulously.

Kyle grinned and shrugged. "It's just one of those things you get used to", he said. "It's like forgetting whether or not you've had breakfast!"

"I never forget whether or not I've had breakfast", laughed Carly.

Kyle smiled again and pushed open the cabin door. Carly followed behind him. She gasped as she walked into the living room - it was a complete mess. The furniture had been turned upside down, there were items from the kitchen strewn all over the floor and everything had been totally ransacked. "Wow, what were they looking for?" she said in shock.

"Probably trying to find out if we had left any clues to where we were heading", replied Kyle.

"Go and get some clothes then", said Carly. "I don't think the others have been back here but it's hard to tell."

Kyle sniffed the air. "I can't smell a recent scent from any of them", he said. "Wait here then."

He turned and walked into the bedroom he had shared with Carly, whilst she stood in the living room surveying the damage. She felt a bit useless just standing there so she began to straighten the upturned furniture and pick up the books that were lying on the floor. A few minutes later Kyle came out of the bedroom. He was now fully dressed in a pair of black jeans and a black t-shirt emblazoned with the logo of a rock band.

"You look nice", said Carly.

"You prefer me with clothes on", said Kyle with a laugh. "That's ironic!"

Carly blushed. "I like you either way", she said, smiling. "I'm getting kind of used to seeing you wandering around in the nude now!"

Kyle chuckled and winked at her. "I'm just going to see if there has been any sign of Seth having been back in his room", he said.

"Like what?"

Kyle shrugged. "I dunno. Can't hurt to look though. Maybe I'll spot something. I wish I knew where he was!"

Carly sat down on the sofa to wait for Kyle while he wandered into Seth's bedroom.

"What the...?" Kyle's voice came floating out of the open

bedroom doorway.

Carly stood up and immediately hurried to Seth's bedroom. "What's the matter?" she asked.

Kyle didn't say anything but held up a jacket. It was the same jacket Carly had stumbled on several nights ago when she had been snooping around amongst Seth's things; the jacket Kyle's dad had been wearing in the photo Kyle had in his wallet.

"Th...th...this is my dad's jacket!" said Kyle looking pale.

Carly didn't know what to say. She wasn't sure if she ought to pretend she had never seen it before or to admit that she knew what it was. "Is it?" she said at last, opting to seem ignorant. "Does Seth wear a lot of your dad's things?"

"No," said Kyle, "he doesn't. I have no idea why he has it." He held up the jacket to his nose and sniffed it. "It smells like... blood...I think", he said. He carefully examined the jacket. "Pretty sure those are very old blood stains there." He sounded a little unsure and thrust the jacket out to Carly. "Here, see what you reckon."

Carly took the jacket and stared at it; there were certainly some small brownish black stains on the collar but it was hard to make out what they were. She carefully touched her nose to the material and breathed in deeply. "It smells a bit like...copper," she said at last, "but it's extremely faint".

"That's what I thought", said Kyle. He sat down on the edge of Seth's bed and rubbed his forehead. "I don't understand..." he said.

Carly sat down next to him. "Did you think that your dad had this jacket himself?" she asked, "or did your dad leave it in the house when he left?"

"He wore this jacket all the time", said Kyle. "He never went out without it. Maybe Seth met up with him at some point and dad gave him his jacket?"

Carly could imagine there was another explanation why Seth had their father's blood-stained jacket but she didn't want to even voice what she was thinking. "Maybe", she said quietly. She didn't believe what Kyle had said when they first met - that he didn't care about his dad; he wouldn't have a picture of their whole family, with his dad present, in his wallet, if his dad meant nothing to him.

"We need to find Seth", said Kyle, standing up quickly. "I need to ask him how he got the jacket and if he saw dad."

"We don't know where Gary, Ian and Devon are either", reminded Carly.

"I know, we can look for them all at the same time", said Kyle.

WHAM!

Carly felt as though she had been hit by a car. She was suddenly sitting at a table eating some sort of broth. Gary was by her side and her right butt-cheek felt distinctly uncomfortable. 'I'm Devon', she realised. It seemed, of course, quite normal to her that she should be Devon, for her mind was now intermingled with his. She looked around the room and knew exactly where she was. She was in the Native American reservation. It was very confusing for poor Carly. Part of her was aware that the hunter was somewhere on this reservation also. However the part of her that was entwined with Devon's mind had absolutely no idea of this and wasn't even aware the hunter was still alive.

"Thank you very much again for taking us in - it's kind of you", Gary was saying to an elderly Native American lady across the other side of the table. She smiled and nodded but Carly wasn't sure whether she had any comprehension of what he was saying.

"I'm going to go and check on Ian", said Carly pushing aside Devon's now empty soup bowl and standing up. Carly found herself wishing that she were with Seth and the other wolf pack. She felt unsure whether or not Seth would still be with the other pack but she assumed he would be. She walked into another room. It was dark as the windows were covered by drapes. Ian was lying on a bed looking weak. "How you feeling?" asked Carly. She didn't particularly care but she was asking out of obligation.

"I've been better", whispered Ian.

"Not shaping up to be a good week for you, is it buddy? First your leg, now your shoulder! Third time unlucky - you'll not make it next time!" she laughed.

Ian didn't look impressed. "You didn't need to say something like that", he retorted crossly. "There won't be a next time!"

"I'm just joking, lighten up!" 'That guy has no sense of humour', thought Carly. "Look at me, I got shot in the butt! At least you can sit down!"

"It's not a contest about who got shot in the most awkward place Dev", said Ian. "I think I'd like to rest now if that's alright with you."

Carly shrugged and walked back out of the room without saying bye to Ian.

"Carly, snap out of it!" Kyle was gently shaking Carly's shoulders.

She opened her eyes and felt the softness of Seth's bed beneath her head. "Hi", said Carly, feeling a little dizzy.

"Hi you! Were you having a vision or did you just pass out?"

"Ian, Gary and Devon have been taken in by the Native Americans", said Carly. "Ian has been shot in the shoulder."

"Holy shit! The same reservation where that hunter is?"

"Yeah, I think so," said Carly, "but I don't think they realise that he's there; they're in a different part of the reservation".

"Seth isn't with them?" asked Kyle.

"No, as far as I could tell he wasn't. Listen, Kyle, why am I having so many visions lately? They seem to be increasing in frequency and lasting longer each time!"

"That's because it's getting closer to the full moon", explained Kyle. "I told you that the run up to your first lunar change would be full of strange experiences."

"Strange experiences is definitely an understatement", muttered Carly.

"The closer it gets to that full moon the more visions you will have. You might even get other peculiarities happening. I really don't know, it's different for everybody."

"What did you get when you were in the lead up to your first full moon?" asked Carly, hoping he had gone through something similar.

"It's different for werewolves who are born this way", explained Kyle. "Nothing kicks in until we first change - literally nothing. It just hits us all of a sudden when the first full moon rises after our thirteenth birthday. There's nothing during the run up to it. Werewolves that have been bitten though, like you, have an intermediate stage of being not quite a werewolf yet no longer a human."

"Hmm", pondered Carly. "So other turned werewolves, do they experience visions like I am having?"

"Some do", said Kyle. "Women tend to experience things more to do with the mind and emotion whereas men tend to experience things in a more physical way. I've seen a few people go through their first change."

"Did you see Seth go through his first change?" asked Carly.

"Oh no. He kept that to himself. Besides I was only ten, he had other friends that he used to hang around with at the time. He was a moody teenager who didn't have much time for me or Gemma."

"Do you think his other friends knew what he was…is?" asked Carly.

"Hell no, I don't think so", said Kyle. "Seth has always been very strict about us keeping our identities secret. It's dangerous for werewolves you know!"

"Oh I know", said Carly, casting her mind back to the hunters. "I've had my fair share of danger over the past couple of weeks!"

Kyle put his arms around her and gave her a hug. "Well, I don't suppose we need to worry about Gary, Ian and Devon for the time being then. As long as they stay away from that hunter they should be alright. If Ian is hurt like you say, the Native Americans will be able to look after him well. They are very skilled in medicine."

"I suppose it was handy to find out where they are", said Carly.

"Yep, your visions are very useful", agreed Kyle. "You wanna have another one now and find out where Seth is?"

'I know damn well where Seth is likely to be', thought Carly. "It doesn't really work that way", she said. "I have no control over the visions. I don't know why I'm seeing the people I'm seeing or why it happens at certain times and not at other times."

"I know I'm only kidding. It's probably quite random, these things generally are. Though I must say yours have been pretty handy at saving our bacon lately, so maybe it's not a coincidence, who knows? We ought to get moving though if we want to find Seth. Are you hungry?"

"Yes!" said Carly, her stomach beginning to growl with the all-too familiar rumble that she was starting to grow accustomed to. The mouse she had eaten earlier really hadn't been terribly filling.

"We'll catch something before we go then", said Kyle. They headed out of the cabin and into the forest again. It was raining.

Carly shivered as the water dripped down the back of her neck. "I hate the rain", she said. She had never been fond of wet weather. Before becoming a werewolf she had always carried an umbrella around if the clouds looked even the slightest shade of grey, but she was standing in the pouring rain without even a hood on. It wasn't cold but she felt uncomfortable and damp.

Without saying a word Kyle bounded straight back into the cabin and emerged with one of his own jackets a minute later. "I don't have any hats," he said, putting the coat around her shoulders, "it's the best I can do".

Even though the jacket was hoodless, Carly felt a little better for not being just in her t-shirt in this weather. Luckily the thick canopy of trees above their heads prevented the rain from hitting them as quickly as it would have done if they had been out in the open. Even so, Carly felt herself wishing she were under a shelter. "Maybe we could wait in the cabin until it stops?" she asked hopefully. She knew that she was stalling, not just because of the rain, but also because she didn't really have any desire to find Seth.

"It's just rain Carly. I really want to find my brother - please understand!" said Kyle, sounding a little upset.

"Okay, okay, let's find him then", conceded Carly.

Kyle took her hand and they set off walking across the forest. Kyle's hand felt warm and soft against Carly's skin. She marvelled at how well their fingers intertwined together. She had never quite felt that her hand had fitted properly with Rob's. Somehow it had always seemed as though their fingers were the wrong shape or something; it was hard to describe. With Kyle though, their hands appeared to be made to hold each other. Carly felt a little silly having thoughts like this; it was not as though she had been in the middle of a romance movie but it made her smile nevertheless.

They stopped for a moment so Carly could catch something to eat. Despite her protestations, Kyle had insisted she had to catch her own food this time. He said it would be good practice for her. She didn't doubt that, but as it was still raining she thought she was never going to catch anything. Most of the forest creatures were taking shelter from the rain. It seemed there wasn't anything to catch! Eventually though she managed to grab a small rabbit which had ventured out of its burrow.

After polishing off the rabbit the pair set off again. Carly thought she recognised the way they were walking but she wasn't sure why. After a few minutes she remembered this was the path she had taken when she had followed Seth a few days ago. They were walking straight to the camp-site of the other werewolf pack! Carly experienced a surge of mixed emotions that made her involuntarily squeeze Kyle's hand. He looked down at their hands surprised and gave her hand a little squeeze back. 'If Kyle sees Seth with the other wolves he'll have no choice but to believe me!' thought Carly somewhat excitedly. She felt sad Kyle hadn't believed her about Seth's betrayal but at least he wouldn't be blinded by his sense of loyalty to his brother any longer once he saw evidence of the truth. She wished he didn't have to find out this way but it was better that he knew.

Unfortunately, after walking half an hour along the route that Carly had recognised as the road leading to the other pack's campsite, Kyle decided to divert his route and follow a new trail

"I don't think we should go that way", said Carly, tugging at Kyle's hand to try and steer him back onto the right path.

"Why not?"

"I dunno, I just prefer this path," said Carly, "less brambles!"

Kyle looked puzzled but did as Carly suggested and returned to the path she wanted him to take. "You're odd sometimes", he said, half laughing. "I don't see how the paths make any difference since have no idea where we're going!"

Carly didn't reply; she was too busy trying to remember the way without having to resort to sniffing bushes. That would have been far too obvious. She tried to picture the forest the way it had looked in the dark and where the moon had been positioned at the time above the treetops. "Tree shaped like a tiger, brambles at knee height, clump of nettles…" she muttered, counting off visible landmarks on the fingers of her free hand.

"What are you doing?" asked Kyle.

"Oh nothing, just taking note of things I'm seeing", said Carly trying to sound nonchalant. Kyle didn't look terribly impressed but he carried on walking with her regardless.

At last Carly spotted the tree she had sat behind when she had first stumbled on the other pack's camp-site. She knew that, beyond that tree, the other wolves had their tents pitched. She could barely even dare to look and see if they were there. She couldn't hear anything coming from that place though and she didn't think she could smell the aroma of other wolves or humans; at least no recent smell in any case. "Nobody's here!" she said in surprise. Kyle let go of her hand and stared at her.

"Did you have any particular reason to think there should be someone here", he asked raising an eyebrow.

"'Course not!" said Carly, again trying a little too hard to sound natural. "Come on." Plucking up her courage she walked out from behind the tree towards the territory of the other wolf pack. There were no tents, no werewolves, nothing to suggest they would be making camp there again at any point in the near future.

"I don't know quite what you were expecting to find", said Kyle, noticing the look on Carly's face.

Carly knew she was gawping a little but she couldn't help it. She had truly believed they would come across the other wolf pack here. "Do you remember when I said I followed Seth to the other wolf pack?" she asked.

"That again? I told you that wasn't real!"

"It was real, very real", insisted Carly. "This is where the wolf pack was. This is where Seth came."

"Carly, stop it, just stop!" Kyle sounded firm and almost angry.

Carly gulped. "I'm not just making this up Kyle, I wish you would believe me."

Kyle turned away from her and began to walk through the clearing. Suddenly he stopped and crouched down to look at something lying on the earth at the side of his shoe.

"What have you found?" asked Carly. She wanted to scurry over to him, but she was afraid he would be snappy with her again if she did so.

"A ring", said Kyle. He held the ring up in a chink of light that was shining down into the forest from a break in the leafy canopy above. "It can't be", he muttered.

Carly walked up to him. "Can't be what? What is it?" she asked, gently putting her hand on Kyle's shoulder.

Kyle handed her the ring. Carly inspected it. Engraved inside were the distinctive initials 'S. T.' "Our surname is Thompson", said Kyle quietly.

"This is Seth's ring?" asked Carly.

Kyle didn't reply but the look on his face told her everything she needed to know.

"That means he has been here then", she stated.

Again Kyle said nothing. He stared at her with a slightly stunned expression etched on his face.

"Umm…do you believe me now? About Seth being in contact with the other werewolf pack?" she asked.

"How do you know the other wolf pack was even here?" he blurted out. "Maybe there was nothing here at all and Seth just happened to be here at some point."

"Look around you Kyle. You're a skilled tracker! I'm not, yet even I can see that the ground has been used for a campsite. There are flattened leaves and holes that have clearly been used for tent pegs…Kyle just *look!*"

Reluctantly Kyle glanced at the ground. Carly could see in his eyes the dawn of realisation setting in. "I can smell that they've been here", he admitted, sounding upset.

Carly took his hand. "I would never lie to you and I'm not making it up", she said. "He really was here with them."

"I didn't want to believe you; Seth is my brother."

"I know."

Kyle was quiet for a few moments. "So he has some sort of double life then…but why? To what end?"

"I dunno Kyle but I don't think it's for anything good."

"Tell me exactly what it is that you saw or heard."

"Well…" Carly hesitated, "I think it has something to do with skinwalkers".

"What are skinwalkers?" asked Kyle. "The hunters mentioned those as well but I didn't know what they were talking about."

Carly explained everything that the Native American, Pat, had told the hunter during her vision. Kyle listened attentively, at times seeming fairly shocked. When she had finished he took a deep breath.

"You're not suggesting that the other pack is a pack of skinwalkers are you?" he asked.

"I don't know," said Carly honestly, "but Seth was saying that the hunters were using the wrong weapons. That ties in to the legend of how skinwalkers can only be killed by white ash."

"I don't understand why Seth would be mixed up with skinwalkers though", said Kyle. "What can he hope to achieve?"

"The hunters said that the skinwalkers were looking for the wolf born," said Carly, "and they were looking for the wolf born themselves".

"That's Seth though isn't it?" said Kyle, "so what is he doing with the skinwalkers? Why haven't they used him for whatever it is they plan to use him for? Don't they know he's the wolf born?"

"I was thinking the same thing to tell you the truth", said Carly. "I can't get my head around it. Maybe he hasn't told them for some reason; maybe he's planning something?"

"But what though?"

Carly shrugged; she had no idea whatsoever. "I've actually had a vision that I haven't told you about", she said, feeling a little nervous.

Kyle raised an eyebrow.

"I was seeing through Seth's eyes. He was talking to some of the other members of the other pack; he's their leader it would seem."

"Their leader?" Kyle sounded incredulous.

"I know; it's bizarre. He was saying how the world would be their oyster after the full moon."

"I wonder what's happening on the full moon, other than it being yours, Gary's and Ian's first lunar change?"

"I dunno, I didn't get to hear him say anything about that", said Carly. "Actually there's more."

Kyle slumped down to the ground. "I don't know if I can handle any more!" he said.

"Seth said that the hunters had been after him for a while ever since he killed two of them - a girl and her mother."

"That's not true, it can't be", said Kyle turning pale. "He's never told me that. Surely if that were true he would be tormenting himself about it? Why wouldn't he have confided in me? I'm his brother!"

"I think I know who he killed", continued Carly. She felt as though she was dropping bombshell after bombshell on Kyle. She wondered if it was a bit much for him to hear all at once. On the other hand the can of worms had already been opened. She might as well tell him everything now. "In the vision when I was seeing through the eyes of the hunter, I...sorry I mean he...was telling the Native American about how he became a hunter. It turns out a werewolf killed his wife and one of his daughters."

Kyle's mouth fell open. "Seth killed the hunter's family?"

Carly looked at the ground. "Well, it would seem that Seth killed three members of his family at least; I killed his other daughter, remember."

"Geez Carly, that was self-defence!"

"She had her back turned to me."

"All right, it was defence of the pack! Do you suppose the other sister and the hunter's wife were attacking him? Maybe that was self-defence too?" Carly could hear the desperation in Kyle's voice; he so obviously still badly wanted to believe in his brother.

"The way the hunter recounted the story...it doesn't seem likely that it was self-defence. I'm really sorry Kyle."

Kyle shook his head sadly then suddenly his face changed as though he had snapped out of it. "We've got to get to that Native

American reservation", said Kyle. "If the hunter has a personal vendetta against werewolves because of Seth killing his wife and daughter, he won't hesitate to slaughter Ian, Gary and Devon if he discovers they're there in the reservation as well. The Native American reservations are usually neutral territories but somebody who has lost their family will probably be too filled with vengeance to actually respect that."

Carly felt a chill run through her. "Oh hell", she said. "That didn't actually occur to me. I thought the Native Americans would be able to keep the peace."

"Well it's possible," said Kyle, "but we can't take that chance. It's up to me to look after the pack."

"You're not the pack leader though", pointed out Carly.

Kyle snorted. "Well we can't very well rely on Seth! Come on, let's go." He stood up, took hold of her hand and they began to walk through the forest.

"Do you even know where the Native American reservation is?" asked Carly.

"Umm…I have a vague idea", said Kyle. "I've only been that way twice though a few years ago. It's nowhere near our cabin and it's not on route to town either, so I've had no real need to head that far."

"Is it near the campsite where we pitched last night?"

"It's further than that - maybe two hours walk past that clearing."

"It's going to take us a while to get there then", stated Carly.

"Hmm, yeah, maybe you should ride on me."

"That sounds kinky", joked Carly, trying to make light of the situation.

To his credit, Kyle laughed. "Plenty of time for that", he chuckled, "but first we've got things to do!" The smile vanished from his face quickly and Carly realised that it probably wasn't the best time to try to cheer him up. He whipped off his clothes and handed them to Carly. "Don't lose them this time", he quipped.

Carly ensured she had hold of his clothes and watched as he changed into wolf form before her eyes. She never tired of seeing him do that. It was fascinating the way his limbs morphed into their new shapes and how his fur seemed to sprout from his body so quickly. It was almost like watching a plant grow on one of those nature documentaries where everything is shown speeded up.

She was so caught up with watching him and daydreaming, she quite forgot to climb onto his back. A sharp whine from Kyle brought her back down to Earth. Quickly she scrambled up onto him and held on tightly. Kyle began to run faster and faster, so fast that at last Carly could barely see. She knew she couldn't yet move at such a speed herself, though she longed for the day when she would be able to. That was one thing she was looking forward to in regards to her first lunar change; afterwards she would be able to do a lot more. It was that freedom she craved. Being a semi-werewolf (as she had been inwardly calling herself), was certainly more liberating than being a human, but she knew she could be (and would be) so much more. The terrifying prospect of losing control during the first lunar change was the only thing worrying her, but she knew she would be able to change at will into a wolf after that.

He ran on and on never seeming to tire. What would have taken a good five hours walk or more was cut down to a mere hour and a half's run. Carly began to pick up scents of other people who had passed through that area recently. The smells were unfamiliar. A faint waft of cooking drifted in the air also. Kyle slowed down to a stop. Carly disembarked from his back.

Kyle gave a little wriggle and changed back into a human again. Carly handed him his clothes and he slipped back into them. "Thanks", he said. "I sure could use a drink after that!"

"I bet you could. I could use a bite to eat actually", admitted Carly. "That smell of cooking was quite appetising."

Kyle cocked his head to one side. "I must admit I've very rarely eaten anything cooked since becoming a werewolf. You're right it did smell pretty good."

Carly hadn't considered that until now. She had not eaten a single bite of cooked food for the past eleven days. All the meat they had caught had been eaten raw. "I miss spaghetti bolognese",

210 - N. Gosney

she said wistfully. "Is that strange?"

"Course not - wolves are omnivorous. Didn't you ever have a pet dog when you were a child?"

"My mother was allergic to dogs", said Carly. "We had a few goldfish. Actually we had eight goldfish and one black fish. My mom believed in feng shui. Apparently that's the luckiest configuration of fish to keep."

Kyle looked at Carly as though she had just spoken a foreign language to him. "Feng what?"

Carly sighed. Nobody ever seemed to know what that is. Her mother's interests in Chinese beliefs and the way she had decorated her house to help the flow of positive "chi" energy, had meant a lot of her friends had asked her about it when she was younger. She couldn't be bothered explaining it all to Kyle right now though. She told him this.

Kyle just looked baffled. "Well," he said, sounding unsure of himself, "dogs are omnivorous. You can give your dog leftovers from the table and it'll eat it, whether it's vegetable, meat, whatever. Wolves are therefore also omnivorous. Just like dogs, wolves can eat food that is cooked or uncooked but, as wolves cannot start fires, they tend to eat everything raw. So what that means for us, your average standard werewolf, is that we're like trash cans."

Carly laughed. "I get the picture", she said. "I do love the meat I've been having, but I must admit, having something else from time to time wouldn't go amiss."

"It's only raw meat that will keep your hallucinations at bay though," warned Kyle, "so bear that in mind. Once you've gone through your first lunar change, it won't matter what you eat. You won't get the insatiable hunger that comes during your transition period. Actually I don't get hungry as often nowadays as I did when I was a human."

"Well I'll make sure to keep eating raw meat then, don't worry", said Carly.

"Right, come on, let's just get ourselves to the reservation. We've got to speak to the others."

CHAPTER TEN

They moved silently through the forest not knowing exactly how far they were from the reservation. Carly had the strange sense of being watched or followed but when she spun around nobody was there. Even with her acute sight, hearing and smell, she couldn't detect anybody, yet she couldn't shake the feeling that somebody was present. "Kyle," she whispered, "I think somebody is following us".

Kyle turned to look behind. "I can't see anybody", he whispered back.

They kept walking despite Carly feeling somewhat agitated. At last she caught a glimpse in the distance of a wooden building. It was much larger than the cabin where she had previously been staying. It had multiple stories, much like a house rather than just a simple cabin. As they neared she realised that there were several such houses grouped together to form a small village. "That's a very small reservation", said Carly in surprise. "I thought it would be larger, the size of a town perhaps."

"Usually they are but this is just an offshoot from a larger reservation I believe", replied Kyle.

"Will they be hostile to us?" asked Carly feeling a little nervous.

"I shouldn't imagine so."

Taking a deep breath, Carly walked up to the nearest house. It helped immensely that Kyle was by her side. She would have been too afraid to approach it on her own. There didn't appear to be anybody around which she thought was strange.

"Why do you come here?" asked a voice behind them. Carly and Kyle both spun around in surprise. Behind her stood the Native American named Pat who Carly had seen during her vision.

"You've been following us", stated Carly.

Pat smiled. "Your senses are quite in tune for an initiate wolf."

Carly was floored. "Y…you know what I am?"

"We are at one with the spirits, and know the spirit of the wolf. Of course we know what you are, and your friend here too", he said, motioning to Kyle.

"Don't you know why we are here then?" asked Kyle.

"We are many things, but we are not psychic", said Pat smiling.

"We're here to see our friends, Gary, Ian and Devon", replied Carly, hoping the hunter was nowhere around.

"Ah yes. We picked them up last night. Ian was hurt so we have tended to his wounds."

Carly nodded; she knew this already. "May we see them please?"

"We seem to have quite the pack gathering in our small village", said Pat. "Allow me to introduce myself; I am Pat."

"Nice to meet you", said Kyle, offering his hand for a shake. Carly did the same. Pat shook hands with each of them in turn.

"I'm Kyle and this is Carly", Kyle continued.

Pat stared into Carly's eyes. "There is something familiar about you", he said.

Carly flushed with embarrassment. "I can't imagine why, we've never met before", she pointed out.

"Then why do you look at me as though you know me?" asked Pat.

Carly was astonished. She hadn't realised she had been doing that at all. "I'm sorry, I didn't mean to!" she stammered. "I don't believe we've met before."

Pat continued to stare at her; Carly felt uncomfortable as though his eyes were trying to bore into her very soul. Finally though he blinked and broke his gaze. "We had better get you to your friends", said Pat. He walked forward a few steps and then stopped abruptly. Carly, who had been walking directly behind him, almost bumped straight into the back of him.

Pat spun around to look at Kyle. "Come to think of it," he mused, "you also seem familiar".

Kyle pulled a doubtful looking expression. "I've never actually met any Native Americans", he said. "I've learned of your culture but I've never actually met any of your people."

"Hmm", said Pat. "I cannot put my finger on it. It will come back to me I am sure." He turned around again and began to walk across the courtyard (or at least it was a courtyard of sort. Carly could see that some attempt had been made to lay gravel down in between the buildings although it was far from being a professional job by the look of it). At the far end of the courtyard was a building. The aroma of food was stronger from here than anywhere else in the reservation. "This is the dining area", said Pat. "Come, eat; you must be hungry. I shall find your friends and ask them to join you here."

Carly and Kyle entered the building. There were rows of tables and benches all carved from wood neatly laid out within the room. The tables were bare. Over to one side of the room were wicker baskets filled with cutlery. Carly felt as though she was in a high school canteen of some sort. "Where's the food?" said Carly.

"In the kitchen. John shall bring you some," said Pat, "please sit".

Carly and Kyle did as he suggested. They sat down on a bench facing each other at the nearest table. Pat smiled and left out of the door they had just come through. The room was quiet now and Carly and Kyle sat in silence, waiting. Around ten or fifteen minutes later, a door in the far side of the room opened. An elderly Native American man entered the room. His long white hair was plaited and his face was brown and wrinkled like a walnut. He walked slowly to their table carrying in each hand a plate of dinner. Carly craned her neck slightly to see what was on the plates. She thought she could make out some sort of steak with potatoes and vegetables. As the man set the plates before them on the table, Carly could see that this was indeed the case.

"Thank you sir", said Carly. Kyle echoed her.

"You are welcome," said the man, "I am John. Pat tells me you are here looking for your friends."

"Yes," said Carly, "Ian, Gary and Devon".

"Ah yes, they like my soup", said John, chuckling. Kyle smiled politely. "I will leave you now to eat", said John. He shuffled away before either Carly or Kyle had chance to say anything further.

Carly was staring at her plate. It looked so delicious. She had actually missed eating vegetables. Quickly she grabbed a carrot and popped it into her mouth. She was chewing vigorously, enjoying the flavours, when she realised Kyle was grinning at her. "What?" she asked, instantly paranoid.

"Nothing," he sniggered, "it's just…"

"Just what?"

"You haven't bothered to get any cutlery", he said.

Carly felt a little embarrassed. She had become so accustomed to eating raw meat with her bare hands that the thought of using a knife and fork to eat her dinner just hadn't occurred to her.

"I mean, I don't mind at all," continued Kyle, "we are werewolves after all, but seen as how we're eating at tables, from plates…"

Carly leapt up from her chair and dived over to the baskets of cutlery. She quickly grabbed two knives and two forks and brought them back to the table. She handed one set to Kyle. He still had an amused expression on his face.

"Shut up!" said Carly, half jokingly.

"What? I didn't say a word!" protested Kyle in feigned outrage.

Carly had a strong urge to fling some potato at him but decided that would be positively unladylike, so she refrained from doing so.

"Kyle! Carly!" The sound of Gary's voice instantly made Carly look up from her dinner. There, standing in the doorway that they had entered the room by, were Gary and Devon.

"Guys! Great to see you!" Kyle stood up and gave them both an awkward sort of hug teamed with lots of back patting.

'A manly hug', thought Carly, finding it quite funny. She also stood up and found herself being embraced by quite a strong bear hug from Gary. "Hi Gary, I'm glad you're all right", she said warmly. She was genuinely pleased to see him. She had begun to feel quite fond of Gary (in a platonic sort of way of course). Gary released her from his tight grip. She looked over to Devon standing beside him. "Hi Devon", she said. Devon made no attempt to hug her but gave her a smile and greeted her in return. Carly felt wary of Devon considering he also had some connection to the other pack. She wasn't going to mention it though.

"Sit down, finish your meals", said Gary. "We can chat while you are eating."

"So, how did you end up here?" asked Gary.

"We could ask you the same question", said Kyle with a laugh, chewing a mouthful of steak.

"Well when we went to look for Ian, as you know, we searched where we had left him being sick, but he wasn't there. We followed his scent and it turned out he had wandered for miles! He must have been running to have come so far. We could smell somebody else as well though we didn't know who. After a long walk we discovered Ian lying in the forest with a bullet in his shoulder. We concluded there must have been a hunter still alive somewhere. Devon went to see if he could find him and I stayed with Ian trying to tend his wounds. There was little I could do - I had no equipment. Besides I have very few first aid skills."

"We were too far from the cabin to get any supplies of course", interjected Devon. "I found the hunter though who had shot him."

"I suppose you killed him?" asked Kyle.

Devon nodded. "He won't be bothering us any more. I think he was the last of them - he must have been."

"Actually," said Kyle, "he wasn't, but we'll tell you about that later. Carry on with your story Devon."

"I headed back to where I had left Ian and Gary..."

"...and Devon had only been back with us for about two or three minutes when Pat came out of the forest, from nowhere so it seemed, and offered us help. He said he could heal Ian and told us to come with him. So we did, we had no choice really", finished Gary.

"Is Ian all right?" asked Kyle.

"He's doing really well now yes", said Devon.

"They know what we are", said Gary. "The Native Americans... they know!"

"Yep, we gathered", said Carly. "They knew about Kyle and I as well."

"What's all this business about there being another hunter still alive?" asked Devon. "That doesn't sound good. Did you have a run in with him?"

Carly and Kyle exchanged glances. "Not exactly", said Carly.

"He's...well...he's here", said Kyle.

"What?" gasped Gary. "Here in the reservation? How do you know that? What's he doing here? Why are you not panicking about this?"

"That's why we came to find you, we had to tell you", said Carly.

"Carly had a vision about him", explained Kyle. "He was injured and Pat took him in to heal him just as he did with Ian."

"Why would he be healing that vile man?" spat Devon angrily. "Hunters hate our kind. Native Americans have always been sympathetic to werewolves, so why would he help him?"

"Probably because he couldn't stand back and let the man die", said Kyle. "There is one more thing...it's the same hunter who shot you in our cabin."

Devon's eyes flashed and he let out a guttural sounding noise from deep within himself. "I should rip him to shreds", he snarled.

"You will do no such thing", said Kyle firmly. "We are guests here and the Native Americans have treated us all well, not to mention the fact that they have tended to Ian's wounds. It would be completely disrespectful of us to betray them by bringing violence to their reservation."

Carly admired Kyle for what he had just said. He sounded like a leader. She couldn't help thinking he would have made a much better head of the pack than Seth had ever been. "I agree with Kyle", she said, taking hold of his hand.

Devon snorted. "Well you would", he said, sounding bitter.

"I agree as well", said Gary.

'He doesn't sound very confident, but at least he's in agreement, which is better than nothing', thought Carly. "We have no right to cause a fight scene here in this peaceful place", she said.

Devon's shoulders sagged as he realised he was outnumbered. "I don't like it," he muttered, "I don't like it at all".

"You don't have to like it Devon," said Kyle, "but if you have any gratitude towards the Native Americans for how they have helped Ian and have been kind to you, then you'll agree that what I am saying is the most sensible thing".

Devon grunted again, a sign that Kyle clearly took to be acceptance, as he smiled and nodded. "Good, that's settled then. We should just stay away from the hunter, wherever he is, and stick to wherever Pat tells us is safe. If the hunter learns that we are here though I'm not so sure that he will not start a fight with us regardless."

"And we're just going to stand there and take it, are we?" asked Devon sarcastically.

"No, of course not. I didn't mean that; I meant we shouldn't start anything", said Kyle. "If we have to protect ourselves then obviously that's what we should do, but it would be preferable if it didn't come to that in the first place!"

Carly realised that her dinner was beginning to go cold, so she fell silent and tucked into it whilst listening to the others making small talk about their journeys and what terrible weather the rain-storm had been earlier. She wasn't as keen on the meat as she thought she would have been; despite her having missed cooked food. For some reason a grilled steak just wasn't as appealing as a raw one. Certain dishes she craved, like the spaghetti bolognese she had been pining for earlier, but a plain cooked steak just wasn't a patch on a raw steak. The meat was far too chewy and gristly and its flavour was nowhere near as succulent as the steaks she had been used to recently. Still, she ate it anyway. She didn't want to seem ungrateful for John's hospitality at having prepared meals for them.

Sneaking a look over to Kyle, she could see that he, too, was struggling to chew the meat on his plate. He was giving it quite an admirable attempt though. One thing that Kyle had which Carly did not, were sharper and very slightly longer teeth. It wasn't something immediately obvious, but when he laughed or spoke, if you stared at his mouth really carefully, you could just about see his teeth were somewhere in between being human-like and wolf-like. Carly's on the other hand were still very much human.

When the meal was over, after Carly and Kyle had taken their plates to the kitchen (where John had cheerfully relieved them of them whilst enthusing about how carefully he had cooked the meat that he was sure they must have enjoyed), they returned to the table where Gary and Devon were waiting for them.

"Would you like to see Ian?" asked Gary. "He's in one of the recovery units."

"Recovery units?" asked Carly.

"Well that's what Pat calls it", explained Devon. "It's really just a bedroom with some medicines and potions on the shelves."

Kyle shrugged. "Sounds as good a recovery unit as it's going to get. Sure, yes, it would be good to see Ian. I'd like to make sure he's okay."

"Oh he's alright", said Devon. "And I'm feeling much better myself, thanks for asking", he muttered under his breath.

Carly heard what he had said and raised an eyebrow. She looked over to Kyle and saw him gritting his teeth whilst avoiding Devon's gaze. 'It's a bit petty of Devon to say something like that. He's clearly jealous of Ian having people show concern about him', Carly thought.

"Let's go then", said Gary, seemingly quite oblivious as to the sudden awkwardness in the room. They all trooped out of the dining room in single file; first Gary, then Kyle, then Carly. Devon brought up the rear. Carly felt once again as though they were a family of baby ducks following their mother. Gary led them across the courtyard to another building. It was smaller than the last one. The door to the building was closed. Gary knocked twice, waited a moment, then pushed the door open. The others went inside and Devon closed the door behind him.

The room was familiar to Carly, just as the dining room had been. She remembered she had seen it a few hours ago in her vision. Ian was still lying on the bed although he was looking rather perkier than when she had seen him last through Devon's eyes.

"Kyle! Carly!" Ian exclaimed as he saw them. A huge beaming smile spread across his face. "I'm so glad you're all right! I was worried hunters may have found you."

"Hunters, pah! Hunters don't scare me!" joked Kyle, smiling back. "How are you feeling?"

"Well, it hurts a fair bit," said Ian, indicating his wounded shoulder, "but I'll live. I've already had my leg shot and now my shoulder, let's hope the third time it's nowhere more serious!" Carly felt as though she was experiencing déjà-vu considering Devon had said virtually the same thing to Ian previously.

"There won't be a third time buddy", said Gary reassuringly.

Devon shuffled on the spot looking a little uncomfortable.

"Devon," said Kyle, not meeting his gaze, "would you mind very much going to ask John if he could prepare us another one of those steaks? They were delicious."

"They were n…" began Carly, who had intended to voice her absolute disagreement on quite how delicious those steaks were! However she didn't manage to get as far as that, for Kyle (who was standing directly next to her) subtly but very painfully pinched her arm. "*Nice!*" yelped Carly. Her arm stung a little. "*Very very nice! Delicious steaks!*"

Gary, Ian and Devon stared at Carly in surprise. "Erm, Carly, are you feeling okay?" asked Gary.

"I'm great", said Carly trying to laugh it off. "I just really loved the steaks!"

"Talk about enthusiasm!" said Ian laughing at Carly. Then he groaned and grabbed hold of his shoulder. "Ouch!" he moaned. He quickly stopped laughing and sank back into his pillow. "It twinges a bit!" he explained.

Kyle looked at Devon in earnest. "Would you mind?" he repeated.

"How many steaks?" asked Devon.

"Well, just one for me please."

"Better make that two then Dev," Gary said with a grin, "considering how desperate Carly is for another steak as well!"

Devon raised an eyebrow at Kyle's strange request, but he nodded and said he would do as he was asked. He left the room and closed the door behind him.

Kyle tiptoed over to the door and put his head against it to listen. He waited a minute or so then motioned for the others to huddle closer to Ian's bed. "I need to be quick with what I'm about to tell you", said Kyle in hushed tones. "Devon won't be gone long."

Carly wondered if Kyle was going to tell the others about Seth. She was right, he did. The look on the faces of Ian and Gary when they heard that Seth was part of the other pack and that Devon was also somehow connected to them, was a look of pure astonishment.

"What does that mean?" asked Gary. "Are we not allowed to meet with the other wolf pack?"

"I didn't even know there *was* another wolf pack", said Ian, sounding quite stunned.

"Well it makes sense", mused Gary. "We can't possibly be the only werewolf pack in the whole world. Otherwise, where did the first werewolves come from? Seth and Kyle's dad, how did he become a werewolf?"

Ian shrugged. "From his dad?"

"Don't be silly, it has to be traced back to somewhere, some point of origin. The further back in time, the more likely that it would have spread out - through descendants or from biting or scratching people. There'd be more than just Kyle and Seth's dad by now who would be werewolves."

"Shh!" said Kyle. "You can ponder the origins of werewolves later. I've got more to tell you, about skinwalkers."

"What are skinwalkers?" asked Ian. "You haven't finished explaining yet why Seth is with the other wolf pack."

Just then the door opened. In came Devon carrying a plate of two cooked steaks. Carly caught her breath. 'Shit, I hope he didn't hear any of that', she thought, biting her lip.

If Devon had heard anything of their conversation, he was doing a good job of acting to the contrary. His expression never faltered. "John was delighted you liked his steaks so much", he said, handing Kyle the plate. "He said the secret is that he puts a pinch of thyme onto the steaks while they are cooking."

Kyle chuckled. "Oh really? Well I'll bear that in mind." He picked up one of the steaks and took a bite out of it. "Mmmm", he said, making appreciative noises.

Devon looked at Carly expectantly. "What about yours Carly?"

Carly forced a smile onto her face. "I'm trying not to seem

greedy", she said, hoping to make it sound convincing. Eating another tough steak was the last thing she felt like doing, but she knew she had to eat it otherwise Devon would be suspicious. Kyle held the plate out towards her. She picked up the other steak. It was quite a large steak. Carly realised that Kyle had taken the slightly smaller one for himself. 'Jerk!' thought Carly, slightly disgruntled. Kyle grinned and winked at her. Carly resisted the urge to punch his arm. Lifting the steak to her mouth, she took a large bite, hoping she could finish it as quickly as possible. "Good heavens!" she exclaimed aloud, as she chewed the meat which vaguely resembled shoe leather.

"That good eh?" said Devon.

Carly couldn't say any more - her teeth were busy trying to get through the tough steak.

"Look at that, she can't even speak she's enjoying her food so much!" exclaimed Kyle, whilst making short work of his own steak thanks to his sharp teeth.

Carly managed to tackle half the steak then put the rest down on the plate. She simply couldn't take it any longer. "Ohhh," she groaned, "I'm so full. As delicious as it is, I can't manage another bite. I'm rolling!" It was a complete lie of course; she could easily have managed the rest but she definitely didn't want to! She genuinely had jaw ache now after all that chewing.

"I didn't know pre-turn werewolves could get full!" said Devon, sounding surprised.

"Erm, that's because it's cooked meat", piped up Kyle, coming to Carly's rescue. It was a good thing he did for Carly hadn't known what to say. "Pre-turn wolves have an insatiable appetite for raw meat but anything else is more filling. Only raw meat stops the hallucinations though."

Devon looked impressed. "Well, waddya know, I had no idea", he said. "When I was turned I didn't touch anything other than raw meat until my first lunar change."

"You were turned three days before the full moon", pointed out Kyle. "It's not as though you were living on raw meat for very long, nor did you experience a large number of hallucinations."

222 - N. Gosney

"True", agreed Devon.

"Besides," continued Kyle, "I think it's different for women. Men can eat more."

'Shut up Kyle,' thought Carly, 'he believes you. Just stop talking now, that's enough!'

As though he had read her mind, Kyle chose that moment to stop talking. An awkward silence settled on the group. "Have you met Pat?" asked Ian, breaking the tension.

"Yes, we have", replied Carly. "He was the first Native American Indian we met actually. Other than that we've only encountered John in the kitchen."

"Pat is a nice guy, he really helped me", said Ian. Gary nodded in agreement.

"Yeah he seemed like a decent guy", said Kyle.

Devon grunted. "Oh sure, so decent", he said sarcastically. "That's why he's keeping that wolf-slayer here and looking after him."

"What is he talking about?" asked Ian.

Kyle sighed. "The old hunter guy is staying in this reservation. He's alive and wounded."

Ian went pale. "You have to be kidding?" he exclaimed incredulously. "Why would Pat take him in?"

"He's a Native American", said Kyle. "They have honour and are not likely to leave a dying man in the forest unaided."

"Stupid if you ask me", grumbled Devon. "They respect the spirit of the wolf, yet Pat goes and brings in a hunter, of all people."

"Your friend Kyle is wise." A voice behind them made Carly jump. They all spun around in great surprise. Pat was standing there with a slightly amused smile on his face.

"How long have you been there?" asked Kyle.

"Oh, long enough", said Pat.

Carly felt her cheeks redden. 'He knows we have been talking about him', Carly thought, feeling very ashamed. 'It was rude of us to question his judgement on taking in the hunter, considering how kind he had been to us.' Although, granted, it was really only Devon who had been grumbling.

"Where did you come from?" she asked. Pat stepped to one side to reveal another door behind him. "Oh, I didn't know there were two doors", said Carly, feeling stupid.

"So you are aware of our other guest", said Pat. "He will not harm you, though I would not go paying his room a visit. I do not think he would be pleased."

"We had no intention of it", snarled Devon.

Pat looked at him with surprise. "There is no need for the hostility Devon. We are all connected you know. He is your brother."

"He's not my fucking brother!" snapped Devon. "He's a dirty no good werewolf hunter who should have died last night like the other hunters." Devon's eyes were beginning to flash brightly now and the expression of rage on his face was growing. "I've had enough of this shit. I'm outta here!" With that, he turned and stormed out of the cabin, slamming the wooden door as he barged through it.

Kyle looked extremely apologetic. "I'm so sorry for his behaviour", he said, hanging his head. Carly could tell he was too ashamed to lift his head to look Pat in the eye. "I don't know what came over him."

Pat smiled. "You have nothing to be sorry for", he said. "Devon is responsible for his own actions, just as you are responsible for yours. Devon has a lot of deep anger inside him, I can tell."

Nobody said anything. It seemed to Carly nobody knew what to say. She certainly didn't.

"Come, let me show you to your rooms", said Pat at last. "There will be time to spend with Ian this evening. Perhaps you would like to rest first and refresh yourselves."

Carly thought that sounded like a wonderful idea. She was aching and badly needed a bath. She felt so very grubby. She and Kyle followed Pat to another room which was laid out like a dormitory with several beds in a row. Gary, who of course already knew where he would be sleeping, stayed behind with Ian. The rest of the afternoon was much more peaceful. Carly had a bath. It was the most luxurious bath she had had for a while - with actual hot running water and bubbles. She felt as though she had floated to heaven. She rested her head back against the side of the bath, closed her eyes and allowed herself just to think of absolutely nothing.

By the time evening fell Carly was feeling much more relaxed. The Native Americans had given her and Kyle some clean clothes to put on (the ones they had given Carly weren't exactly her style, but they fit her at least), and had taken their own clothes to wash. Much to Carly's relief, cooked steak with thyme was not on the menu for their supper. Instead they were given a more appetising dish of fish stew, which Carly wolfed down with relish. She was beginning to feel a little jittery though and she mentioned to Kyle that she needed some raw meat. Kyle said that they would head out directly after supper to hunt deer and that they would also bring back some meat for Ian and Gary. Carly was surprised that Ian and Gary had managed to last as long as they had without any raw meat and without hallucinating. When she asked Gary about it he told her he had actually managed to catch some rabbits earlier that day, not long before Kyle and Carly had arrived at the reservation.

Devon wasn't seen a great deal that evening. He made a brief appearance during dinner but it was only to tell them all that he was going for a walk and that they shouldn't wait up for him. John had seemed quite wounded that Devon hadn't wanted to try any of his fish stew but Devon didn't appear to care. Kyle apologised once again for his friend's behaviour, but nobody had blamed Kyle. Carly told Kyle to stop saying sorry on behalf of Devon but Kyle had said he felt obligated to do so.

Carly met a large number of other Native American Indians that day, all living on the reservation. Pat's wife, Olivia, was a sweet lady with smiling eyes who seemed to instantly click with Carly. It didn't take longer than five minutes before she was clucking around Carly like a mother hen. Carly felt slightly as though she were a little child again the way Olivia was fussing over her, but she couldn't deny that it was quite nice being pampered. She was reminded of her own mother and Carly realised she really did miss her family.

After dinner, Carly, Kyle and Gary headed back to Ian's room.

They hadn't needed to go hunting after all. John had rather intuitively taken it upon himself to bring out a bowl of raw rabbit for each of the werewolves shortly after their dinner, a gesture for which they were most grateful. As they entered Ian's room they noticed Devon was nowhere to be seen. Kyle filled Gary and Ian in on what they had learned with regard to skinwalkers. Gary and Ian had been very intrigued by this, though somewhat horrified at the possibility that Devon and Seth had been mingling with such evil people.

"Are you sure the other wolf pack contains skinwalkers?" asked Ian. He seemed quite afraid and Carly couldn't say she blamed him.

"No," said Kyle, "not a hundred percent sure but it seems quite likely considering the conversations Carly overheard".

"So, you get visions Carly, and I just get excess perspiration and the need to pee every fifteen minutes", commented Gary. "Hardly fair is it?"

"The visions aren't exactly a barrel of laughs", said Carly. "I think I'd rather have what you've got!"

By the end of the day Carly was more than ready to go to sleep. She made her excuses to the group and headed to the dormitory. Olivia had left a pair of green floral (quite hideous looking yet very comfortable) pyjamas on her bed, which she slipped into gratefully. She was about to climb into bed when she felt a pair of strong arms wrap around her waist from behind her. "Ooh!" she squealed.

"You look great in those pyjamas", said Kyle, his lips very close to her ear.

Carly laughed and spun around. "Don't I just though?" she agreed jokingly. "Height of fashion."

"They're nice and soft", he said, running his hands down them and grabbing hold of her bottom.

"Kyle!" said Carly, looking around furtively. "Somebody could be watching!"

"Pfft! Spoil sport!" teased Kyle, giving her a peck on the lips. Carly hesitated for half a second then kissed him back.

"This is a shared dorm you know. We can't just…"

Kyle laughed. "I know, I know. But you really do look so sexy in those pyjamas!"

"Are you making fun of my pyjamas?"

"Hell no! I'm being serious!"

Carly swatted playfully at Kyle then skipped lightly around to the other side of her bed.

"Ooh you little minx," he said grinning, "you better get to sleep before I say to hell with the shared dorm".

Carly giggled and climbed into her bed. "Goodnight Kyle", she said, and closed her eyes.

Kyle bent down and kissed her forehead. "Goodnight Carly", he said.

CHAPTER ELEVEN

Carly was completely unaware of anybody else entering the room or going to bed. She was out like a light the minute her head hit the pillow and she slept through the night completely undisturbed. The next morning the sound of hustle and bustle woke her. She opened her eyes. For a few minutes Carly was completely disorientated; it took her a while to remember where she was. Then it all came back to her. She yawned, stretched and sat up in bed. All the other beds around her were empty and neatly made. "Wow I wonder what time it is", she said aloud. Then the chair at the side of her bed caught her eye; on it was a stack of neatly folded clothes which Carly recognised as her own. Olivia must have crept in and left them for her whilst she slept. Carly resolved to find Olivia as soon as possible to thank her for washing and drying them.

Quickly she wriggled out of the soft green pyjamas and pulled on her clothes. She made her bed neatly, folded the pyjamas and placed them underneath her pillow. She wished she had a watch. Her internal body clock was all out of synchronisation. She was hungry but this alone was no indication of time. She was very frequently hungry nowadays. It certainly didn't necessarily mean she had missed breakfast.

After a quick trip to the bathroom, Carly headed to the dining area but nobody was around. It was so cloudy outside that Carly couldn't even use the sun to judge what time it was. It felt late though. She decided to pay a visit to Ian for she thought she might find Kyle, Gary and Devon there. She headed across the courtyard and knocked on Ian's door. She heard Ian's voice inviting her to come in. He was sitting upright in bed reading a book; he was alone.

"Hi Ian, how's the shoulder?" she asked.

"Not too bad now thanks", said Ian. "I want to be up and about but Pat and Olivia keep insisting that I rest. It's a little boring in this bed."

"I bet", said Carly. "Listen, you haven't seen Kyle and the others by any chance have you?"

"They're out looking for Devon", said Ian.

"Looking for Devon?"

"Yeah, he didn't come back to the reservation after he went for his walk last night. Nobody has seen him all day. Kyle was worried that another hunter might have found him, so he and Gary have gone to see if they can find him."

"Wow", gasped Carly, feeling instantly concerned. "I hope he's all right! What time is it by the way, do you know?"

Ian pointed over to the far wall where a clock in the shape of a star was hanging.

"Ten past four? Seriously? Is that clock right?"

"Yep it's right. We had lunch a fair while ago", confirmed Ian.

"That's crazy though, ten past four?! And nobody woke me up?"

Ian shrugged. "I didn't realise you were still asleep actually as I've been in this room all day. I guess you must have been really tired."

'Wow', thought Carly. 'I didn't know I was quite that tired!' "What time did Kyle and Gary set off?" she asked.

"Erm…just after lunch. They came to tell me they were going. Must have been about one o'clock ish."

'Three hours', thought Carly. 'Surely they should be back by now.' "Do you think I should venture into the forest to see if I can find them and help look for Devon?"

Ian shook his head. "I wouldn't if I were you. They could be absolutely anywhere. What are you going to do? Track their scents through the entire forest? What if you get spotted by a hunter yourself? Then we'd be sending out search parties looking for you! At least Gary and Kyle are together - there is safety in numbers you know."

"So my mother always used to tell me", said Carly.

"Where is your mother these days?" asked Ian. "Do you think she'll be missing you?"

"She moved abroad nearly two years ago. Bought a house, found a new husband, the whole works."

"Ah I see", said Ian. "My parents live about an hour away but I never see them. We've not had any contact with each other since I moved out four years ago. We weren't close when I was growing up; we just bickered all the time. I couldn't wait to leave to tell you the truth."

"What about your girlfriend? Won't she be wondering where you are?"

"Fiancée", corrected Ian. "Sarah." Ian's expression changed to one of wistfulness as he spoke of the girl he loved. "We've been engaged for two months, though we're not planning on getting married for a few years yet. She wants a big wedding so we need to save up." A tear rolled down Ian's cheek. "What am I even saying?" he said angrily. "We're never going to get married now. How can I marry her? I'm a werewolf!"

Carly felt her heart twinge in sympathy for Ian's situation. 'It must be so hard for him, being apart from Sarah and knowing their life together would never be the same again', she thought.

"Maybe you should go back to her", she said softly. "Explain to her what you are and how it happened. If she loves you surely you can find a way to make it work somehow."

"It's not exactly ideal is it?" snorted Ian. "What is she going to do when I go through the lunar changes? Am I going to attack her? I won't be in control of myself!"

"Well, when that happens you could always just go alone into the forest for the night so that you are nowhere near her. Surely there's a way you can be together."

"Seth says it's too dangerous in the town", said Ian. "We're supposed to stay in the forest away from humans."

"We're with humans here in this reservation", pointed out Carly.

"That's not the same though. The Native Americans - they worship the spirit of the wolf. They know what we are. We're part of their culture. We won't be so accepted among other people

230 - N. Gosney

though I expect."

"It's not like you'd be telling everybody what you are - it would only be Sarah."

Ian looked doubtful.

"Don't you think she would understand? She loves you, doesn't she?"

"Yes, she does", agreed Ian.

"Well then, you should tell her. You should be with her."

"But Seth says…"

"Screw what Seth says!" scoffed Carly. "He hasn't exactly been honest with us now has he? Sneaking off to that other pack! Who knows what he's really up to anyway? Not to mention that for a pack leader he's kind of a jerk!"

Ian sniggered. "You're right, he is a jerk!"

Carly was enjoying chatting with Ian. She realised she knew very little about him up to this point. It was good just to sit and talk about themselves. "So, are you going to go back to Sarah?" she asked.

Ian sighed. "I want to, I really do. I miss her so much."

"Hell, if it makes you feel better, why not turn her into a werewolf too? She can come and join the pack." Carly was only semi-serious when she said that. On the one hand she didn't think that turning somebody into a werewolf against their own volition was a great idea. After all, she had been given no choice in the matter herself and in a sense she felt almost as though she had been violated, though she accepted that Rob hadn't realised what he was doing. On the other hand though, she actually quite liked being a werewolf despite having not experienced a change yet. The enhanced senses were incredible and the feeling of freedom she got when running through the forest was like nothing that any human had ever experienced. She couldn't imagine that Sarah wouldn't enjoy that as well.

Ian however looked quite horrified at her suggestion. "You have got to be kidding me?" he said, incredulously. "Do you honestly think I'd subject Sarah to this life?"

Carly shrugged. "Do you hate being a werewolf?"

"No, but that's not the point!"

"What's the point then?"

For a moment or two, Ian gaped at her like a goldfish, his mouth opening and closing as he tried desperately to think of something to say. "It's dangerous!" he blurted out at last. "There are hunters after us!"

"Well, okay, there is that," conceded Carly, "but most of them are dead."

"There'll be more I bet. I've had more dangerous adventures in the past week and a half than I have had in my entire life. I've been shot twice! I don't want to put Sarah in harm's way like that."

Carly understood what he was saying. 'He only wants to keep Sarah safe, which is completely understandable. Wanting to protect the people you love is a very natural reaction.' Although, Carly couldn't help thinking that Ian was still being a little over-cautious. 'Most of the hunters were dead. Surely the worst of the danger is over? Perhaps we could, at some point, make peace with the remaining hunters? Then we would be able to live out our lives without having to look over our shoulders at every turn.'

"Have you spoken to Gary about how you're missing Sarah?" asked Carly.

Ian shook his head. "We've never been all that close really", admitted Ian. "I was always better friends with Rob than I was to Gary, but I wasn't impressed when he started seeing that other girl behind your back. He changed then - he wasn't acting like himself. It was as though he was a different person."

Carly shuffled uncomfortably. She didn't really want to think about the fact that Rob had cheated on her.

"Sorry", said Ian. "That was a stupid thing to say. I wasn't thinking. I shouldn't have brought it up."

"That's ok," replied Carly, "but I admit I'd prefer not to think about it". She cleared her throat. "You say you're not that close to Gary, but you seem closer to him than you are to me, if you don't mind me saying so, yet you've just told me about Sarah."

"I know", said Ian, blushing slightly. "I actually don't know why I told you all that. You're a good listener I guess."

Carly smiled. "Well I'm here any time you want to talk."

"Thanks", said Ian.

Carly looked up at the clock again. Nearly five o'clock. Kyle and Gary still weren't back yet. She was beginning to feel very anxious about them. She admitted this to Ian.

"Kyle knows that forest pretty well," reassured Ian, "and he has had to avoid hunters before. Don't forget, he has been a werewolf now for quite a long time. I'm sure they're alright. He knows what he's doing."

Carly nodded, feeling only the very slightest bit reassured. "I just wish I knew where they are", she said.

"Why don't you go and get something to eat? You must be absolutely starving", said Ian. "Have you eaten anything today?"

Carly shook her head.

"Shit you're gonna start spacing out soon if you don't eat some meat! Go on, go and catch a squirrel or something."

Ian was right and Carly knew it. She had already started to feel very light-headed and she had started wondering how it was that a hallucination had not already crept up on her. She felt the grumble of her stomach as it protested about its emptiness. Carly decided it would be very foolish to ignore it for much longer. "Okay", she said giving him a gentle pat on the hand. "I'm going. Do you want me to bring you anything?"

"Bit of meat would be lovely", he said. "I've already had some earlier, but…"

"But more is always welcome?" finished Carly with a laugh. "You got it. Meat coming right up." She left the room and headed to the outskirts of the reservation where the houses met the trees. It didn't take her too long before she had been successful in catching a rabbit and a squirrel. She swiftly broke their necks and ate the rabbit greedily. It was so delicious and tender - much nicer than the cooked meat she had been forced to eat twice yesterday. She couldn't imagine a time when raw meat would have seemed unappealing to her, though she remembered when this was the case. She was a different person then; the world no longer seemed the same.

When she had eaten her fill she picked the squirrel back up and walked back towards the reservation and to the room where Ian was. She went in and handed him the squirrel. "One freshly caught squirrel!" she announced; then she noticed that Ian had a tray on his lap and was eating something that looked like stew. "Oh", said Carly, feeling a little flat. "You're eating dinner."

Ian grinned at her. "Yes I am, but I'm still going to need raw meat. That squirrel looks great, thanks so much."

Carly smiled back and handed it to him. Putting down his knife and fork and leaving his stew for a few minutes, Ian bit into the little creature and ate it remarkably neatly considering he was tearing it apart with his teeth. Carly watched fascinated as he nibbled on its legs as though he was skilled in the art of fine dining.

Just then, Ian's bedroom door slammed open. In trooped Kyle and Gary. Both were sweating and looked tired.

"You're back!" exclaimed Ian and Carly simultaneously. Carly felt a strong urge to say 'jynx' at this point, as she would have done when she had been about eight years old, but realised that was ridiculous so she didn't.

Gary sat down on a chair at the foot of Ian's bed. Kyle, looking around but finding nowhere to sit, sank down on the floor. "Could use a drink", said Kyle, panting slightly. Ian handed him his cup of water from his tray and Kyle drank it dry. "Thanks", he said, handing it back.

"Where have you been? Did you find Devon?" asked Carly.

"We looked all over", said Gary. "We covered a fair chunk of the forest but we couldn't find him."

"The forest is huge though. We're will have to look again tomorrow", said Kyle. "At least we didn't find his body, so that's something!"

Carly shuddered. "That's not a nice thought", she said. "Has it occurred to you that he might be with the other pack?"

Kyle's eyes narrowed. "Yes I had thought of that", he said. "We didn't find the other pack either as it happens." He sighed. "The thing is that until we know for sure he's safe, even if he's with the other pack we can't really stop looking for him. We're his pack as far as I'm concerned; we have a duty to make sure he's safe. He hasn't told us that he's leaving our pack so we have to assume he's still with us. We don't know what he's doing with the other pack and we don't know what Seth is doing either."

"Isn't it really Seth who has a duty to make sure that he's safe?" asked Carly. "Come to mention it, Seth has a duty to make sure that we're all safe, doesn't he? Yet I don't see him here."

"Yeah, well…" Kyle tailed off mid-sentence. "We'll carry on looking for Devon tomorrow. Right now I'm starving and kind of tired. This week has been hectic."

"You can say that again", agreed Gary.

"Have you both had dinner?" asked Kyle, looking at both Carly and Ian.

Ian held up his tray. "Stew today", he announced. "Oh and Carly very kindly just caught a squirrel for me."

"What about you Carly? Have you eaten?"

"I caught a rabbit but that's all I've had today."

"All you've had the entire day?"

"I got up quite late", said Carly feeling quite sheepish. Really, she had been shocked at what time she had woken up. She felt as though she had committed the deadly sin of sloth, it had been so late in the day!

"Well shall the three of us go to the dining room and see if there's any stew left?" asked Kyle. "You don't mind do you Ian?"

"No no, you guys go and get some dinner. The stew isn't bad actually", said Ian, taking a large forkful of it from the bowl on his tray.

Carly followed Kyle and Gary to the dining area where John and two other Native Americans were clearing away the large tureen of stew that was standing on a table near the cutlery baskets.

"Oh, erm, excuse me", said Kyle. They turned to look at him as he spoke. "I'm sorry, but would you mind if we had some stew before you tidy it away?" he asked.

John muttered something under his breath about how he would never have dreamed of arriving late to dinner when he was a young man, but he put the tureen back down on the table. "Go on then", he said, sounding a little grumpy.

"Thank you so much", said Carly. She walked to him and put her hand on his back. "Your food is so delicious, we really appreciate it." She knew she was sucking up to him slightly but she did genuinely like the old man, even if his steaks left a lot to be desired. She didn't want to offend him in any way. Thankfully, John seemed appeased by her praise of his culinary talents and he smiled back broadly, then left them to serve themselves.

After a delicious stew (and having helped themselves to seconds, or in Gary's case thirds, for Ian had been right, the stew was quite tasty), Carly was roped into performing a fair number of household chores in the reservation. She had offered her services to Olivia who had happily accepted and set her to work sewing and mending clothes. Carly hadn't liked to confess that she was quite terrible at sewing. She felt she ought to be helping the Native Americans and earning their keep, so she did the best she could at mending tears in trousers and sewing patches onto frayed material.

"Ouch!" she exclaimed for the third time as the needle pricked her finger. Olivia looked up from her sewing; she was sitting in a rocking chair opposite Carly. They were both in a large room littered with all manner of textiles, for the Native Americans were, as they explained to her, quite self sufficient in many ways. They made their own clothes a lot of the time, grew their own vegetables and fished in the nearby lakes, streams and rivers. They liked to save money wherever possible so mending clothes was quite normal. Carly found this unusual. She had been brought up in quite a throw-away society, where trousers with holes in would be quickly replaced by new store-bought trousers rather than any attempt made at mending them. She found this new way of thinking made her better appreciate everything she had had in her life more than she had done before.

"Are you okay?" asked Olivia.

"Yeah, fine", said Carly, struggling with the material that kept slipping off her knee.

Olivia laughed. "You're giving it a good try I can see that, but maybe you should head off to bed now. It's getting late and you must be tired." Carly could tell that this was Olivia's tactful way of sparing Carly from destroying any more garments with her absolutely appalling needlework.

Carly wasn't tired in the slightest but she was far too ashamed to admit that she had slept until mid afternoon. She didn't want to seem lazy. "I'm alright for the time being", she said instead. "I'd really like to help if you have anything else you would prefer me to do."

Olivia wrinkled her forehead and appeared to be thinking. "You could go to see if Pat has anything that needs doing", she suggested. "Our house is just next to the dining area, on the right, with the green door."

Carly decided to take her advice; she figured it was polite to at least ask him. Keeping busy made her feel less useless. She walked in the direction Olivia had instructed her, towards the dining area. She easily saw the house with the green door to the right of it. She had never been inside it before; indeed she had not dared to venture into any of the buildings aside from her dormitory and bathroom, Ian's room, the dining area and this evening the textiles room with Olivia, for the simple reason that she had no idea where exactly the hunter was staying. She had no desire to bump into him inadvertently.

She knocked on the green door and Pat opened it. "Hello," he greeted her, "what can I do for you?"

"I was just wondering if there were any chores you had that need doing? Olivia told me to ask you. I've been sewing with her but I'm afraid I'm not very good at it."

Pat laughed. "I do not have anything that needs doing. You are welcome to come in and talk if you prefer."

Carly couldn't see why not. 'A sit down and a chat will pass the time at least', she thought.

"Where are your friends?" asked Pat.

Carly didn't actually know where they had gone. They had wandered off somewhere after dinner but it was possible that they were with Ian. She told Pat this and he nodded.

"I see", he said. "Leaving the woman to do all the work!" he tutted, but he had a smile on his face showing Carly he was only jesting with her. "Come and have a seat", he said. He ushered her into the cosy inviting living room. The house had a very rustic and warm feel about it which Carly found immensely comforting. She sat down in an oversized brown armchair and marvelled at how soft and comfortable it was. An antique looking mahogany sideboard to the side of her caught her eye. She turned her head to look at it. There were framed photographs all along the sideboard - some of Olivia and Pat, some of them with some other Native Americans, presumably their friends and family, but one in particular caught Carly's eye. It was a small photograph in a silver frame of Pat standing next to a man. Carly peered at it curiously; the man next to Pat seemed awfully familiar. She racked her brains trying to think where she had seen him before.

"That's Richard", said Pat, making her jump. "He was my best friend."

"Was?" asked Carly, still trying hard to recollect the man's face.

"He is dead now," said Pat, sounding a little sad, "around fourteen years ago. I found the body myself. He was a werewolf like yourself actually."

Suddenly, that was it! It was as though a bolt of lightning had struck Carly and she instantly knew where she had seen the man before - in the photograph that had fallen out of Kyle's wallet. Richard was Kyle and Seth's father! She gasped sharply; she hadn't meant to but it came out involuntarily.

"What?" exclaimed Pat. "What is it?"

Carly didn't know what to say. She didn't want to blurt out to Pat that his best friend's son was here, not without speaking to Kyle about it first. She struggled to stand up from the soft armchair, then hastily excused herself and told Pat she would be back in a few minutes. She ran as fast as she could out of the house, leaving a very baffled looking Pat standing gaping after her scratching his head.

Carly raced over to Ian's room and barged in without knocking. Sure enough Gary and Kyle were there with him; they appeared to be playing a game of cards and they looked up as she entered the

238 - N. Gosney

room.

"Kyle...I...gotta..." she gasped, trying to get her words out.

"Woah, slow down", said Kyle.

Carly forced herself to stand still and to slow her breathing down. After a couple of moments her heart rate returned to normal and she had stopped panting. "I need to speak to you about something", said Carly to Kyle. "It's really important."

Kyle shot an apologetic shrug at Ian and Gary and put his cards face down on the floor in front of him. "No cheating", he said with a grin. He stood up and followed Carly out of the room. "What's up?" he whispered as soon as they were alone.

"I didn't know whether you would want Ian and Gary to know this just yet", whispered back Carly. A knot began to form in her stomach. It had only just hit her that she had to tell him his father was dead. How do you go about breaking something like that to somebody? Carly certainly didn't know. It wasn't something she had had to do before and it wasn't something she wanted to do now!

"Know what?" asked Kyle.

"I've got some bad news", said Carly. "You may want to sit down for this."

"Oh my God! Is it Seth? Is it Devon? Are they alive? What's happened?"

"It's not Seth or Devon", said Carly. "It's about your dad."

"My dad?" said Kyle in a shocked tone. "What about him?"

"He's...he's dead."

Kyle's mouth dropped open. He stared at Carly with a look of horror in his eyes. "How do you know that?" he asked at last.

"I was in Pat's house and there's a photograph of them both on his sideboard. He said that Richard was his best friend and that he has been dead for about fourteen years."

Kyle brought his hand up to his mouth and shook his head. He didn't say anything but looked as though he might fall over. Carly put her arm around him to steady him.

"I'm so sorry Kyle", she said. She felt terrible. She could tell that what she had told him had hit him badly.

"Kyle cleared his throat and brought his hand back down. He had a semi-vacant expression now as though he had retreated a little within himself. His eyes were wide and there were no tears in sight. His bottom lip was not wobbling but his voice when he next spoke was trembling. "Did Pat say how my dad died?" he asked at last quietly.

"No, I didn't get as far as to asking him that", she replied. "I just ran straight over here to tell you."

"I guess that explains why he disappeared before I had my first lunar change", said Kyle. "I thought he had just walked out on us and abandoned the family but he didn't, did he?" It sounded like a rhetorical question so Carly didn't answer it.

"Do you want to come and have a talk to Pat about it? He might have more answers for you", suggested Carly.

Kyle nodded blankly still seeming in shock. Carly took his hand and led him over to Pat's house. She knocked on the door and Pat opened it.

"Where did you run off to?" he asked. "Was something the matter? You looked as though you had seen a ghost."

"Can we come in?" asked Carly. "There's something we need to tell you and things we need to ask you about."

"Very cryptic", said Pat. "Yes sure, come in."

Carly and Kyle entered the house. Carly sat down. Kyle didn't though; he just stood in the living room. His gaze was aimed in the direction of the photograph on the sideboard of Pat and Richard. He stared at it as though he could not take his eyes off it.

"This has got something to do with Richard, hasn't it?" asked Pat. He walked over to the sideboard and picked up the photograph. "You know," he said thoughtfully, "Richard looked a lot like..." he looked up at Kyle and realisation spread across his face. "Oh...wow", he said aloud. "You are the son of Richard!"

"Yes", replied Kyle. His voice was flat and devoid of emotion.

"Oh my poor boy! You did not know your father was dead?"

Kyle didn't move. Pat ushered him over to a chair and Kyle sat down in it quite stiffly. "How did he die?" asked Kyle.

"Umm..." said Pat. "He was shot..." Carly could hear in Pat's voice he wasn't telling the whole truth about what had happened. Apparently Kyle could hear that too.

"What aren't you telling me?" he asked sharply. "You're holding something back."

"I am not sure now is the right time to…" began Pat, but Kyle growled.

"I want to know. I need to know", he said angrily. Then he caught himself and his frown softened. "I'm sorry", he said. "Please tell me, I can take it. I just need to know what happened to him."

Pat sighed. "I had arranged to meet up with him for a chat and a drink", said Pat, "he was supposed to be coming to my house but he did not show up. I assumed he was busy. A few hours later I went into the forest to head for the river where I intended to catch some fish. I stumbled upon his body. He had been shot with a silver bullet laced with aconite. He had been…"

"He had been what?" demanded Kyle.

"Skinned", mumbled Pat.

You could have heard a pin drop. Carly couldn't believe what Pat had just said. She looked over at Kyle and he was as white as a sheet. He stared at Pat with his eyes as round as saucers. Finally he whispered "which way is your bathroom?"

Pat pointed to a door. Kyle walked slowly towards it as though he was a zombie. He opened it, went through it and closed it behind him. Then Carly heard terrible retching sounds coming from behind the door. Both she and Pat waited in silence.

Eventually Kyle emerged from the bathroom. He leant against the doorframe seeming in need of support. Carly got up and walked over to him. She couldn't even begin to empathise with how he was feeling nor did she particularly ever want to experience anything as horrific as that. She put her arms around his waist and pulled him towards her for a hug. "Are you going to be okay?" she asked. Kyle shrugged.

"Come, sit back down. I will get you some water", called Pat. Kyle nodded, headed over to an armchair and sat down. Carly perched next to him on the arm of the chair and put her arm around his shoulder. He took her hand and looked at her gratefully.

Pat stood up, left the room and returned with a glass of water for Kyle. He drank it rapidly." I am sorry, I have nothing stronger", said Pat.

"That's ok, thanks", said Kyle clearing his throat. His voice sounded hollow to Carly's ears.

"I think maybe we should continue this conversation another day. You have suffered a huge shock Kyle. I am not sure we should talk about this any further this evening."

"No, please, I need to know everything", insisted Kyle. "Who did this to him?"

"I do not know", admitted Pat. "At the time I thought it may have been hunters, but over the years I have become less and less sure of that. It is not like hunters to skin werewolves."

"A hunting trophy perhaps?" suggested Carly.

Pat shook his head. "This would be unusual. Hunters who hunt for sport, moose or deer perhaps, then yes, but werewolf hunters generally have their own agenda for hunting. It is not often for sport."

"Then who...?" Carly tailed off as a thought entered her mind. She looked at Kyle. As their eyes met she could see that the exact same thought had just occurred to him also.

"Seth", they said in unison.

"It can't be", groaned Kyle, hanging his head in despair. "No, I don't believe it; I can't believe it. He wouldn't...he couldn't!"

Carly wished with all her heart that they hadn't found Richard's jacket in Seth's wardrobe but the evidence spoke for itself.

"Who is Seth?" asked Pat.

"My eldest brother," said Kyle, "our pack leader".

"You think your brother did this?"

"We found their dad's jacket in Seth's wardrobe", explained Carly. "It had some very tiny old faint spots of blood on it."

"Why would he do this?" wailed Kyle. He was sobbing now quite openly. Carly tightened her squeeze around his shoulders and he clung to her arm as he cried.

"Skinwalkers are the only people I can think of who would skin a werewolf", said Pat. "They use pelts of animals to transform themselves into that creature, at least superficially."

Kyle's sobs subsided slightly and he looked up at Pat. "We think Seth is involved with some skinwalkers", he said, sniffing and wiping at his eyes with his arm. Pat passed him a Kleenex.

"Are you sure?" asked Pat. "They are dangerous, extremely dangerous. Your brother could be in danger if he is mixed up with skinwalkers."

"We're not completely sure," admitted Carly, "but it's a very strong likelihood".

"Why did he kill our dad though?" asked Kyle despairingly, tears falling from his eyes. "Why not kill another werewolf? Why our dad?!"

"I don't know", said Carly. "Maybe there weren't any others werewolves in the area and some of the skinwalkers needed pelts?"

"He'd sacrifice our own dad to help the skinwalkers? I just can't believe it!"

"I do not think you will get the answers you are looking for by sitting here and dwelling on it", said Pat. "I wish I knew what to tell you. Your father was the closest friend I ever had."

"How come we never saw you come to the house?" asked Kyle. "If you were his best friend, wouldn't we have met you?"

"Your father and I had many discussions that would not have been appropriate for you to hear at the time", said Pat. "He had fears for his children in the future. He did not know if you would handle becoming werewolves. He loved you very much and did not like keeping things from you, but it was not yet time for you to learn about what your father was. You may have been afraid and might not have understood. If I had come to your house he would not have been able to speak freely with me."

"So when was he going to tell me?"

"He was waiting for you in turn to reach the age of your first lunar change. He planned to take you under his wing once that happened. Unfortunately he died, presumably before learning that you had changed."

"He left a few years before my first lunar change", remembered Kyle. "He went out and just never came back."

"I am sorry Kyle", said Pat. "It must have been hard for you to go through your change without the guidance of your father."

Kyle nodded. "I lost my sister the day I changed", he said. He looked so upset. Carly's heart felt as though it was physically aching for him.

"What happened to your sister?" asked Pat.

Kyle seemed choked. "I…" he stuttered. He shook his head and couldn't finish what he was saying.

"Kyle accidentally killed his younger sister during his first lunar change", filled in Carly.

"Oh I am so sorry Kyle, that is a heavy burden you carry", said Pat softly. He sat and thought for a few moments. "Listen, I think you both should get some rest now. Kyle, I am so sorry about everything you have learned tonight. You should know that all hurts heal in time, but for now I just want to offer you my condolences. His spirit did not die though. Take comfort in it."

Kyle didn't really seem to have taken in what Pat said. His focus had gone and his eyes were listless. Carly helped him to his feet, bade Pat goodnight and guided Kyle out of the door. They walked across the courtyard and towards the dormitory. Inside they found Gary who was lounging on his bed reading a book. "Ian was tired so I thought I'd read for a while", he said. "What happened to you two?"

Carly shook her head at Gary indicating that he shouldn't ask too many questions. Gary nodded understandingly and quietly wished them goodnight. He had obviously noticed Kyle's sombre expression and knew better than to pry.

Carly gave Kyle a hug again and he laid his head on her shoulder. "Goodnight Kyle", she whispered. "I'll be right here in the next bed if you need anything."

Kyle softly kissed her shoulder and hugged her back. "Thank you", he whispered back. Then he let her go and climbed into his bed fully dressed and closed his eyes. As Carly watched, a single tear crept out from underneath his eyelids and trickled down his face.

Carly didn't know what to do to help him. Really there was

nothing that could possibly ease his pain at the moment. If she had a magic wand she would gladly have waved it to take away his suffering. In a single night his brother had betrayed him in the worst possible way and he had lost his father. Granted, it might have been many years since his father had been killed, but that didn't mean the hurt that Kyle felt inside was any less real than if the murder had taken place yesterday. All these years Kyle had believed his father had abandoned him just when he had needed him the most; he had been trying to hate him for the past fourteen years. Now, to find that his father hadn't left after all must be indescribably difficult to deal with.

Carly picked up her pyjamas and headed into the bathroom to get washed, changed and ready for bed. It didn't take her very long and she soon quietly padded across the rugs in the dormitory to her bed. Gary had stopped reading his book now and appeared to be asleep. Carly flicked off the light switch and lay down on her bed. Thoughts of their previous conversation with Pat swirled around in her mind. She couldn't shake the feeling of needing to know what had driven Seth to kill his father - a man who apparently had done nothing wrong within his family previously.

CHAPTER TWELVE

After lying awake for about half an hour, Carly drifted naturally into a disturbed sleep. At first it was filled with nightmares about being skinned alive and being chased through the forest by hunters and skinwalkers. Later in the night she woke up suddenly and realised she was once again having a vision through another person's eyes.

It was dark. Carly looked down at her scuffed black trainers. She recognised the trainers but still wasn't sure who she was. 'Who am I?' thought the part of her that was still detached from the body she had found herself in. She was sitting inside a tent on her own waiting for something to happen…but what?

Suddenly she remembered. She was waiting for Seth to give the signal that they were to make their move toward the Native American reservation. When she had arrived at the pack's camp earlier that day she had told Seth what she had overheard at the reservation. Upon hearing that the others now knew about Seth being part of the other pack and that they had mentioned the word skinwalkers, Seth had indicated that they were not going to hesitate any longer with capturing Kyle.

"If he knows about us then our initial plan of trying to lure him back to the camp isn't going to work", Seth had said. "He won't come willingly if he no longer trusts me."

"So what do you propose we do?" another man named Oscar had piped up.

"Tonight, before he has a chance to talk to any of those Indians and figures out any more about us, we have to go there and get him. We can't afford for him to leave. We don't want to be chasing around the forest looking for him. We need him ready for the ceremony."

So here she was now just waiting with anticipation for Seth to announce that they were ready to leave. The rest of the pack were eager to be off but Carly (who had now figured out that she was in fact Devon owing to various thoughts rattling around in his mind which were pretty transparent), felt a slight sense of nervousness knotted inside his stomach. Devon didn't know what was wrong but he had a feeling that something was amiss. He had begun to question how much he could trust Seth despite being essentially his right hand man. He was so quick to sell out his own brother. That made Devon uncomfortable as it indicated a level of selfishness that led him to wonder if Seth was truly looking out for the well-being of his followers.

Regardless of that Devon was eager for the full moon to take place. Seth had promised that his monthly curse would be lifted if he took part in the ceremony. There was nothing Devon wanted more than to be free of the burning pain, memory loss and lack of control that came every time the moon was full.

"Just imagine - you'll have the power of the beast and it will be harnessed. No longer will you be a slave to the actions of the creature. No longer just a puppet unable to take control. You will be at one with the beast! It will be painless and you will be strong. You'll remember everything you have done and you will be so powerful." Seth had said. Devon had thought that sounded fantastic and had readily agreed to help his best friend with the preparations for the full moon.

As Carly (entwined with Devon's mind) was pondering all of this, she heard rustling coming from outside the tent. The zip opened and Seth stuck his head through the hole. "Come on then", he said and promptly disappeared again. Carly clambered out of the tent and looked around. An army of animals had begun to form just on the outskirts of the camp. There were several werewolves but Carly could also see bears, grey wolves (which were notably smaller than their werewolf counterparts) and even a few bald eagles circling the group overhead. As Carly peered closely she could make out various different venomous snakes draped along the branches of trees near the group.

In a way Carly was surprised to see so many different types of creatures. Even Devon had only ever seen the group in werewolf or human form but then it occurred to her that many members of the pack never changed from human to werewolf, generally because they did not have their own werewolf pelt. Skinwalkers can only change into a certain creature if they own that type of pelt. For an attack on the Native American reservation to be successful, Seth needed an army big enough and strong enough. The Native Americans were plentiful in number, not to mention that there were four werewolves there in the way of Kyle, Carly, Gary and Ian. The hunter at the reservation could also be a problem, though which side he would choose to fight for in a battle scenario was anybody's guess. Clearly the members of this pack who did not have werewolf skins to wear had resorted to turning into other creatures. Humans are not the strongest form to be when fighting!

Carly, now in Devon's body, gave herself a shake and promptly turned into a very large black wolf as she had seen him do many times before. Devon was not a skinwalker and did not have to resort to wearing skins to change form as they did. She headed towards the group and found Seth still in human form giving instructions to the rest of the pack. He greeted Devon with a smile as he approached him. "Are you all set?" he asked. Devon nodded his head. "Great", said Seth. "Just think, in just two nights' time we'll reap the rewards of all this!" Carly didn't move and Seth took Devon's silence positively. "Right - our objective is to bring my brother Kyle back here alive. I cannot stress to you how important that is. Everybody else at the reservation is disposable."

A chorus of animal noises cheered Seth who swiftly turned into a werewolf. His outer garments ripped and fell off his back. Throwing back his head he howled loudly and began running through the forest. Carly and the other animals followed behind.

Carly woke with a start panting furiously. Sweat poured from her. "Oh my God!" she said aloud, and dived out of bed. She knew there wasn't a moment to lose. Fumbling in the darkness she flicked on the light. Gary and Kyle were fast asleep, and several other Native Americans were asleep in their single dorm beds around the room. "WAKE UP!" she yelled as loudly as she could. Instantly everybody in the room bolted upright.

"Carly, what the fuck?!" exclaimed Gary. "You've nearly given me a heart attack!"

Several of the Native Americans were looking stunned. Almost everybody was squinting, shielding their eyes from the light with their hands.

"I've just had a vision", she announced. (At this point she couldn't have been less bothered whether everybody knew about her visions or not).

"I take it this vision was important enough for you to wake us all up so dramatically at…" Kyle looked down at his wrist for a non-existent watch, "…at this ungodly hour!"

"Devon must have been eavesdropping on us the other day when we were telling Gary and Ian about Seth being part of the other pack", gasped Carly, her words tumbling over each other in her desperate attempt to fill them in as quickly as possible. "He went back to the other pack. He told him that we know about them. Seth and the rest of the pack have decided to come here and kidnap you!"

"Kidnap *me*?" squawked Kyle in astonishment. "Why do they want me?"

"Hell Kyle I don't know!" said Carly in frustration. "They are on their way right now!"

"Oh God," muttered Gary, "this is seriously not good".

"That's not all", continued Carly, "pretty much the whole pack is made up of skinwalkers. It's a huge pack. They're coming as all different animals - bears, wolves, werewolves, eagles, snakes…there are loads of them!"

"Well we don't stand a chance then", said Gary.

"We must tell Pat", piped up a Native American boy who couldn't have been older than about fifteen who had been listening attentively. "I'll do that." The boy had already pulled on his clothes and was half-way across the room.

"Tell him we need his help", said Kyle. "We can't fight them alone."

The boy nodded and ran off as quickly as he could. It didn't take long for everybody in the reservation to get dressed and assemble in the dining area. This was the only place in the reservation large enough to hold everybody together at the same time. The only notable absence was the hunter who had presumably not been informed about what was about to happen. Even Ian was present, his shoulder well bandaged (though he insisted that it barely hurt at all now). Pat and Kyle were both standing on chairs at one end of the room so that they could be seen. Carly could hear ripples of fragmented discussion about skinwalkers and werewolves floating through the crowd. When Pat held up his arm the room fell silent.

"Some of you may not actually know quite what is going on here", announced Pat in a loud voice. "I shall briefly fill you in, for we do not have a great deal of time. Our friends, Kyle, Carly, Gary and Ian, need our help. I do not need to point out what you already know about them, but there is an army of skinwalkers coming, apparently with the aim of capturing Kyle. As of yet we do not know what they plan to do with him, but it is clear that they must be protected. We have always been friends and loyal allies of the werewolves. We must help them fight against this enemy. If anybody wishes to leave they are free to do so now, but know this… if you leave, you abandon our teachings and our beliefs. You will not be welcome back at the reservation." Pat paused for dramatic effect and looked around the room. Nobody moved, nobody left. Carly allowed herself to exhale as she realised the Native Americans were indeed going to help them fight the skinwalkers.

The Native Americans remained in the dining area for a while after that, planning their defences and discussing amongst themselves what their strategy should be. Pat took Kyle, Carly, Gary and Ian aside to talk to them.

"I think I need filling in a bit more here on everything you know", said Pat. "I know we discussed this earlier, but you had a vision Carly…what was it about?"

Carly relayed everything she had seen in her vision. Gary and Ian in particular listened intently. They had not yet even been informed that Kyle and Carly had discovered that Kyle's father was dead so they needed a fair amount of catching up. Their mouths dropped open when they heard about everything Kyle and Carly knew.

"Oh God Kyle, I'm so sorry buddy", said Gary. Ian expressed his condolences also.

Kyle thanked them but also shrugged off any grief that he might be feeling. "We don't really have time for me to feel sad right now!" he said solemnly. "Unfortunately we have bigger problems on our hands."

"I still don't understand why they are coming for you Kyle", said Ian. "You say that the skinwalkers are after the wolf born. Seth is the wolf born though so what use are you to them?"

"Well, Seth isn't the only person who was born from a werewolf", pointed out Gary. "Maybe they need another person who was wolf born."

"But Seth is older than I am", puzzled Kyle. "He's the natural leader so by default he's the most likely choice."

"But if he's orchestrating this ceremony he's hardly going to use himself as the wolf born", said Carly. "So maybe they're settling for you?"

"What is this ceremony for anyway?" asked Ian.

"It's going to rid the werewolves in the group of the pain and lack of control that happens during the lunar changes", said Carly. "At least, that's what I learned from my vision when I was inside Devon's mind."

"What good is that to the skinwalkers?" asked Gary. "From what I gather, that pack is made up of a large majority of skinwalkers. The number of werewolves in the pack is few, am I right?"

"Yes, I believe so", said Carly. "In fact I'd hazard a guess that Seth and Devon are probably the only werewolves there."

"Exactly," said Gary, "so why is it beneficial to the skinwalkers to do this ceremony? Surely it's only beneficial to Seth and Devon?"

Pat, who had been sitting quietly during this conversation, now piped up. "This particular upcoming full moon is actually one of the rarer full moons we shall see for a long time. There is going to be a lunar eclipse, but even more importantly, it coincides with the heliacal rising of Sirius, the Wolf Star."

"Wow", said Carly, "I take it that doesn't happen very often?"

"No, it does not," confirmed Pat, "a lunar eclipse at the same time as the heliacal rising of Sirius is a rare occurence".

"So does that actually tell us how the skinwalkers benefit from this ceremony?"

"No," admitted Pat, "nor does it tell us what the ceremony will involve, though we know it has something to do with Kyle. At least it gives us a reason why they have chosen to do it on this particular full moon rather than any other. Sirius is the star which governs over all dogs and wolves, so it has special links with werewolves also."

Gary sighed. "That's not really a great help to us though", he said. "Do you have any writings about skinwalkers that might tell us about their rituals or ceremonies? Something that can give us a better idea about what we're dealing with?"

Pat shook his head. "We do not like to speak about skinwalkers", he admitted. "I have never spoken of them so much in my entire life as I have done in the past few days. It makes me nervous I must say. We do not keep any books about them here, no, though many have written about them in the past. Those books would probably be in libraries I should imagine or posted on the Internet for the world to read about. Skinwalkers are dangerous creatures. We want no association with them here."

"Unfortunately we're going to be associated with them here all too soon", said Ian with a touch of irony. Pat visibly winced at the thought.

A man in his late twenties rushed up to Pat and interrupted their conversation. "They've been spotted about twenty minutes from here", he said breathlessly.

Pat stood up sharply. "Right", he said. He clambered onto his chair again, turned to face the rest of the room and waved his arms in the air. "Grab your weapons, they are nearly here!"

Gasps and shouts emerged from several people. A scuffle of noise and motion broke out as everybody fumbled for weapons they had prepared previously. Some had guns, some had bows and

252 - N. Gosney

some had crossbows. All the arrows and bullets, explained Pat, were laced with white ash. This would be as fatal to a skinwalker as aconite is to a werewolf.

Carly herself had been given a small gun by Pat. "Do you know how to use it?" he had asked her. She had shaken her head. "Just point and shoot!" he instructed.

Carly wasn't sure that she would be much good at pointing and shooting but she didn't exactly have time for a firearms lesson. She took the gun and vowed to be careful not to accidentally shoot an ally with it. Kyle did not have a weapon at all. He was, of course, going to be in werewolf form during the battle. Gary and Ian both had guns like Carly.

In single file everybody left the dining area and assembled just on the outskirts of the reservation. They formed several defence lines with Kyle and Pat heading the front of the group. "Do you think somebody ought to tell the hunter about all this?" hissed Gary to nobody in particular.

"Quinn needs to rest", said Pat. "He was badly hurt during the last fight he was in. He is not a werewolf like you four - it will take him much longer to heal. He has broken ribs."

"He's going to hear all this commotion though, surely", pondered Carly out loud. She didn't have time to say any more, for the distant sound of branches breaking and leaves rustling came to her ears. She looked at the Native Americans and realised they couldn't yet hear what she could hear. Carly breathed in a deep intake of air. The smell of various animals wafted into her nostrils. "They're coming", she whispered. Carly wasn't sure she had ever been quite as petrified. She wondered if this was how ancient knights must have felt when facing an army of enemies or whether they were just full of bravery and valour. Carly felt far from brave. 'Then again', she reasoned, 'I'm not a knight either'. The waiting was churning her stomach, waiting for something to happen - for that first attack to take place. "Do we charge at them or just stand here until they approach?" she muttered to Kyle.

He didn't look as though he knew though. "We should stand defensively", he said.

"Maybe they'll want to negotiate", said Ian hopefully.

Pat raised an eyebrow. "Skinwalkers? Negotiate?" he scoffed. "That is not going to happen."

Suddenly out of the trees a huge black wolf emerged. It was Seth. Behind him slowly walked his army of skinwalkers with Devon at the front, also in wolf form. Upon seeing the group of Native Americans behind the werewolves, Seth took a few steps backwards. For a brief moment Carly wondered if the size of their group had put Seth off fighting, but then he threw back his head and howled. Kyle instantly turned into a wolf beside her, his clothes falling in ribbons to the floor.

Animals of all shapes and sizes rushed past Seth and ran straight towards Carly and the rest of their group. "Oh my..." gasped Carly. She screamed as a huge bear lunged towards her.

"Carly!" shouted Ian. He barrelled into the side of her, knocking her away from the bear. Carly hit the ground with a groan. She looked up just in time to see the bear's massive paws lifting into the air, ready to bring them down with claws outstretched onto Ian's head.

"BANG!" Carly heard a gunshot very close to her. She had shot the bear. At first she hadn't even realised it had been her shot; the way she had reacted had been instinctive. Gone was the bear. In its place was a man lying dead at the side of her. A bear pelt was draped over him, trailing on the ground. "Shit, I must have hit him in the heart!" she muttered aloud.

A growl from behind her made her spin around quickly. A grey wolf had bitten the leg of a Native American woman who was now screaming and clubbing it around the head frantically. Carly didn't hesitate and shot the wolf directly in the head. As she did so though, she felt the wind being knocked out of her as another wolf barrelled directly into her stomach. Her gun was thrown from her hand and she felt the wolf clamp down on the first bit of flesh it came to, which happened to be her arm.

The searing pain coursed up her arm causing Carly to scream involuntarily. Tears sprang to her eyes. She reached out with the other arm trying to prise the wolf's jaws away from her. Suddenly,

254 - N. Gosney

another wolf shot into view. Carly screamed again thinking this was the end for her. She wouldn't be able to tackle two wolves, she was certain of that. But this wolf didn't attack her. Instead it lunged for the throat of the wolf that was still clinging to her arm. In that instant Carly realised it was Kyle.

The wolf let go of Carly's arm and let out a whine of pain. It thrashed and growled and lashed out with its paws, but Kyle clung fast to its neck, sinking his teeth in deeper. Kyle, being a werewolf, had the advantage of size and strength but the smaller grey wolf wasn't making it easy for him. Carly looked down to the ground, spotted a large stick, and grabbed it. She began to smack the wolf on the head and eventually their combined efforts sent the wolf slumping to the ground. Carly assumed it must be dying as it wasn't moving, though it hadn't changed back yet into a man. Carly wondered if it was clinging to its last breaths.

Gunshots were ringing out all around her and Carly whirled around in a daze. So much was going on she didn't know what to do; everything was a blur. From the corner of her eye she caught sight of three eagles swooping down and attacking Gary. He was powerless to do anything to protect himself from them as he was fending off a wolf with a stick. Carly spotted her gun lying on the ground where it had been flung. She dived to get it just as a snake lunged at it with its fangs. Snatching it up she jumped to her feet, kicked at the snake and shot at the wolf in front of Gary. It yelped and limped away. Carly cursed the fact that she hadn't managed to kill it but at least Gary was able now to hit the eagles with his stick and protect himself.

A loud roar behind her made Carly's eyes open wide. The noise was so terrible Carly almost didn't dare turn around. In fact she would not have had the chance to turn for suddenly she felt something very hard smash into her back. The sheer force knocked her to the ground. She felt as though the skin had been torn from her back. She writhed in agony face down on the forest floor. Then another roar from above her sent shivers down her spine. She tried to get up, but in vain, and fell back down. The force of her own impact against the ground shot through her body. She groaned loudly. She propped her torso up with her arms and began to drag herself slowly on her belly. She was still fearfully anticipating another attack from the creature when gunshots behind her head half-deafened her. The ground shook as a huge bear fell next to her. Blood was pouring from its head. It magically changed back into a man before her eyes and the bear pelt he had used for his skinwalker appearance altering spell slipped off him exposing his naked body.

"Carly", said a voice. It was Pat; he stooped to take her arms and help her to her feet. Carly could see a huge gash across his face from where some claw or other must have gouged into him.

"Argh!" cried Carly. At that moment she genuinely thought that her back had been broken. "I can't stand up!" Her own voice sounded strange to her ears. "My back…"

"Can you move your legs?" asked Pat. Carly managed to wiggle her legs a little and nodded. "You'll live then", said Pat. With surprising strength he hoisted her up over his shoulder. Next minute though both Carly and Pat were sent sprawling to the ground as a huge black wolf barreled into them, snarling and growling.

"Seth!" gasped Carly. "Seth, please, don't hurt us; don't do this!"

Seth paid her no heed though and advanced towards them, head down, teeth bared. He pounced. Carly squeezed her eyes shut tightly waiting for the end to come.

BANG! BANG!

The end did not come but rather Seth emitted a small howl. Carly dared to open her eyes. To her amazement there stood the hunter, bandages and all, brandishing a rifle. Seth was no longer in front of them. Carly just managed to catch sight of him disappearing into the battle scene before her.

"Don't just sit there, get up!" the hunter barked sharply at Pat and Carly. Pat quickly stood up, but Carly, despite her best attempts, could not move. Her back felt as though it were on fire.

"She is hurt", said Pat. "We need to move her."

Without saying another word, the hunter took hold of Carly and began to try and haul her up. Pat went around to the other side of her. Together they dragged Carly a little way away from the fighting and propped her up behind a tree out of sight. She felt completely useless just sitting there. "Wait here", said Pat. Then he and the hunter rejoined the combat disappearing into the fray. Tears began to run down Carly's cheeks as despair overcame her. The sounds of the fight raged on behind the tree and Carly knew she couldn't stay where she was. She had to try to get up. She had to try to fight.

Scrabbling in the dirt beside her, Carly found a strong thick stick and picked it up. Clamping it between her teeth, she struggled to her knees. The pain was indescribable and Carly bit down hard on the stick. Sweat was pouring from her forehead. She could hear the groans coming from her own throat, yet they sounded as though they belonged to someone else. Slowly she managed to cover some distance, still on her knees, and emerged from behind the tree.

The scene before her was horrific. A large number of Native Americans were lying dead on the ground, many of them torn to pieces, their entrails hanging out of their guts, some with their throats ripped out. Likewise the corpses of dead skinwalkers were scattered everywhere, their pelts lying beside them. The battle was far from over though. Fighting was still taking place. It was difficult for Carly to see what exactly was going on. It was dark and everyone still standing mingled together, so Carly could not tell who was who. One blurred into the other and Carly could hear the screams of the dying.

As she watched, a figure she recognised came running towards her, hotly pursued by a skinwalker in werewolf form. "Ian!" screamed Carly, dropping the stick from her mouth. "Look out!"

Ian turned to face the werewolf and pointed his gun directly at its head. Carly let out a sigh of relief; he was going to be okay - he was going to shoot the skinwalker. Her relief turned to horror as Ian pulled the trigger; the gun, out of bullets, clicked uselessly. The next few seconds appeared to take place in slow motion. "NO!" Carly wailed. The werewolf's massive paws knocked Ian to the ground and it sank its teeth into his neck. Ian gurgled something incomprehensible. Blood gushed from his mouth and he stopped moving. "Oh God Ian no! Please no!" Carly sobbed uncontrollably as she realised Ian was dead.

The werewolf was still standing over the body but it heard Carly's cries and bounded swiftly towards her. Carly tried to force herself to stand up but her legs buckled. Her hand managed to make contact with a sizeable rock that was on the ground next to the tree and she flung it with all her might at the werewolf. Chance was on her side - it hit the werewolf smartly on the nose. The werewolf yelped as it struck him and he took a few steps backwards. "Take that you fucking skinwalker!" screamed Carly, the adrenaline pumping around her body. She knew she didn't stand a chance against a brute of that size but she figured that if she was going to die she was going to go down fighting. "You're just pathetic, attacking me like this when you're ten times bigger than me. Why not make it a real fight? Show me what you're made of! Take off that skin and fight me properly."

The werewolf looked a little stunned. To Carly's great surprise, he took off his skin and instantly turned back into a human. He dropped the skin on the ground and faced Carly. He looked somewhat younger than Carly, maybe sixteen or seventeen. Ian's blood was smeared across his face and his hair was dirty and dishevelled. "You're female", he said, scorn in his voice. "It wouldn't be a real fight no matter which way you look at it. I'm stronger than you as a human or as a werewolf so it makes no difference. I'm still going to kill you."

"Kill me then", said Carly, trying to sound braver than she felt. "But just so you know, Kyle will never take part in your ceremony."

"What do you know of the ceremony?" asked the guy. "You don't know anything."

"I know everything", bluffed Carly. She wanted to keep him talking as long as possible. If he was talking to her, he wasn't killing her!

"Doesn't matter if you do", said the skinwalker. "Kyle hasn't got any choice in the matter. He's going to be sacrificed and then we're going to have the power of the beast. Even you puny werewolves don't have control over that. The beast controls you, but we will control the beast. You think you're better than us just because we have to wear a skin in order to change, well you won't be thinking that soon." He paused for a moment then grinned. "Not that you'll live to see it happen mind you."

He reached down and picked up the werewolf skin he had been wearing on his back and flung it over his shoulders. He closed his eyes and muttered a few short words in a language Carly had never heard before. Then instantly he had gone - in his place stood a werewolf. He snapped his jaws at Carly and growled menacingly. Carly had only seconds to think about what he had said. The frustration of knowing she would not be able to tell Kyle what the boy had said was too much to bear. 'I'm not going to fucking die like this', her inner voice screamed in her head. She let out a tremendous roar and lurched to her feet. As the werewolf pounced at her she dived out of the way, then swung around and grabbed hold of his back.

The werewolf spun around in circles like a dog trying to catch its own tail, snarling and snapping at Carly as she clung to the fur on his back. She constantly remained just out of reach from his sharp teeth but the pain in her back was so extreme that Carly wondered how long she was going to be able to hold on for. She felt her hands losing their grip. She tumbled to the ground with a thud. She saw the world growing dark around her and knew she was about to pass out. Everything went black. The next thing she knew she was being shaken awake by somebody calling her name. "Carly, Carly, wake up!" It was a woman's voice.

"Olivia?" said Carly blinking. "Am I dead?"

"No you're not, though you would have been if I hadn't shot that skinwalker that was about to take a bite out of you!"

"How long have I been unconscious?"

"Only about two minutes."

Carly shook her head. It seemed longer than two minutes. She felt as though she had had a full nights sleep. "My back hurts", she said, trying to sit up. Olivia took hold of her arms and pulled her to a sitting position. This was agony for Carly but she bravely fought against the pain. Around twenty or thirty metres away from her the fighting was still raging. Everybody was so intent on what they were doing that they were not currently bothering to attack Carly or Olivia. "The skinwalkers are planning to gain the power of the werewolf's beast side", said Carly. She felt as though she needed to tell somebody, even if it was Olivia. If something happened to her and she didn't make it, maybe somebody else like Pat or Kyle could make use of the information. "That's why they are so keen to help Seth with the ceremony."

A slightly confused expression crossed Olivia's face. "I don't know what you mean Carly", she admitted. "Pat and I haven't exactly had time to talk, so much has been going on."

"If something happens to me you must tell Pat what I've said," insisted Carly, "and tell Kyle as well. They have to know."

Olivia nodded and hushed Carly. "I will, but it won't come to that. You can tell them yourself when this is all over."

An eagle flew overhead, heading straight towards the rear of Olivia's head. "Watch out!" yelled Carly, pointing to the sky. Olivia turned around as fast as lightning and whipped out her gun. Pulling the trigger she shot the eagle, which instantly dropped onto the ground. As it hit the floor it changed back into a human, his eagle feathers lying beside him. From such a close view Carly could see his veins bulging under his skin. His eyes were rolled back into his head. She shuddered at the grotesque sight.

"It's the white ash", explained Olivia. "It instantly poisons their blood and enlarges their veins. Death is instant."

"It's not the same as aconite to werewolves then?" asked Carly.

"No, aconite kills werewolves a little slower. The werewolf is certain to die if he is shot by a bullet laced with aconite, but it has to travel around the body first. The hunter on the other hand…his rifle is filled with silver bullets laced with aconite. Those are useless against skinwalkers so he's not doing much good down there. It's a miracle he's still alive."

"He shot Seth", said Carly. "The aconite and silver would work on him. Is that it then? Seth is going to die? Do you think it will all be over when he does? Surely, if he's leading the skinwalkers, they will retreat if their leader dies."

"I don't know", said Olivia. "I…" but her words were cut short as Gary came rushing up towards them.

"They've got Kyle!" he panted. "I saw Seth and another two wolves attack him. I thought he was dead at first but then Seth picked him up by the back of his neck and dragged him, with the help of a bear, into the forest somewhere."

"Seth's alive? What the hell? He was shot by the hunter with aconite! How is he still walking around?" cried Carly. "Why didn't you stop him?"

Gary turned around to reveal huge scratches gouged into his back. "I was dealing with a bit of a problem at the time!"

"Seth must not be a werewolf", said Olivia, voicing what they were now all thinking. Carly agreed with her but she was also puzzled. She had noticed a glaring inconsistency. Of course if he had been seen with a pelt about his person previously it would have been so obvious what he was, but he had never worn one at all, despite the fact that he must somehow be shifting into a werewolf by using Richard's pelt. Indeed, she had seen him change into a werewolf countless times during her first week spent at the cabin and he had always appeared to change in the same way as Kyle and Devon.

Carly peered into the darkness; it looked as though most of the remaining skinwalkers had begun to run away back into the forest. The Native Americans were giving chase and shooting at them. A couple of the skinwalkers fell to the floor like flies as the bullets and arrows hit them, but the Native Americans themselves were tired and spent. They couldn't run after them very far before stopping and collapsing to the ground from exhaustion.

Due to the lack of belligerents, just like that, the battle was over. The wounded Native Americans dragged themselves over to where Carly, Olivia and Gary were. They sat down beside them. Some were being crudely tended to there and then, on the ground, though lack of first aid equipment made this difficult. Others, who were even more seriously hurt, were carried away by their comrades. Carly looked at the group - it seemed so small compared to such a relatively short time ago. The carnage was immense, with bodies piled upon bodies. It made the devastation after the hunter and skinwalker battle a few nights ago seem quite tame in comparison.

Gary began to look around in a panic. "Where is Ian?" he asked. Carly's eyes met his and she could see the realisation hit him.

"Ian didn't make it", she said quietly. Gary didn't say anything but his bottom lip began to tremble. He bit it in a brave attempt not to cry, but a sole tear escaped from his eye and trickled down his cheek.

"Pat?" said Olivia suddenly. "Pat? Pat?" She began to call into the group gathered there.

"He's here", said a male voice from behind several people. Olivia got up and hurried over. Carly couldn't see what was going on as there were people in the way, but her keen ears could hear everything that was being said. "He's in a bad way," continued the voice, "I found him lying on the ground like this".

Olivia let out a small stifled sob. "Pat", she said. Carly could her despair in her voice. "Oh Pat, no!"

"We need to get him back to the reservation, we can treat him there", said the man.

Carly didn't need to hear any more. "The wounded need to be tended to properly", she announced in a loud voice to the group. "Let's get back indoors." Truth be told, the main priority in her mind was to go after the other pack and finding Kyle, but she couldn't do much about that right now.

Gary got to his feet. "Agreed", he said. He held out his hand to pull Carly up but she shook her head, knowing she couldn't stand. "I think I've broken some bones in my back", she said. As it happened, she was feeling mostly numb now. The feeling in her back was so intense, it was as though her mind had shut the pain down, creating some sort of mental block against it. She could barely feel her legs, but with some force, she could just about move them. There was no way she could walk though. She knew that, with injuries this severe, had she been human, she would very likely be dead. It was only the rapid werewolf healing power she possessed which was keeping her alive.

"You should be healed in a few hours time", said one of the men sitting next to her.

"How do you know that?" asked Carly.

"We know much about werewolves", he replied. "Every young Native American in our tribe is taught from an early age to worship the spirit of the wolf. Learning about werewolves is part of our culture. Werewolf bones heal very quickly."

Carly felt a surge of relief. "That means I'll be able to go and find Kyle soon", she said aloud, largely talking to herself.

"The skinwalkers will kill you if you go near them", said the man. "They're so strong."

"I'll take my chances", said Carly obstinately. Her heart felt constricted at the thought of the skinwalkers sacrificing Kyle. She knew that no matter what, she had to do everything in her power to try and get him back. She wouldn't be able to live with herself if she didn't.

"You're not going alone", said Gary. "I'm with you till the end if necessary!" Bending down he gently picked up Carly and began to walk back towards the reservation. Behind them the other Native Americans Indians dragged themselves to their feet and helped take the wounded back to where they could be treated.

CHAPTER THIRTEEN

Once inside the reservation Carly was taken to her bed and set down carefully on it. "Thanks", she smiled at Gary. He smiled back thinly, his brow furrowed. "I'm going to miss him too", said Carly, understanding that he was thinking about Ian.

"He had a fiancée, did you know?"

Carly nodded. "Yes, he told me about her", she said. A twinge of sadness filled her as she remembered the conversation she had had with Ian about his life. "He loved her so much", she said. "He didn't like the fact he had just upped and left her when he became a werewolf. He told me how concerned he was that she would be worried about him."

"No doubt she probably is", said Gary. He hung his head, "I wish things had been different. He didn't need to die tonight. I wish we had never become werewolves."

"I think Ian wished that too", said Carly softly. Then another thought crossed her mind. "Did you notice if the hunter was still alive?" she asked.

Gary shook his head. "I don't think he was, though I can't be sure. He wasn't with us when we gathered after the battle, I know that much."

"I suppose he must be dead", said Carly. "I wonder why he helped us."

Gary shrugged. "I don't know", he said. "Maybe he didn't realise he was helping werewolves. After all, we're in human form and we were fighting alongside the Native American Indians. He probably assumed that the skinwalkers were werewolves."

"Most of them were bears, or birds, or snakes", pointed out Carly. Her mind flicked to Kyle. "I wish I could just get out of this bed and go after Kyle", she said. "I feel so useless lying here."

"Well they're not going to hurt him yet," pointed out Gary, "they need him for the ceremony. Besides, Kyle is Seth's brother - there must be something inside him that still cares about him?"

Gary didn't sound sure of that last part and Carly certainly didn't agree with his sentiment. "Seth is a selfish bastard who cares about nobody but himself", she said bitterly. "He killed his own father!"

"I don't understand how Seth isn't a werewolf," said Gary, "how could that have happened?"

"I have no idea", said Carly. "Could he have been adopted? Pat told the hunter while I was in his mind that skinwalkers have to kill a family member to become a skinwalker in the first place. I guess he must have killed his dad and then pretended to Kyle that he was a werewolf rather than a skinwalker."

"Why would he do that? That's just sick", said Gary.

"God knows what's going on inside his head", said Carly. "He needs some serious help!"

"I don't think there's anybody qualified enough to help somebody like that", said Gary wryly. "Anyway Carly I think you had better get some rest. You want to heal those bones as quickly as you can."

"You'd better get some rest yourself", said Carly, thinking of the deep scratches on Gary's back.

"Actually…" said Gary, as he lifted up his t-shirt and turned around. To Carly's surprise the scratches had faded and were very nearly gone.

"Wow", she said, impressed. "They healed quickly!"

"Yeah, isn't it great being a werewolf?"

Carly could sense the sarcasm in his voice; she knew how he felt. Certainly the advantage of rapid healing was a marvellous advantage they had over human beings, but the amount of stress she had faced since being a werewolf was quite ridiculous. Thinking back to her conversation with Ian she understood why he had not wanted to bring his fiancée into this life. "Goodnight Gary", she said.

"Good morning Carly!" he replied.

Carly widened her eyes in surprise. "What time is it?" she asked.

"Put it this way," he said, craning his neck to look out of the window, "dawn has already broken".

"Ugh", groaned Carly. It seemed she had almost turned nocturnal since becoming a werewolf! Gary gave her shoulder a gentle squeeze, then turned and climbed into his own bed. Carly wriggled painfully down under her blankets and drifted off into a troubled sleep. She slept without experiencing any visions but her dreams were fragmented and disturbing. She saw images of mutilated bears running around tearing into people. At one point, an army of Seths all screaming danced around in her minds eye. When Carly finally woke from her sleep, the sweat was pouring from her. She was glad to be back in the real world.

Carly looked around the dormitory. Most of the Native Americans in there were still asleep. Gary, too, had his eyes closed and was breathing deeply. Carly didn't know how long she had been asleep but the room was much brighter than it had been earlier. Tentatively, she tried to sit up; the unpleasant sensations in her back were not as extreme as they had been previously, but it was still difficult for her to move without wincing. 'I suppose I just need to rest a little longer', she thought. She needed the bathroom but found that she couldn't get out of bed without some help. "I'm not waking Gary up", she whispered to herself. "He doesn't deserve that. I'm just going to have to…" She tried swinging her legs out of the edge of the bed, but as she did so, she lost her balance and ended up falling completely out of bed onto the hard bedroom floor. Frustration and rage that had been building up inside her suddenly forced their way out and she began to cry. On and on she cried, desperation washing over her like a sea crashing over rocks on a beach. There she was sprawled on the floor, unable to even get up, and Kyle needed her. How useless she had turned out to be! She brought her hands to her face in a desperate attempt to stem the flow of tears that were now pouring freely from her red, sore eyes, but to no avail. It was as though somebody had broken a dam inside her. She simply could not stop crying.

As she cried, her eyes clamped shut, she became aware of a

whooshing sound around her. Her highly sensitive ears tuned into the noise and she realised that what she was hearing was not whooshing at all. It was whispers. She had heard whispering like this only once before. She shuddered as she remembered it was when she had entered the land of the dead just after Rob had died. "Oh man", she said aloud, and opened her eyes. Shadows surrounded her and her sobs died down out of fear and shock. "I've gone and done it again", she said, speaking only to herself. As scared as she was though, she wasn't as afraid as she had been the first time it happened. She turned her head to look around, expecting to see the spirit of Rob, or even Ian, heading towards her. What she saw, though, was neither of them.

A young girl and a middle-aged man floated near her; they were holding hands. Carly knew she had never met them before in her life, yet she recognised them instantly. "Y...y...you're Kyle's sister and father", she stammered. The girl smiled and nodded. Carly was amazed they had understood what she had said. When she had seen Rob he hadn't appeared to have heard a single word she had said. 'Either I'm getting better at this, or these are way more powerful spirits or something!' thought Carly.

"Seth has lost his way", said the man. His voice didn't come from his mouth and Carly was sure that his lips hadn't even moved. It was a sort of telepathic communication she was having with the spirits.

"He cannot be saved", added the girl. She sounded sad but there was no doubt in her tone.

"Is there hope for Kyle? Can Seth be stopped?" asked Carly desperately. "Can you help me?"

"We can't help you, no, but there is one who can, though it won't be easy to persuade him", said the man.

"Who?" asked Carly. She would take any help she could get right now!

"He can be found in the town sitting outside the supermarket."

Carly was puzzled at this at first. "Sitting outside the sup..." and then it hit her. "The homeless guy Kyle told me about?"

The girl nodded. "He is not what he seems to be", she said. "You should speak with him."

The man and girl began to fade now and Carly tried in vain to ask them to stay and explain to her how a homeless man could possibly help her. It was no use. Just as it had been when she had seen Rob, they disappeared out of view, leaving her frustrated but with renewed hope that she might be able to save Kyle. As the real world phased back into view, Carly was surprised to see a large pair of feet beside her. She had almost forgotten she was lying on the floor. She had felt more as though she had been floating during her trip to the land of the dead.

"Carly, shit, are you all right? Did you fall?" The voice belonged to Gary. His strong arms lifted her up and sat her back onto the bed.

"I needed the bathroom", she admitted, feeling a little silly.

"Were you crying when I found you?" he asked. "I thought I heard something but then it stopped. I didn't know where you were. It was as though you had vanished."

Carly told him all about what she had just seen and what Kyle's father and sister had told her.

"Did they say how the homeless guy could help us?" asked Gary.

Carly shook her head. "No, they didn't even say what his name was", she confessed. She wished she were able to will herself back into the spirit world so that she could question them again, but she didn't think she would be able to. It had been difficult enough just to phase herself into the next level when the three hunters had infiltrated their cabin, let alone being able to visit the land of the dead at will. She thought it was probably pointless even attempting it. "I think our best bet is to just head to town and see if we can find him", she said. "We're running out of time before the ceremony takes place and the town is several hours away, so we need to go as soon as possible."

"You're not in any fit state to go just yet", said Gary sensibly. "You couldn't even get off the floor!"

"I should be healed soon though", protested Carly.

"Well, I should imagine you would heal more quickly if I brought you some meat."

268 - N. Gosney

Meat! Yes, Carly was starving. For a fleeting moment a thought crossed her mind that perhaps it had only been a hallucination seeing Kyle's father and sister. She couldn't really be sure that it hadn't been. After all she had seen stranger things during her hunger-induced visions. However she couldn't afford to take the risk of not pursuing the lead about the homeless man - if he could help them that was something to their advantage. "I'd love some meat, thanks Gary", she said gratefully. He helped her to reach the bathroom and returned her to bed, then left to hunt for something for them both to eat.

One by one the other occupants of the dormitory woke up and left the room. They told Carly they were going to set about burying the dead who were lying still outside the reservation in the forest. It was already well past lunchtime but nobody seemed to be concerned with the fact they had slept late, considering what time they had gone to sleep. Carly didn't envy them their task. The battle-ground had been a bloody grisly scene indeed.

Gary seemed to take ages to return and Carly was beginning to wonder how much longer she would be able to hold out before having a hallucination. Her stomach was hurting and noises of protest like the rumbling of some strange monster emanated from deep within her. This would have been somewhat embarrassing if there had been anybody present in the room left to hear them! At long last though the door of the dormitory opened. Carly pulled herself up as best she could in eager anticipation. To her surprise though, it was not Gary, but Olivia, who poked her head around the door-frame. She looked tired, as though she hadn't slept a wink.

"How are you feeling?" asked Olivia, coming into the room. Although Carly was pleased to see Olivia she couldn't help feeling a little frustrated that it wasn't Gary with any meat. "I'm not so bad", said Carly. She was still in pain but she felt that it would have been insensitive of her to say so considering the state that Pat had been in last night. "How's Pat?"

Olivia pulled a worried expression. "He's hanging on", she said. Her voice quivered. "We're just not sure if he's going to make it or not. We've done everything we can for him. As far as we can tell he's stable but he's still unconscious and he's not showing any signs of actually improving."

"Do you think you should take him to a hospital?" asked Carly. "Maybe the doctors there would be able to help him?"

Olivia shook her head. "He would hate that", she said. "He is very much in favour of our traditional remedies and healing techniques. Trust me, he wouldn't thank me for taking him to a hospital!"

"Whether he thanks you or not, perhaps you should do it anyway?" suggested Carly quietly. She didn't know what sort of a reception this suggestion would glean but she thought it needed to be said.

Olivia shook her head again though, quite vigorously. "I'm not going against his wishes", she said firmly. The look in her eye told Carly that this discussion was over. She bit her tongue and held back from making any further suggestions.

"Do you know a homeless man in the town?" she asked instead, wondering if perhaps he was somebody that Pat and Olivia might have known.

Olivia wrinkled her brow. "No I don't think so", she said. "That's a peculiar thing to ask me. Why do you want to know that?"

Carly told her about her visit to the land of the dead and Olivia looked thoughtful. "Richard was always a very sensible fellow", she said. "If he tells you that this homeless man, whoever he is, might be able to help you, then you would be wise to heed his advice."

At that moment Gary returned. Carly would have thrown herself out of bed and hurtled towards him if she could have done, so eager was she to get hold of some meat. As it turned out, her wait had been worthwhile. Gary had rather spectacularly managed to kill three rabbits, two badgers and four squirrels. Carly felt as though she were attending a banquet with the amount of meat he presented her with! Olivia left them to eat and said she was going to go and check on her husband's condition.

The strength that ebbed into Carly as she devoured the meat was like nothing she had ever felt before. Almost instantly she could literally feel her bones fusing themselves together again. It hurt, but in a good way - like pulling out an infected tooth. It filled her with a sense of relief she had never experienced before. "I can't believe how much better I feel!" she said in astonishment, her mouth still full of meat, blood dripping down her chin. She had tucked straight into a rabbit, for no other reason other than the fact that it had been the first creature she had grabbed hold of.

Gary smiled as he, too, tucked into a delicious looking rabbit. "Give it a couple of hours and you'll be up and about. Then we can head to the town."

"Are you coming with me?" she asked.

Gary seemed surprised that she had even questioned that. "Of course I am!" he said, sounding astonished.

Sure enough, by late afternoon, Carly was feeling virtually a hundred percent mended. Her back wasn't even bruised any longer. Aside from clicking slightly when she bent over and re-straightened herself, there appeared to be no lasting damage at all. After having a shower and changing her clothes, she decided it was time to set off to find the homeless man. Gary asked her if she wanted to take anything with them but Carly politely declined. They would be able to catch animals to eat along the way. With a bit of luck they would be back at some point in the night or early hours of the following morning, so it wouldn't be necessary to take any supplies. A few of the Native Americans offered to go with them, but Carly, after thanking them, refused their offers. She felt guilty enough about the fact that so many of their people had died during last night's fight; in the event that something should happen to them on their way to or from the town, she didn't want it on her head that any more of the Native Americans should die.

Carly and Gary began walking through the forest in the direction of their cabin. Carly was still not skilled enough at navigating and tracking to be able to find the town directly from the reservation. She thought she could find the way back to the cabin though. From there she would be able to retrace the steps that she and Kyle took several nights prior when they went to town together. She thought there was likely to be a quicker, more direct route straight from the reservation, but she didn't want to risk them getting lost.

On and on they walked, neither saying very much, both lost in their own little worlds. Carly had about a million thoughts flying around in her mind - thoughts of Kyle, of Ian, of the ceremony, of Rob...just of everything that had happened recently. She didn't think that Ian's death had properly sunk in for her yet. She knew that Kyle's capture hadn't completely hit her either. It was the only explanation, she figured, as to how she was managing to keep herself together rather than emotionally falling apart.

As they plodded through the forest she caught sight of Gary wiping his eyes a few times. She assumed he must be thinking about Ian but she didn't ask him. She just reached out her hand to him and gave his arm a gentle squeeze. He smiled at her gratefully but she could still see tears in his eyes.

The trek back to the cabin was uneventful. They didn't go inside though. They carried straight on with Carly following the trail she had taken when she had visited the town with Kyle. She had expected it to be quite hard to follow given that several days had passed. She had thought it likely that their scents would have faded quite considerably. She was right, this was the case, but it was fairly simple enough to know which was the right way to travel, as there were a great deal of broken branches and disturbed leaves and mud thanks to the team of hunters that had passed through that way as well.

After many hours of hiking through the forest, stopping only briefly to catch rabbits and drink at a stream along the way, Carly and Gary reached the outskirts of the forest. In some small way Carly had hoped that they might have bumped into the skinwalkers somewhere. She desperately wanted to see Kyle but she knew it would have been disastrous for them to have done so. The two of them alone wouldn't have stood a chance at rescuing him. Carly knew this, but the irrational part of her still felt just a tiny bit disappointed.

The sun had already set. Street-lights were lit along the roadside lighting up the shops and houses nearby. Some larger shops were still open, though all the smaller ones had shut a few hours ago.

Carly and Gary hid behind some large trees as there were a few people still dawdling around doing some last minute shopping.

"We can't let anybody see us", whispered Carly.

"Why not?" asked Gary, his confusion apparent.

Carly sighed. "Just think about it - we both went missing almost two weeks ago and nobody has seen us since. There's bound to be some people who have noticed that we aren't around. Jackson's girlfriend was hysterical after you guys all disappeared. I bet the police are looking for us!"

"That's a good point", agreed Gary. "Okay, so what are we going to do? We can't stay here all night."

Carly thought for a moment. "Not all night, no, but at least until most of the people have gone home. The stores shouldn't be open too much longer and I expect it'll be much quieter by then. We'd better stay put for now."

Gary slumped to the ground and Carly did the same. They waited, quietly, with one or the other of them peering out from behind the tree every now and again to see whether or not it was safer for them to emerge. After some time had passed, Carly saw that the street appeared to now be empty. The stores that had been open were now closed; their shutters were pulled down and there was no sign of any life coming from them. Even most of the houses had their curtains closed, although lights were still visible from behind the drapes. "I think we can probably go now," she whispered to Gary, "as long as we try not to bump into anybody". Carly wasn't sure exactly what time it was. She estimated it might be around ten or eleven o' clock. The pair crept out of the forest and hurried along the paths, trying to keep to the shadows as much as possible. Once or twice they almost bumped into other pedestrians but they kept their heads down and avoided making eye contact. Nobody appeared to recognise them.

"Where is this guy supposed to be?" asked Gary.

"Kyle said that he often sits outside the supermarket", replied Carly. "I expect he probably moves around though. We'll have to hope that he's there when we arrive."

The supermarket was a good half an hour's brisk walk through the town, but Carly and Gary managed to get there in less than fifteen minutes for they moved much more swiftly than they would have done when they were humans.

"There it is", announced Carly, as the supermarket came into view.

Gary, who had previously had his head down and had been staring at the ground as he walked, now looked up at the sound of her voice. "Is he there? Do you see him?"

Carly peered closely but couldn't see anybody near the entrance. "No, I don't think so."

"That's just fucking marvellous", cursed Gary.

They carried on walking regardless, just in case they were wrong. "Maybe he's sheltered behind something there", suggested Carly, not feeling terribly hopeful. Unfortunately though, as they approached the supermarket it became all too apparent that the homeless man was not there.

"Fucking marvellous", repeated Gary.

Carly couldn't blame him. She felt exactly the same way. Frustration boiled within her and she kicked a dustbin as hard as she could. "UGH!" she grunted loudly.

"SHHHH!" came a voice from around the side of the building. "Do ya want t' ave police come 'ere? They'd lock me up again an' am right fed up o' that 'appenin. So shut up would ya!"

Carly and Gary looked at each other in surprise for a brief moment. Then they ran around the building to find the owner of the voice. There, at the side of the supermarket, were some large dumpster bins. Squashed in between the bins, covered in a brown blanket as well hidden as he could be, was a dirty unkempt looking man. His beard and hair were overgrown and looked as though they hadn't been washed or groomed in a long time. An unpleasant odour emanated from the man's body. Carly wrinkled up her nose in disgust as the foul stench wafted up her sensitive nostrils. A quick glance at Gary told Carly that he, too, had caught a waft of the pungent smell.

"It's you!" said Carly, feeling a little foolish. Now that they had found him she didn't have the faintest idea how to ask for his help.

She wished she had rehearsed a small speech of some sort along the way.

The man raised an eyebrow at Carly. "To be sure I am meself," he said gruffly. "I 'aint never been anybody but me."

Carly couldn't place the man's accent but he didn't sound as though he was local to the town. She wasn't even sure that he was American. "We…need your help", she said hesitantly.

"What wi'?"

"Have you ever met somebody called Richard?" she asked.

The man wrinkled his nose. "'Av probably met a lot o' people wi' name o' Richard over the years", he muttered. "It 'aint an uncommon name."

"This one was…" began Carly, not knowing quite how to phrase it. "He was a…"

"…a werewolf", interjected Gary. Carly looked at him sharply but Gary just shrugged. To Carly's surprise though, the man didn't seem at all shocked by this.

"Oh aye, were 'e now? I did know a werewolf called Richard once, aye, but that were a very long time ago."

"He said you would be able to help us", said Carly, feeling a little more optimistic.

"'Ow is 'e?" asked the man. Carly couldn't understand what the man was asking.

"Sorry, what did you say?" she asked politely.

"OW IS 'E?" bellowed the man more loudly, as though assuming that extra volume would help them to understand his accent. He had apparently forgotten about keeping quiet.

Carly shook her head, looking blank. She felt as though she was being terribly rude by not understanding what the man was asking her, but she genuinely had no idea what he was saying.

"Unfortunately, he's dead, I'm very sorry to tell you", said Gary, who clearly had better comprehension skills than Carly did. She shot him a look of admiration.

"Dead? DEAD? Shit!" muttered the man to himself. "Poor bastard!"

"Actually it's his sons who need your help now", said Gary.

"Well, one of them really, Kyle. He is going to be sacrificed in a skinwalker ceremony tomorrow night. We have to rescue him!"

The man's eyes had widened as he heard the word 'skinwalker'. He shook his head vigorously. "Sod that, no way! I 'aint gettin' involved wi' any skinwalker shit."

"But you know Kyle! He comes to the supermarket sometimes at night and he brings you food and drink!"

"That kind lad is Richard's boy?"

Carly nodded.

The man grunted. "E's good to me is that lad. Keeps me goin'. I look forward to 'is visits."

"So you'll help us rescue him?"

The man didn't answer, but pushed off his blanket and stood up. He began to walk around the side of the supermarket leaving Carly and Gary standing in the alley staring after him. After a few steps the man turned around. "Well come on!" he called.

Carly and Gary wasted no time and trotted after him as he walked around to where the back entrance (the goods entrance) of the supermarket was located. "You're both gonna 'ave t' get me some stuff from inside", he said, his voice now lowered to a whisper. "This 'ere is 'ow your friend gets in an' out. There's no security cameras on this door."

Carly put out a hand to the door; it was locked. She took hold of the handle and tugged on it as hard as she could but the door didn't budge. "Maybe it's a push door", she mused aloud. With all her strength she pushed the door. Instantly, the internal locking mechanism gave way and the door flew open. Carly tumbled headlong into the dark room in front of her.

"Are you okay?" asked Gary.

"Ya broke the door!" exclaimed the man. "That 'aint how your friend does it! 'E picks the lock!"

"Well I don't know how to pick locks!" said Carly crossly, picking herself up off the floor and brushing down her dusty knees. She turned to face the man. "What is it that we need to get for you?"

The man scrunched up his forehead as though he was thinking.

"A pestle an' mortar," he said, "tarragon, sage, candles, matches…" he paused, "an' whiskey. Also gonna need a tree an' a live animal but you 'aint gonna find those in there."

"Is that it?" asked Gary. The man nodded.

"Okay, let's go", said Carly. She assumed from his list of requests that the man had the ability to cast spells of some sort. She figured there was enough time to ask him about that after they collected his ingredients. Right now she just wanted to get in and out of the supermarket without getting caught. Her heart was pounding wildly. She felt as though she was doing something very wrong, which was sort of crazy considering everything that had happened during the past couple of weeks. She had never broken into a building before though, let alone stolen anything. She felt a strange sort of thrill whilst at the same time being a little scared.

The storeroom of the supermarket was dark. Carly couldn't initially see what she was doing. Despite the fact that her eyes were particularly sharp it still took a few seconds for them to adjust to the blackness. "Ouch", she whispered, banging her hand on something hard and sharp.

"Careful!" hissed Gary.

"We're never going to find what we need", she said, a little despairingly. Her eyes had now managed to focus on what was in the room. She could see it was extremely large and full of large metal crates. These, in turn, were stacked to the brim with cardboard boxes of stock for the supermarket.

"I think our best bet is to try to find our way onto the store floor itself", said Gary. "We have no idea what are in all these boxes but at least we can navigate our way around the supermarket shelves."

Carly agreed that was probably the most sensible idea so together they made their way to the edge of the room. The wall seemed to be endless but with no doors, so they began to walk along, keeping the wall to the side of them. At last they came to (as they knew they would) a large set of double doors. To their surprise they were not locked; in fact they didn't even close properly, but rather the doors just flapped backwards and forwards freely when they were pushed. 'This seems a little too easy', thought Carly, but then she paused and reconsidered. "I suppose this stockroom must be only used by the people who work here", she said aloud. "No customers would come through the doors in any case." As they pushed the doors open and walked through, Carly turned around to check if her prediction had been correct; it had. There in large red letters were the words 'NO ENTRY - STAFF ONLY'. "I guess that's why they don't need to have locks on the doors", she said.

Gary didn't comment - he was too busy peering at the signs above the aisles. "Cereals, Produce, Entertainment, Bread, Soft Drinks..." he read aloud. "What are we looking for again?"

"Herbs, candles, matches, whiskey and a mortar and pestle", clarified Carly. She wasn't even entirely sure that the shop would have any mortar and pestles, but they had to at least look.

"Okay, herbs are bound to be near the vegetables in the Produce aisle", said Gary. "Whiskey will be in the Alcohol aisle. Candles and matches...hmmm." Gary furrowed his brow and continued to scan the signs. "Seasonal Goods, Fish, Poultry, Household Goods..."

"That'll probably be it!" exclaimed Carly, "and we might find the mortar and pestle in Kitchenware, if they have such an aisle here."

"Yes there it is", said Gary, pointing at a sign a little way from them.

"Okay - you get the candles, matches and whiskey. I'll get the herbs and mortar and pestle", said Carly.

They split up, each hot-footing it to different parts of the supermarket. Carly opted to head to the Produce section first. She thought she would have a better chance of finding tarragon and sage than she would have of finding the mortar and pestle. Sure enough the herbs were not difficult to find, although Carly dithered slightly for a moment wondering whether or not to opt for the dried or fresh varieties. "Well, surely spells are cast using fresh ingredients", she pondered. She grabbed a couple of packets of each herb. She wasn't sure of quantity either but she assumed (and hoped) that she had probably taken enough. 'Right, now to get the mortar and pestle', she thought. She headed straight towards the Kitchenware aisle and began to search amongst the pans, crockery and cutlery stacked neatly on the shelves. "No, no, no, that's not it", she muttered, her eyes quickly scanning up and down the shelves. Finally, near the end of the aisle on the bottom shelf, she spotted a lone mortar and pestle. 'Thank God!' thought Carly. She snatched it up quickly as though she was expecting somebody else to come along and buy it. She acknowledged that this was ridiculous as the store was closed. "I've got them!" she hissed, hoping Gary could hear her. He must have done for he now came bounding back up to her. He was clutching a set of six vanilla scented candles in glass candle holders, a bottle of Jack Daniel's whiskey and a packet of matches. "Vanilla candles?" asked Carly.

Gary shrugged. "They only had scented candles and I happen to like the smell of vanilla."

Carly smiled then followed him as he began to make his way back to the storeroom entrance. Before she knew it, they were outside and standing in front of the homeless man once again.

"Ya got it all?" he asked, coughing slightly.

"Yes", said Carly.

"Tree an' animal now. Rabbit or summit will do."

"What's your name?" asked Gary. Coincidentally Carly had been wondering the same thing.

"Ee now there's a question!" said the man. "S'pose my name is James, but I've been known as other things before."

"Such as…?" asked Carly. She wondered whether or not he knew that Kyle had referred to him as the rather strange name of Scully Jim.

"Dunt matter really, just call me James", said the man.

"Okay James. Well, if you need a tree and an animal you'll have to come with us to the forest. I can't think how we're going to bring a tree to you here!"

"Ya got whiskey?" asked James. Gary handed him the bottle. James quickly unscrewed the lid and began to drink. Carly and Gary exchanged worried glances.

"I think we ought to get on with…erm…whatever we're doing", said Gary. James didn't respond - he was too busy drinking.

"What exactly do you need all this stuff for anyway?" asked

Carly.

"Your friend 'as bin kidnapped, right?"

"Yes", confirmed Carly.

"So them what's taken 'im, they need a dose o' morality I reckon."

"So that's what you're going to make? Some sort of morality potion? To do what? Make them see the error of their ways?"

James smiled and winked at them.

"How do you even know how to do that?" asked Gary sceptically.

James sighed. "I were raised by me mam an' dad an' they knew of such spells. I dint question it like, I just picked it up. I were living in England but I married a Yankee lass when I were in me early twenties an' moved t' states, but she died 'bout five year ago...'" James's voice was tinged with sadness and he tailed off at this point.

"Is that why you're sleeping rough?" asked Carly kindly.

James sniffed. "I dunt wanna talk 'bout it no more", he said, suddenly clamming up defensively. "Let's go, we 'avent got all day!"

Carly and Gary led the way back through the deserted streets towards the direction of the forest. James followed behind, sipping whiskey as he walked and swaying slightly.

"If a cop sees him like that he's going to get arrested", said Gary in hushed tones.

"Let's just get him safely into the forest as quickly as we can", said Carly. "With a bit of luck we won't bump into any police. Once we're among the trees it wont really matter if he wants to drink his whiskey."

"We still need him coherent enough to do the spell!" said Gary urgently.

Carly took the point. She stopped walking for a moment or two to let James catch up. "I think we should move a little faster", she suggested, trying to be tactful. "How about if you put the lid on the bottle for now. You can have some more after you've done this spell."

James pulled a face. He muttered some slurred obscenities under his breath but he did as she had requested. Carly took him by the arm and guided him forward.

"I can do it mesen!" roared James, altogether entirely too loudly.

"Shhh!" hissed Carly desperately. She let go of his arm in an attempt to appease him but he promptly tripped up and went sprawling onto the ground.

"Oh for goodness sake", said Gary, exasperated. He came over to help lift James up. "We haven't got time for this!"

James seemed to subdue at Gary's stern voice and allowed them both to propel him towards the forest; Gary at one side of him, Carly at the other, both gripping his elbows firmly. Thankfully the forest was in sight now. They ushered him into the dark cloak of the trees.

"I can't see!" exclaimed James.

That was a good point - Carly realised that James didn't have the same visionary abilities she and Gary had. "I don't have a torch", she said, feeling slightly at a loss.

Gary winked at her. "Oh how quickly they forget", he teased. He struck a match he had been carrying and lit one of the vanilla scented candles.

"That's better", said James. Groaning, he eased himself onto a mossy patch of earth. "Right, I need a small animal, squirrel or summit o' that sort, an' I need a tree."

"You're surrounded by trees", pointed out Carly.

James looked around in surprise. "Oh, aye, so I am!"

"I'll catch an animal", said Carly. She felt as though she could do with a good run to clear the cobwebs from her mind. She was finding it hard to concentrate on anything other than the thought of Kyle.

"Don't eat the fecker, I need it alive!" called James, unscrewing his bottle of whiskey and having yet another drink.

It didn't take long before Carly had managed to pounce on a young rabbit. She resisted the urge to sink her teeth into it. She was rather peckish but instead she brought it back to James.

"He hasn't stopped drinking since you left", whispered Gary, as Carly returned with the rabbit. "He's been going on and on about pirates and pixies. I don't think he is going to be able to help us!"

Carly walked up to James - he was now semi-recumbent. She placed her hands on his shoulders and shook him relatively vigorously. "Pull yourself together", she barked in an authoritative tone of voice. "We need you to help us; you have to do the spell!" James closed his eyes and dribbled slightly. Carly let out a small squeal of frustration and yanked him to a more upright position. "JAMES SNAP OUT OF IT!"

James jumped and opened his eyes. "Sarah! How lovely t' see ya!" he slurred.

Carly rolled her eyes. She didn't care what he called her as long as he sobered up enough to create the potion. She waved the rabbit in front of his face. "You have to create the morality potion", she said, trying to speak as clearly and concisely as possible to him. "I have brought you a rabbit."

James grabbed hold of the rabbit. He almost ended up releasing it as his hands were so unsteady. Then he offered it back to Carly. "Well watcha give me it for?" he asked in surprise. "I dunt need it yet!" Taking hold of the mortar and pestle Gary had placed beside him, James muttered an incantation that Carly thought sounded vaguely celtic. Then he turned to Gary. "Put candle on t' floor in front o' me", he requested. Gary obligingly placed the candle on the ground. James closed his eyes and Carly wondered if he was going to begin chanting or something of that sort. To her great irritation though he let out a snore. She leant over and gave him another shake.

"Wake UP!" she cried, wondering if he was actually going to be able to get through this at all. James' eyes shot open once again and he nearly knocked over the whiskey beside him. Carly thought that wouldn't have been such a bad thing!

"Okay, okay, okay", he grumbled, sounding somewhat disgruntled at having been disturbed. He opened the packets of tarragon and sage and put a few leaves of each into the mortar and pestle. Mumbling more celtic sounding words, he began to grind them up finely until they no longer resembled leaves. Then he threw the pestle to the ground. "Help me up!" he said, and held out his hands to Gary and Carly. They pulled him to his feet and he unsteadily staggered a few steps forward. Carly put out a hand to steady him. He appeared to temporarily regain composure. Without saying another word, he snatched the rabbit from Carly with one hand and clutched steadfastly to the mortar with the other hand. Carly was quite sure he would drop one or the other of them. To her surprise, he began to dance haphazardly around the nearest tree whilst singing a strange celtic sounding song.

Gary shot Carly a slightly bewildered glance but Carly tried not to let his mistrust cloud her judgement. Richard and Gemma had told her that this man could help them so she had to believe what they said to be true. After a few minutes, James' erratic dancing slowed to a stop. He handed the mortar to Carly. She took it unquestioningly and watched as James held the quivering frightened rabbit high above his head. He spoke a few words Carly didn't understand, then he gently lowered the rabbit, kissed its head and released it to run free into the forest. He picked up the candle and brought it over to the mortar in Carly's hands. He attempted to turn the candle upside down and set fire to the ground up herbs, which was very difficult considering the shape of the glass candle holder. Try as he might it simply wouldn't work. In the end Gary tore a small strip of material from the bottom of his t-shirt, held it to the flame, and quickly used it to set the herbs alight.

"Ouch!" he yelped. The fire had flared up the cloth and singed his fingertips. Carly winced in sympathy but James paid no attention to Gary's discomfort. Instead he took the mortar from Carly, chanted a few more strange words then blew out the flames within it. Then he looked up and smiled.

"Put these burnt 'erbs in t' drink o' whoever you want to gain a few morals!" he said, handing it to Carly. She looked at the small amount of blackened powder in the mortar.

"There isn't much there", she remarked. "The skinwalker pack is pretty big. I think we're going to need more than this really."

James shook his head. "No, no, no!" he said firmly. "I 'aint doin' no more! Now take me back t' supermarket."

Carly sighed, then realised she was probably being a little ungrateful. "Thank you James for the spell", she said politely. "It was very kind of you to take the trouble to help us."

James barely appeared to have heard her though. He had picked up the whiskey again and continued to drink it.

"We should go then if you want to get back to the supermarket", urged Gary. James began stumbling deeper into the forest, merrily singing a slurred song.

"Ugh", muttered Carly. Gary quickly strode after him and began to steer him back in the right direction.

"Wait there," he told her, "no point both of us going. I'll be back in a few minutes."

Carly nodded, and watched as James and Gary left the forest; Gary trying desperately to quieten James down so he wouldn't attract any attention as they walked through the town. As she waited, Carly studied the burnt herbs once again. She wished she had a bag or pouch of some sort to carry them in. She was afraid that they would blow out of the mortar. Luckily it wasn't a particularly windy night, but she knew that an unexpected gust would send the ashes through the air very easily. She held her hand over the bowl. It seemed to suffice, though she realised she wouldn't be able to run very easily whilst holding the mortar in that position. Soon Gary returned and the pair began to hike back to the Native American reservation as quickly as they could.

CHAPTER FOURTEEN

It was morning by the time they arrived back at the reservation. Several men ran to greet them as they came within sigh. "We've been looking out for you", one of them explained. "Pat is awake now, he wants to speak to you both."

"Did you find the homeless man?" asked another. Carly realised that Olivia must have filled everybody in on what she had told her about her latest visit to the land of the dead, and what Richard and Gemma had told her.

"I did find him", affirmed Carly. "I should go and see Pat."

She knew the Native Americans might think that she was being a little evasive but she didn't really have time to stop and explain about the burnt herbs or about James to everybody individually. Time was of the essence - the full moon was due that night. Carly had to find the skinwalker camp as quickly as she could if she wanted to stand a chance of rescuing Kyle before the start of the sacrificial ceremony. Apologising hurriedly for her briefness, Carly hurried towards Pat and Olivia's house in hot pursuit by Gary. About twenty Native Americans also followed them, apparently eager to hear what they had to say. Carly knocked on the door and Olivia opened it. She greeted Carly and Gary warmly and hugged them both.

"Was he able to help you?" she asked, referring to James.

Carly nodded. "He did help, but perhaps I should tell you all together. I hear that Pat is awake, that's wonderful!"

Olivia smiled. "He's still quite weak", she warned, "but yes he is awake. He was asking for you."

"Did you tell him where we went?"

"Yes", replied Olivia. "Come and see him."

Carly and Gary stepped into the house. The rest of the crowd pushed forward as though to enter also but Olivia held up a hand to them. "I'm sorry but Pat is still fragile. He cannot have such a large group of visitors at the same time."

"But we want to help", piped up one man, whose name Carly had quite forgotten.

"I'll fill you all in when Carly and Gary have spoken with Pat", promised Olivia. Carly knew they would abide by her decision. Pat was the chief of the reservation and Olivia, being his wife, was a highly respected lady. The group disbanded and left the house. Olivia closed the front door. "Don't get him too excited, I don't want him to rupture anything", warned Olivia. She walked down a short passageway with Carly and Gary behind her and headed for a wooden door ahead of them. They followed her inside and there they saw Pat lying in a bed. His face was pale despite his naturally tanned complexion and he sported various cuts and bruises. His eyes looked heavy and tired. He had a bandage around his head and his arm was in a pot and sling.

'Poor Pat', thought Carly. It was quite a shock to see him like this - he usually seemed to be such a strong man. Once again she felt a pang of guilt at the thought of the amount of trouble her pack's arrival had brought upon the people of the reservation.

Pat managed a weak smile as they walked up to his bed. "Olivia told me you had gone to town", he said, his voice quiet and shaky. It seemed to Carly that he had aged overnight.

"I had a visit from Richard and his daughter Gemma", explained Carly. "They told me to find a homeless man in the town; they said he could help me."

Pat didn't seem at all surprised to hear this. Carly assumed that Olivia must have filled him in on it already. "And did he?" he asked.

"He gave us some herbs, some burnt herbs", said Gary. Carly held out the mortar for Pat to see into. "He said that if somebody drinks them, they will obtain a dose of morality", Gary continued.

"There isn't a great deal there though", said Carly, feeling a little dismal.

"There doesn't need to be", wheezed Pat. "You only need to

286 - N. Gosney

target Seth. He is their leader."

"Did Olivia tell you that Seth isn't a werewolf?" asked Carly.

Pat nodded, then winced at the movement. "Only skinwalkers would be unaffected by the hunter's aconite-laced silver bullets", he said. "I actually had my suspicions when I saw him get shot by the hunter and yet didn't die. He would have needed to be shot by one of our white-ash bullets in order for it to be fatal."

"I don't understand how it is that he isn't a werewolf though", said Carly. "It makes no sense. Kyle told me that werewolves pass down their legacy to their children."

"They do," agreed Pat, "so that only leaves one explanation".

"Richard wasn't Seth's father", said Carly, the pieces suddenly sliding into place. "That means…he isn't the wolf born, Kyle is!"

"Do you suppose that's why Seth killed Richard?" asked Gary, rubbing his chin. "Perhaps he found out he wasn't his father."

"Christ that seems harsh!" said Carly. "After all, it wasn't Richard's fault! Surely that couldn't be the reason why."

"Harsh maybe, but look what he is doing to Kyle", pointed out Pat. "Anyway, enough speculation, you two have to rescue Kyle. It is now…" he checked his watch, "twenty past ten. I think you should both have a nap for a couple of hours, then wake and have a bite to eat."

"Are you kidding?" said Carly incredulously. "We don't have time to sleep! It's the full moon tonight!"

"I know, but the heliacal rising of Sirius will not occur until just before sunrise. That will be when the sacrificial ceremony will be due to take place. It would be useless for them to carry it out sooner than that."

"What time is sunrise?" asked Gary.

"Tomorrow morning the sun will rise at 5:05am", replied Pat.

"That only gives us just over eighteen and a half hours!" cried Carly in alarm. "In fact less than that. Our own lunar change will happen at midnight!"

Pat reached over to her with his one free arm, and took hold of her hand. "Two hours sleep is not much, but it will refresh you a little. You cannot take on this great challenge if you are plagued with fatigue. You must rest."

"Maybe he's right", said Gary. "I can feel my eyes beginning to close and you look really tired."

"Thanks a lot", retorted Carly, a little indignantly.

"You must sleep", said Olivia. "Not another word of argument - go to your beds now. You can leave the herbs here for safe keeping." She propelled them out of the room before they were even able to say goodbye to Pat and waved to them from the house. She watched to make sure they went straight to their dormitory.

"Okay", agreed Carly once they were inside. "Two hours, that's all. You had better wake me up after that!"

"Don't worry, I will. I'm a light sleeper so I tend to wake up every couple of hours anyway."

"That must be inconvenient", remarked Carly. "Goodnight Gary."

Carly was truly exhausted. Nights of broken sleep had taken their toll on her and last night they had, of course, been occupied with James. Her body was desperately in need of some rest. She fell asleep almost instantly and found herself once again occupying the same body as somebody else. She was sitting on a chair and was tied up with chains. They burned and cut through her skin and flesh and she felt as though she had been hit by a bus. It was a strange feeling of déjà-vu as she remembered being tied up in a very similar manner by the two younger hunters several days prior. She tried to move her head to see where she was and what was happening around her, but she didn't have the strength to raise it. Instead, it was hanging forward and her eyes were fixed on the floor.

"Seth, please let me go", she pleaded. Although she couldn't see him she sensed that Seth was in the room with her. She could smell his unmistakable odour - a scent she recognised so easily, in much the same way a dog recognises his master. Seth made no reply. Then she heard his footsteps walking away and fading out of earshot. 'I'm going to die', she thought, despair washing over her. 'He's going to kill me and I don't even know why.' "What have I done to deserve this?" she cried aloud. Her words stuck in her throat as emotion overcame her. She closed her eyes and began to concentrate very hard. She allowed the feelings of anger, confusion, fear and sorrow to wash over her like waves. After a few minutes she heard a sound that was both familiar yet unfamiliar. Whooshing noises and whisperings flittered close to her ear, completely surrounding her. Carly, in her own mind, knew what the noises were, but within Kyle's mind she did not recognise what was happening. Kyle's eyes shot open in fright and he forced his head up from its bowed position. What he saw did not bring him any comfort or reassurance.

Shadows everywhere danced around and Carly forgot that her actual self had seen this before. The part of her mind that was at one with Kyle was dominant. He was terrified. Carly felt as though this must be the end. 'I'm dead! He's done it, he's killed me', she thought in a panic, channeling Kyle's fears. The notion that she had crossed over into the land of the dead whilst still being alive simply didn't occur to her at that moment. All at once a figure appeared before Kyle; a pretty little girl aged about ten years old. Her long sandy coloured hair flapped around her delicate features as though it were being blown in the wind. She wore a pair of pink pyjamas with a cat on the front. Kyle gasped, his mouth gaping open like a goldfish. "Gemma", he said, unable to believe his eyes.

Gemma smiled at him and reached out her hand to his face. Though Carly couldn't feel it, the fact it was there filled her with joy. She experienced something else though as well - an intense feeling of shame and guilt. She couldn't distance herself from these emotions, though they belonged to Kyle and not her. Kyle turned his face away, unable to continue to look Gemma in the eye. "Oh God, Gemma. I…" he was so choked up that he almost couldn't finish his sentence. His tears began to fall freely. "I'm so sorry Gemma. You must hate me as much as I hate myself!"

"I don't hate you at all", said Gemma. "You did nothing wrong."

"How can you say that? You'd still be alive if it weren't for me."

"Kyle, when you turned into a werewolf that night you didn't hurt me. You made a great big hole in the house and ran away. I was still in your bedroom wondering what had happened."

Kyle slowly raised his head, unable to believe his ears. "I don't understand!" he said. "When I came back you were buried under the rubble. You were dead!"

Gemma crouched down in front of him. "You didn't do it though", she replied.

"Then who...how?"

Gemma looked hard at him. All at once Carly and Kyle together both knew what Gemma was trying to tell him. "Did Seth kill you?"

"He needed to kill somebody in our family. He knew you would blame yourself for my death and wouldn't suspect him of doing it, so he killed me when you turned into a werewolf."

Carly felt the heart began to beat furiously inside Kyle's chest as rage swelled up inside him. "Why would he do that?"

"To become a skinwalker", came a voice from behind Gemma. Carly peered around and saw the shining outline of Richard.

"Oh my God...dad!" Carly felt Kyle clamp a hand to his mouth and began to cry in earnest now. Tears of joy at seeing Gemma and Richard and of the intense feelings of distress he was having at learning all these things about Seth. Although Carly knew deep down that all these emotions belonged to Kyle, it was almost as though she was sharing his soul.

"Kyle, I need to show you something", said Richard gently, sitting down on a chair next to him. "You have to close your eyes."

Hesitantly, Kyle closed his eyes.

"Try to free your mind of any thoughts. Just listen to my voice."

Kyle did his best to obey what he had said. Richard was speaking gently but neither Carly nor Kyle could make out what he was saying. Carly felt as though she were floating on water, gently bobbing and swaying. All at once an image appeared in Kyle's mind's eye. He could see Richard and Seth; Seth looked only about thirteen years old. They were standing in a wood together and Richard had his hand on Seth's shoulder.

"I'm going to show you something but I don't want you to be afraid", said Richard. Seth nodded solemnly and puffed his chest up, as though he was trying to appear more grown-up and manly than his tender years allowed.

"I will not hurt you, just remember that."

Seth's eyes widened but he nodded again and stood up straighter. Richard began to take off his clothes.

"Dad, what are you doing?" exclaimed Seth, losing all composure.

"I know it's a bit strange but bear with me", replied Richard. Having finished undressing he now held up his hand. It began to grow dark brown fur. Claws started to protrude from his fingertips.

Seth began to breath heavily. "Holy shit", he gasped. Richard raised an eyebrow, apparently a little irritated by his son's use of profanities, but he said nothing to chastise him for it.

"Watch", said Richard. Then he smoothly turned all of himself into a large dark brown wolf. He shook his fur, threw back his head and howled loudly.

"Oh my God!" said Seth. Carly could see the fear in his eyes. He stood as rigid as a statue staring at the werewolf before him. Then, just as quickly as he had changed into a wolf, Richard turned back into a man again.

"Oh my God!" repeated Seth. "What the hell was that?"

Richard didn't respond at first but began to put his clothes back on. Once he was fully dressed he sat down on a tree stump and indicated for Seth to do the same. Seth hesitated for a few moments. Very slowly he sat down on another tree stump close to Richard.

"I'm a werewolf", stated Richard in a matter-of-fact tone of voice. "Being a werewolf is passed down to their children."

"I'm going to be a werewolf?" said Seth, his voice filled with awestruck wonder.

"Becoming a werewolf occurs on the first full moon after a boy or girl's thirteenth birthday. It just so happens that tomorrow is a full moon."

"And I turned thirteen two weeks ago", said Seth, his eyes as wide as saucers.

"Have you been noticing anything strange lately?" asked Richard. "Any visions or enhanced hearing, anything like that?"

Seth shook his head.

"Hmm, well no matter, it's different for everybody."

"I'm going to turn into a werewolf tomorrow night?" The boy was obviously still reeling from the shock of learning about his heritage.

Carly watched as Richard explained to Seth the difference between changing into a wolf, and the lunar change, which brings about the transformation of the beast. Seth visibly trembled at times but Carly could see from the look on his face as the conversation progressed that Seth had warmed to the idea of being a werewolf. As Carly continued to concentrate on the vision being shown to Kyle, the scene faded. A new scene formed in his mind. Again Richard and Seth were standing in the forest, but their clothes were different so it couldn't have been the same day. It was dusk.

"You remember everything I told you?" asked Richard.

"It's going to hurt a lot, it's dangerous, stay in the forest, don't stray near anybody else…" said Seth, sounding as though he was reciting a set of instructions he had memorised.

"This is your first time - are you excited?"

"Hell yeah", said Seth, his face brightening up. "I couldn't sleep all last night thinking about what you told me yesterday. I can't believe you turned into a wolf dad, that's so cool!"

"I can't stay with you tonight, you know that don't you?" said Richard. "I don't know what would happen if two werewolves came together in beast form. It's very possible that we would fight each other and that would very likely end badly!"

"I know dad, it's okay, I'll be alright."

"I know you will, you're a big boy now. I remember my first lunar change, I didn't have the luxury of knowing the things I'm telling you."

"And you were fine, so there you go", said Seth, smiling up at Richard.

"I'll come back to this spot in the morning and we can go home", said Richard. "I told your mom we were going camping together so we had better return together!"

The scene faded again and another scene flickered into Kyle's subconscious.

"Seth, how do you feel?" asked Richard approaching Seth. The sun was beginning to rise above the trees, its light casting beams on the forest floor below.

"That was amazing", said Seth grinning. "It hurt like hell though!"

"I know, I'm sorry about that. If there was one thing I wish, it's that you didn't have to endure the pain of the lunar change."

"That's okay dad", said Seth. He gave Richard a hug. "I'm so glad you passed this down to me. I love you."

"I love you too", replied Richard, returning Seth's hug.

A fourth scene replaced the previous one. Richard was running through the forest in wolf form, his brown fur streaking past the bushes, darting in and out of the trees. As he neared the Native American reservation, Carly heard a gunshot fire out. Richard dropped to the floor, blood pouring out of a wound in his side. Seth appeared from behind a tree and walked up to Richard, who was writhing on the floor in obvious agony. "You lied to me", said Seth. His face was contorted in anger and his voice quiet but dangerous. "You told me I was like you. I'm nothing like you. You are not my father!" He lifted his hand to reveal a silver knife clenched in his fist. Holding the hilt firmly, he bent down and began to skin Richard alive, ignoring the dying wolf's howls of torture.

The scene faded away. Carly felt Kyle's mind being brought out of the trance it had been in. They both became aware of Richard's voice and Carly heard him telling Kyle to open his eyes.

"I didn't know at the time, but Seth was right - he was not my son", said Richard, his voice heavy with sadness. "Your mother had an affair I didn't know about, but we won't go into that now."

Kyle was feeling extremely nauseous from what he had just seen but he forced himself to speak. "So Seth didn't change then on the full moon? He lied and said he did?"

"That's right", replied Richard. "I learned after my death that Seth had tried to find me that night because he didn't change. Instead of finding me though, he found a pack of skinwalkers.

They welcomed him in and persuaded him to tell them what was the matter. He told them about me and that he had not turned into a werewolf. They told him that I must not be his father but rather an impostor. They convinced him that real werewolves are evil creatures and told him about how much better skinwalkers are. They told him he needed to kill me to obtain my pelt, for that is how they shift into other creatures, with pelts. They also explained that he needed to kill a family member in order to become a shapeshifter like them. Seth knew that couldn't be me, because I was not really his father."

"So he decided it had to be one of us instead", piped up Gemma, who had been sitting quietly all this time. "He was too scared to do it though - he thought he would be found out. So he stayed away from the skinwalkers after that and just hid the pelt and dad's clothes in a cabin he came across in the forest. It was a cabin that belonged to dad. He pretended that nothing had happened and we all assumed that dad had left us. Seth was still afraid he would be caught for killing dad; but when you turned into a werewolf three years later, Seth suddenly got jealous and angry that you were a werewolf and he wasn't. After you jumped through that hole in the wall that you made, he smashed me over the head with a brick and killed me."

"Carly, wake up! It's half past twelve." A voice in her ear instantly dragged her away from Kyle and back into herself. Her eyes shot open with a start and her gaze immediately fell on Gary's face hovering above her. She could still feel the remnants of Kyle's intense anger boiling inside her.

"ARGH!" she exclaimed aloud, and sat bolt upright in bed. Gary's expression turned to one of alarm as Carly punched her blankets.

"What's the matter?" he asked sounding alarmed.

"Seth!" exclaimed Carly, as though that explained everything. She wasn't sure she wanted to divulge the details of Kyle's family history to Gary but she couldn't withhold her anger either. Gary raised an eyebrow, seemingly wondering if Carly was going to elaborate on this statement. She opted not to. 'I can't go around blabbing about something like that', she thought. She felt as though she wasn't really entitled to know about it herself. Richard had obviously intended to show these private family matters only to Kyle, his son, but it wasn't as though Carly had been eavesdropping on purpose. She flung herself out of bed and raced past Gary to the bathroom. Ten minutes later she was ready. She emerged raring to free Kyle from his black-hearted brother. 'Half brother', she mentally corrected herself.

"Are you going to tell me what that was all about?" asked Gary.

Carly shook her head. "Not right now", she replied. "Let's just say that Seth is an even bigger asshole than we thought he was."

Gary looked perplexed but he shrugged and said nothing further about it. Carly was sure she was giving off an aura of fury that deterred him from prying too intently.

"We need to get going", she said. "We have got to somehow get Seth to drink the herbs. Heaven knows he could do with a dose of morality!"

"What about the rest of the skinwalkers?" asked Gary.

"Well, we'll deal with them later. Seth is their leader so lets focus on him."

Together they crossed the courtyard and headed for Pat and Olivia's house. Olivia opened the door and welcomed them in. "Did you sleep?" she asked. Carly and Gary both nodded. "You'll be wanting to set off then I suppose."

"Yes," replied Carly, "we haven't a moment to lose. We don't know how long it will be before the herbs take effect. We need Seth to have a change of heart and release Kyle before the heliacal rising of Sirius."

"You should take some of our young men with you", suggested Olivia. "They are all eager to help."

"No", came a croaky voice from down the corridor. Olivia turned and walked towards Pat's room. Tentatively, Carly and Gary followed. Pat was still lying in bed. "It's going to be difficult enough to sneak into the skinwalkers' camp without adding even more people to the venture", he pointed out. "You are far better going alone, just the two of you. The fewer people to be seen, the better."

Carly thought that sounded like sound sensible advice, and told him so. He smiled wryly. "Let's just hope it keeps you safe then!" he replied.

"You're going to need your burnt herbs back", said Olivia. She handed Carly a little brown leather pouch, bound at the neck with brown string. "I put them in this for you. You can't exactly be carting a mortar around with you everywhere - they'll blow out."

Carly took the pouch, thanked Olivia and placed it in her pocket. "I can't tell you how grateful we are for everything you have done for us", said Carly, feeling quite unexpectedly emotional. "You risked your lives to fight for us. That means so much! Whatever happens, always remember this."

"Now then, don't go saying things like that as though you're not going to come back", said Olivia giving her a hug. "Everything is going to be alright, I'm sure."

"You can't know that for certain", pointed out Gary. "What Carly said is true though. It was a very kind and brave thing your people did for us, so thank you."

Olivia released Carly and gave Gary a hug now. "Hush boy", she said, trying to subtly wipe away a tear which did not go unnoticed by Carly.

"Take care", said Pat.

After arming themselves with an arsenal of weaponry all laced with white ash, Carly and Gary bade the Native Americans farewell and set off through the forest. They followed the scent of the skinwalkers in the direction they had taken when they had retreated with Kyle after the fight. The scent was still quite easy for them to track despite having been a day and a half since the skinwalkers passed through this area. They walked for hours. They even reached the edge of the forest at times and had to cross over roads before returning to the forest on the other side, but the roads were quiet in any case. It was rare that travellers ventured to these parts. They passed a huge lake - at least double the size of Wolf Lake. Where Carly had grown up there hadn't been any lakes like this; she marvelled at its vastness.

"Where on Earth are they?" asked Gary as they stopped to catch something to eat.

"I guess we just have to keep going until we find them", replied Carly. Admittedly she had been wondering the same thing. She hoped they hadn't camped too far away, though she suspected it wouldn't be exactly next door to the reservation!

After they had eaten and drank they continued to walk. Gary pointed out that they were heading in an easterly direction. He could apparently tell this from the position of the sun. Carly was impressed - she had never been very good at that sort of thing, not to mention she could barely see the location of the sun through the branches above their heads. Eventually, after about four hours of brisk walking, Carly began to notice that the smell of skinwalkers had begun to be more potent than it had been previously. "They mustn't be too far away now", she said, automatically lowering her voice.

Gary lifted his nose and sniffed the air, breathing it in deeply. "They've been here recently, within the past few hours", he said. "It wouldn't be this strong a smell if they hadn't."

"We ought to be careful", said Carly. "What time is it?"

Gary looked at his watch. "Just gone five O'clock", he said. "Perhaps we should wait until dusk to make our move."

Carly shook her head. "That won't be for at least two and a half hours", she replied. "What are we going to do for all that time? Sit and twiddle our thumbs?"

"We don't want to be seen though", said Gary. "We have the advantage of being able to see in the dark. The skinwalkers may not be able to."

"The ones who are in werewolf form will," pointed out Carly, "or any who have taken the pelts of nocturnal creatures".

"Okay, so at least not all of them will be able to", conceded Gary, sounding a little subdued. "I suppose it makes no difference then really."

"Yeah", agreed Carly. "If some of them can see us, it hardly seems worth waiting until the sun has set. We might as well go now."

They set off again following the scent. Less than ten minutes later Carly heard voices ahead of them. She couldn't see anything yet for the dense collection of trees before them obscured her view but she could definitely hear talking. It sounded like quite a number of people. "Try and get a little closer without being seen", whispered Carly. She hoped against hope that none of the skinwalkers had the ability to hear sounds as clearly as she and Gary could. They both inched forwards, moving at what Carly now felt was an incredibly irritatingly slow pace. She knew they couldn't risk barrelling into the skinwalkers camp though as they would be seen. That would mean capture and certain death for both of them. They were painfully aware that the skinwalkers outnumbered them greatly. Instead, they moved silently, hiding behind trees and staying in the shadows, until at last the campsite came into view.

Carly counted around ten tents - each looked large enough for approximately two people to share. She didn't know how many skinwalkers had escaped unscathed from the fight the other night, but clearly from the look of the site they still had at least twenty men accounted for. Carly half wished that the Native Americans had accompanied them. The tribe in its entirety would probably have been greater in number now than the skinwalkers. Clearly though this wasn't something they could have anticipated without coming to view the campsite. There simply wasn't enough time for them to return to the reservation and rally an army, so Carly knew this was now something she and Gary were going to have to do on their own. She felt a wave of fear overcome her. The pit of her stomach lurched and she wondered how they should make their move. She closed her eyes for a moment to let the feeling of dizziness pass.

"Carly", Gary hissed, breaking through Carly's light-headedness. "Come on then! We've got to try and find a way to get this morality stuff into Seth's drink."

"What if he doesn't have a drink?" asked Carly, her nerves now completely getting the better of her. "What if he goes to a lake to drink or something?"

"He always had a flask with him in the cabin", replied Gary. "He must have brought it with him. I doubt he's left it behind."

Carly had forgotten about Seth's flask; it was a small silver thing that Seth had hanging from his belt. Carly had no idea what was inside it but she assumed it was some sort of alcohol. He drank from it frequently, though Carly didn't know where he kept his supply of liquor, if that was indeed what was in the flask, for she had never seen any at the cabin. "How are we going to get to his flask? He keeps it with him at all times!"

"Not when he's masquerading as a werewolf he doesn't", pointed out Gary.

That was perfectly true, Carly mused. Seth had to be naked before shifting into a werewolf, just like a real werewolf would. She sat and pondered for a moment. 'How can we force Seth into wolf form?' she thought. "We need to get him angry", she said at last. She wasn't entirely sure that was a great idea but she didn't see any alternative.

"Pardon?"

"We need to get him angry", she repeated. "If he gets angry enough, he'll probably flare up and change into wolf form."

"So then what? We steal his flask, put the herbs in it and replace it...all without being seen?"

Carly cringed slightly; when he put it like that it did seem that there was quite a high risk of failure, but she couldn't think of any other way around it. "We have to at least try," she said, "unless you can think of a better solution?"

Gary wrinkled his nose in concentration, but at last he, too, admitted that there didn't seem to be another method of getting to Seth's flask. "I'll make him angry then," said Gary, "and you go for the flask".

"I think it would be better the other way around", said Carly. When Gary began to protest, Carly held up her hand firmly. "Seth has no quarrel with you", she said. "I've already caused him to flare up - I seem to have that affect on him."

"He didn't turn into a wolf though", Gary pointed out.

Carly did realise that but she hoped he would if he were sufficiently riled up. "Look," she said, "we can either sit here debating this all night or we can give it a try. What do we have to lose?"

Gary gulped. "Do I really need to spell it out?"

He didn't, of course. Carly was well aware how dangerous this was, but every fibre of her being screamed to get Kyle away from these awful people. She had to do everything she possibly could. "I'll rile up Seth, and you get the flask", she said.

Gary nodded and Carly reached into her pocket for the pouch of dried herbs. She passed them to Gary. Then, on the count of three, they began to move nearer and nearer to the campsite, trying to make as little noise as possible. The closer they got the more people Carly could see but she couldn't yet see Seth. They couldn't go into the campsite to look for him, of course - that would alert the other skinwalkers to their presence. What they needed was some way of drawing Seth into the forest.

Suddenly, there he was. Carly's head shot up and Gary had to grab her to pull her down to the ground beside him. Seth was not alone; three other skinwalkers, all in human form, were walking beside him talking. Although they were far away, Carly could make out what they were saying. It was quite a mundane discussion about collecting firewood. Seth was being as bombastic as ever and was clearly making use of his authority toward the other skinwalkers by bossing them around.

"Go and fetch some firewood", he ordered, waving them away. Carly couldn't help thinking that Seth's inflated sense of ego was quite ludicrous. She wondered how he had come to be the leader of the skinwalkers in the first place. Surely they had already had leaders when he had joined up with them as a boy. Of course there was no time to think about this further - now was their ideal opportunity. Seth was standing alone with no other skinwalkers in sight. Her heart beating wildly, Carly impulsively picked up a stick and threw it in Seth's direction. Gary immediately took his cue from this and dived out of sight behind another tree.

Seth jumped as the stick hit him squarely on the leg. His eyes flashed and he growled softly. "Who did that?" he said angrily. He began to walk in the direction the stick had come from. Then he stopped and laughed - a frightening manic sort of laugh. "Carly my dear, I know it's you. I may not be able to smell you while I'm in human form, but you don't have to be a werewolf to realise you would come after your precious Kyle. In fact I've been expecting you."

Carly didn't reply. She flung another stick at him, and another, and then another. Each one hit Seth quite forcefully. He growled again, louder this time, "Stop it Carly, you know this is futile." Carly threw another stick. This time Seth's face changed to display an expression of complete anger. "You wanna play with the big boys, little girl? Fine!" He roared and tore off his clothes. Flinging them aside he immediately changed into a wolf. Carly briefly wondered how he had managed to achieve this without having any visible pelt, but she didn't time to think about it for long.

"Oh shit!" muttered Carly and dived off the ground. She began to run through the forest as fast as her legs could carry her. She could hear the soft pads of Seth's paws closing in. She could practically feel his breath panting behind her. Carly knew she didn't stand a chance at outrunning him. He had the speed of a werewolf but she would not be able to run as quickly as that until after her first lunar change. She changed direction and darted left and right amongst the trees, hoping to confuse Seth with her erratic motions. It did nothing to help. 'It's too bad he's not an alligator', she thought (Carly had once read a book which informed her that alligators have a hard time chasing somebody who is running away from them in a zig-zags. How reliable the book was, Carly wasn't entirely sure). She realised this was a ridiculous time to be thinking about alligators! "Aaaahhhh!" she screamed, as Seth's razor sharp teeth clamped down on one of her legs. She turned around and punched him in the face. He growled at her viciously and continued to hold onto her appendage. Blood was seeping through the leg of her trousers and it stained the fur around Seth's mouth. Carly's stomach lurched as the pain seared through her. "Get off me you lowlife!" She spat the words out at him, struggling to catch her breath. "What's the matter? You just jealous because your little brother got the girl? Who'd have you anyway? Look at you, you're vile!"

Seth retaliated by biting down on her leg even deeper, which made Carly cry out again. The pain was not dissimilar to when she had injured her leg earlier that week in the trap. Seth began to walk back to the skinwalker campsite, his jaws still holding fast. Carly found herself being dragged along the ground on her back. Her body scraped across every stick, twig and bramble bush as they went. She grabbed hold of a strong stick and began to hit Seth's back with it as hard as she could manage, but although he flinched it simply wasn't sufficient enough to force him to release her leg.

As they neared the campsite, Carly felt her heart rate increase. All the other skinwalkers came out to see what had been happening. They had obviously heard the racket that Carly and Seth had been making in the forest. Devon was there also and Carly called out to him as she was dragged past. "Devon, help me, please!" but her cries fell on deaf ears and he turned his head away. Finally, Seth stopped walking and opened his mouth. This movement in itself caused a new wave of agony to course up her leg. She tried to block out the intense pain from her mind and made a valiant effort to scramble to her feet, but she realised she had nowhere to run as she was now surrounded by skinwalkers.

"I could kill you now," said Seth, who had turned back into a human again, "but then you wouldn't get to enjoy my little show tonight", he smirked. Then he paused as though remembering something. "Ah yes, of course, it's your big night tonight as well isn't it! Well I can't very well kill you until you've experienced your first time - that would be very…unsporting of me."

"What are you going to do with me?" asked Carly through gritted teeth. Her leg felt dangerously close to buckling underneath her. In fact she was amazed she was able to stand at all. She attributed it to sheer willpower and adrenalin. She didn't know whether she was more angry or afraid at this point.

"Well my dear, first of all you can witness our beautiful ceremony. Then in the morning, with my new abilities…let's just say we're going to play a little game of cat and mouse. I'll be the cat!"

"You're going to obtain the ability to shift into the beast and then you're going to kill me?" said Carly in horror.

"Oh I'll give you a fair chance", said Seth. "I like a good chase!"

Carly felt her blood run cold. He planned to hunt her down like a dog chasing a fox. Even if she was in wolf form in the morning, the beast form of the werewolf would rip her to shreds. "I'd rather you just killed me now and have done with it", she muttered.

"Well unluckily for you, bitch, you have no say in the matter", snarled Seth aggressively. He nodded his head and two skinwalkers stepped forward to bind her wrists together behind her back with a silver chain. Instantly the burning sensation flooded through her arms. Carly gritted her teeth; she didn't want to give him the satisfaction of hearing her cry out.

"Don't worry, tomorrow will come along soon enough", said Seth. He grabbed hold of her long hair and yanked it viciously.

Carly couldn't help herself - she yelped and tears sprang to her eyes. "Where are you taking me?" she cried. Her unwilling feet had no choice but to walk in the direction she was being pulled. Every step sent a wave of agony through her injured leg. The pain was explosive. Carly began to see black spots forming in front of her eyes. She wondered if she was going to lose consciousness. Her head was twisted backwards so she couldn't see where she was going. She stumbled and tripped as they went.

"You don't think I was naive enough to think that you wouldn't show up? I took the liberty of preparing a guest room for you." They came to a stop. Before Carly could even straighten up and get her bearings, Seth shoved her forcefully and she felt herself falling through the air. She let out a shriek as she slammed into the floor below; the impact shuddered through her body and the pain intensified to the point of numbness. She lay still for a moment, unsure as to whether or not she had broken any bones. "Enjoy your stay", taunted Seth. Then Carly heard his footsteps walking away.

CHAPTER FIFTEEN

Slowly Carly moved her unharmed leg. Her arms were still tied together with the silver chain. She didn't dare move her injured limb for it was so painful. Her chest hurt. She suspected she may have cracked a rib, but she knew it ought to heal relatively quickly. She attempted to sit up but was aware she would have to push both feet against the floor to succeed. Summoning all her courage, she dug her heels into the hard soil and managed to hoist herself up into a sitting position. She let out a blood-curdling scream as a new wave of pain shot through her leg. Her only consolation was the realisation that, in much the same way as her ribs, the bite would heal reasonably quickly. Carly could now look around and analyse the situation. She was in a deep rectangular pit. 'Seth must have had this pit dug out on purpose', she thought. 'What else could contain a werewolf during the lunar change? A tent wouldn't work!'

At first Carly fought to remove the bonds which cruelly tied her arms behind her back. The silver was burning her skin. She tugged and pulled with all her might to wriggle free of the accursed chain. It was to no avail though. She sighed with frustration and leant back against the pit wall. The sky was still light above her head but she knew that wouldn't be the case for much longer. She wondered where Gary was and whether or not he had managed to slip the ashes of herbs into Seth's flask. "That's pretty much our only hope now", she said aloud. To make matters worse, Carly still hadn't even seen Kyle. She had vaguely caught a whiff of his scent as she had been taken through the campsite though so she assumed he must be relatively close by. There was nothing she could do now other than wait. Her stomach rumbled loudly, reminding her that it would be wise if she caught something to eat, Of course that was impossible. The waiting was agony. Carly had no way to tell the time, but as the sky began to darken and the stars became visible, she figured it must be around half past seven. 'Four and a half hours until midnight.' Already her toes were feeling slightly numb and her fingertips were experiencing pins and needles. She didn't know if the latter was as a result of her arms being bound or whether or not it was some sort of pre-change side effect. Either way it was a little disconcerting.

Darkness fell. Carly had just about given up hope and assumed that Gary had left, or worse yet been killed, when she heard a noise above her. "Psst! Psst!"

Carly looked up with a start. "Gary?" she whispered.

"Yeah", came back the hushed reply. "I'm going to see if I can get you out of there."

"Did you manage to get to the flask?"

"Not now, we'll talk about it when you're free!" he hissed. Gary prowled around the edge of the pit, looking for a way to get in and out easily. The walls of the pit were very steep; not even a wolf would be able to jump out. The earth was crumbly so climbing to freedom was not an option.

"Well then, what have we got here?" A voice from behind Gary made them both jump. It was Seth. "I should have known you would tag along you pathetic sheep."

Even from within the pit Carly could see that that Gary's shoulders had stiffened with indignation at this last comment. He let out what could only be described as a roar and lunged himself forward, presumably straight at Seth. Carly could see none of the ensuing fight, but after a few minutes she found that she had company; Gary had come sailing down into the pit. He landed a few feet from her and twisted his neck awkwardly. Carly inwardly cringed. "Christ, are you all right?" she asked, shuffling on her bottom towards him. Thankfully the pain in her leg had eased slightly and she was able to move without too much difficulty.

Gary let out a groan in response and rolled onto his back. "That was a joyful reunion", he said sarcastically, pain etched on his face. Carly tugged again at her chains, annoyed at not having her hands free to be able to tend to her friend.

"Let me get those for you", said Gary, who had no chains himself. Carly slid around to face away from Gary and waited patiently as he removed them for her. They must have been burning his hands as he did so but he didn't complain.

Carly's intense relief at having the chains no longer touching her skin was short lived when she learned what Gary had seen. "I managed to sneak the herbs into the flask no problem", said Gary. "Then I hid in the bushes to watch Seth fetch his clothes; but Seth didn't come back for his clothes at all. He caught you instead and brought you here."

"Do you know if he went back for them after that?" asked Carly. "Perhaps he had a drink then."

Gary shook his head. "I was there for ages and then I saw Devon coming. He picked up the clothes. Seth must have given him orders to fetch them for him."

"So did you follow him to see if Devon gave Seth the flask as well?"

Gary looked grim. "He drank from it", he muttered.

"What? Devon did?"

"Uh-huh."

Carly's stomach flipped over. "I think I'm gonna be sick", she said. "Our entire plan rested on Seth drinking that stuff."

"I know", said Gary. He sounded utterly despondent, exactly the way Carly was feeling. They sat in the pit together in silence.

Carly racked her brain trying desperately to think of some way out of this predicament. She had to admit it seemed hopeless. "We're gonna die", she said. Carly didn't want to die. In fact she was terrified of dying. The prospect of no longer being alive hadn't so far seemed to be anything more than a surreal notion that couldn't possibly happen. Even during the fight with the skinwalkers, bearing in mind how close that young skinwalker werewolf had come to killing her, a voice in the back of her mind had niggled at her that she couldn't possibly die - not then, not there. Now though it was different; for the first time since becoming a werewolf it had finally hit her. They were going to die! She wanted to scream and cry and punch somebody. Gary said nothing but kept his head slumped forward, his eyes staring down at the ground. This did nothing to raise Carly's spirits. Carly fell silent again and listened to the hustle and bustle of the skinwalker camp above as they busied themselves ready for the ceremony. Finally, after a couple of hours, Carly's ears pricked up at the sound of a familiar voice.

"Get off me you asshole."

Kyle! It was Kyle! Carly leapt to her feet and rushed to the edge of the pit. Frantically she tried once again to climb up the steep walls, but to no avail. "Kyle!" she yelled. "Oh God Kyle, are you all right?"

"Carly? Shit what are you doing here?" Kyle's worried voice called back to her. Clearly he had no idea that Gary and Carly had come to the skinwalkers' territory.

"Shut up you!" a voice snarled from above Carly's head. Carly heard Kyle yelp in pain.

"Leave him alone!" she cried, her heart in her mouth. She couldn't bear the thought they were hurting Kyle. It seemed so unnecessarily cruel considering they planned to slaughter him. Did they have to make his last few hours so painful?

"You shut up as well or I'll come down there and deal with you."

"Just try it", called Gary. "There are two of us down here!"

The skinwalker, whoever he was, didn't bother replying. Carly listened to various noises above her head that she couldn't identify. Eventually she caught sight of something above the pit. "What the hell is that?" she said aloud. Then she realised what was happening; the skinwalkers were raising a large wooden pole into the air. Half way up the pole was Kyle. He was tied to it with silver chains, way up in the air, with his arms high above his head. Chains were wrapped around his wrists, neck, waist and ankles. Even from far below in the pit, Carly could see with her enhanced vision that his skin was blistered where the chains were touching him.

"Oh my God", said Gary clutching Carly's arm. She flinched as his hand touched her wrist - it was still very sore from where she had been tied up. "Sorry", said Gary, immediately letting go.

"Carly, I'm sorry, this is all my fault", said Kyle relatively quietly. Though he was high in the air above the pit, Carly and Gary could of course hear him perfectly well with their enhanced hearing.

"Don't be silly, it's not your fault at all", replied Carly. "If anything it's our fault! Our rescue plan didn't exactly work."

"It's nobody's fault", said Gary firmly.

"I'm scared", said Carly, voicing what was on everybody's minds.

"Yeah, me too", agreed Kyle. "We'll figure something out I'm sure."

"Your optimism is a bit unrealistic don't you think?" replied Gary glumly.

The three werewolves had nothing further to say for a few minutes. Then a thought came to Carly. "Are Gary and I going to kill each other?" she asked, her voice trembling. "We're both going to change at midnight, aren't we?"

"I don't know what's going to happen", said Kyle. His voice was beginning to sound strained as his body bore the brunt of being strapped to the pole. "I've never known two werewolves share close proximity during a full moon before."

"Chances are we're going to rip each other to shreds", said Gary.

Carly kicked him slightly. "You're not making me feel any better!" she said. Gary stopped talking and once again silence descended upon the trio. Time ticked by; Carly was practically counting the minutes in her head - five minutes, twenty minutes, forty minutes...closer and closer to midnight. She could hear the skinwalkers above chanting and talking, apparently waiting for their opportune moment to begin the ritual. She kept asking Gary at intervals what time it was. Finally he replied that it was five to midnight.

"Oh hell", said Carly. She stood up and began to pace around the pit. Gary did nothing but remained seated, as he had been, stony faced. Carly glanced up at Kyle - he had his eyes closed. She could see him moving slightly, gritting his teeth against the pain from the chains. "I'm really scared", she said again. Tears began to form in her eyes. She thought about all the plans she had made in her life. She wanted to travel around the world, get married one day perhaps and maybe even have children. None of these things would ever happen now though she suspected deep down that she had lost her opportunity to fulfill her dreams when she had become a werewolf. That wasn't much consolation at this time though.

"One minute", announced Gary. His deadpan expression was virtually impossible to read.

'Sixty, fifty-nine, fifty-eight, fifty-seven,' Carly began to count down in her head. She only got as far as forty-two though when a pain unlike anything she had ever experienced before surged through her body. It was as though she had just plunged into a vat of burning acid. She screamed aloud and dropped to the floor. A roar from Gary beside her told her that the lunar change had hit him as well.

"I thought you said we had one minute!" she gasped, struggling to speak. "Your watch is forty two seconds slow!"

Another wave of agony coursed through her body. Carly could hear terrible cracking noises coming from her legs as she felt her limbs contorting in entirely the wrong direction. With the corner of her eye she glanced down at her feet just in time to witness spurts of blood gushing from her toes, as huge black claws emerged from underneath her skin, tearing it back as they grew. She threw back her head and tried to scream, but instead out came a deep guttural sound. Carly thought that she could make out some similar noises coming from Kyle on the pole, but she was too consumed by her own torture to take much notice of what was happening around her. Even Gary now had become insignificant, as she writhed on the floor wondering when this hell would stop. She still had full control of her mind at this point but her body was another matter. RIP!...

Carly heard her clothes tear from her body; they fell away from her in shreds as though they were made of paper. Then she was naked, half monster and half human; her once slender feminine form now sprouting hair and contorted strangely. Her chest felt as though it was about to explode, and as her bones broke and shifted into new positions, her stomach jolted with nausea. Suddenly, Carly became aware that her mouth felt strangely too full of teeth; among all the other sensations she was enduring, at first this was merely uncomfortable rather than painful, but unfortunately this was not to last. As the first stinging wave of discomfort rippled through her gums, Carly realised that this would only intensify as her new fangs grew; she was right. Within a matter of seconds the sensations within her mouth were so agonising she couldn't hold back the nausea any longer. She lifted her hands to cover her mouth. As she did so, claws protruded from each finger sending blood spurting through the air and her finger joints twisted and snapped. She retched as her body tried to vomit, but was held back, as if to cause even more torture.

She couldn't even make a sound now other than pant, for the pain was too intense. Her heart was beating so fast she thought it would explode. As her rib cage contracted within her chest, Carly began to see darkness envelop her and she passed out. She couldn't have said how long she was unconscious for; it seemed to be both instantaneous and endless at the same time. When she opened her eyes she was dazed and confused. Her hands tied above her head had gone numb from having been raised for so long. The instinct to feed, kill and rip apart anything in her path was so strong.

She looked down at the pit and was horrified by what she was seeing. Two enormous black beasts were wrestling with each other with their claws bared. These monstrosities looked like the stuff of nightmares with their massive bulks of muscle and sinew covered with fur. Their elongated snouts snarled and their protruding yellowish teeth were snapping at each other, drool dripping from their up-curled top lips. A ridge of spiked hair ran up both of their backs. Carly caught her breath as she realised that she was looking at the pit she had just been in; this meant the monsters were her and Gary. They danced around the pit on their bowed hind legs, lashing out at each other in cumbersome movements. One of the beasts lifted its paw and struck out at the other's face.

"Argh!" thought Carly. Her cheek began to sting and she let out a roar. This didn't make any sense to her. She was tied to a pole not down there in the pit. 'How am I able to feel that hit?' she thought. Her mind and Kyle's mind both struggled to make sense of what was happening. As the thoughts swam around their now shared consciousness, Seth approached the pole. In his hand he was holding something which emitted a strange glimmer of green light, though Carly couldn't initially make out what it was.

"You may have noticed little brother that you are still very much aware of yourself", he said smiling. "That was the first part of the ritual; to make you self aware while being in beast form." Seth began to twirl the object around in his fingers, passing it over his knuckles as though it were a quarter. The moonlight struck it and Carly could see that it was some sort of shining unusual crystal. She had never seen a jewel gleam at night the way this one did. Seth chuckled. "This little beauty is the reason you're not running around like a crazed dog right now", he sneered. "You should be grateful actually - I'm practically doing you a favour by sparing you from a night of amnesia!" He cleared his throat. "Lesson one in skinwalker traditions", continued Seth as though he were a school-teacher. "The leader of the skinwalker pack holds all the pack's magic in a crystal. If he is killed by another, they gain the crystal and the position." He smiled proudly. "The last pack leader never even saw me coming!"

Carly opened her mouth to speak but all that came out was a howl.

"That power of yours, that strength, there's nothing like it on earth", Seth marvelled. "Soon all that will be mine." Carly thought that he sounded like a villain from a cheesy movie. She growled and strained with all her might at the chains binding her to the pole, but they held tight. "No matter how strong you are though you're not going to get free", said Seth. "Even in beast form you are still weakened by silver."

Carly felt a sudden sting in her shoulder and she looked back over to the pit. One of the beasts was pinning the other to the ground. Its huge claws sunk deep into the earth, stopping the subdued werewolf from moving. Its teeth clamped down into the shoulder of the creature beneath it, at which point the pinned monster bit back into the arm of its attacker and they both rolled away from each other. 'I've got to do something about this', thought Carly, who had by now realised that she and Kyle were both occupying Kyle's beast form. She concentrated on Carly's body, which was thrashing around wildly attacking Gary, totally out of anybody's control. 'Stand still', she thought. Nothing happened. Carly's body continued to lunge at Gary, swinging her massive paws around and stomping her enormous feet. They were both huge, much larger than werewolves in wolf form but more cumbersome. 'Come on, stand still.' Still no effect; Carly's real body continued roaring and lunging at Gary as though a demon were puppeteering it. Carly took a deep breath. 'Come on Kyle,' she thought to herself, 'and come on Carly! You can do this!' She no longer knew precisely whose mind was in control though she felt as though she was Kyle. Either way, she was aware that somehow Carly's mind needed to be reunited with its true form. She closed her eyes and began to meditate in a way that Kyle was well practised in. He used a similar technique when he wanted to phase out from this plane of reality and into the one they had hidden in when the hunters had come to the cabin. Together, Carly and Kyle as one concentrated on Carly's body.

"What are you doing?" called up Seth sounding confused. Carly heard him once but then blocked out the sound of any further noises. She closed Kyle's mind from any outside distractions.

"Stand STILL", she commanded, channelling her energy into her real body. She opened her eyes and peered down into the pit. To her amazement, Carly's body was standing completely still. Unfortunately, her relief at having been able to remotely control her own body was short-lived by the fact that Gary was still raining down his blows onto her. If she had not been in beast form at that time, he would have certainly killed her. It was only the fact that werewolf beasts seemed to have unnaturally tough hides that acted as a shield in her defence. "Look out!" cried Carly in alarm, but the only sound that came from Kyle's lips was a long loud howl. Gary lunged at her again in a flurry of teeth and claws. Of course her real body did nothing though. It merely stood where it was, as she had willed it to, and took the hit.

"OWWWW!" screamed Carly as she felt the burning agony of Gary's attack – even from within Kyle's body. 'Okay, I've got to do something!' she thought desperately. Summoning all mental strength, she willed her real body to walk forwards. It did so. As Carly got the hang of what she was doing, she found she was able to control her own body quite well even though her mind was not inside it; it was almost as though she was playing a computer game of sorts. She ducked and weaved from Gary's attacks, all the while trying desperately not to hurt him. The beast's instinct to attack any living thing within its reach was still strong. At times when her concentration slacked slightly, the beast snarled and snapped of its own accord, but she was able to quickly rein it back into check. "We're not damn well dying here tonight!" she said aloud. Again, no words came out, just a beast-like snarl. It didn't seem to matter. It took every shred of thought-power contained within Kyle and Carly's minds to do what they did next. Carly's beast form took two steps forward, then in one swift motion it grabbed hold of Gary and hurled him upwards and out of the pit. Even for a strong werewolf that was no easy feat. Carly instantly felt the strain hit the muscles of Kyle's upper forearms, as though Kyle's body and Carly's were as intertwined as their minds were.

Far below the pole the skinwalkers screamed and fell over each other in their scramble to get away from Gary. The rampant beast grabbed a skinwalker, who was puny in comparison, and in the blink of an eye ripped him apart and began to devour his remains. Some skinwalkers had managed to get hold of their pelts and had shifted into various creatures. As Carly watched, still trapped inside Kyle's head and still tied to the pole, on the ground below two grey wolves jumped onto the massive werewolf's back and began to bite him and tear at his flesh with their teeth and claws. Gary's beast form howled loudly and began to jerk around, looking as though he was trying to throw them off him. One of the wolves was flung from him and skidded across the ground on its belly. The other wolf clung on, its teeth sunk deep into the great brute's neck.

Carly howled in frustration not knowing what to do. If only she could break free of the chains that held Kyle's body captive. In vain she pulled at the chains, pleading to the heavens for a miracle to happen. She looked back down at the ground and did not see Seth. 'He must have run away when Gary was flung out of the pit', she thought. That figured - just like a coward to run away. Carly could feel Kyle's hatred for the brother he once loved filling his mind and soul.

Watching Gary fight the skinwalkers, Carly felt useless. She wanted to help and tried to meditate again to return her mind fully into her real body, but it didn't work. It seemed she had no control over this; it came and went seemingly at random and it was stubbornly refusing to put her back in the right place.

Below her, the beast shook the wolf from its back and managed to claw at it, instantly tearing it in half with its huge powerful talons. The skinwalkers who were still in human form were screaming in fear as the werewolf lunged towards them. Stretching out its rippled fur-covered arm, the beast grabbed hold of the nearest man and sank its claws deep into the pale white flesh of his shoulder. Dark red blood poured from the man's wounds immediately and ran down his back; his desperate cries of terror filled the air. The werewolf dragged its prey towards it and with one powerful snap of its jaws it severed the skinwalker's torso in two.

Carly felt a strange combination of sensations bubbling inside her - a mixture of relief that the werewolf appeared to be coping quite well alone with the onslaught of attacks from the skinwalkers, and a burning desire to join in and sink her teeth into some of them herself and savour their flesh. She was horrified at this second thought but she couldn't dismiss it; the instinct to kill which had arisen when she had turned into a werewolf, was so intense that it was almost overpowering. The smell of the fresh blood from the man that the beast had just ripped apart wafted up to Kyle's nostrils. Carly felt his mouth begin to salivate.

The huge creature lifted its head from chewing on its latest victim's intestines and howled; it was a sound that pierced through the night like a siren. Carly jumped, startled. Then without knowing why she did so, she threw back her head and howled in response. The noise, which came from her throat, was low, guttural and very loud. The werewolf on the ground raised its arms upwards, almost in a gesturing motion, as though it had heard her. The skinwalkers around it in various animal forms were desperately trying to launch themselves at the beast with their teeth bared, but the huge creature momentarily appeared to ignore them. Then it drew a long slow breath, paused for a moment and roared with all the power of a miniature tornado. The skinwalkers physically lifted off the ground at the force of its breath and were flung back several metres. One skinwalker in the form of a snake slammed into a tree, impaling itself on a sharp branch. It fell dead onto the moss below in human form. Carly caught her breath at the sight of the werewolf's extraordinary strength.

The pole began to shake. She tried to see what was causing this to happen, but vertically downward was not an angle she could turn her head to because her neck was also tied to the pole. The shaking continued and Carly realised that somebody was climbing up the pole. All sorts of visions danced in her mind, not least of all scenes of a skinwalker slitting Kyle's throat in order to complete the ritual.

'Don't be ridiculous', she tried to rationalise with herself. 'It's nowhere near dawn. It can't be much past one in the morning. They wouldn't complete the ritual just yet, surely?'

She didn't have time to reason with herself any longer though, for a hand grabbing her ankle sent an impulsive roar to be emitted from her. She wriggled her legs but they were tied too solidly for her to be able to move very much. She thrashed around and suddenly she found that her legs were able to kick freely! Somebody had removed the chain from her ankles!

"Who are you?" she cried out, but to her dismay she was still roaring and howling. It was so exasperating not being able to speak!

Far below the blood-curdling screams of the skinwalkers continued to resonate. Out of the corner of her eye Carly could see their numbers had dwindled. Dismembered bodies were scattered on the grass. The werewolf in the midst of this gruesome scene had ripped off the leg of another skinwalker; holding it by the ankle it began to chew away the flesh, guzzling it down as though it were a leg of lamb. The wounded skinwalker himself, barely alive, had huge claw-marks down his back. As he dragged himself along the ground on his stomach, blood poured from these wounds and from his ragged stump.

The pole began to shake dangerously; whoever was climbing the pole had now moved around to the back of it in order to continue climbing without Kyle's body being an obstruction. Carly felt the chain fall away from around Kyle's waist. No doubt about it, somebody was freeing them. She didn't have the faintest idea who it could be. Was it Pat or Olivia? One of the Native Americans? Had they sneaked into the skinwalkers' campsite in a bid to free Carly, Kyle and Gary?

Just a few moments later Carly's neck had been freed; she was now dangling by her wrists alone. The strain on her wrist bones was terrible considering all of Kyle's heavy beast-like body was pulling down on that chain. Carly felt that Kyle's wrists would certainly end up broken. The pain only lasted a short time though as the chain slackened, and down, down, down Carly fell to the ground with a thunk.

She lay stiffly where she had landed. Kyle's whole body was wracked with pain. She blinked, her head on the ground. A face appeared before her eyes.

Carly gasped in horror - it was another werewolf, another werewolf in beast form. Gary? No, it couldn't be Gary; Carly could still hear him growling and snarling several feet away from her.

'Devon!' she realised. 'But how?' Then it hit her - of course, he had drunk the morality potion. It must have triggered self-awareness in him also. They stared at each other for a few moments. Then just like a flash Devon had gone.

Carly struggled to sit up; she had to move because the destructive beast was very close by. The scent of the mutilated skinwalkers teased her nostrils. She paused for a moment, drawn in an almost hypnotic state towards one of them lying nearby. She licked her lips at the sight of the blood and she took a step forward. A bellow from the rampaging werewolf in the distance shook Carly out of her trance. She stumbled away from the dead skinwalker, fighting her urges to feed. She didn't want to risk an encounter with the monster that had caused this mayhem.

A branch from a tree came flying past her head and smashed onto the ground a few yards from where Carly was standing. Kyle's body reacted almost instinctively; immediately its fur stood on end and its muscles tensed. Carly felt its mouth open as though to roar, but she forced it to close and remain silent, overriding Kyle's involuntary actions. She didn't want to alert the other werewolf to her presence for it couldn't be far away.

A movement between some trees caught her eye and Carly caught sight of the beast. Another apparently lifeless skinwalker was dangling from its mouth. This one seemed to be largely in one piece and was simply being carried. It reminded Carly of a dog retrieving a pheasant or duck. With a grunt the creature dropped the man. He gave a small groan. The werewolf growled and immediately bit the man's neck. He gurgled and blood began to ooze out of his mouth. His wide-open eyes had a look of frantic desperation in them but he was not to suffer for long. Within a few seconds the skinwalker had stopped moving; his expression of terror still etched on his now motionless face.

Forcing Kyle's body to move, Carly staggered over to the pit. Looking in she could see her own body hurling itself around the pit, clawing at the walls and trying to get out. The mindless beast had taken over again since Carly had broken her concentration in controlling it. She scrutinised it with a mixture of disgust and awe; it seemed incredible that this massive hideous monster was her.

The creature's eyes glowed a dull red and it looked up at her for a moment. Carly had a sudden surreal feeling of being in two places at the same time.

'You stay there for now', she mentally told it. 'You're safer in there than you are out here!'

A howl unlike anything Carly had ever heard came from behind her. It was the single most horrible sound she could imagine. She prayed she would never hear a sound like it again. She spun around just in time to see the huge monster holding a skinwalker up in the air with its huge claws. The skinwalker had his mouth open wide as if screaming, but nothing came out. The look of sheer terror on his face and his drained pale complexion showed the dread he felt.

In one swift motion the beast pulled in two directions, ripping the skinwalker in half. After a second of pause the creature flung the two halves of the bloodied husk to one side revealing the cause of its anguish, dropping to its knees with an arrow sticking out of its chest.

"NOOOOO!" screamed Carly, though it sounded like a great roar. She rushed over to the fallen werewolf immediately. The beast toppled sideways onto the ground and its breathing became laboured; it was clear that the arrow had struck it very close to the heart.

"Gary! No, don't die, please don't die!" begged Carly wordlessly. She could feel sobs beginning to build up inside Kyle's throat but the only sound she made was an anguished whine. The beast's gaze fell upon Kyle's face. Carly thought she could see a glimmer of recognition in its eyes. A small choked noise escaped from its lips and it drew its last breath with a shudder. Almost immediately the creature changed back into its human form. Carly winced to see the arrow protruding from Gary's naked body.

"Silver tipped with aconite", said Seth proudly, standing a few feet away, brandishing a crossbow at her. "Got this from the hunter I managed to kill yesterday. The pathetic bastard was wandering around in the forest looking for me; no doubt he had realised I was the one who killed his family." Seth continued to soliloquise sounding very smug. "Pretty little thing his daughter was but she just point blank refused to join with us. Said she didn't want anything to do with skinwalkers. So she had to go. I couldn't have her running off and telling people of our existence - that would never do. Her mother, the interfering old busy body, she just got in the way!"

Seth pulled another arrow from behind his back and loaded it into the crossbow he was holding. He pointed this at Kyle's body. "Now listen to me, you're going to do this ritual with me otherwise I will shoot you."

'What difference does it make?' thought Carly, 'he's going to kill Kyle anyway regardless!'

As though he had read Carly's thoughts, Seth continued. "Oh

and I wouldn't bother trying to play the hero, because if you don't comply your girlfriend in the pit will be joining you. When I'm done with you both I know a certain reservation I can get my hands on. But if you do as I say and be a good boy, Carly can go free and I'll leave the Native Americans alone." With that, Seth changed the direction of his crossbow and aimed it at Carly's real werewolf body in the pit.

Carly fought to separate her thoughts from those of Kyle. Kyle's mind was wondering if Seth might be genuinely planning to let Carly go after the ceremony, providing he went along with it and sacrificed himself. Carly, of course, knew otherwise. Seth had already told her what he intended to do with her. The two conflicting sets of information were bouncing around inside the same brain. Carly felt as though she was getting a migraine.

She faltered, feeling terribly confused. Kyle wanted to believe his brother; Carly knew this because she felt his emotions. Despite everything that had happened, everything that Seth had done, despite all the lives he had been responsible for ending including Gemma and Richard's, Kyle was still clinging to a hope in the pit of his stomach that his brother could be reformed and that he could change - that he wasn't just pure evil through and through. He hated his brother passionately but a very tiny part of him still saw Seth as his older brother, as his pack leader, as somebody he ought to care about. He knew Seth had no real right to be called a pack leader - he wasn't even a werewolf. Kyle was the real alpha. That was fine in theory, but for years Kyle had looked up to Seth. He was now finding it difficult to change his old way of thinking.

Carly wrestled against these feelings of Kyle's. She needed clear rational thoughts, not a misguided sense of loyalty to a monster. She tried to access the part of her mind containing Carly's memories instead of those belonging to Kyle. Slowly, with much mental pushing, a small crack broke through to separate the two consciousnesses. Carly remembered she already knew that Seth meant to kill her. Sweat poured from her brow from the strain of the mental exhaustion which was almost physically painful.

'If he already means to kill Carly,' thought Carly, involuntarily retreating back into Kyle's mind again, like a rubber band snapping back into place after having been stretched, 'then chances are he won't hesitate to slaughter the Native Americans either once he has obtained the power of the beast'.

Having just watched Gary slay at least two thirds of the skinwalker tribe single handedly, Carly now knew how powerful the werewolf beasts were. It was likely that the only reason Seth had been able to shoot him was because Gary was not in control of his own body. A werewolf beast in full control was quite a different story. Carly knew that she, right now, could easily finish off the entire rest of the skinwalkers including Seth, were he not aiming an arrow directly at Carly's real body. She didn't dare to make a move in case that crossbow ended up being fired.

Thinking logically though, if Seth was going to kill Carly and the Native Americans, regardless of whether or not the ritual was to continue Carly realised that she and Kyle both had nothing to lose. She lowered her head and walked slowly forward toward Seth, trying to appear as though Kyle were offering his submission. Seth hesitated for a minute then adjusted his stance slightly to a less aggressive pose, though he still kept his crossbow trained on the pit. "So predictable little brother", he sneered. "Willing to give your life to save others. Very commendable." His voice dripped with sarcasm. It took every ounce of Carly's will power to hold back from tearing him apart then and there.

The remaining skinwalkers were beginning to gather around again. Carly counted perhaps seven or eight of them, no more than that. Devon was nowhere in sight, though Carly hadn't spotted his body amongst the fallen skinwalkers. She wondered if he had run away into the forest, or even whether or not Seth had noticed the disappearance of his wing man.

Seth motioned with his head towards what could only be described as a sort of makeshift altar to the far end of the campsite. It consisted of a large rock, large enough for a big werewolf to be able to lie down on; the top had been smoothed away so the surface was flat. "Get on that", he commanded Kyle, still keeping his crossbow pointed at Carly's beast form. Carly wondered how he had been planning to tie Kyle to that altar from the pole in the first place if everything had gone according to his plans. Perhaps he would have shot Kyle with a tranquilliser she supposed. Despite herself, she was actually a little curious about the ritual, though not to the extent that she wanted to witness it first hand! She wished she could ask Seth about it but of course that was impossible.

Looking at Seth, Carly found herself remembering, via Kyle's memories, when he and Kyle used to play together as cowboys and indians and chase each other around the garden. They must have only been around three and six years old - when Gemma was only a baby. Things had been so much simpler then. Seth had been a brilliant older brother up until he was about eleven years old. Carly recalled when Kyle had celebrated his eighth birthday - Seth had sneaked off during the party and smashed up all Kyle's birthday presents because he had been jealous. That was the end of their childhood games together. Seth had acted pretty much like a selfish jerk ever since. Carly felt a tear come to her eye as she experienced Kyle's sadness and nostalgia.

"Get on it!" barked Seth sounding impatient. Carly growled and reluctantly headed over to the stone. She took a deep breath then heaved herself onto it.

"Lie down!"

Carly lay down. As she watched, another skinwalker brought some heavy silver chains over to Seth.

"Do you want me to tie him up?" he asked.

Seth furrowed his brow. "I'll do it myself", he said after a moment's thought. "I don't trust anybody else to tie him up after the fiasco we had earlier with him somehow managing to escape from that pole."

'So he doesn't know Devon untied me?' thought Carly in surprise. 'He assumes I just managed to break free?' It would make sense she supposed, considering all the chaos that had been happening at the time with Gary rampaging through the camp.

Seth looked slyly now at Carly. "I don't think you're likely to be going anywhere in a hurry while we have your girlfriend under our...protection...as it were," he said, "but having you wrapped in silver just adds a certain something to this performance, don't you think?" He smiled, a twisted manic looking smile.

With that, Seth handed his crossbow to another skinwalker to the side of him. "Keep this bow trained on that pit", he snapped. "Any funny business from this one and you shoot her." Then he took the chains from the first skinwalker.

'This is it', thought Carly. 'It's now or never.'

She gritted her teeth, wondering how badly it would hurt when that aconite laced arrow struck her real body. Then just as Seth lifted his hands to place the chain around Kyle's body, Carly dived off the rock as swiftly as she could and sank her teeth into Seth. She had been aiming for his neck, but he had managed to move his head so her first bite only dug into his shoulder.

"ARGH!" screamed Seth, wrestling with the beast's clamped jaw. Still holding fast, Carly spun around to look at the pit in horror, though she was prepared to sacrifice herself if necessary. The skinwalker fired the crossbow into the pit. It seemed to be heading straight for the beast within, but somehow Carly's body, which had been aimlessly roaring and stomping, sidestepped the arrow quite by chance and it skimmed past her arm and fell short of its mark.

Oh my God!' thought Carly, 'he missed! I'm alive!'

She didn't have time to celebrate. Seth was lunging a series of punches and kicks at her as the monster's teeth sank further into his shoulder. The blows didn't hurt particularly but suddenly she felt something behind her. She roared loudly as another skinwalker (who was now in werewolf form) bit Kyle's flesh. She released Seth and charged at the man who was still brandishing the crossbow, ignoring the pain she felt from Kyle's back. She knew it was vital to reach that weapon - it contained the aconite-laced silver tipped arrows which were so deadly to werewolves.

The skinwalker holding the crossbow screamed and stumbled backwards, dropping it to the ground. Carly seized the opportunity to bat the crossbow away from anybody's reach. It flew a good ten metres into the forest, so powerful was the force of her whack.

Then, without any warning at all, Carly was surrounded by high walls made of earth. Gone were the skinwalkers around her though she could hear noise from the fight still continuing somewhere above her.

'What the hell?' she thought, quite disorientated and alarmed. Then she realised she was back in the pit looking through another beast's eyes. She was in her own body and somehow her self awareness had been carried across with her on leaving Kyle's body - she wasn't just a mindless creature the way Gary had been.

She bellowed with frustration and punched the pit wall as hard as she could, causing a small avalanche of earth to crumble away at the force of her blow. She couldn't even see out of the pit to find out what was going on so there was no way she could help Kyle. Throwing back her head she howled loudly. An answering howl came in return; it was Kyle, he was acknowledging that he knew she was safe in her own body.

CRASH! A loud thud made Carly jump as a large pole came sliding down beside her, slanted with the top still sticking out of the pit. It was the pole Kyle had been tied to - he must have grabbed it and thrown it down for her! Wasting no time Carly scrambled up it to the ground above.

The bodies of skinwalkers lay scattered on the ground, each a gory sight to behold. Just three were left alive including Seth. The two other skinwalkers were both in the form of grey wolves but Seth remained as a man. His hand clung to the peculiar green crystal. He appeared to be patting up and down his body, looking for somewhere to put it. As the great beast lunged once again at him, Seth hastily crammed the crystal into his mouth and swallowed hard. He instantly changed into his usual black werewolf identity, his clothes tearing from his body in shreds as he fell on four paws; without a second thought he leapt at the monster in retaliation. Carly had noticed earlier that the skinwalkers liked to carry their pelts in draw-string bags on their backs at all times, so Carly gathered that they must have been able to grab them and put them on. Not Seth though; Seth never wore a pelt.

'How is that possible?' thought Carly again. She really couldn't understand how a skinwalker could change without having the skin of another animal.

Seth and Kyle were wrestling with each other; Seth prancing around on his hind legs (and Kyle naturally as a biped in beast form) as though they were taking part in a type of ballroom dancing competition. The other two skinwalkers were snapping at any part of Kyle they could get hold of; his tail, his legs, his flanks. Carly ran up behind them and leapt at one, sinking her long sharp claws into its back and ripping its throat out with one fluid motion. Only a single high-pitched whine escaped its jaws. The other grey wolf immediately swung round and snarled before launching itself at the huge monster standing before it. They rolled around on the ground, claws flying, teeth bared, jaws snapping. The grey wolf was much smaller than Carly's enormous beast form but had the advantage of being nimble and light on its feet. By contrast the werewolf's massive bulk was almost tank-like in movement. Most often when Carly turned to bite it, the wolf ducked out of the way, leaving the beast snarling with teeth clenched in thin air. Finally though she managed to knock it to the ground. The wolf lay stunned just long enough for her to plunge her claws into its stomach and disembowel it. Immediately the wolf turned back into a man and his blood stained wolf pelt detached itself from his lifeless body.

Carly instantly turned her attention back to Kyle and Seth. The gigantic werewolf was wildly swinging its arms at Seth trying to knock its opponent to the ground, but the smaller black wolf was too quick and deftly avoided the blows. The wolf snapped at the heels of the beast, clamping down hard and drawing blood. The werewolf howled in pain and kicked the wolf in retaliation. Carly leapt over to Kyle's side and lashed out at Seth, her monstrous claws gouging the side of his face. Seth yelped and stumbled backwards reeling in agony; Carly could see fresh blood dripping from the gashes on his cheek. Kyle lunged for Seth's throat in one swift movement which seemed almost impossible due to his huge cumbersome form. His teeth missed their target though and instead he yanked something from around the wolf's neck which had been hidden under its shaggy black fur; it was Seth's pendant.

The very moment that this happened the wolf turned back into a man. His gold chain hung limply from Kyle's mouth. The capsule pendant which had fallen from it had split open on the ground to reveal ash and small particles of fur. 'He must have cast some sort of spell to enable the power of the pelt to be concealed within a necklace', thought Carly. Perhaps he had burnt the pelt and taken some fragments in his pendant. It seemed the most likely explanation; skinwalkers were shaman after all, capable of spells and rituals. Seth had stopped fighting now and instead was backing away from the beast with a terrified expression on his face.

"Please don't kill me Kyle", he said. "I'm your brother. You wouldn't do something like that, I know you wouldn't - I'm all you have left."

Carly could see the beast faltering as it listened to Seth's words. "No, don't listen to him", she pleaded, but all she could manage was a rasping noise from the back of her throat. She tried to will her thoughts into Kyle's mind again but it was too late for that - there was no mental link between them any longer.

The werewolf lifted its paw as though to strike Seth, but then lowered it and its features softened. It motioned with its forearm that the skinwalker should leave and Seth's face lit up with delight. "Oh Kyle, I knew you couldn't kill your big brother!" he beamed. Carly peered hard at his face though. She had seen an evil smirk hiding behind his apparently grateful expression. Her stomach contracted and an uneasy feeling came over her.

They watched side by side as Seth headed off towards the forest. When he had walked a short distance he stopped and turned to face them. He sprung into a swift forward roll grabbing something from the ground in the process; in his hands was the crossbow pointing at them. Carly could see the arrow hurtling straight towards Kyle's head; it was as if it was travelling in slow motion. "LOOK OUT!" she screamed, but the only sound she made was a howl. Leaping instinctively she slammed her body into Kyle's, knocking him to the ground as the arrow parted the fur on his head, shaving a few strands and lodging itself in a tree behind them.

Carly blinked and Kyle was gone. She sprang to her feet and saw that with incredible speed the beast was charging towards Seth. Its legs were so long that it only took a few massive strides before it reached the skinwalker. Carly could feel the ground slightly vibrating at a rapid pace like a pneumatic drill, shaking with every step that it took.

Seth opened his mouth to protest but it was too late, he had shown that he could not be trusted. The beast swiftly grabbed the skinwalker lifting him high above the ground with one arm, its huge claws penetrating his chest and back. Blood began to spurt from Seth's mouth and he gurgled in desperation, his hands flailing weakly as he tried to fend off the enormous werewolf.

The creature threw the skinwalker down to the ground. Seth lay there, stunned, his ugly gaping wounds clearly visible. Carly caught a delicious whiff of his blood and restrained herself from leaping towards him hungrily. Saliva began to dribble down her chin and she took a few steps backwards, not trusting herself not to act on her animal instincts.

Kyle raised his huge paw. He was about to bring it down across Seth's torso to finish him off, when Seth's stomach began to lurch violently. A horrible retching noise came from within his throat. The monster, obviously confused, lowered its forearm and stared at the man writhing around on the ground beneath it. Seth rolled onto his side and with a loud sickening sound he vomited in a projectile manner. A flash of green from within the regurgitated mess caught Carly's eye; it was the crystal Seth had previously swallowed.

A hint of a smile began to form at the corners of Seth's lips and he painfully scrabbled at the crystal with his fingers, trying to grip hold of it. Kyle was still looking bewildered so Carly sprung into action. She didn't know what Seth planned to do with the crystal but she could sense it was probably something she wanted to avoid happening.

As quick as a flash, Carly bounded towards the skinwalker on the floor. She could feel the muscles in her powerful legs clenching as her huge paws slammed into the ground. The look on Seth's face as he noticed her approaching turned to one of absolute panic.

It suddenly dawned on her that he had no idea that she had self-awareness.

'He thinks I'm out of control the way Gary was', she realised.

She took a step closer to Seth - a look of panic was etched on his face. Carly quickened her pace and Seth began to fumble in the dirt all the more frantically, trying to reach the gem. Just as his fingers made contact with the shining jewel, Kyle lunged forward and brought his massive foot down hard on top of Seth's hand.

With a smash, the crystal was crushed; it shattered into thousands of tiny shards. Seth shrieked in pain as the bones in his hand made a sickening cracking sound. Kyle lifted his foot and a shimmering viridescent light glowed from underneath Seth's bloody broken fingers. Within a matter of seconds the light had faded and disappeared. Seth, his face contorted in agony, gave a new cry of horror as he realised what had happened to the gem.

For a moment Carly stared at the scene before her; Seth's petrified expression looked frozen onto his face and that moment seemed to last an age. The last thing she heard before she lost consciousness was a haunting howl from the werewolf near her, as both she and Kyle succumbed to their beasts.

When Carly finally came around she was lying on her back on the floor of the forest completely naked, once again in human form. She could see the beautiful colours of the sunrise beginning to streak across the sky. Carly realised that the Wolf Star, Sirius, must have been and gone, and now the effects of the full moon had worn away with the coming of the new dawn. Beside her, Kyle, too, was lying on the ground, his eyelids just beginning to flutter. With a sigh of relief Carly took in his familiar features; no traces of the beasts remained. The smell of blood was heavy in the air and she caught sight of a gold flash. She sat up and looked over at the object - Seth's chain.

Chunks of human flesh were lying all around them. Carly knew that Seth wouldn't have stood a chance against the two huge werewolves. She had a strange empty feeling inside her stomach. It was all over, but at what cost? She thought of Gary and Ian and a tear began to trickle down her face. She closed her eyes and tried to take a deep breath.

An arm around her shoulder made her jump slightly. "Hey, it'll be alright, we have each other", said Kyle softly, kissing her forehead. Carly buried her head against his chest - it felt warm and comforting. She knew it was true, they had each other and they were alive - those were the most important things.

Wiping her eyes with the back of her hand, she sniffed loudly and nodded. "Yes," she echoed, "it'll be alright".

About The Author

Natalie Gosney was born in 1983 in Paris, France in a small private clinic just off the Champs-Élysées. When I was three years old I moved to Leeds, England with my parents where I spent my childhood climbing trees, playing make-believe and reading lots of books. My passion for books only grew as I got older, and with this passion came the desire to tell stories of my own. I attended Leeds University where I studied French with Teaching English To Speakers Of Other Languages.

Later I studied Classics in addition to courses in Writing Short Stories and Creative Writing. I began my working career in 2003 at the age of 19 in a commercial estate agents which sold only *fish & chip* shops. Since then I have had various jobs, and got married in 2005. I relocated to South Yorkshire with my family in 2010. Now I am a full time writer and mother, and I wake up to the sound of cows lowing in the morning from the nearby farmer's field.

To find out more about The Wolf Born Saga™

Visit our Facebook page at:
http://www.facebook.com/WBSaga

Visit our website at:
http://www.wolfborn.co.uk

Follow us on Twitter at:
http://www.twitter.com/WolfBornSaga

This novel is the first in a series. The second novel is called Wolf Witch, the third is Wolf Blade and the fourth is known as Wolf Bane.

Acknowledgements

Many thanks to my husband Philip Gosney for helping me with the publishing side to this book. After all, what use is a book if it is merely stuck on someone's computer, unable to be set free into the world? I would never have been able to bring Wolf Born to life without his typesetting and layout skills, not to mention his encouragement whilst I was writing which gave me the boost I needed to continue.

Another big thank you to my dad Gérard Tourtois. Being a writer himself he took it upon himself to proof-read my book to within an inch of its life, for which I am most grateful. For those of you interested, you can find his books at the following address.

sites.google.com/site/theesterelledynasty/

Thanks to my mam for drilling into me the importance of spelling and grammar when I was a child, and for her support.

I am most grateful to all my friends online who have been behind me every step of the way whilst I was writing this book.

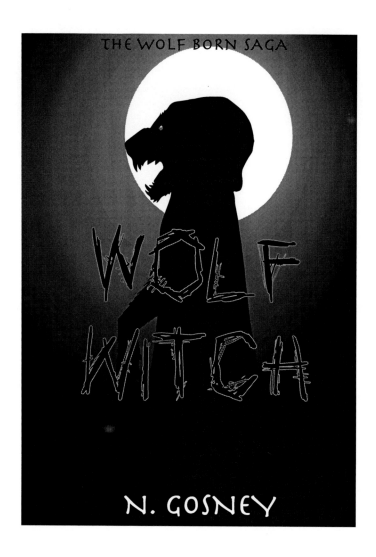

Wolf Witch, the second thrilling novel in this series, known as The Wolf Born Saga, is now available to buy from all good retailers.

ISBN-13: 978-0-9575273-2-4

Lightning Source UK Ltd.
Milton Keynes UK
UKOW04f0647200116

266731UK00001B/48/P